WITCH-WAY
By
CEANE O'HANLON-LINCOLN

A Sleuth Sisters Mystery

Book five in the bewitching series

A Magick Wand Production
"Thoughts are magick wands powerful enough
to make anything happen– anything we choose!"

This book is lovingly dedicated to time travelers everywhere ~
And to my husband, Phillip R. Lincoln, who bought me my ticket.

Warm gratitude and blessings bright and beautiful to:
My husband Phillip,

And to my muses Beth Adams; Carrie Bartley; Janet Barvincak;
Sandy Bolish; William Colvin; Nancy Hrabak;
renowned psychic and High Priestess Kelly M. Kelleher;
Dr. Cassandra Kuba, professor of anthropology/forensic
anthropologist at California University of Pennsylvania;
Kathy Lincoln; Marla Mechling; Jean Minnick; Robin Moore;
and songstress, poet and author extraordinaire,
Rowena of the Glen ~

For all the reasons they each know so well.

Witch-Way

By

Ceane O'Hanlon-Lincoln

A Sleuth Sisters Mystery

"Watch with glittering eyes the whole world around you because the greatest secrets are always hidden in the most unlikely places. Those who don't believe in magick will never find it." ~ Roald Dahl

"Life is too, too short to be cynical. So smile, dare to *believe*, and leave the door open for– *magick!"* ~ The Sleuth Sisters

The bewitching Sleuth Sisters Mystery Series:
~By Ceane O'Hanlon-Lincoln~

In this paranormal-mystery series, Raine and Maggie McDonough and Aisling McDonough-Gwynn, first cousins, are the celebrated Sleuth Sisters from the rustically beautiful Pennsylvania town of Haleigh's Hamlet. With their magickal Time-Key, these winning white witches are able to unlock the door that will whisk them through yesteryear, but who knows what skeletons and dangers dangle in the closets their Key will open?

One thing is certain– magick, adventure, and surprise await them at the creak of every opening door and page-turn.

The Witches' Time-Key, book one of the *Sleuth Sisters Mystery Series*

Fire Burn and Cauldron Bubble, book two of the *Sleuth Sisters Mystery Series*

The Witch's Silent Scream, book three of the *Sleuth Sisters Mystery Series*

Which Witch is Which? book four of the *Sleuth Sisters Mystery Series*

Witch-Way, book five of the Sleuth Sisters Mystery Series: A chance encounter on the train home from the "Witch City" of Salem, Massachusetts, with a woman from the Sleuth Sisters' hometown of Haleigh's Hamlet, Pennsylvania, leads the Sisters into a web of intrigue and danger. At the mysterious woman's request, they delve into the unsolved ax murders that terrified their Hamlet in 1932. Before long, a string of "coincidences" lead the trio of savvy sleuths to believe that the whole bloody mess is veiled in witchcraft and black magick– their investigation opening a Pandora's box of mystery, mayhem, and murder!

Watch for *The Witch Tree,* book six in the bewitching series– coming soon!

Amazon Books / www.amazon.com/amazon books

"It is important to remember that we all have magick inside us."
~ JK Rowling

Also by Ceane O'Hanlon-Lincoln:

Autumn Song, a harmonious medley of short stories threaded and interwoven by their romantic destiny themes and autumnal settings.

Each tale in this compelling anthology evokes its own special ambiance– and sensory impressions. *This book is a keeper you will re-visit often, as you do an old and cherished friend.*

O'Hanlon-Lincoln never judges her characters, several of whom resurface from tale to tale. These are honest portrayals, with meticulously researched historic backdrops, intrigue– *magick*– surprise endings– and thought-provoking twists.

For instance, in "A Matter of Time," on which side of the door is the main character when the story concludes?

From the first page of *Autumn Song*, the reader will take an active role in these fascinating tales, discovering all the exciting threads that connect them.

How many will *you* find?

Available at Amazon Books / www.amazon.com/amazon books

~~~

And the award-winning history series:

County Chronicles
County Chronicles Volume II
County Chronicles Volume III
County Chronicles Volume IV
County Chronicles: There's No Place Like Home!

"If you haven't read this author's *County Chronicles*, then you haven't discovered how *thrilling* history can be! With meticulous research and her "state-of-the-heart" storytelling, Ceane O'Hanlon-Lincoln breathes life into historical figures and events with language that flows and captivates the senses." ~ Mechling Books

"I write history like a story, because that's what history is – a story– or rather, *layered* stories of the most significant events that ever unfolded! Each volume of my *County Chronicles* is a spellbinding collection of *true* stories from Pennsylvania's exciting past." ~ Ceane O'Hanlon-Lincoln

"Love and magick have a great deal in common. They enrich the soul, delight the heart, and they both take practice." ~ Nora Roberts

WITCH-WAY
~ Cast of Characters ~

Raine and Maggie McDonough, PhDs– Sexy, savvy Sisters of the Craft, who *are* more like sisters than cousins. With sorcery in their glittering emerald eyes, these bewitching Pennsylvania history professors delve into the unsolved ax murders that terrified their Hamlet in 1932, their investigation opening a Pandora's box! Will the Sisters be able to solve the Hamlet's dark secret *and* the mix of present-day mayhem and murders they are certain are connected to it?

Aisling McDonough-Gwynn– The blonde with the wand is the senior Sister in the magickal trio of Sleuth Sisters. Aisling and her husband **Ian**, former police detectives, are partners in their successful Black Cat Detective Agency.
The Gwynns have a preteen daughter **Meredith** (**Merry**) **Fay**, who mirrors her magickal mother. Merry was named for the McDonough *Grande Dame* "Auntie Merry," who resides in the "Witch City" of Salem, Massachusetts.

Aisling Tully McDonough– The Sleuth Sisters' beloved **"Granny"** was the grand mistress of Tara, the Victorian mansion, where Raine and Maggie came of age, and where they yet reside. Born in Ireland, the departed Granny McDonough left her female heirs a very special gift– and at the enchanting Tara, with its magickal mirrors, Granny is but a glance away.

The Myrrdyn/Merlin Cats– Descendants of Granny McDonough's magickal feline Myrrdyn (the Celtic name for Merlin), these "Watchers" are the Sisters' closest companions. Wholly *familiar* with the Sleuth Sisters' powers, desires, and needs, the Myrrdyn/Merlin cats faithfully offer moral support, special knowledge– and timely messages.

Cara– The Sleuth Sisters' magickal ragdoll companion. Will the ancient poppet's magick prove powerful enough to help Raine, Maggie, and Aisling untangle the web of evil that threatens to ensnare them as they get closer to solving their current mystery?

Thaddeus Weatherby, PhD– This absent-minded professor and head of Haleigh College's history department has an Einstein mind coupled with an uncontrollable childish curiosity that has been known to cause unadulterated mischief for the Sleuth Sisters. Thaddeus and Maggie are lovers and reunited kindred spirits.

Beau Goodwin– Raine's dashing **Beau**, soul mate, and next-door neighbor is a superior veterinarian with an extraordinary sixth sense. After all– his patients can't tell him what's wrong. An Old Soul, like Raine, Beau has a way about him that keeps Raine– *enchanted.*

Hugh Goodwin– Beau's semi-retired veterinary father– whose acute sixth sense matches his son's– has an avid appetite for mystery novels and an astonishing aptitude for solving them that the Sleuth Sisters find absolutely "wizard."

Betty Donovan– A retired librarian, Hugh's attractive companion shares his intense love of mysteries and is fast becoming his equal in solving them.

Hannah Gilbert– The Sleuth Sisters' loyal, protective housekeeper is a fountain of homespun wisdom. Her quirky purple sneakers and garish muumuus are indicative of her colorful personality.

Kathy Wise– Known throughout Haleigh's Hamlet as "Savvy Kathy," this receptionist at the Hamlet's Auto Doctor sets the Sisters rolling on the path to discovery.

Eva Novak– The Gypsy Tearoom lady's own special brew of "Tea-Time-Will-Tell" is not the only sustenance the charismatic woman delivers to the Sleuth Sisters.

Sophie Miller– The owner of the charming Sal-San-Tries café-deli is a terrific cook, but has she a recipe among her delectable **sal**ads, **san**dwiches, and pas**tries** for murder? The sweet-looking Sophie, it seems, has a couple of bad, downright *rotten*, apples on her proud family tree.

Belle Christie– Haleigh Hamlet's most popular beautician and its theatre's makeup artist knows more than she's telling about her own ancestor, and others, in the elite circle of moguls who once lorded it over the entire Pittsburgh area. Belle's peels, concealers, and masks are *not* confined to her craft.

Dr. Benjamin Wight– Braddock County's fastidious coroner finds himself suddenly overwhelmed by some pretty messy murders!

Dr. Elizabeth Yore, PhD– This Margaret Mead figure, with her long, signature cape and tall, forked staff, can only be described as something betwixt and between an impish witch and a stern schoolmarm. As joint head of Haleigh College's archaeology and anthropology departments, Yore is forever posing questions. However, the haunting questions begging here are: "Whose hoary bones were those unearthed in Haleigh's Wood?" And "Are the Hamlet's unsolved murders from the past connected to the ones with which the rustically beautiful village is presently plagued?"

Nellie Triggs– The mysterious woman the Sleuth Sisters encountered on the train home from Salem asked the Sisters to delve into the unsolved ax murders of her namesake and ancestors slaughtered in the Triggs' Hamlet home in 1932. But has Nellie neglected to share with the Sisters a secret or two about her great-aunt and her gory tale?

Mada Fane– The great-granddaughter of the affluent Fane couple for whom the murdered Nellie worked in 1932 holds doctorates in both archeology and anthropology, in addition to countless accolades for her acclaimed books. Independently wealthy, she is, like her ancestors, a world traveler– a quintessential free spirit without a care in the world. Then why does she appear to be ensnared by fear?

Adrian Fane– Known and respected across the entire Pittsburgh area, Mada's great-grandfather was an esteemed industrialist and munificent philanthropist. During the Hamlet's heyday, his assets included railroads, banks, coal and coke lands, as well as various real estate holdings across the globe. His dealings and great wealth stimulated his keen interest in travel and collecting curiosities from around the world– some of which will shockingly surface.

Elsa Fane– Adrian's wife owned the antique and curiosity shop– Enchanting Things– that specialized in the unusual and highly collectible– that the ill-fated Nellie managed. What will the Sleuth Sisters unveil about Elsa that may prove a bit more than unusual?

Henry Moretti– The interview with the Hamlet's former band director hits a sour note when the Sleuth Sisters pose a particular question. What information, over the long years, might *his* family be hiding about the village's unsolved ax murders?

J.D. Means– During the Roaring Twenties, the Hamlet referred to J.D. as "Jim Dandy, the Millionaire-Maker." The bank run that caused his bank to fail during the Great Depression resulted in J.D. taking his own life. *Or did he?*

Josie Means– J.D.'s granddaughter, a prolific author of historic works, is shocked when she learns that the Sleuth Sisters have unlocked what she calls a "Pandora's box of evil and intrigue."

Dale Hardiman– The direct descendant of the axed woman's brother Clyde is furious that the Sisters should *dare* to dwell on that Pandora's box.

Beatrice Hart– Ms. Hart is the progeny of the cousins who took axed Nellie's orphaned son, Billy Triggs, into their home after he had been traumatized by the ax murderer. Beatrice has some shocking stories to share with the Sleuth Sisters.

Jake Swain– This great-grandson of one of axed Nellie Triggs' suitors is not exactly enamored by the Sleuth Sisters.

Harry Valentine– Harry's great-grandfather was Nellie's rejected suitor whom many believed was the Hamlet's ax murderer.

Chief Fitzpatrick– The Chief of Police of Haleigh's Hamlet is ever amazed by the Sleuth Sisters' uncanny ability to solve a mystery.

The Keystone Coven– As they have for past Sabbats, the Sleuth Sisters invite their very special friends and fellow sisters of the moon, the Keystone Coven, to Tara for the May Day celebration of

Beltane. Will the High Priestess' premonition and glittering gift–
together with the Sisters' own talismans– suffice in protecting our
"mystery magnets" against the powerful evil that targets them?

"Don't make me release the flying monkeys!"
~ Dr. Raine McDonough, *Witch-Way?*

"Evil comes to all us men of imagination,
wearing as its mask all the virtues."
~ W.B. Yeats

"Any time women come together with a collective intention, it's a powerful thing …
when women come together with a collective intention–
magick happens."
~ Phylicia Rashad

"Careful! Careful what you *witch* for!"
~ Ceane O'Hanlon-Lincoln

~ Prologue ~

Known far and wide as the "Sleuth Sisters," raven-haired Raine and redheaded Maggie McDonough, cousins who shared the same surname, residence, and occupation, as well as a few other things in what could only be termed their *magickal* lives, were busy in their kitchen. As they prepared a salad to take to a spontaneous supper and brainstorming session connected to their current mystery, they could already sense that one of their most *chilling* adventures was about to unfold.

Recently returned from a thrilling sojourn on the remote isle of Eynhallow in Scotland's windswept Orkney Islands, the Sisters concluded their trip in the Witch City of Salem, Massachusetts, where they attended the 100th birthday bash of their great-aunt Merry McDonough. Spring break from their teaching duties at Haleigh College had allowed these winning white witches to solve back-to-back nerve-jangling mysteries, proving yet again their merit as super-sleuths.

Now, as they chopped fresh veggies and mixed greens for the salad, Raine drew a faint breath of relief, collecting herself for a moment before stating with certainty, "We both know, Mags, that there are no accidents in life. Everything happens for a reason. And the reason we encountered Nellie Triggs on the train home from Salem was so *we* would be given the opportunity to solve the mystery that has tormented her family and baffled our Hamlet for so many years."

Maggie tipped the celery she had finished chopping into the salad bowl. "The unsolved ax murders happened so long ago, in 1932." She sucked in her full lower lip, turning to face her cousin. "I only hope we can–"

"Fiddle-dee-dee! We'll solve that old whodunit in jig-time! Otherwise, why did it fall into *our* laps? In any case," Raine quipped, "people don't call us the 'Sleuth Sisters' for nothing!" The Sister plunked chopped black olives into the large bowl with a bit of a flourish.

"It's an awful cold case. Absolutely *frozen*," declared Maggie with a raised brow. "And as we said earlier, nary a clue has ever surfaced."

"We don't know that for sure," Raine said after a rapt moment, though not entirely in response to Maggie's remark. Her thoughts were yet on the mysterious woman from the train, on her sad eyes and smile. "I kept getting the feeling that Nellie was holding something back about her great-aunt and namesake. Maybe she has a secret or three of her own. She gave the impression she did. I seem to recall a faint note of bitterness underlying her words."

Maggie cocked her red head. "Oh, everyone has a chapter of their lives they don't read out loud, darlin'."

Raine shrugged and picked up a radish, the corners of her pouty mouth lifting as she commenced to slice it. "I'm quite looking forward to the challenge of solving our historic Hamlet's mulish mystery. All in all," and her eyes, as green as any cat's, glittered, "weren't *we* the ones to finally solve the mystery of our Hamlet's eighteenth-century hermit?"

"We were," Maggie answered, reaching for the fresh arugula that she had soaking in cold water. "Indeed we were!"

Raine's smart phone, programmed to sound with the music of *The Faerie Circle*, interrupted the Sisters' conversation.

"Dr. McDonough," her deep voice rumbled into the phone. "It's Beau," she mouthed aside to Maggie. "Hey, big boy, what's up?" Mischief played on her sexy voice.

Raine listened for a few moments, responding with one of her throaty laughs. "You know I do." She listened again, answering, "I'm counting on that. We'll be walking over in about an hour or so. Crafting your requested salad as we speak."

Beau interjected something, resulting in Raine's retort, "Sounds delicious! Your father's a wizard … uh-huh, like his son," she exclaimed, concluding, "and a thumpin' good one at that! I'd better ring off, still a few last-minute things to do. I love you too. *Ciao*, baby!"

She ended the call, slipped the phone into the pocket of the Gothic black skirt she was wearing, then reached down and picked up the Sisters' magickal doll, Cara, that had materialized next to them on the kitchen counter. "We want you to house-and-cat-sit tonight, Cara. We're going next door later to Beau and Hugh's for dinner and a brainstorming session. With lady-friend Betty's help, Hugh's whipping up a great meal– chili and jalapeño corn bread. We're bringing the salad, Thaddeus the sangria. What's Aisling and Ian bringing, Mags?" Raine smoothed the poppet's faded yarn hair.

Maggie thought for a moment. "They've been swamped at the agency. Three ongoing cases, so they're planning to stop at Sal-San-Tries for one of Sophie's delectable desserts on the way over."

"I'm proud of Aisling," Raine stated, leaning back against the counter. "She and Ian have really made a success of their Black Cat Detective Agency."

"Sure 'n ye'd best remember t' bring me sumpin' good t' eat, lass!" the ragdoll retorted, looking up at Raine, its smeared, crooked mouth seeming to convey a wily grin. The bewitched little doll's speech was a lilting Irish brogue.

Raine's pouty full lips curved upward. "Do we ever forget about you?" She truly loved Cara and occasionally fretted about losing her. Now she gently tapped the doll's mop-top head. "See you keep out of mischief, poppet!"

Before Cara could answer, Maggie, with head cocked in a musing attitude, replied, "Your comment to Beau about Hugh being a wizard reminded me of our Hamlet's real Wizard, senior advisor to the Keystone Coven." She thought for a long moment. "Dear sisters of the moon," she added, using the term in the Craft for female practitioners. "I wonder if we'll *ever* discover who the Keystone Coven's Wizard guru really *is*?"

"That's a sentence you don't hear every day!" Raine giggled. She was feeling a bit giddy, and she wondered if it was because yet another mystery had befallen them.

Maggie wiped her hands on a paper towel. "Never having met the Wizard in person, the Coven doesn't even know who he is! Now *there's* a mystery!" the redheaded Sister exclaimed, picking up Raine's thought.

Raine made a face that was so kittenish, it brought a twinkle to Maggie's emerald eyes. "That might just be the one puzzle we *never* crack. Sometimes I think it's Thaddeus, other times Hugh, and then," her eyes narrowed, and her voice dropped, "there are ... *fervent* times, I'm downright convinced the Wizard is my Beau."

"Well, darlin'," Maggie responded with her favorite endearment, "if you ask me, Beau, Hugh, or Thaddeus are each mighty good candidates. You know what keen sixth senses Beau and Hugh possess, the pair of them. It's why they're such good veterinarians. After all, their patients can't tell them what's wrong! As for Thaddeus," her Mona-Lisa smile transformed her face to sexy-mysterious, "well ... suffice it to say he's a recurrent wizard. The man's forever surprising me!"

"All we and the Coven are certain of, is that their senior advisor lives in our Hamlet; but as we've said before, just because, over the years, the Coven has referred to their enigmatic advisor as the 'Wizard,' doesn't necessarily mean it's a man." Raine lifted one ebony brow. "It could well be a *sister* of the Craft."

"True." Maggie got to her feet and rolled her aching shoulders. "I can image Dr. Yore as the Wizard. C'mon, let's get this salad done. I'm *dying* for a cup of tea."

Raine started to say something when her words were silenced by their poppet.

"Whist! I'm goin' t' supper an' th' brainstormin' session wit ya!" the ragdoll screamed, twisting partway round to face Raine, from where she was propped against the backsplash of the counter.

Cara was bestowed on the Sisters by their Hamlet's mysterious eighteenth-century hermit, a fellow sister of the moon whose violent murder the Sleuth Sisters solved when they time-trekked, several months prior, to the perilous Pennsylvania frontier.

Approximately eleven inches tall, the doll's head bore a mop of what used to be, over two centuries earlier, bright-red wool yarn for hair, faded now to a pale orangey hue. The rag-stuffed head and body were fashioned of a coarse, age-darkened muslin. Two faded, but still faintly visible, black ink dots represented the eyes; and the mouth, smeared undoubtedly by countless childish kisses over the tumbled years, was somewhat crooked, giving the evident impression of a *mischievous* grin.

A green vest, the design in the cambric long claimed by Time, was pinched in at the waist by a narrow, rope-like cord. The poppet's uneven skirt was pinked and somewhat tattered, the purple-ish color nearly gone the way of history; and though the doll sported no shoes, the ink-blackened feet were shaped as though it did, the soles turning up at the toes evoking the notion of a leprechaun.

A scowling Raine stood staring at the doll, her hands on her hips. "I already told you, you're going to remain here at Tara to house-'n-cat-sit this evening."

Tara was Raine and Maggie's nineteenth-century Victorian home, a stately Queen Anne, located in the quaint, picturesque village of Haleigh's Hamlet– a historic southwestern Pennsylvania town that conferred countless glimpses of the past.

The wily poppet drew herself up to her full height, resting her wee mitts on her own hips and planting her elfin feet in what could only be read as a fighting stance.

Raine instantly recognized a declaration of war, which sent her own Irish flying high. "You are *not* coming with us! We'll summon you, if we need you," Raine concluded, giving Cara a patronizing pat on the head that brought a decided grimace to the poppet's cloth face.

The raven-haired Sister sat the doll firmly back down on the counter, then covered the salad Maggie had just completed with cellophane and foil before placing the bowl in the fridge to await their departure.

"We'll carry the dressing with us," the red-haired Sister stated. "Always best to add the dressing right before we're ready to eat."

"Come up to the tower room for a few moments with me before our tea break," Raine voiced to Maggie as that Sister was putting the finishing touches to her creamy, homemade Southwest dressing. "I want to show you what I found on the Internet about the ax murders. I'll run everything off– newspaper accounts, as well as our own notes I typed from what axed Nellie's namesake shared with us on the train. Want to print the sheets off now, so we'll be ready to go promptly out the door when Thaddeus gets here."

"Splendid idea," Maggie said, as she set the container of dressing on the refrigerator shelf, next to the salad.

A few moments later, the Sisters entered Tara's tower room where they did their paperwork. From floor to ceiling, bookshelves encircled the high, round chamber, where the tall windows, crisscrossed with ecru lace curtains, let in plenty of light. The carpet and walls were a rich hunter green, and the woodwork, as throughout the manse, was a dark and durable English oak.

Raine read aloud, snappily and selectively, perusing from five separate sheets printed from their computer. She handed a duplicate set of the printed papers to Maggie, saying, "*That's it.* It's all the info I could garner thus far. Not much, is it? I hope the great Goddess aids us in untangling this web of evil that has tainted our Hamlet for so long. It would be wonderful to be able to tell our present-day Nellie that we solved her great-aunt Nellie's murder … and not just *her* murder, but her aunt's daughter's and elderly mother's murders too."

The sexy redhead stretched in her feline fashion, the black knit dress she was wearing accentuating her voluptuous figure. "We've got to keep to the path of the Great Secret. That's how we ferreted out the Time-Key," she pondered, brushing a finger across the large Herkimer Diamond– the talisman of researchers– they kept on the claw-footed law table that held their computer. "It's how we crafted our thesis on time-travel so that it was accepted by our fellow colleagues of letters, and how we defended it successfully to gain our doctorates. Not to mention the run of wicked murders we solved in the past few years. We did it *all* by keeping to the path of the Great Secret."

"You bet we did!" the more petite Raine returned with vigor, and her emerald eyes sparkled through a veil of thick, inky-black lashes. "And through it all, we've successfully guarded the Time-Key and its secret."

It had become the Sisters' habit to throw themselves into spirit-boosting pep talks when tackling a new mystery, for it quite bolstered their confidence. "In keeping with the Great Secret," Raine was fond of saying, "the real magick is believing in oneself!"

Now she too stretched, cat-like. Tilting her dark head, her fair cheeks suddenly took on a rosy tint. "We've safeguarded the Time-Key through, I might add, *four* nerve-jangling time-travel quests." Raine ran her ringed fingers through her short, sassy asymmetric hair– as black and lustrous as their cats– the point-cut bangs dipping seductively over one eye. "And this new adventure, challenge though it is, I just *know* we'll chalk up to yet another victory!"

Maggie had drifted over to the tower's tall windows. There, her green eyes swept the glorious spring panorama below– the woods bursting with the splendor of the season, the redbud trees ethereal and faerie-like in the yard. Turning from the windows, she glanced at her watch. "We've been rushed off our feet since that spur-of-the-moment call from Hugh, inviting us to supper with our sleuthing set tonight. Let's be off downstairs for that bracing cup of tea before Thaddeus gets here, and we have to set off through the woods to Hugh and Beau's place."

"OK, but let's not tarry. We want to leave ourselves enough time to consult Granny before we go," Raine said excitedly, and spinning on her heel, she headed for the door.

"Right," the less talkative Maggie replied, "I just need to duck into my room to slip these notes into my purse." She tossed one last glance out the window, remarking, "I love our Hamlet all year, but isn't spring an enchanting symphony of green!"

An enchanting place *any* time, Haleigh's Hamlet was a cluster of Victorian, castle-like homes, replete with gingerbread and old money, all built during an era when help was cheap and plentiful, and the owners, coal and railroad barons (the life's blood of the village during its heyday), could well afford a bevy of servants.

To folks who lived elsewhere, the Hamlet's kingly mansions, each occupying a triple-sized wooded lot, were ever mysterious, bringing to mind secret rooms revealed with a touch to a certain "book" on a shelf and hidden staircases exposed by the twist of a latch disguised as a wall sconce. There was never any danger of anyone undesirable moving into one of the Hamlet's manors– the cost and upkeep warded off that problem.

The day was a glorious one in late April. Rays of sun, through one of the home's many stained-glass windows, cast jewel-toned light on the McDonough pair, as the windowsills sparkled with rows of vari-colored crystals– each charged with strong magick.

Among them were amber for vanquishing negativity, disease and dis-ease; amethyst for healing and inducing pleasant dreams; aquamarine for calming the nerves and lifting the spirits; citrine for cleansing; moonstone, "wolf's eye," for new beginnings and intuition; peridot for release from guilt; rose quartz for unconditional love; tiger's eye and falcon's eye for strong protection; sapphire for insight and truth; emerald for bliss, loyalty, and wealth; and ruby for energy, passion, and vigor.

On a center sill, a small smoky-glass dish held Apache tears. To the Ancient Ones, these were frozen tears lost in the sands of time, the magickal stones proffering grounding, good luck and protection, as well as the ridding of negativity that held back realized dreams. Like amethyst and tiger's eye, Apache tears protected the Sisters against psychic attack– also known as the "evil eye."

Here too the Sisters kept a large Herkimer Diamond, which, despite the name, was not really a diamond at all but a powerful clear crystal. The Sisters understood that "Herkies," perfect conduits of the Universal Life Force, were exceptional healing crystals– the high-energy seekers of the crystal world that amplify the influence of other gemstones.

From the waning day's azure-blue sky, the lowering sun splashed rainbows through the Queen Anne's jewel-like windows, spilling a cornucopia of color on the already vibrant collection of curious things the old mansion held within its sturdy walls.

In her woodsy-themed bedroom with its large, green-marble fireplace, Raine slipped her notes into her purse, a black shoulder bag with the word *Goddess* spelled out in clear, glittering rhinestones. Turning partway round, she checked her appearance in the tall cheval glass. *I'll stop wearing black when they invent a darker color,* she laughed to herself. *Black is my happy color!*

The raven-haired Sister often donned Gothic attire, the style suiting her to the proverbial "T." Beau called her witchy chic "Raine gear." (Witches have always known that wearing black neutralizes dark, negative energies.) Today a black blouse, with stand-up collar, coupled with a long Victorian riding skirt showed off her trim figure to perfection. Raine loved witchy shoes and boots, and the vintage, high-button boots she sported today possessed all the witchy-woman wow that she fancied.

Shadowing Maggie down the hall, the Goth gal repeated thrice, more to herself and the Universe than to her cousin and sister of the Craft, "We've bested evil before! We can do it again; that's for sure!"

Raine was referring to their vanquishing, the previous year, of the ancient *Macbeth* curse from Whispering Shades, the Hamlet's "little theatre in the woods," that resulted in the most terrifying of battles. Besides ousting a bane of evil from their beloved theatre and Hamlet, they managed, in the bargain, to soothe Whispering Shades' resident ghost.

En route down the ornately carved staircase, the pair swept past the framed oil painting, mounted on the stairwell wall, that Maggie had done of the famous Irish dolmen Poulnabrone, the prehistoric set of huge stones resembling a portal to the netherworld. A gifted photographer and painter, Maggie executed the oil painting from a photograph in which she captured the setting sun just as it flashed, star-like and centered, beneath the horizontal slab of the great standing stones.

Over two years earlier, Raine and Maggie had made the most significant journey of their lives– a trip to mystical Ireland, where they happened upon more than they had bargained for. There, they sought and found answers to the haunting questions connected to a very special quest of their own– and to a series of murders and legendary lost jewels at Barry Hall, a noble, old estate in County

Clare. It was in Ireland where, after years of research, the pair ferreted out the magickal Time-Key, which, when properly activated, whisked them through the Tunnel of Time to yesteryear– to *any* year that they encoded.

When the Sisters re-entered Tara's generous, high-ceilinged kitchen, the opalesque stained glass in the tall cabinet doors shimmered with sunlight, as the two women busied themselves with the tea things. It was a happy-feeling kitchen, and Maggie hummed merrily to herself.

Introduced to them years before by their beloved Granny McDonough, teatime was something these steeped-in tradition ladies enjoyed whenever and wherever they could.

The spacious kitchen's focal point was the charming, sky-blue, hooded stove, restored to its Victorian splendor, that had been their granny's pride and joy. The old house had most of the modern conveniences, but in the kitchen especially, Raine and Maggie preferred the Old Ways– trusted, tried and true.

Above them, bunches of dried herbs and flowers dangled from the dark, massive ceiling beams of abiding English oak. A small herb garden thrived year-round in the kitchen's bay window, and affixed to the brick chimney, a broom-riding Good Luck Kitchen Witch warded off the bad and invited the good.

A besom-riding witch topped Tara's highest gable too. Celts have always been superstitious, as well as deeply spiritual. The tradition of the witch weather vane, imbued with Irish and Scottish folktales of enchanted old women flying over castle and field, casting spells and weaving magick, dates all the way back to the 1300s– or even earlier. Legend has it that if a passing witch saw such an effigy, she knew she could rest on the chimney top and consequently would cast no mischief upon the household.

Whilst the majestic manse's waterspouts channeled rainwater from Tara's slate roof and rust-colored brick walls, these conduits also served as watchful gargoyles, their mouths open in the silent shrieks that warded off evil.

Protective holly grew by every one of Tara's entrances and near the rear gate leading into the garden, where, upon a faerie mound, spell-cast items were recharged under the full moon's energizing glow.

Like a bubbling cauldron, Tara *overflowed* with magick, casting its spell over anyone who set eyes upon it. Invisible to non-magick people, strong energies encircled and protected the house and its occupants.

Surrounded by a black, wrought-iron fence with fleur-de-lys finials, the turreted 1890s home was crowded with antiques, the cousins' vintage clothing, and a collection of *very special* jewelry, all of it enchanted, most of it heirloom and quite old.

The "McDonough Girls," as the Hamlet called them, had a charismatic flair, each for her own brand of fashion, each possessing the gift to *feel* the sensations cached away in their collected treasures, "As if," they were prone to say, "we are living history."

A long line of McDonough women possessed the gift for sensing, through proximity and touch, the layered stories and energies of those who previously owned the antique articles they acquired. Attired in their vintage clothing, these women were all gossamer and lace– but, make no mistake, they bore spines of cloaked steel.

Plainly put, the McDonoughs ran to women of strong personalities– generation after generation. For the most part, they ignored convention, were headstrong and willful– with every intention of staying that way.

The family was an old one, full of tradition, mystique, and fire that dated back to the *Ard Ri* of Tara– the High Kings of Ireland.

The grand old lady who named the house for Ireland's sacred Hill came, decades before, from County Meath, bequeathing her female heirs a special gift– and a great deal of magick.

Tara, as it became known, was a grand old house, one of the Hamlet's great houses. In all honesty, it was not the most beautiful residence in the district but, unquestionably, it was the most unique– *as were its mistresses.*

McDonough women could make magick just by walking into a room. They had ages of it behind them, following in their wake like the long, fiery tail of a comet. *Samhain*– Hallowe'en– was their favorite holiday.

And then there were the cats– known in the world of the Craft as "Watchers," though some might say "Familiars," five at the moment, three of which, Black Jade and Black Jack O'Lantern and Panthèra, were descended from Granny McDonough's big tom, Myrrdyn, the Celtic name for Merlin. After all, it was a commodious old house– and it literally *purrred* with love.

Back in the day, when Granny McDonough entered a room, the theatre, a shop, restaurant, or hall, whispers abruptly broke out like little hissing fires throughout the space. The villagers used to babble that Granny McDonough's "big ole black cat" assisted her with black magick. Black cats do that to some people, the un-magick anyway, rendering them shivery and illogical, while conjuring up all sorts of dark-night superstitions.

"Psychological poppycock! I have no patience with that sort of talk!" Granny used to cite– Granny whose magick was forever white. Tittle-tattle never bothered Granny McDonough, who, inclined to laugh it off, advocated, "You might as well get the benefit of it– gossip liberates you from convention."

But that's the way of any small town– people talked, and they always would; their tongues were never idle. Not to say that the folks of Haleigh's Hamlet didn't like the McDonoughs. They very much did, some even going so far as to flaunt pride for this longstanding Hamlet clan. Despite the whisperings of the townfolk, many were the times someone of them came knocking at the backdoor, under the veil of darkness, for a secret potion or a charm.

Over the long years, the McDonough family home gathered within its stout brick walls its fair share of arcane, esoteric, and cloak-and-dagger mysteries. Without the least bit of puffery or purple prose, Tara could be summarized as a house that embodied a *myriad* of veiled secrets– old and new.

The greatest secrets are hidden, the most significant, powerful, things in the Universe unseen, and those who do not believe in *magick* will never experience it– will never uncover its mysteries.

Years before, at least three generations of the Hamlet's women found themselves drawn to Granny McDonough, wanting to confess *their* secrets to her in the shadows of her porch, where the sweet-smelling wisteria still grew thick in spring and summer, gracing the lattices with cascading, grape-like blooms.

And the Hamlet men, though they might scoff at such things, believed secretly, then and now, that on occasion a beautiful, young Aisling Tully McDonough, before she became known as "Granny," visited their dreams, igniting their carnal desires or whispering to them ways in which they might succeed in their careers.

The Hamlet learned that they could trust Granny McDonough with their secrets, and she conscientiously passed that torch on to her three granddaughters– to her namesake Aisling, to Maggie, and to Raine.

Granny had always looked straight into the eyes of anyone with whom she spoke, and she never minced words either, leaving "… sugar-coatin' to the baker and elegance to the tailor." It was quoted far and wide that Granny McDonough was a wise woman and a healer– of many things. Hamlet folks had feared her, yet they sought her out, over time learning to love her, even going so far as to believe that if her long, black cloak brushed against them, as she passed on the street, its mere touch brought them good fortune for the remainder of their days.

Suffice it to say that the Celtic history of healing is a rich and powerful one, and *Celt* is synonymous with "free spirit."

Once when Raine was sent home from school for thrashing a fellow student, a boy much bigger than she, who had relentlessly teased her for being a witch, Granny sat her down and said, "Always be yourself, me darlin'. An original is always better than a copy. And remember that you not only have the *right* to be an individual, as a McDonough you have an *obligation* to be one." When Raine, drying her tears, remarked that all she wanted was to be "normal," Granny pulled herself up and expounded, "Me darlin' girl, I'll tell you, here and now, that bein' 'normal,' as you call it, is utterly *ordinary*! And I'll tell ya flat out, lass– it rather denotes a lack of courage."

That's all it took. The willful, ofttimes hoydenish, Raine was cured forever of wanting a "normal" life!

After Grandpa McDonough passed on, Granny, who spoke to the end of her life with a brogue as thick as her good Irish stew, never wore anything but what the Hamlet referred to as her "widow's weeds."

With her shadowy cape billowing out behind her, she often walked her big, black tom on a leash after supper in the magickal owl light of evening. To the amazement of the villagers, the cat pranced– tail held high to form a question mark, neither twisting nor turning in any effort whatsoever to escape– at the end of a long, black velvet lead that was fastened to a fancy, jewel-studded collar around his neck, the other end wrapped several times round Granny's bejeweled hand. As self-important as you please, proudly and demurely did that tom swagger, with attitude and expression that clearly stated, "I am Granny McD's cat if you please– or if you don't please!"

Granny fathomed what most here in the New World of America did not– that gently stroking a black cat nine times, from head to tail, brought good fortune and luck in love (that went triple for *Samhain*/Hallowe'en); treating cats kindly– with the respect they deserve– and warmly sharing one's home with cats of any color brought a multitude of blessings from the great Goddess.

Granny taught her granddaughters many useful things about cats, including the fact that they love to curl up and nap within a circle. Indeed, they will intentionally remain inside a circle for long periods, sitting almost trancelike.

Granny McDonough's love of cats stayed with her all her life, just as the musical lilt of Ireland lingered on her tongue, and given that she raised Raine and Maggie, some of Granny's expressions and patterns of speech carried over and became part of them.

Cat tales abound in the McDonough and Tully clans, and Raine especially enjoyed spinning the colorful yarns– complete with Granny's brogue.

One year, for instance, when Mrs. Jenkins' tabby gave birth to kittens that everyone *knew* Myrrdyn had sired (when he darted out the door one crisp autumn night under the enchanted light of the Hunter's Moon), it surprised the kibble out of a suddenly-younger-acting Gypsy and her owner. That tabby had thirteen years on her, if a day, and well past her kitten-bearing time was she. "The old fool!" Mrs. Jenkins had complained to anyone who would listen.

But there were kittens all right– *and what kittens!* The villagers took to calling them "faerie cats," and to be sure, there was something *magickal* about those glossy kittens, black as midnight each one, and shiny as patent leather, with bright pumpkin-colored eyes that seemed to bore clean through whomever they regarded. Every child in town had fussed for one, and all these years later, Myrrdyn's charmed progeny still inhabit a few of the Hamlet's quaint old mansions. It's funny how things can stick in the mind over the jumbled years– but that story has real sticking power.

Closer to the moment, Raine and Maggie were bustling about Tara's kitchen, where the former lit a thick, red candle-in-a-jar labeled "Witches' Brew" that smelled suspiciously like Dragon's Blood incense, filling the space with a wonderful cinnamon tang. Raine had just pulled the new candle from its box, and she wanted to light it straightaway, for Granny had taught that it was unlucky to keep a candle in the house that had never been lit.

Granny instilled many, what some might call, "flights of fantasy" or "old wives' tales" into her three granddaughters, such as a toppled chair upon standing was a bad omen. Spilled salt was too, unless you promptly tossed a pinch of it over your left shoulder to stave off the bad luck.

Remembering Granny, as she always did at teatime, Maggie poured herself and Raine each a fragrant cup of the first-flush Darjeeling the pair ordered from abroad. Nary a tea bag ever found its sorry way into Tara's traditional door! As was their habit, the pair used the eggshell-thin cups their granny had carefully carried, years before, from the "Old Country." At Tara, tea was never taken from a mug, or as Granny used to call it, a "beaker."

"I was just thinking of Granny's special water-cress sandwiches she used to serve at teatime," Maggie mused. *And her cucumber sandwiches.* She sighed. *We miss you, Granny.*

Raine gave a knowing nod. "While we're having our tea, why don't we review a bit about the ax murders?" the raven-haired Sister suggested. Her eyes shone brilliant green as she finished her candle-lighting task with a flourish of hand, her rings catching a beam from the setting sun that sparked a rainbow off a stained-glass window.

There was *magick* in candlelight. Its soft glow not only transformed a room into an enchanting space, its illumination raised psychic awareness, and most significantly– a lit candle released energies.

Having arranged on a tray the tea things, Maggie sat at the kitchen's antique table– a heavy, round, claw-footed affair that matched the oak, pressed-back chairs around it. Immediately the stunning redhead began to run through her mind the details of their current mystery; but reading her thoughts, it was the ever-more loquacious Raine who began.

"As I mentioned earlier, after Nellie shared her story with us on the train, I couldn't help feeling that she'd purposely left something out about her aunt." Raine took a swallow of tea. "And the more I think about it, the more I'm convinced of it."

Maggie looked absorbed, reaching up to flick back the wave of fiery hair that often dipped toward her eye. "Hmmm, I know what you mean. I sensed that too."

"I can't tell you why exactly. Body language, I suppose." Raine's steady gaze met Maggie's.

"Uh——**huh**," Maggie remarked, raising a brow. "That often speaks clearer and louder than words. I hope we can ferret out enough clues to solve this mystery, or as much of it as we can, before resorting to our Time-Key. I mean we must be careful, *discriminating*, in how we use the Key. It's crucial that we never abuse its sacred use now that we have the ability to unravel History's most stubbornly shrouded mysteries."

Raine gave a brisk nod. "Auntie Merry's powerful crystal ball will be a huge help to us, Mags." After a pensive pause, she said suddenly, "I know the ax murders occurred a long time ago; but surely, there are others, besides Nellie Triggs, still living in our area whose ancestors had some connection to the ghastly tragedy."

Maggie set her teacup down in its saucer. "If there are, we'll find them and speak with them. Nevertheless, you thought of something else a moment ago … something you've yet to share with me."

Raine shrugged. "Nothing. Just puzzling over a few little things." She ducked her dark head to drink her tea, keeping her eyes downcast to prevent her cousin from easily reading her brainwaves.

Maggie pressed. "Hmmm, well I *know* you. You're stirring a cauldron of notions in that wily brain of yours. Give! What is it you're struggling to keep from me?"

Raine gulped the rest of her tea then rose to put their cups in the sink, still avoiding Maggie's eyes. When she turned to again face her sister of the moon, her expression was somber, and her deep resonant voice sounded even lower in timbre. "There are several people yet in our neck of Penn's Woods," she said, using the old name for Pennsylvania, "whose families have connection to those murders, and …" her voice drifted off, as a cold sensation, like icy skeletal fingers flitted down her spine.

"And?"

Two pairs of intense green eyes met and held.

"I have a keen Irish feeling that we had better be extra cautious whilst investigating this case."

"Aren't we always?" Maggie's expression mirrored her sudden concern.

"Yes, but this case feels different to me. Different from all our others."

"How do you figure?"

"I don't figure. *I know.* I can't tell you how or why, but I just know it feels different. I fret a bit before every sleuthing venture, but–" she suddenly switched gears. "Let's just be extra careful this time. That's all I'm saying." Raine forged a smile that came off as just that.

"*This* coming from the Sister known to throw caution to the wind, to laugh in the face of danger!" Maggie twisted to cast an eye to the kitchen clock. "Thaddeus will be here before we know it."

Raine tossed the dishtowel she had picked up aside. "Let's go conjure Granny while we're still alone."

"Right," Maggie answered, at a loss for what else to say.

En route to the attic, Raine, who could communicate with animals– it was her very special gift– began brooding over the Merlin cats. *They've been alerting me to approaching danger all day!*

Snatching only the last fragment of her cousin's thought, Maggie shuddered as an especially cold frisson skittered down her spine, making the hair on the back of her neck rise. "If I were to be honest, I've been getting a stronger and stronger feeling, too, that this mystery is going to be our most challenging to date and–" Her look clouded as she stopped herself from expressing the concern aloud– *most perilous of all.*

Briskly, Maggie brushed the errant swirl of rich, red hair away from her face as though to shake off the qualms that, truth be known, were plaguing her since they had encountered the mysterious woman on the train home from the Witch City of Salem. "We shan't worry ourselves about any of this now, darlin'. We're not keeping to the path of the Great Secret if we allow negative thinking to lead us. We don't want to program anything bad for ourselves or anyone else."

With a nod, Raine continued, wordless, toward the attic stairs.

Wordless, however, was a rare condition for the verbose, brunette Sister. Often effusive, always bold, and ever more-than-ready for a new adventure, Raine was a sexy, somewhat naughty pixie who was destined to keep her looks and her youthful appearance. Pixies, after all, are enduring as well as endearing.

Maggie was another of those women whom capricious Fate had ordained would be forever young– and she too was most definitely sexy. Perchance it was her sense of humor that helped retain her beauty and allure. Maggie laughed often.

However, the short laugh she had just pitched Raine was not her usual expression of amusement, a laugh that was almost musical. This laugh carried trepidation. "God and Goddess grant that we don't encounter anything as evil as we did in our Macbeth adventure, or as risky as our last two quests. Stuff and nonsense!" she quickly amended, catching the flicker of concern that flashed in Raine's eyes. "We'll program our way to be smooth. It's merely the usual apprehension we experience before each pursuit." She started to say something else then stopped herself a second time, the unspoken portion of her thought seeming to trail through the house after the pair like a dark, looming shadow. *I just hope we won't be opening a Pandora's box!*

Raine picked up the fragment of fear but quickly blew it off, not allowing it to take root.

Their ability to read each other's minds, bonded Maggie and Raine; and though they sniped at one another on occasion, they were close, much more like sisters than first cousins.

For one thing, the magickal trio– Raine, Maggie, and Aisling– had identical eyes, arresting to anyone who looked upon them. The "McDonough eyes" the villagers called them– tip-tilted and vivid green, the color of Ireland itself, fringed with long, thick, inky lashes and blazing with insatiable life.

"God's fingers were sooty when he put in the eyes of my three lovely Irish granddaughters," Granny had been want to say.

As their blonde cousin Aisling, raven-haired Raine and redheaded Maggie accentuated their eyes with intense makeup, too theatrical for most– signature for the Sleuth Sisters. And like their granny before them, all three McDonough lasses had beautiful complexions– rich cream, glowing and flawless– that, together with their hair and matchless emerald eyes, rendered each dramatically stunning.

From the moment of birth, Granny had recognized how extraordinary each of her granddaughters was– even for a Tully or a McDonough– predicting that they would be able to see what others, including their own kind, could not.

And from the moment each of the McDonough girls entered puberty– it was like bees to honey! Boys suddenly couldn't keep away from them. Just looking at them rendered most males so giddy, they acted like they'd had too much of old Buck Taylor's 'lectricfyin' applejack. Would-be suitors followed the McDonough gals home from high school and college, tied up their phones evenings, and fought with each other over who would invite them to dances and such.

Perhaps it was Granny's special olive-oil soap the threesome washed with that made their skin so luminous and rendered their auras so bright that people– well, those who believed in magick, anyway– virtually saw them in dazzling, sparkly radiance, like the beautiful leaders of splendor and light they actually were. Or maybe it was simply the self-confidence Granny instilled in her granddaughters that made them shine so. Poise has a way of doing that. Whatever the reason, the McDonough lasses radiated something that was impossible to ignore.

Their artsy theatre friends summed them up by saying, "Raine, Maggie, and Aisling have that intangible *je ne sais quoi* that makes them unforgettable."

No one ever forgot a McDonough woman.

In all fairness, they did not collect hearts as one collects seashells or butterflies, and yet …

A second ago, Raine, who was usually fearless about plunging into tomorrow, felt that fantastic McDonough confidence and optimism slip a notch. *A Pandora's box!* she echoed Maggie's earlier thought, the disquiet making itself evident on her face.

Instinctively her hand rushed to the antique talisman suspended on a thick silver chain around her neck. She brushed her ringed fingers across the large emerald embedded in the center of the amulet's broad silver-and-black-enameled surface. A colorful sprinkling of tiny, pinhead-size gems of moonstone, garnet, emerald, ruby, sapphire, amethyst, citrine, and various hues of quartz and topaz glittered in the treasured heirloom. For a long moment, Raine regarded the piece, as if seeing it for the first time.

"Everything will work out the way it's supposed to. It always does," Maggie purred, stopping before the large stained-glass window on the stair landing. She flicked her heavy, shoulder-length hair away from her face. The dark-red flame of her crowning glory, in certain luminosity such as this, rippled blue lights through the thick waves. "Even if this were to prove the most challenging mission …" her voice trailed away for a quiet moment in meditation. "We'll handle whatever comes."

The fleeting shadow lifted from Raine's countenance, and she nearly shouted, "Yes we will!"

Raine worried the most before an adventure; yet, true Aries that she was, continually proved herself the most daring of the Sleuth

Sisters. Beau always teased her that the mere mention of a mystery quickened her pulse.

Maggie declined to respond, except to comment that the Merlin cats, perfectly aligned, were following them up the steps to the attic, the steady, slow purr of their escort of magickal felines growing louder.

For a time, both women were silent, listening to the familiar, and somehow comforting, sounds the old house was prone to issue.

"Black Jack is telling me that a pair of red cats will figure into our current puzzle," Raine said suddenly.

"*Red* cats?!" Maggie shrieked. "Whatever do they mean?"

Raine lifted her shoulders in a shrug. "I suppose we'll find out. Sooner or later."

At the door to the attic, it was Maggie who shrugged. She pulled open the creaking attic door, and the pair entered, followed by the glossy black Merlin cats, Black Jade and Black Jack O'Lantern, with the more elusive Panthèra.

It was dark. They needed the lantern Maggie had seized from the bottom attic step.

At the top of the stairs, the two women slipped into the black ritual robes they kept on pegs on the attic wall.

Raine cocked her head. "You realize that at some point we might *have* to travel back in time to witness who wielded an ax against Nellie's great-aunt and her household."

Maggie gave a half-nod, not wishing to commit to that alternative yet. From under her clothing, she extracted the talisman she habitually wore on a strong silver chain around her neck.

Maggie's heirloom piece matched Raine's exactly, save that the large center stone in hers was a blood-red ruby. Tracing a finger over the amulet's bejeweled Triquetra surface– or rather, her talisman's *third* of the Triquetra design– she said, thinking of their consummate Leo cousin Aisling, "There's indeed something to be said for having the mystical Power of Three."

"Levitation!" Raine rallied. "For the life of me, I don't know why we get ourselves into such a dither before each new undertaking! Me especially!" Dipping her head, she waited for her cousin's reaction, watching her from under the bristly veil of her lashes. "I mean, we–"

"We'll prove ourselves yet again," Maggie managed to insert with quiet Scorpio force. "We've got to. Granny left us more than just this house and a great trust fund. We were summoned to unlock a mystical portal, a gateway that unveils a world of ancient mysteries and hidden knowledge! To guard the Time-Key's secret and its power, and to use it for good."

Raine flashed her cousin and sister of the moon an understanding grin, deepening her dimple. "To repeat Granny's wisdom, 'Everything will work out the way it's supposed to.'"

"Because it *is* our destiny," Maggie interposed. "So mote it be."

A sudden surge of witchy-woman power fired Raine's confidence, and now it was her turn to repeat the charmed phrase, "So mote it be." *Woman In Total Control of Herself ... that's what it means to be a witch. And what a delicious word it is!* she reflected. *A witch is a healer, a teacher, a seeker, a giver, and a protector of all things.*

She reached down and picked up one of the black cats that on silent paws had shadowed her to the attic room. Gazing into the depths of Black Jack O'Lantern's mesmerizing pumpkin-colored eyes, the raven-haired Sister recited her favorite tale, "Once upon a time, there were two pioneering college professors and one former police detective turned private eye– young but possessed of very old souls– from an unheard-of little hamlet in the backwoods of Pennsylvania. Nonetheless, the good works of this magickal threesome were widely noted, winning them the well-earned soubriquet the 'Sleuth Sisters.'"

With the cat content in her arms, Raine, from force of habit, walked deosil– clockwise– the circumference of the attic room, casting a strong circle of protection around the sacred space, whilst Maggie went with lighted lantern to the wooden bookstand that held their ultra-thick *Book of Shadows.* The huge book's black leather cover was embossed in gold gilt with full-blown Triquetra, the ancient Celtic knot symbolizing all trinities– *and infinite power.*

Supporting their *Book of Shadows* and occupying a place of honor before three grand stained-glass windows, the vintage bookstand had been treasured by their granny because it was the lectern used by the celebrated orator William Jennings Bryan when, at the turn of the last century, he had come to speak at the Hamlet's Addison McKenzie Library.

The redheaded Sister swished, in her black robe, across the attic space to hang the lantern, from an oak beam, on a hook above the lectern; then she clicked on a pair of porcelain table lamps, splashing the colorful, hodgepodge room with the soft glow of light and the mystery of shadow.

A former maid's quarters, Tara's attic was dominated by its trilogy of stained-glass windows, the tall center one the largest, displaying the symbol and soul of Ireland– a golden harp. The two smaller, flanking, stained-glass windows each depicted a bright-green shamrock, another symbol of Ireland, and one of the supreme Trinity. There were two stairways, the "front" and the "back" (the back being the "servants' stairs") leading to this attic room that the Sisters referred to as the "Heavens." It seemed a fitting name since it was the place where they did most of their spellcasting, weaving powerful magick; and it was here they conjured their dearly-loved granny.

The spacious room's furniture was an assortment of odds and ends, touched by Time and not fitting enough for the rest of the manse, but too steeped in memories to cast away, such as a green velvet couch and two somewhat lumpy, but still comfortable, easy chairs in a rich claret shade of a fabric that had come from *Belle Époque* Paris. An antique spinning wheel stood in one corner, and in another was a stack of curious old hat boxes, a couple from Edwardian London that held cunning little hats with veils. Maggie, especially, enjoyed sporting those hats, from time to time, for the added mystery their veils lent her.

Atop a pair of small cabriole end tables rested the set of porcelain lamps Maggie had switched on. Chipped from decades of use, the glowing lamps' bases depicted romantic scenes of eighteenth-century lovers engaged in a waltz. Two domed, ornate trunks occupied places under the eaves, one on each end of the attic room; and the center of the scarred-wood floor was graced by a threadbare French carpet, its floral design faded by Time, sun, and the treading of countless feet.

With a chuckle, Raine recalled what Granny always said about that carpet: "So many waltzin' feet have tripped the light fantastic over this ole rug! It holds so many magickal memories an' energies that I cannot bear to part with it, though it's as old as the hills."

One piece of furniture in Tara's attic room was not chipped, faded, worn or shabby, though it was most certainly old.

This was a tall cheval glass that had accompanied Aisling Tully McDonough, "Granny," as the Sisters called her, on her fateful journey from Ireland to America. The mirror was likely worth a fortune, so ornate was it in carved giltwood with Irish symbols and heroes from the Emerald Isle's turbulent past. It had been Granny's most prized souvenir from the Old Country. The Sisters wanted to preserve as much of her essence with that mirror as possible, and so they kept it in their sacred attic room where they worked most of their magick, draped, when not in use, with a protective ghostly sheet. Hence, no one else ever handled this treasured keepsake.

On one side of the mirror hung Granny's Irish knit shawl; from the opposite side dangled a favorite necklace, a long, thick rope of pure silver from which hung two round, silver Gypsy bells. Granny used to say that the delightful tinkling sound soothed away her troubles and reminded her of the shell chimes that hung in the windows of the seaside cottages on the Old Sod. The shawl, in a spider-web design, was still black as jet and sparkling with dozens of tiny aurora borealis crystals– Granny's widow's weeds had enfolded style, as well as a great deal of magick!

Raine always made it a habit to stand for a few quiet moments at the tranquil trilogy of stained-glass windows, peering out the clear portions to the faerie-tale Hamlet below. In a mysterious way, did a mist oft hover over the beautiful but contrary Youghiogheny River.

She drew a deep breath, letting it out slowly. The late-afternoon had turned dusky with early evening and an impending storm, but the twinkling lights of the town and the boats on the curving ribbon of river never failed to relax her, freeing her mind of unwanted thoughts and anxieties. Once in a while she would hear the lonely, nostalgic sound of a horn from one of those boats, as it navigated the fog pockets. In the fog, sounds carried a long distance, seeming ofttimes to echo. It was a curious thing, that. Sometimes, the raven-haired Sister even imagined she heard voices in the fog. Perhaps she did.

Now what she heard was a faint roll of thunder. It started to rain, falling straight and steady, as she stood quietly watching it. Raine lingered a moment longer at the window, spinning out the time and reliving a treasured memory of their granny that would serve as the "juice" needed to conjure the grand lady.

"Ready?" Maggie's soft voice asked. Carefully, she removed the sheet from the treasured mirror, unveiling it in all its splendor, after which Raine reached out and touched the glass wistfully, a whispered supplication on her lips.

"Granny."

With her wand, Maggie drew a second circle of protection around the attic room, calling upon the God-Goddess, their angel and spirit guides, as well as the guardians of the watchtowers— the spirits of the four elements— to secure their sacred space.

After lighting four white, beeswax candles, Raine touched her lighter to a Frankincense-and-Myrrh incense cone in its burner. With the aid of a large, purple feather, she fanned the smoke, allowing the aromatic fragrances to permeate the entire area. At once, Maggie lit, in a fan-shaped seashell, a bundle of white sage and, carrying it in a clockwise motion, cleansed the room of negativity, all the while chanting a smudging mantra. "Negativity that invades our sacred place, we banish you with the light of our grace. You have no hold or power here. We stand and face you with no fear! Be you gone forever, for now we say— this is our sacred space, and you will obey!"

The Sisters then positioned themselves before their *Book of Shadows,* as Maggie quickly thumbed to the desired page at the beginning of the massive tome.

Holding crystals in their hands, the Sisters took a few moments to clear their minds of fears and worries. They called upon Archangel Michael to protect them from all harm and evil and to keep their circle secure. They called once more on their angel and spirit guides to surround and protect their blessed space.

Raine also felt compelled to summon Black Panther, her chief animal totem. Black Jack, meanwhile, was content to sit in the center of the protective circle. There he would remain till the Sisters completed their magick.

Protected, centered and grounded, the Sisters knew they could now invoke the wise and gentle spirit of Aisling Tully McDonough; and joining hands, they chanted and called forth, using the invocation taught them years before by their granny.

Gazing into the room's tall cheval glass and ringing a small silver bell, they chanted in unison, "In peace and love, and by the Supreme Majesty of the God-Goddess, we evoke and conjure thee, Aisling Tully McDonough! Come hither and appear before us, in this mirror, in the fair and comely shape we know ye to be! Come ye forth; we conjure thee, Aisling Tully McDonough! Come ye forth!"

Suddenly, a strong wind sprung up to rattle the windows of the old mansion; and in the distance, a train whistle, from the Hamlet's busy station, sounded a protracted, mournful wail. An unearthly sensation came over the Sisters, as they focused on their intent and believed with all their essence, imaging their grandmother in their minds, and feeling the strong love they held for her in their hearts.

As always when they conjured their granny, the candles began to flicker wildly. Oblivious, the Sisters continued gazing into the tall, antique glass until the entity, at last, accompanied by a blast of cold air in the otherwise temperate attic, manifested in full figure, cloudy at first, then clearly– the beloved image of Granny McDonough.

Like her eldest granddaughter and namesake, this Aisling was a statuesque woman, cameo pretty, with a pleasant face and classic features, a woman who bespoke strength and dignity along with eternal beauty.

Using the proper comportment when conjuring, as taught by Granny, Raine and Maggie asked, their voices blending, "Spirit, what is thy name?"

In the easy, kindly manner with which Granny McDonough had spoken in life, the music of County Meath yet on her tongue, she replied, "My name is Aisling Tully McDonough, and I have come at your beckoning, Granddaughters." The image smiled then, with posture tall and unbent; the cloud of soft white hair in its loose bun; the familiar, unlined, pink-and-white face– angelic and so dearly loved by the two young women poised before the glass.

This day Granny was dressed in a long white robe topped by a glittery white cape, the voluminous hood draping lightly over head and shoulders to gracefully frame her face. This was a sign to the Sisters that Granny had been temporarily excused from an important Celestial summit. Their session with her would be brief.

"In love and peace we welcome you, Grandmother! Stay within this mirror for as long as the elders permit; we entreat you, for we seek and need your wise counsel yet again."

"I have been summoned to aid you, and this I shall do, though today," she swept a bejeweled hand along her shimmering white attire, "as you can see, I cannot tarry." The reflection smiled; and the Sisters knew, now that the required ritual rules had been properly followed, their spiritual encounter with their grandmother could take on a less formal tone.

"Granny," Raine began, her voice breaking slightly, "we miss you so!"

"I'm with you always, me darlin's, all three of you," she asserted with her enchanting Irish inflection. She blew them a kiss that passed through the glass as soft, fine faerie dust– silver and gold, glittering and diamond-bright. The crystalline particles cascaded over Raine and Maggie, swirling around them– a Heavenly hug– as the Sisters felt their granny's warm love and protection.

"We are grateful," the two present of her granddaughters replied with fervor.

Maggie, whose Scorpio love was intense, pulled a handkerchief from the pocket of her black ritual robe to dab at her tear-stained face.

"Granny," Raine voiced anxiously, "we need your guidance." Without preamble, she launched into the encounter with the mystery woman on the train home from Salem, concluding, "What can you tell us about the unsolved ax murders that chilled our Hamlet into a state of fear in 1932? As always, we ask that you assist us in any way you can. Have you advice for us before we delve into this new mystery?"

"Make use of every protection I taught ya, and I taught you well. Concentrate your intentions *as one mighty force*. Have faith in th' supremacy an' goodness of the God-Goddess and in their army of archangels an' spirit guides you will summon to assist you. *And*, by extension, have faith in yourselves, in your own capabilities. *Believe* with all your essence."

Granny McDonough lifted a hand to point a cautionary finger at the Sisters, her keen gaze holding them. "Never lose faith in your *own* powers, me darlin's. That is my advice, and it is tried and true."

"Well, Granny," Raine quipped with the vivacity of an Irish storyteller, "whenever life turns us upside down and around, and we feel as though we've passed through the Looking Glass once again, with your guidance, we always emerge with a bit more wisdom."

"*Tré neart le chéile– together strong!*" Granny's voice took on a somber note. "Now *I* must warn you that there will soon be more evil for you to deal with than the dark an' bloody complexities of th' past."

"Surely not–" Maggie abruptly stopped herself.

Holding up a hand for silence, Granny's eyes softened benevolently, revealing a soul sated in wisdom and love. "My dear child, rest assured I shall be with you through the confusion."

Raine pursed her lips. "Once more, mystery and mayhem have landed in our laps."

Granny gave a quick nod. "*Och*, f'r sar-tain, but niver f'rget that y' have the sacred Power of Three, and *if* you hold fast to the Great Secret an' keep control of your fears, you will succeed in annythin' you set your minds upon."

After a brief silence, Maggie spoke. "Granny, I've been feeling something dark– something *exceedingly* wicked. In fact, today I began sensing a wicked web of shadows forming, entwining and tangling all around us."

"*Aye*, your sentiments ring true, child," Granny answered. "Mind you wear your talismans continuously. Still, you must proceed with *extreme* caution. The evil you'll be facin' this time will be especially virulent, more so than anny in th' past; and," the reflection raised a hand to again point directly at the Sisters, the eyes penetrating, "*you and Aisling– **all three of you**– will be its **particular prey**.*"

Maggie and Raine exchanged looks.

"Take heed," Granny said sternly; "use *every* precaution. You have what it takes to defeat this evil."

"But, Granny," Raine blurted, "what–"

"***Whist**, lass!*" Granny McDonough lowered the hood of her white, diamond-bright cape to tilt her snowy head and cup a hand over an ear, listening to something the Sisters could not perceive. "*Och*, me darlin's, I must go. I am called. Remember, there are no secrets that Time or," her green eyes flashed, "*time-travel* does not reveal." With that, she raised the hood of her celestial cloak and shook her head sadly, her voice taking on a sinister note as she pronounced the dreaded words they had heard from her in caveat before–

"*Murder. Murder most foul.*"

Then turning on a heel, and with a swish of her sparkly white cape, Granny was gone, sending in her wake, through the mirror, a swirl of silver and gold glitter to embrace them.

Fifteen minutes later, Raine set her purse down next to Maggie's in the entrance hall near Tara's front door, Granny's parting words replaying in her mind and heart– "Take heed; use every precaution." She glanced at her watch. Thaddeus would be pulling into Tara's circular driveway any second. Then, they planned to walk the well-worn path through the woods to Beau and Hugh's place next door for supper.

The storm was over; the night would be clear, though it was unseasonably chilly, more like autumn than spring. Or was it Granny's warning that chilled her? Raine breathed a sigh of relief that, at last, they were ready to set out for the evening's gathering.

She and Maggie had been so rushed the past several hours that their minds were swirling. When they received Hugh's phone invitation to break bread and brainstorm over their current mystery with their sleuthing set, she and Maggie were just leaving the Haleigh College campus. Though their teaching duties had been satisfied for the day, they had to grocery shop for the ingredients to make the huge salad that would be their dinner contribution; return home, wash, chop and mix the veggie medley together; then conjure Granny with all the questions that were buzzing in their heads.

Raine caught a glimpse of Maggie through the door that led into the kitchen. She was taking the salad dressing out of the fridge.

The raven-haired Sister strode past the life-size knight-in-armor to the oak-pillared entry that led into Tara's spacious, old-fashioned parlor with its heavy Victorian furnishings, green velvet drapes, and wall of books, the shelves crammed with leather-bound tomes spilling over with esoteric, arcane knowledge. Instantly her eyes locked with the pair, so like her own, of her grandmother whose fascinating portrait hung above the ornate fireplace.

The oil painting by Charles Dana Gibson captured Aisling Tully McDonough at the height of her beauty, the soft cloud of red hair, upswept in the famed Gibson-Girl coiffure of the era, graced the flawless oval of the face, the low-cut, off-the-shoulder, green velvet gown accentuating the hour-glass figure. Streaming down over one white shoulder, a long tendril of fiery red hair formed a perfect question mark. Gibson had entitled the captivating image *The Eternal Question*, and thus read the neat, brass plate at the base of the portrait.

There Raine lingered for a solemn moment, thinking aloud. "Granny, as Maggie and I make ready to embark on our next adventure, we know, this time, we must be extra careful to protect ourselves and our Time-Key. We promised you we'd be especially cautious and vigilant, and we shall. But oh Granny, that can be *soo* tricky.

"It's *empowering* to know, from our past efforts, that we can travel down the Tunnel of Time, at will, to unlock the door that'll whisk us through the thrills and chills of yesteryear. Pretty exciting stuff! And that's why, Gran, we ask your continued guidance. Aid us, as you faithfully have, in making prudent choices."

The attractive brunette paused for a beat, moving closer to the portrait. "I know I can be impetuous and impulsive, too daring at times, so I guess what I'm asking for is a bit more guidance than usual. It's hard for me to admit that to Maggie," she whispered.

The eyes in the portrait seemed to kindle, and a little cat smile curved the corners of Raine's pouty, candy-apple-red mouth. "I can't help my feeling that, though this adventure will be more dangerous than our past pursuits, we'll advance to a whole new level of skill and achievement. She gave her normally husky voice a thick coat of drama, "And as I always say– who knows what skeletons and dangers dangle in the closets our Time-Key will open? Along with those secreted perils, magick, adventure and surprise await us at the creak of every opening door." She finished with an eerie laugh, sending the portrait a saucy wink. "You see, Granny, I can laugh in the face of danger and still be cautious. Laughter is, after all, the Goddess' medicine."

"Just so your laughter doesn't drown out your witchy intuition."

Raine had been so rapt in reverie, she hadn't heard the light footfalls behind her. "Mags! You startled me. I swear you're like a phantom. I seldom hear you enter a room. How long have you been standing there?"

The redhead's full red lips twitched to a smile. "Long enough."

Raine's ebony brows rushed together in a grimace, and she opened her mouth to retort, when–

Maggie waved her cousin's unspoken words aside. "If we run into a snag untangling our Hamlet's unsolved ax murders, we'll make good and proper use of *all* our magickal tools, including our Time-Key. And as you so aptly stated, with it **and** the powerful crystal ball gifted us by Auntie Merry, we should be able to solve virtually *any* mystery that History has cloaked in shadow! One thing's certain– our lives are never boring. Once again, we've some exciting days ahead."

"Danger? Sure, but we've faced high danger in the past. And even if it's going to be worse than before, we're *better* than before." Raine's eyes lifted once again to the painting. "Remember what Granny *always* told us– 'To be forewarned is to be forearmed.'"

"True," Maggie, who opted for an economy of words whenever possible, concurred with a brisk nod, her eyes, too, on the riveting canvas. "And we know she is always with us."

Raine shifted her gaze from Granny's portrait to the striking redhead beside her, as her voice took on an even stronger element of anticipation, and her heart beat excitedly. "I'm feeling ever more confident we'll be able to handle everything and anything that comes at us. So mote it be!"

With her Mona-Lisa smile and a witch's fiery passion, Maggie repeated the time-honored phrase— **"So mote it be!"**

"I kept getting the feeling that Nellie was holding something back about her great-aunt and namesake." ~ Dr. Raine McDonough, PhD

Chapter One

Kissing Maggie lightly on the lips, Thaddeus remarked, his eyes seeming to spark with appreciation as they scanned his lady-love in the form-fitting, black, hooded dress she was wearing. "You look ravishing, as usual. Is everyone going to be there this evening?" he asked. "I remembered the sangria." He raised the two large bottles of the dark-red wine he was holding.

Maggie's full, glossy-red lips curved in her beguiling smile. "Yes, I think everyone will be there. Aisling and Ian may be a tad late however. They have to stop off in town first to pick up a dessert at Sal-San-Tries." She slipped the strap of her designer bag over her shoulder and picked up the salad dressing in its sealed container from the counter. "You look rather enticing yourself, darlin'," the redhead purred, adjusting the Indiana Jones hat she had bought him, her emerald gaze skipping happily over his tweedy attire.

As the esteemed head of Haleigh College's history department, Dr. Thaddeus Weatherby had been the perfect advisor to Raine and Maggie when they were working toward their doctorates in history. His mentorship bonded him with the Sisters and aroused his passionate love for Maggie. As the Sisters came to discover, most often to their delight, the distinctive Dr. Weatherby possessed a wide variety of talents.

Moreover– and to the point– Dr. Thaddeus Weatherby, PhD, was an absent-minded professor with a mind like a steel trap. To put it another way, the highly respected Dr. Weatherby was a bona fide genius, and like most geniuses, he retained his quirks. For instance, he occasionally displayed a childlike nature or more precisely what, owing to his passionate curiosity, colleagues *mistook* for a childlike nature that, at times, drove those in his department a little crazy. But then, as those of the Craft know well, the secret of genius is to carry the riddle of the child into old age. One of the things Dr. Weatherby was fond of saying was, "You're never too old to enjoy a happy childhood. Take time every day to do something amusing!"

And one of the most special things– *and there were many*– about the professor was that he possessed extraordinarily accurate and vivid recall, both visual and audial, an "eidetic memory" some might call it. And that sharp Scorpio wit, along with the remarkable man's courage, or as Hemingway penned it, "grace under pressure," served the Sleuth Sisters well on more than one hair-raising occasion in the past.

A wiry and surprisingly muscular, middle-age man, Thaddeus' iron-grey hair, thanks to Maggie's influence, was no longer reminiscent of Einstein's; rather it was professionally styled. "It doesn't look as if you comb your hair with firecrackers anymore," Raine teased when first she'd seen Thaddeus' new look.

His once careless manner of dress was now "country gentry," Irish tweeds replacing the rumpled, mismatched "Weatherby wear" about which his students used to genially jest. However, he did retain, regardless of what he was wearing, his signature, cherry-red bow tie. Due to his significant other's sway, nowadays he sported a van dyke mustache and beard, and though he wore his contacts more often than he used to, today his bright blue eyes peered from behind his workaday Harry Potter spectacles that adjusted to light.

"Ready, Raine?" Maggie called to her cousin and fellow sister of the moon. She picked up the bright red, old-fashioned railroad lantern the Sisters used evenings to traverse their rural property. Though it was barely dusk, they would need the lighted lamp in the deep woods.

With a farewell wave to the poppet Cara, still sitting on the kitchen counter, the raven-haired Sister pulled open Tara's backdoor, picked up the large, covered bowl containing the salad, and the three of them headed for the woods, through which a maintained path led to the Goodwin's.

Raine's Beau Goodwin and his semi-retired father, Hugh, lived just across the connecting woods from Tara, where the Goodwin Veterinary Clinic was attached to their home.

"I suppose Hannah's sitting with Merry Fay tonight," Maggie commented as she followed Raine onto the well-used path. The trees had sprouted their leaves now, and the woods were in deep shadow.

"Yes, that's what Aisling told me earlier today on the phone," Raine answered. The Sisters were referring to Hannah Gilbert, the McDonough family's longtime, devoted housekeeper and sitter. "Beau's last appointment is at five-thirty today, so barring any emergency farm calls, he'll be able to join us for supper and our brainstorming session."

A few paces behind, on the narrow trace, Thaddeus pushed his spectacles further back on his nose. "I never tire of watching you walk away or following you, Maggie. Each is an ecstatic experience."

Their arrival at Beau and Hugh's long ranch-style home was met with loud and excited barking as Hugh's sibling German shepherds, Nero and Wolfe, greeted them at the backdoor.

Raine sent the dogs a telepathic message to settle down, and within seconds, the pair complied, standing quietly with tongues lolling, as Raine, Maggie, and Thaddeus filed into the Goodwin's rustic kitchen.

Hugh and Betty Donovan, Hugh's companion, were at the sink, washing up the dishes they had used to prepare the chili that was simmering nicely on the stove, with delicious aroma wafting to the arrivals.

Sniffing the air like a hungry wolf, Raine pronounced, "Your chili smells *wonderful!*" She set the salad bowl on the kitchen island to give Hugh and Betty a joint hug.

Betty Donovan and Hugh Goodwin became a couple due to Raine's magickal finagling. They had just seemed so right for one another, both widowed, both animal lovers, and both enthusiastic mystery buffs. Before long, Betty's Irish setter Boru, nearly impossible for her to manage after her husband passed away, heeled perfectly when they walked with Hugh and his two shepherds, Nero and Wolfe; and Betty and Hugh both slept better nights after companionable sessions of reading aloud with discussion of whatever whodunit they were currently unraveling.

A retired librarian, Betty was an attractive lady with short, casual, salt-and-pepper hair and eyes like polished turquoise. She had a penchant for artsy Southwestern fashions and bold silver-and-turquoise jewelry that suited both her coloring and her adventurous Sagittarian personality.

Tall and robust like his son and their Highlander ancestors, Hugh Goodwin's once-ebony hair was now an ennobling silver, as was his full, what-used-to-be-called "cavalry mustache." Indeed, the dear man carried himself in a smart, soldierly manner.

Under wiry, expressive brows, the deep blue of Hugh's eyes had faded some with age, but the years had not diminished his zest for life, not perceivably anyway. In truth, Time had been gracious to Hugh Goodwin; and there were those ladies in his Pennsylvania Hamlet who considered him handsomer now than when he was young, and they had all vied for his attention. But women have always been attracted to men with cavalry mustaches and soulful "bedroom eyes."

A virile, inventive Aquarius, Hugh was a good, upright man, a lover of life and all living things. If he had a fault, it was that he sometimes spoke gruffly– and those times he would huff his salty words into his mustache with gusto– but he was never deliberately unkind, and his words carried truth.

They carried truth now when, turning to Betty, he remarked, "I think, lady, that your supper is about to become a huge hit." He leaned over to plant a kiss on her cheek.

Betty laughed, patting the side of Hugh's chiseled face, "If so, you deserve half the credit."

Nero and Wolfe were eagerly pawing at Raine, their cold, wet noses questing her hands. From her pocket, she pulled a couple of treats, which she bestowed on each dog. "I'm starved!" she exclaimed, snatching a stick of stuffed celery from a platter on the counter.

"You can eat most of us under the table. For the life of me, I don't know where you put it. What's your secret, girl?" Betty joked.

Raine chose to answer with a grin, thinking to herself– *magick!*

By the time Aisling and Ian arrived, everything was ready to serve– the chili simmered to perfection; the jalapeño cornbread cut into wedges, warm and waiting for the seasoned butter, savory with garlic; and the salad tossed with Maggie's homemade, creamy Southwest dressing.

When the doorbell rang, Raine nearly shouted, catching sight of the senior Sleuth Sister and her husband through the glass, "Aisling and Ian are here!" Both she and Maggie sailed to the front door.

The archetypical tall, cool blonde, Aisling McDonough-Gwynn, stretched her long legs to alight from the passenger side of the black SUV. As she strode across Hugh's driveway toward the house, carrying the cardboard box that held their dessert, her long, silvery blonde hair and the knit black cape she was sporting, over ebony jeans and sweater, billowed out behind her in the brisk April wind. At the door she gave Raine and Maggie each a quick peck on the cheek as the magickal trio paused on the stoop, waiting for Ian to lock the vehicle.

"Whad'you get us for dessert?" Raine queried, peering inside the low box. "Anything Sophie whips up at Sal-San-Tries will be welcome, however."

"Believe it or not, she made Spanish flan." Aisling's McDonough green eyes glittered with magick. "I'd programmed that she'd make something that would complement chili and jalapeño cornbread, and," she glanced down at the box she was holding, "*aquí está!* We bought enough for everyone to have seconds."

"Evening, ladies," Ian stepped onto the stoop, holding the door for the Sisters, as they all entered the house.

Ian was a burly ex-cop with a mellow Leo personality that harmonized well with his wife's feline persona; and though he could be fanciful at times, like Aisling, he had no wishbone where a backbone ought to be. His coloring was entirely red-gold. Thick, wavy reddish-gold hair covered his Leonine head, while his hazel eyes flashed bright gold glints. Even his weathered skin gleamed golden, though it could instantly flame red with stirred emotion.

Several years earlier, Aisling and Ian had met on the Pittsburgh police force where they worked together as detectives, the stepping stone to their present career. The Gwynns' Black Cat Detective Agency was a flourishing operation; and all in all, these master sleuths were a well-matched, lionhearted couple. Aisling often said that she and Ian were true soul mates, and anyone seeing them together knew instantly of the bond and the love they shared with one another, as well as with their precocious little Fay of a daughter. Merry Fay mirrored her magickal mother– in more than just her charming looks.

Raine was just about to duck through the door in the alcove that led into the veterinary clinic when it opened, and Beau stepped in.

"Babe," he said, bending to her height to kiss her. "Done for the day." He slipped her a wink. Cast a spell for me that I'll be free for the rest of the night, and we'll be good to go."

"Mmm," she purred, her deep voice leaving her throat in an even lower timbre, "we'll be good to go all right. Maggie's staying at Thad's tonight, so how about you staying over with me? Hmmmmm, big boy?" She spun the wink back to him, though hers was loaded with sexy suggestion.

He pulled her closer, whispering into her ear, his mustache playing sensory sport with her skin. She slid her hands up his chest as a sigh escaped her partially opened lips, her head thrown back.

Beau Goodwin was a big man– tall and powerfully built with the jet-black hair and hot-blue eyes of a long line of Scottish and Scotch-Irish ancestors. In his thirties, his body was lean muscle– muscle that moved with the kind of intensity and power that comes to men who get plenty of exercise a good deal of the time outdoors. His relentless farm calls afforded him continuous bodybuilding workouts; and like Raine, Beau enjoyed spending his free time, the turning wheel of the seasons, in Nature's company.

There was something, simply put– *special*– about Dr. Beau Goodwin that people– and above all, animals– noticed straightaway. Animals reap a "knowing" when a human possesses a good and pure heart through the vibrations the human emits, and this provides the "fur, fin, and feather people" with a safe feeling in the company of that human.

Along with his animal patients, people remembered the softness that peered from Beau Goodwin's eyes. Beau was a healer, and like the Sisters, he was an Old Soul.

Raine often experienced a keen Celtic knowing, just as he frequently did of her, that he had come from somewhere else– somewhere not of this earth. To be sure, each created magick in a singular way, and together these two Star Children enkindled an utterly magickal *Raine-Beau*.

Like all starseeds, who are intrinsically programmed to find others like themselves, both preferred to work in the esoteric and creative fields, using their innate but heightened talents– healing, helping, and searching for their own truths. "Truths beyond the ken of men," as Beau liked to quip.

Raine had a saying of her own regarding their relationship. "It's said some lives are linked across time, connected by an ancient calling that echoes down the ages. We're like magnets, Beau and I, with each incarnation, reaching out and leaping across space to be together."

Magick calls to magick.

The couple shared several common denominators, and though there had been others in each of their lives, this was *why*, after so many years, Raine and Beau were still mutually enchanted.

Only a few things triggered Dr. Beau Goodwin's temper, causing him to lose his Leo chivalry– animal cruelty (he did *not* tolerate animal cruelty in the least) and, at times, Raine's too-daring, impetuous Aries disposition, along with her unwavering outlook on the woes of marriage.

The rare times Raine had dated someone else, she could not squelch the memories of Beau's scorching kisses, and those reminiscences alone could send a multitude of thrills coursing through her.

There's no denying he has power over me, she was thinking, as she always did when she gazed into his piercing, lapis eyes. *Much more than I let him know. Will **ever** let him know. He can burn me up alive. It's part of his appeal, and he can do it in the time it takes to wave a wand.* She stroked his thick ebony mustache, his intense regard holding her captive. Her eyelids fluttered and fell before his searching glance. *There've been times, several times, when I'm almost convinced that my enchanting Beau is the–*

"Wiz-zard!" she exclaimed when her glittering green eyes caught sight of the foil packet peeking out of his shirt pocket. "You remembered to bring me some kitty immune booster!"

He grinned. "Do I ever forget? Just crumble each soft chewable into their food," he said, handing her the packet. "Cats like this liver flavor the best, I think. No more than twice a day, once in the morning food, once in the evening."

"Thank you, baby. It really helps Black Jack especially now that it's allergy season again. I'll see to it you get paid later," she whispered, trailing her hand down his chest.

"Come and get it!" Hugh called from the adjoining kitchen.

"My sentiments exactly," Beau replied, his grin morphing positively wicked.

***

"Start the cornbread round the table again, dear," Hugh said, as he handed a fresh platter of the hot bread to Betty before sitting back down at table.

"You've outdone yourselves tonight," Maggie smiled at Hugh and Betty, with the latter replying her thank-you.

"Glad you're enjoying it. We make a great team," Hugh added. "But now it's your turn to treat. Betty and I are chompin' at the bit to get to the new mystery. How about giving us the scoop?"

Raine, ever the more talkative, began the tale of how she and Maggie had encountered the strange woman on the train home from Auntie Merry's 100th birthday bash in the Witch City of Salem.

"Why *strange*?" Betty interposed. She helped herself to another wedge of the spicy cornbread, and reaching for the seasoned butter, began swirling it over the still-warm bread.

Raine tilted her dark head in a musing gesture. "I don't know why I said that. I meant *mysterious*. She seemed to be holding something back about what she shared with us concerning her great-aunt. After all, it was *she* who approached us. Being from Haleigh's Hamlet herself, she recognized us as the Sleuth Sisters." Raine paused for a few seconds, adding, "She gave Mags and me both the impression that she was harboring a secret of her own."

"Why was she on that train; do you know?" Betty asked, more than curious. "That should tell us something about her."

"We learned," Raine answered, "from talking with her later, that she was returning from a writers' conference in Boston. She's an editor by profession."

Betty nodded. "Sorry for interposing like that. Please continue."

"The woman's name," Raine swept on, brushing aside the interruption, "is Nellie Triggs. That was her great-aunt's name too, the one who was killed along with her elderly mother and one of her two children in the unsolved murders that took place back in 1932."

"Ah!" Hugh exclaimed, picking up his glass of sangria, "our Hamlet's infamous ax murders! I must say that, over the years, *no one's* been able to crack that case."

Maggie gave a nod. "Nary a clue has ever surfaced."

"That we know of," Raine amended. "Anyroad, the atrocity was a triple ax murder that occurred, as Hugh pointed out, in our Hamlet on October 12, 1932; and as we said, it is *yet* to be solved. On that fatal Columbus Day, children were home from school. It was a chilly autumn morning, unusually cold."

The raven-haired Sister took a sip of her wine. "Thus eleven-year-old Orlando Moretti's parents sent him to the backyard for coal for the kitchen stove of the family home, which was located near the railroad station on Murphy Road– right next door to the Triggs home. That little kid got the shock of his life when he stumbled, in the alley behind his house, onto the grotesquely sprawled, gore-covered body of neighbor Nellie Triggs. By the way, the poor woman was only twenty-eight years old when she was murdered. The Nellie we met on the train, the great-niece, told us that Henry Moretti told her that his older brother Orlando– and I'll use Henry's words here– '… threw the coal bucket in the air and came screaming back to the house and into the kitchen like he'd seen a ghost.' Henry was only four at the time, but he actually remembered the incident; and, of course, his family's stories about the murders kept the memory alive for him."

Beau gave a low whistle.

Raine cocked her head, raising one ebony brow in emphasis. "Oh, it gets better. Louis Moretti, Henry and Orlando's father, immediately telephoned the police, who subsequently discovered not only the axed Nellie's bloody body, but the hacked dead body of her mother, Amanda Hardiman, who was sixty-three. She was lying in a pool of blood on the bedroom floor of the three-room, Murphy Road bungalow.

"The police," Raine continued, "rushed Nellie's two young children, Sadie, eleven, and Billy, nine, to the Hamlet hospital called at that time Haleigh State Hospital. At first, the officers thought the children had been savagely beaten with a club or something, but they later realized that they *too* had been attacked with an ax. Sadie died that same day, but Billy survived– only to be killed ten years later."

"Nellie, the niece, thought it was 1942 when he was killed in combat during World War II," Maggie threw in. "I looked it up, and that *was* the year Billy died. He's buried in Italy."

"Of course," Raine pushed on with the tale, "the *Hamlet Herald* reported on the horrifying violence of the ax crimes. Train Nellie showed us a well-worn, creased newspaper article she keeps inside a piece of cellophane in her wallet. The headline screamed, 'Two children taken to hospital with their heads battered in! Blood was spattered throughout the kitchen, bedroom, and living room … but only one chair was overturned.'"

"Sounds like the murderer was someone whom the axed Nellie knew and had opened her door to," Hugh put in. "If the woman had no known enemies," he brushed a finger over his mustache, "I'm wondering if she was her own worst enemy."

"What are you saying?" Raine and Maggie turned simultaneously toward Hugh.

"Nellie may have been a *naïve* young woman. *Far too trusting,*" Hugh submitted. His keen blue eyes below the bushy brows looked sharply at the Sisters. "I have a feeling she opened the door to the murderer that night."

"Hmmm, we think the same thing," Maggie replied. "No sign of a break-in. Only one chair knocked over. A clue perhaps that the killer was not an intruder, but rather someone the family knew?" The redheaded Sister shrugged. "We don't know for certain– but the Hamlet shuddered and locked its doors."

Raine made a wry face. "Train Nellie also showed us an old photo of her ill-fated aunt."

"I can image that photograph clear as day. Can't you, Raine?" Maggie asked.

With a bob of her head, Raine answered, "The image showed a dark-haired woman with sad eyes– a mysterious woman– wearing a dreamy expression, a cloche hat, and a high-collared trench coat, the style popular during the Roaring Twenties."

"Axed Nellie was a very pretty girl," Maggie and Raine pronounced simultaneously, as was ofttimes their habit. "And she and her namesake look nearly identical."

"I recall that train Nellie told us that she hopes her life goes in a different direction," Maggie voiced softly.

"Yes, and her remark incited me to think of William Blake's *Auguries of Innocence*. 'Every night and every morn, some to misery are born,'" quoted Raine quietly. "'Every morn and every night, some are born to sweet delight.' I remember it was at that point in the poem when Nellie's dreamy expression changed slightly, taking on an extra measure of sadness whilst she finished the poem with the words, '*Some are born to endless night.*'"

Maggie clucked her tongue sympathetically. "It was as if she was saying that some people were born under the wrong star, or that some people bring bad luck– and her namesake was one of them."

After a reflective pause, Raine again resumed the story. "Police were baffled by the ax slayings from the onset," she declared, "as to what provoked the mysterious murders. A concentrated search was launched for the murder weapon. The Triggs family's ax– and they would've owned an ax, because the bungalow had a wood-burning stove– turned up missing and was never found. Likely carried off the short distance and tossed into the river by the murderer."

"Not necessarily," Hugh spoke up. "That makes the most sense, but if the river was low … ." He thought for a moment, saying, "If the Yough was low, the police would've seen that ax in the water. Hell, the murderer could've tossed the ax onto a passing train, or even buried it. Or … the murderer could've hopped a freight train, then hurled the ax into the river, from the train, some distance away."

Everyone chimed in with an opinion, until Raine got them back on track. "Nellie's face and head had been severely hacked; her collar bone was nearly severed, and her arm was broken, this last perhaps due to the fall– or perhaps she was thrown?– from the kitchen window into the alley."

"More likely she tried to escape the violence and run for help by crashing through that window," Aisling interjected. "It was ground-level and opened onto the alley, right?"

"Correct," Maggie answered.

"According to then-Coroner Wilbur Bauer, all three victims died from fractured skulls," Raine revealed.

While the others mulled the information over, the ebony-haired Sister stopped again to take a long draft of her sangria, soon taking up the story anew.

"A popular theory, over the years, has persisted that axed Nellie, who had been a widow since 1927– her husband Milton died in the veterans' hospital in Pittsburgh, the result of gassing in France during World War I– was murdered by a beau, after a lovers' quarrel. And because they were eyewitnesses, the killer then took the ax to Nellie's mother and children.

"When the police interviewed the neighbors, they discovered that nothing unusual had been seen or heard during the preceding night. The *Hamlet Herald* stated that a long freight train passed through around midnight, and several barking dogs added to the train's loud clanking noise, but other than that, *nothing* had been seen or heard."

"The murderer could well have been familiar with the local train schedule," Ian cut in.

"That's exactly what Mags and I thought," Raine adjoined. "It could've been someone who visited that house often enough to *know* that a long, noisy train, with accompanying barking dogs, pierced the quiet neighborhood midnights. My guess, too, is that he or she also knew *how much time* they would have to execute the slaughters."

Elbows on the table, her chin resting on her palms, Aisling urged, "Do go on."

Raine assented with a nod. "Arrests were made during an investigation that stretched out over months; but, as we said, never were the ax murders solved."

"What about the boy who survived the attack? Did he remember anything?" Hugh queried. Listening intently, he settled back in his seat for a speculative moment to draw a long breath.

"At first baffled and generally confused, Nellie's son Billy– who, as I told you, was nine at the time of the murders– reported to the police, once he was well enough to speak, that his *uncle* had struck him and his sister with the ax. But Nellie's only brother, Clyde Hardiman, had an air-tight alibi– he was at his Cumberland, Maryland, home when the crimes were committed; and his wife vouched for that. So did two neighbors, a married couple, who were playing cards with Clyde and his wife that night at the Hardiman house."

"Perhaps," Ian interposed, "the murderer was someone who *looked like* the boy's uncle." By this point, the seasoned gum-shoe's mind was racing.

Maggie gave an enthusiastic nod. "That's what train Nellie told us her family always believed. It all happened so fast and furiously, and probably in darkness or shadow, that young Billy only *thought* it was his Uncle Clyde. Anyway, two of Nellie's suitors were arrested, but both were eventually released when there was no real evidence to hold either."

"There were subsequent break-ins at the house where the ax murders took place," Raine asserted after yet another pensive pause.

"I wonder," Aisling ventured, "could the murderer have returned to the scene of the heinous crimes to collect something he feared might incriminate him? Or perhaps, thinking Billy might remember something– and though the orphaned boy, likely taken in by a relative, would not have been there– the murderer came back to kill the little boy?"

"We don't know," Raine confessed. "But the murderer wielded muscle; *that* we do know. Thus, police tended to believe the killer had been a man."

"Yes," Maggie cut in, "they associated the idea of such violence with a man; but it's a known fact that, in times of towering passion, a *woman* can achieve Herculean strength." Her beautiful face darkened. "And history shows that women are more capable of extremes than men."

"True," Raine concurred, recalling that she had acquired that kind of strength during a couple of perilous incidents in the business of solving past crimes. "But, on the other hand, if the boy Billy thought the murderer was his uncle, the killer was likely a man." Privately, she ran her mind back over a particular moment from the past, wading through previous mysteries to remember something else from her own experiences, then amended aloud, "*likely* but not positively."

Betty pushed away from the table. "My feeling exactly. Likely but not positively." Her turquoise eyes took in the empty plates. Anyone care for thirds? Hugh and I made plenty."

When there were no takers, Aisling remarked, "I'm saving room for that beautiful flan!"

"Let's let our food settle for a few minutes while we talk," Betty suggested. "Then we'll clear the table and serve the coffee and flan."

Everyone agreed, complimenting Hugh and Betty again on the dinner, after which Hugh leaned back and loosened his belt a notch. A feeling of camaraderie always permeated the sleuthing set when they met, and tonight was no exception.

"At this early stage in our investigation, all we're doing is making guesses. But guessing gets the wheels turning. After all this time, we might never know the answers to some of our queries. Nineteen thirty-two was a long, long time ago," Maggie sighed, but–" she broke off abruptly, then went on, "train Nellie told us that so many times has she wanted to approach *us* about this. You see, after the murder, there was a lot of vicious whispering about her great-aunt. Yet, when the neighbors were interrogated by the police– who, as I said, tried for a long time to gather evidence– they all said they never saw nor heard any 'hanky-panky' whatsoever going on over at Nellie's place. The Moretti family, only steps away, told the police that everyone in the axed woman's family seemed nice, and they could never understand why, and I quote, '… something so terrible would happen to Mrs. Triggs and her family.'"

"But," Raine picked up the tale, "that isn't what most people wanted to hear. They wanted to hear the worst. They wanted all the dirt the mud-slingers could generate. You know how people are ... and especially in a small town like ours. They love gossip, the dirtier, the better; so over the years, the story was embroidered on, as we say in our neck of Penn's Woods, and added to–"

The raven-haired Sister stopped herself, concluding, "Gossip is black magick because it spreads emotional poison, perpetuates fear, and keeps others down. Train Nellie said that episode in her family's history put an indelible black mark on the otherwise spotless family name. Why even today, when she meets someone for the first time, someone from our area, one of the first things they ask her is, 'Are you related to the family who was axed back in the Depression years?'"

Raine's brows knitted in a slight frown. "It doesn't help matters that the surname Triggs is an uncommon one in our area, or that the popular TV show *Unexplained Mysteries and Uncracked Crimes* did a segment on the murders a few years ago. What a sensation that caused! I remember Granny saying–"

Aisling interposed a quick question, "Is the house where the murders took place still there?"

Raine and Maggie shook their heads, with Maggie replying, "Evidently no one wanted to live there after the murders and the subsequent break-ins. Nellie told us the little house was one step up from a shack really. It was boarded-up, then eventually torn down, sometime in the late 1930s."

"Didn't the *Hamlet Herald* run the story for years afterward, hoping someone would come forward with information?" Hugh replied.

"I think I remember Granny mentioning that," Aisling remarked, reaching for her wine and looking to her fellow sisters of the moon for confirmation.

"Oh yes," Raine and Maggie chorused.

"For years, the *Herald* ran articles every October, on the anniversary of the murders," Raine revealed, "but it never brought forth any information, not one shred of evidence, nary a clue– *ever. That we know of,*" she stressed.

The Goth Sister suddenly remembered something, pausing for a beat then saying, "And if the victims' spirits ever returned to demand justice ..." Raine's expression lit up as her voice trailed off fleetingly. "'*I* have never experienced anything,' train Nellie told us. Then she started to tell us something else, that someone in her family *had* experienced axed Nellie's ghost perhaps, but she stopped short, saying that she'd already taken enough of our time. Said it was a *whole* other story." Raine looked to Maggie, "That we intend to get from train Nellie soon."

Oh dear! Raine received a sudden revelation: *Nellie will soon see the same vision of her great-aunt!*

"Y—yes," Maggie, who, reaching into the past, had missed Raine's thought, evoked, "I remember train Nellie telling us that a relative had seen her axed auntie's ghost, then she pleaded with us to solve her family's mystery."

"So, there you have it. That's our puzzle," Raine concluded. She could instantly see from their faces and body language that her audience was enthralled. After a moment, she added, "With Auntie Merry's very special crystal ball, Athena, and our," she swished a quick glance round the room, lowering her voice to a near whisper, "our Time-Key, that will make delving into this ice-cold case a lot less painful."

"Well … somewhat less painful," the pragmatic blonde Sister broke in. "There are so many unanswered questions. By the way, who raised axed Nellie's little boy Billy? You said that his father had died as a result of gassing in World War I. After his mother and grandmother were murdered, he was left an orphan." Aisling, who was a devoted mother to her own child, had posed the most fitting question.

Raine and Maggie exchanged looks, with Raine replying, "We *must* find out the answer to that query. I have my doubts that little Billy went to live with his mother's brother, since the child believed that it was his *uncle* who had wielded the killing ax!"

"Raine and I are hoping there're descendants of the protagonists of our Hamlet's unsolved ax murders still residing in our area." Maggie chewed her lower lip. "Someone in this village knew something … something they harbored– likely due to fear– from the police at the time the murders were perpetrated."

Of a sudden, Hugh, who had been staring at the floor, stirred, an expression of illumination brightening his face, as he murmured something under his breath. "Didn't I hear you say, during dinner, that you had an appointment to take the Land Rover into the Auto Doctor's next week for a tune-up?"

"Right," Raine and Maggie answered in sync.

He snapped his fingers, pointing at the Sisters, "I suggest you chat with Kathy Wise, the receptionist there. Kathy is the **go-to** gal. She's what you young people call a 'mover and a shaker.'" He chortled his next words, "The Hamlet folk don't call her 'Savvy Kathy' for naught. Be sure to ask her if she knows anybody who might be descendants of anyone connected to our Hamlet's mysterious ax murders, in addition to anyone who *knew* axed Nellie." Hugh thought for a second, continuing, "Don't volunteer that you're delving into the unsolved murders–"

"No, we'll say it's a history project or something," Maggie finished. "We need to glean information from several sources, not just from axed Nellie's great-niece."

"We intend to make it a front-burner project, right after our *Beltane* fest, which is day after tomorrow, Saturday ... Saturday night. Sunday's May Day. We've invited our fellow sisters of the moon, the Keystone Coven, to Tara for the festival; and so, first, we must ready ourselves for that, but right after–" Raine raised her glass, "It's full-speed ahead on our current mystery!"

Chapter Two

"Now let's make sure we've done everything on our checklist," Maggie said, after passing round the iced tea. She was speaking to Thaddeus, Raine and Beau, Aisling and Ian, as the group took a break from their *Beltane* preparations at one of the long picnic tables in Tara's extensive back yard. The pleasing scent of freshly mowed grass, mixed with the perfume of the spring flowers that bloomed along the borders, where sweeping lawn met forest, drifted over to the cheery assembly.

The Sisters could hardly contain themselves for excitement with party fever. Even the big, old house seemed to wear an expectant air. Tara had a long memory of merrymaking.

That evening, the Keystone Coven would be arriving for the spring fest, so it was mandatory that everyone pitch in to ready the Sisters' outdoor sacred space for the festival and their guests.

Maggie stirred her tea. "We've made enough floral crown wreaths for the thirteen Coven sisters, as well as for the three of us," she said, nodding at her two cousins and fellow sisters of the moon. "Every sister present will get one. They look lovely on any lady, and they really bring out the Goddess within."

"I like that you left the stems on the flowers, and I think the long ribbons you attached to the back of each wreath was– forgive the pun– the crowning touch," Aisling laughed. "Very *Beltane*. I love your choice of spring flowers too."

"Thanks," Raine answered. "We used daisies, petunias, and irises."

"Nice and colorful." Aisling took a long draft of the refreshing tea. The afternoon had warmed a bit from the chilly morning, and she was thirstier than she thought. "Not to mention that daisies represent innocence. With petunias, it all depends on intent, and Iris is the messenger goddess who rides rainbows."

"The wreaths will remain fresh in the basement fridge with wax paper between them," Raine said. "We'll hand them out as everyone is arriving tonight."

"I ran out of green pipe cleaners on that last floral crown, so I used green craft wire I found in the kitchen junk drawer," Maggie stated. "Worked great."

"Keep going down our list, Mags," Raine prodded. "It'll be time to shower and change into our *Beltane* attire before we know it."

Maggie laughed. "Dear Raine! You're as excited as a child! Granny always said that parcels and parties always bring out the child in you." Maggie's fabulous emerald gaze lowered to the paper on the table before her. She picked it up, her eyes coming to light on the second item. "We checked the back-porch speakers, and they're working fine, now that the guys repaired the loose wire. *Beltane* music CD is ready to pop into the player. We must have music at our fests; it's one of the strongest forms of magick. This year our choice is Rowena of the Glen's album *My Mother's Song* that includes the *Beltane* track "The Witching Hour."

"I love Rowena Whaling!" Raine exclaimed, breaking into a line of the song, "'Oo-oo-oo-ooo, the witching hour.' Her music haunts the soul!" The raven-haired Sister scanned the immaculate yard. "Thank you, fellas, for cutting the grass and doing all the trim and weeding. Our sacred space looks … *divine!*"

The men responded, with Thaddeus remarking that the mower and trimmers had been returned to their proper places in the garage.

"Our *Beltane* Altar is ready and waiting in our outdoor space." Maggie glanced up at the large teepee-shape of heaped wood standing tall inside an encompassing circle of boulders. "I assume the bonfire is ready to light?"

Thaddeus gave a brisk nod. "It is. As you requested, we used nine different types of wood, and the stack is tied with ribbons of many different colors."

All three Sisters looked pleased, with Aisling inquiring, "Do you think it will burn a long time? That's a must at *Beltane*."

"It should," the three men answered nearly simultaneously, though each with different words.

"Splendid!" the Sisters chimed as one.

"Our *Beltane* Wishing Fire will be a perfect size for its intended use." Raine turned to regard the readied cauldron where the Wishing Fire would burn. "Anyone wanting to make a wish should be able to hurdle this small, contained fire easily enough. Doing so will bring good luck to all who leap over it."

"What about the Maypole?" Maggie queried. "Is the pole fixed firmly in the ground? It's made of wood and a good twenty feet tall, so we don't want it to flip and flop and eventually fall when the sisters and brothers start dancing around it. Are the streamer ribbons attached securely to it, do you think?"

"That pole is three feet into the ground," Beau supplied. "It's not going anywhere."

"And the streamers are secure too," Aisling assured. "Ian and I bought twenty-foot ribbons, each three inches wide; and trust me, they are strongly fastened to the metal eyelet we screwed into the pole beforehand. Everyone who grasps a ribbon to dance around our Maypole will be able to do so without losing ribbon or bringing down the pole." She picked up the tea pitcher to refill glasses.

Maggie continued down the list. "Our trusty antler headdresses and Green-Man masks for the men are ready and waiting on the back porch with the *Beltane* music CD and our three *bodhráns*."

The Sisters had purchased the Irish sheepskin drums with wooden tippers in Ireland for use during their festivals. The antler headdresses and leafy Green-Man masks they had found years before at the nearby Highland Games, held annually in the Laurel Highlands of their southwestern Pennsylvania home.

"Ian, Beau and Thaddeus," Maggie cast her beguiling smile on the men, "have agreed to be our drummers this night. To begin, anyway. After a while, they can trade places with three of the brothers accompanying the Keystone Sisters. That way, they can eventually be free to dance with us."

"Raine and I worked on the *Beltane* baskets all week." Maggie waved a bejeweled hand toward the table, on the shaded, screened-in back porch, that held the wicker baskets.

The baskets were filled with cellophane-wrapped bread and pastries from Sal-San-Tries, teas from the Hamlet's Gypsy Tearoom, canned goods, scented soaps, and other sundry items. Each basket was covered with a pretty pastel-colored cellophane and tied with a bright ribbon.

"We've added the last-minute items," Maggie went on, "such as the fresh fruit and vegetables we picked up early this morning from the market. Everyone will take a basket home to deliver to a needy person, needy in whatever way, on the morrow. The basket may be delivered anonymously or in any manner the giver prefers. In the meantime, they'll stay fresh on the cool back porch."

"Thank the great Goddess that it's perfect weather today, not hot, not cold, just right," Aisling commented. "I like a bit of a nip in the air." She popped the sprig of mint from her frosted glass of tea into her mouth.

"Yes, and tonight is supposed to be perfect weather too, brisk, but not bitter, with no rain in the forecast," Ian finished.

"Maggie and I collected *Beltane* dew and rain water in a cleansed new vessel, to wash our hair and faces with, just before sunrise when the Pleiades first appeared on the horizon." Raine dimpled, casting a provocative smile at Beau. "I awoke to birdsong this morning. The cheerful notes seemed to stand both as a promise of profound happiness and the achievement of our hearts' desire."

"Oh, may I take some of that *Beltane* water with me tonight after the fest?" Aisling asked, knowing full well what her cousins would answer.

"We already have a vessel of it ready for you to take home, darlin'," Maggie smiled.

"What about the faerie lights?" Raine queried, looking at the men. "Are they all working and ready to turn on," she glanced at her watch, "in a couple hours?"

"They're all up and ready to switch on," Beau answered. He took a gulp of tea, draining his glass.

"These LED lights will be so much better than the old ones. A lot more economical too," Thaddeus declared, adjusting himself on the hard, wooden picnic-table bench. "Are you going to put cushions on these benches?"

The Sisters exchanged looks, with Maggie answering, "We can. Let me finish going down our list, then we'll get the cushions from the garage. Her eyes returned to the paper she held. "*Beltane* prayers are printed out and ready to hand to each person upon arrival. They're in on the kitchen counter. I didn't want them blowing around the nice, neat yard." Her green eyes narrowed in thought. "That reminds me. Are the garbage cans all emptied and lined with new bags?"

"They are," Beau replied. "And out of sight behind the garage, but near enough for easy use."

"Good," but we can take bags around too, once in a while, to collect trash," Maggie said.

"You ladies haven't commented on our May Swing?" Thaddeus remarked. "Did you notice it?" He jerked his head to the side, indicating the direction the Sisters should look.

When the women trod across the yard to the giant oak tree where the vine-and-flower-bedecked swing was hanging from a stout branch, Maggie and Raine exclaimed, "It's beautiful!" Aisling's hands rushed to her mouth. "I absolutely adore it!"

A sturdy wooden plank provided the ample seat with thick rope suspending it from the branch. On both sides of the swing, the rope held beautiful intertwining vines and May flowers, artificial, so that the idyllic effect would last.

"It's good and strong too," Ian assured, having joined the ladies at the swing. "Strong enough to hold the–" he caught Aisling's warning look, grinning at his wife, "*fleshiest* sister. Would you like to take the maiden flight? I'd be happy to do the honors." He extended his hand, which Aisling accepted with a girlish giggle, seating herself on the swing and carefully gripping the adorned ropes.

The Sisters all took a turn in the swing, with Ian sending each sailing over the *Beltane*-decorated yard with peals of laughter.

"Now," Maggie continued fifteen minutes later, "the last thing on the checklist is the food. Aisling and Ian ran into town earlier to pick up our order from Sophie. A few of the items were not her usual Sal-San-Tries fare, such as the honey cakes and the oat cakes, but she came through for us with the proverbial flying colors. They're first-class."

"Was she able to make the *Beltane* bread with the almonds and cinnamon?" Raine asked. This was her favorite *Beltane* treat.

"She made it, and it looks delicious," Aisling assured. "Ian," she turned toward her husband, "whipped up a marvelous chicken and herb stew. It's in your fridge in a chafing dish, so all we have to do, after we heat it on your kitchen stove, is to light the candle beneath when we set it out on the food table later. I can personally vouch for this dish. It's one of Ian's best. My hubby's a culinary genius." She blew him a kiss. "Merry Fay and I would starve without his cooking expertise."

Ian laughed. "I doubt you'd starve, but thank you, sweetheart."

"We bought a couple dozen of Sophie's fruit tarts too, to augment the cakes," Aisling said. "Ian and I thought them very apropos for *Beltane*."

"Raine and I tried our hands at Granny's asparagus, mushroom, onion, egg and cheese spring quiche; and honestly, we think it turned out rather well," Maggie stated. "Thaddeus concocted, from an old *Beltane* recipe he said he discovered online, our witchy May Wine– a good German white wine to start with sprigs of woodruff and fresh, sliced strawberries added. Oh," she remembered suddenly, "we prepared candied violets too. Pretty good, if I do say so myself."

"The Coven ladies are bringing several different salads," Raine informed, adding, "and a *Beltane* marigold custard, along with homemade mead– their own recipe that goes back generations– along with a nice strawberry crisp. We've ice cream in the freezer should anyone want a scoop with it." She faced Maggie. "Is that it for our checklist?"

"Not quite." The red-haired Sister perused the to-do list. "We've set out, on the picnic tables, plenty of rose and jasmine incense and scented candles for use tonight." She glanced around their outdoor sacred space. "And we've filled several cauldrons with hyacinths." She moved forward the few feet to their Altar, noting, "Spring-green tablecloth in place. Great Goddess, we have to put the other green cloths on the picnic tables! We'll secure them with the heavy floral candles-in-a-jar and the incense burners." Maggie's gaze continued to scan the Altar. "Lots of colorful *Beltane* ribbons. Blue for the spring sky and robins' eggs; yellow for daffodils, forsythia, and dandelions; and the purple of the lilac, with plenty of green interspersed throughout the area.

"Now, let's see," Maggie's eyes swept the Altar, "fertility symbols– antlers, acorns and seeds. Symbolic phallus Maypole centerpiece. Goddess symbols– statue, cup, cauldron, wreath of flowers and herbs of woodruff, blessed thistle, nettle, tansy. Stones of rose quartz, garnet, emerald, and tourmaline. A nice big besom decorated with ribbons. Traditional altar tools in place." Her eyes skipped over the expanse of yard. "Our water-faeries' fountain will be switched on at dusk, with its new faerie lights." She gave a quick nod of satisfaction. "Blessed be. All is satisfactory."

"The Faerie Tree!" Raine shouted. She jumped up to stare a few feet distant, throwing her hand out in surprise. "Beau, surely you can't deny doing *that*." She was pointing to a basket set under their Faerie Tree, an ethereal Pennsylvania Hawthorn, where tiny, glittery bells jingled in the breeze at the ends of the bright ribbons secured in its branches. Beside the basket stood an old-fashioned milking stool, upon which was painted a green pentagram.

He shook his head blankly. "I didn't do it. Maybe it was," he looked at Thaddeus, "Thad?"

"Not I," Dr. Weatherby replied.

"Wasn't me," Ian avowed when the others turned to peer at him.

A look sailed amid the Sisters, ending with Raine regarding Beau suspiciously, whilst Maggie sent Thaddeus a dubious, raised-brow stare.

"Well, who was it?!" Raine questioned, her emerald eyes flashing. The Goth gal was never one for practical jokes. "I know *I* didn't do it, though I'm glad someone remembered our garden and woodland faeries!"

No one admitted to setting up the gift basket or the Wishing Stool under Tara's traditional Faerie Tree. After a moment, Raine shrugged, so used to magick was she at their Tara. "Levitation, perhaps it was the faeries themselves! It's been noted since Neolithic and medieval times that hawthorns possess magickal properties. Whoever chooses to make a wish tonight can do so by sitting under our Faerie Tree and imaging what they want, believing, and thanking. Wish-making requires a gift for tree and faeries to be put into the basket there," she pointed. "Our faeries enjoy spirits, sweets, oatcakes, and anything that glitters or sparkles. An appropriate gemstone is good, a ring, a sweet, or a glass of milk laced with whiskey. You get the picture. Did you remember to set a large bowl of dry oatmeal out, ready to sprinkle around our circle tonight, Mags?"

"Of course, it's ready and waiting on the Altar."

"That just leaves the Sacred Rite," Aisling said. We will do it symbolically, with the Coven High Priestess and her husband representing the May Queen and King of the Forest."

Beau leaned over to whisper into Raine's ear. "And we'll do it the Old Way."

Simultaneously, Thaddeus sent Maggie a look sated with a lover's message that curved the corners of her glossy lips slightly upward in her enigmatic Mona-Lisa smile.

Aisling took a long, peaceful moment to gaze over their handiwork and the rolling green and woodsy panorama. The sun was bright, the sky blue and cloudless, and spring was bursting out everywhere. *Thank you, God-Goddess.* "To quote Laurie Cabot," she intoned aloud, "'May is the time of fertility and new beginnings after a long winter. The faeries are afoot! They dance in the hills and roll in the grass, reveling in the joy of warm May breezes. Our spirits are high with the lust and heartiness of spring. New life is stirring, and appetites are keen.'"

It was after sundown. The Keystone Sisters and their partners had arrived. The Altar was ready, the decorations and numerous floral arrangements in place, the food laid, the introductions made. The great Circle was cast, fringed by the dry oatmeal, and it was time for the *Beltane* prayers.

Thirty-two figures dressed in beguiling Renaissance-fair attire joined hands round the Circle– the women in a rainbow of colors and fabrics, the Sisters' handmade floral wreaths adorning their heads, the men's faces covered with the leafy Green-Man masks, and on *their* heads the antlers, symbolic of the King of the Forest.

In the center of the great ring of sisters and brothers of the moon, the High Priestess, Robin O'Malley (whose witch name was Athena), with her male partner, raised her arms skyward, her long, curly mane of fiery-red hair blowing in the brisk breeze that sprang up to cleanse the atmosphere. A delightful carillon filled the air from the multitude of wind chimes that Raine and Maggie always kept hanging from hooks on both the inside and outside of the screened-in back porch and from the many trees on their property. Like all bells, the chimes helped clear the atmosphere of negative energies.

"Hail Guardians of the Watch Towers! Hail Guardians of this place!" Robin opened. "We come here in peace and with clear intent. We come here to celebrate *Beltane*, the ancient spring ritual. We ask, with respect, that you accept our presence. Hail Guardian Spirits of this place!" The High Priestess looked to her partner.

"We will now make the call for peace," he announced in a deep, resonant voice.

"May there be peace in the North!" the Priestess cried out. Everyone present rebounded the plea.

"May there be peace in the South!" Aisling shouted. The gathering repeated the cry.

"May there be peace in the West!" Maggie called. The others responded in turn.

"May there be peace in the East!" Raine rumbled in her deep voice. The Circle repeated the petition.

The High Priestess gave a satisfied nod. "We who are gathered here, we call for peace in this land. We call for peace in our hearts and minds and toward our fellow men." She looked to the trio of Sleuth Sisters, who advanced to the Altar, where they lit the *Beltane* candles.

Though the Circle had already been smudged with white sage, Aisling, Maggie, and Raine, each grasping a large seashell holding a lit smudge stick, began walking the interior of the huge ring, which encompassed the entire back-yard space. With the smoking sage, they slowly progressed deosil, clockwise, all the while chanting, "We give our energy to this Circle, mingling and communing with those of the spirits of Nature to create a sanctuary of peace and love."

This cleansed the area of any lingering negativity.

"With one voice and one intent," the High Priestess declared in her strong voice, "soul to soul, spirit to spirit, we weave our Circle that none may enter this sacred space this sacred night but those who come in tune with our intention and in peace. So mote it be!"

Advancing to the center of the Circle, to the Altar, the Priestess picked up the water jug, saying, "We give thanks for water. Let this vessel be as the Triple Well of Blessings in this Sacred Grove."

Robin picked up a hand sprinkler and consecrated the Circle and those forming it, moving clockwise.

Next the Priestess lit the rose and jasmine incense. A lovely aroma began to waft across the area. "I light this incense to be a symbol of this sacred time, a symbol of strong magick. Light counterpart of dark *Samhain* that honors Death, *Beltane* honors Life. But like *Samhain*, *Beltane* is a time of 'no-time,' when the veil between the worlds is at its thinnest, when the two worlds intermingle and unite– *and magick abounds!*"

The Circle resonated with **"So mote it be!"**

The High Priestess smiled. "It is the time when the faeries return from their winter respite– carefree and full of faerie mischief and faerie delight!"

Everyone laughed, several adding light comments of their own.

Robin looked pleased, stretching her arms upward, her face, too, tilting skyward. "I call upon the God and Goddess! I call upon the Guardians of the Watch Towers! I call upon our Angel and Spirit Guides, especially upon Archangel Michael! Sister and Brother Muses from the Other Side, in the Summerland, I call upon you as

- 55 -

well! Hear us! I call upon the fur and feather people, our brothers and sisters of the forest! I call upon our revered Ancestors whose songs course through our blood and whose spirits live on through our celebrations and reverence for the Old Ways. We call on you, all of you, to be here with us during our Sacred Rite! So mote it be!"

The Circle echoed, **"SO MOTE IT BE!"**

It was time now for the most sacred segment of the *Beltane* ritual– the invocation of the Lord and Lady and the Sacred Rite. A hush fell upon the gathering, as the High Priestess took a deep breath to center herself. Presently, she nodded to the men among the group, who took out their flutes and began to softly play. Ian, Beau and Thaddeus struck the *bodhráns* with the wooden tippers, and the soft drumming began.

Raine ventured forth to pick up the bow and arrow she had set on one of the long, cloth-covered tables. With Maggie's assistance, she lit the arrow, the tip wrapped with an oil-soaked rag, and shot it into the boulder-encircled, teepee-shaped, ribbon-tied branches of wood– to ignite the *Beltane* Bonfire. Instantly did it flame with the assembly of sisters and brothers of the moon loudly and enthusiastically exclaiming their appreciation.

High Priestess Robin raised her arms once again skyward, her fiery head thrown back in ardent appeal, "I call upon the Lady of the Stars and Moon! The Bringer of Dreams and Twilight! The Weaver of Fates in the Night! I call upon the Lady of Evensong! I call upon Maiden, Mother, and Crone! The Triple Goddess alive and strong!"

"The Goddess!" the Circle resounded with gusto. "The Goddess! **The Goddess!!"**

The High Priestess smiled, as she waited and listened to the sensual sounds of the flutes and drums.

After the pleasurable, though brief, pause, she resumed her invocation, arms and face once again skyward. "I call upon the Lord of the Sun, the Rider in the Sky! I call upon the Lord of the Winds, like the eagle as he flies! I call upon the King Stag, Lord of the Wild Wood, laughing free and wise!"

"The King of the Forest!" the sisters and brothers pealed loudly and with vigor. **"The King of the Forest! Hear us, Lord and Lady!!"**

The flutes with the drums grew louder, only to be again softened via a signal from the Priestess, whose benevolent gaze now swept the Circle. "We are gathered here this night to celebrate spring."

She turned, making a sweeping gesture with her arm, "to the abundance and fertility of Nature that surrounds us. Now," she smiled, "the fires of passion burn strong, and all nature turns to thoughts of love. We celebrate the greening of the leaves, the mating calls of our fur and feather brothers and sisters of the forest– and the union, the Sacred Marriage, of the God and Goddess."

From the Altar, Robin picked up the Athame in her right hand. She paused for a purposeful moment, closing her eyes and letting the music and the spirit fill her essence. Picking up the Chalice in her left hand, she extended the sacred items out in front of her for all to see. "We greet the time for unions and honor the Lord and Lady for their fruitfulness."

Again the flutes and drums increased in intensity …

"Tonight," Robin continued, "we witness the union of Goddess and God!"

The flutes and drums waxed louder …

The High Priestess lowered the Athame into the Chalice symbolizing the Sacred Union, as–

The flutes and drums rose to full crescendo …

"They are ONE! THEY ARE ONE! AND WE ARE ONE WITH THEM!" chanted those in the Circle, to the wild flute and drum accompaniment.

"We offer our gifts of song and wine with our Maypole, Lord and Lady!" High Priestess Robin threw back her head and laughed merrily, her bejeweled hands coming together. "How much beauty we would all miss, if we didn't remember to look up! **Let the festival begin!"**

Raine flicked a switch that illuminated the myriad of tiny, white faerie lights, bringing a stereo sigh of surprise and approval from the gathering, after which the Sleuth Sisters proceeded to the center of the Circle with Robin and her mate, accompanying them to the tables. "May the God and Goddess bless this food and drink!"

Once the blessing was cast, Maggie and Aisling began passing out goblets of mead, whilst Raine dashed to switch on the back-porch speakers. In a twinkling, the *Beltane* music of Rowena of the Glen filled the air with "The Witching Hour."

It was time for the Maypole Dance, the *Beltane* wedding gift to the Lord and Lady. Everyone wishing to participate took hold of a ribbon, and nearly all the guests began sensually weaving in and out of one another and around the staff, symbolizing the union of all things, whilst the entrancing music of Rowena of the Glen wove its magick around the dancers:

"Serpents coil at midnight/ Oo-oo-oo-ooo the witching hour/ Drummers drum the fire light/ Oo-oo-oo-ooo in the witching hour/ Madness does abound/ with the May moon full and round/ The energy whirls/ in the witching hour/ Dancers dance till day-break/ Oo-oo-oo-ooo the witching hour ..."

Darkness had descended by this time; and the May moon, full and round, as Rowena chanted via her song, gleamed in all its splendor upon the fest. Night birds twittered in the surrounding trees, seeming to synchronize with the bewitching music. From all directions came enchanting night sounds. An owl hooted in a nearby tree, whilst the watery splashes of the Sisters' faerie fountain, soothing and relaxing, bequeathed a lulling, most satisfying effect on the senses.

"Leave behind your heartache/ Oo-oo-oo-ooo in the witching hour/ As your body starts to sway/ You'll forever want to stay between the worlds ..."

Raine pointed to the sky, "Look! A shooting star!"

Dancing next to her, Beau glanced upward, catching the silver shimmer as it swished a glittering arc across the velvet night sky.

That very special *Beltane*, the sky was *ablaze* with stars!

As the dancers paused momentarily, round the Maypole, those stars seemed extraordinarily bright and somehow nearer to Earth on this night when the veil between the worlds had lifted.

"Did you make a wish?" Raine asked Beau when she swooped, with ribbon, close to him.

"I did." He cast her his familiar sexy grin.

"What was it?" she asked with a grin of her own, the dimple in her left cheek deepening.

"If I tell you, it won't come true," he laughed, brushing his fingers across the twin globes of her bosom brimming over the top of the green corset dress she was sporting, the handkerchief veil skirt of which blew flirtingly in the spring breeze.

"Two can play that game," Raine giggled. She raised her eyes skyward to chant as she continued to weave and whirl, "Star light, star bright, first star I see tonight, I wish I may, I wish I might, have the wish I wish this night!"

Each holding the end of a brightly colored ribbon, the dancers continued weaving in and out of one another, braiding and wrapping their ribbons round the tall Maypole. When they completed their dance, the couples embraced to seal the ritual marriage with a kiss– and it was then that several of the participants saw the first ethereal figure.

A looming male figure wearing leafy, green, brown and black garments, his head displaying antlers, stood tall and watchful, at the edge of the forest. Everyone noticed the imposing figure now, and no one moved. Rather, every dancer froze in his and her tracks to stare– *unbelieving.*

"Oo-oo-oo-ooo in the witching hour/ A gentle rain, a chant ..." sang Rowena of the Glen.

Of a sudden came the sounds of flutes from somewhere deep within the forest. The silvery notes rose and carried on an accommodating breeze, blending melodiously with Rowena's *Beltane* song and the sounds of the rural Pennsylvania night. 'Twas a light waterfall of notes reminiscent of the faeries' fount.

As alluring as the Siren's song, there was magick in the symphony of sounds the *Beltane* participants were hearing. Mysterious, utterly pagan and primitive, it wound its sinuous way through the air, seductively blending with the sigh of the encompassing forest trees and the soft wind.

Rowena's voice rang out, "Love is everywhere you look ..."

Her magical words drew a second figure from the forest, a female figure draped in sheer, luminous, veils. The May Queen. *The Goddess.*

Beltane. The Eternal Return.

Glancing quickly around, hardly daring to breathe, Maggie noted that everyone seemed to be suspended in time, as Time waited, and the figures came together with a sudden flash of white light that leaped between them– the kinetic gift of the vital life force.

The Lord and Lady. The Sacred Rite.

The King of the Forest bent his antlered head to his Lady's height and, lifting the veil from her face and folding it back over her floral crown, kissed her a long, deep passionate kiss ...

"The day uncurls ... in the witching hour/ Lovers feast at twilight/ Oo-oo-oo-ooo the witching hour/ A goddess sings in delight/ Oo-oo-oo-ooo the witching hour/ As the purple shadows move/ feel your spirit soar and groove/ The spiral swirls in the witching hour."

As Rowena's song ended, the ethereal couple broke apart, and the Lady took a step toward the trees.

Again Time waited, as she slowly turned. From the depths of the forest, the sound of the flutes and drums rose seductively, bidding the May Queen and King of the Forest enter to consummate their love. The Lady inclined her head, and from her gown of ethereal veils, a luminous white arm appeared, the graceful hand extending toward the waiting Lord, who came immediately forward to grasp the hand.

The flutes and drums sustained their sensual appeal as the King of the Forest led his bride to their leafy bed, and the pair melted into the shadows– and disappeared.

Raine, always so daring, ran partway across the lawn toward the woods, stopping suddenly, when she felt someone jerk on her arm. Turning partway round, she saw, in the moon's silvery glow, that it was Beau. By the look in his piercing eyes, she realized with sudden clarity that she, that no one, was meant to follow.

Something had been revealed to each of them that magickal *Beltane* night– something of a deeper metaphysical reckoning than anything previously experienced.

As she stood, staring into the night-black woods, Raine heard the final few notes of the flutes, accompanied by a tapping of the *bodhráns*– fleeting but effective.

"The Lord and Lady are gone," she whispered more to herself than to Beau, her essence tumbling down into the here and now.

"No," he answered, "they are here."

She saw that he had laid his hand over his heart.

Along with the others, still frozen in place round the Maypole, they listened, but–

All was silent.

***

In their own bower of bliss within the beckoning cloak of forest– their Renaissance attire draped over a nearby branch– Beau looked long upon his lady-love. He had never felt more keenly about Raine than he did at that moment. He had never felt so close, so near to her, not by mere touching, but spiritually and intellectually joined to her. How extraordinary she was– his Raine.

She was lying on her back on a thick blanket, as a sweetly scented breeze wafted over her body. Her eyes were closed. When she opened them, she could see the silvery-white moon exquisitely veiled by a lacy black network of tree branches.

There was such powerful magick in *Beltane*– strong and very old magick, even in the creaking of the surrounding trees and the rustling of leaves.

The Beltane wind is the great Goddess' breath, she thought. "Bless our love, oh, Three-Fold Goddess!" she whispered.

Suspended over her on one knee, Beau could smell her familiar scent, so like the forest itself. He could still taste the honeyed mead on her lips when he kissed her. And now, he couldn't stop kissing her. Never had she felt more desirable. Never had he wanted her more.

Unlike Raine, this night she seemed to be waiting, waiting to submit to the desires of her … what? *Spouse?*

He made up his mind that next *Beltane* would bring him the long-awaited hand-fasting ritual that he yearned for with this little witch. Come what may, he would make that happen!

She regarded him through half-closed lids, and, as if she read his thought, a ghost of a smile curved her lips.

"My favorite part of *Beltane* is my very special journey to the 'little black forest,'" he murmured against her temple.

"Hmmmm," she purred, "magick can be found in the smallest places."

The *Beltane* music from the fest drifted to them on the wind, and a night bird joined in with its song. He ran his strong hands along her bare arms, her sides, over her breasts and down her belly, little sparks of heat and energy flashing where they connected. She drew in a tiny breath like a virgin bride on her wedding night.

But when he took her it was not the chaste young bride that he took. Rather 'twas the quintessential witchy-woman versed and capable in all the joys of love– as accomplished a lover as any man could wish for.

When Raine and Beau returned, in a glow, to the gathering, the festival was at maximum merry mode. Who else among them had chosen to perform the Sacred Ritual in the Old Way, they did not know, but suffice it to say that there were several satisfied expressions among the gathering.

Sisters and brothers were grouped across the large expense of lawn, the tiny white faerie lights and flaming *Beltane* fires illuminating the happy faces. Chatter and laughter shared the air with the splash of the fountain and the soul-reaching music of Rowena of the Glen.

Spying Thaddeus and Maggie, Raine and Beau stirred to join them at the food table.

"I think everyone is enjoying themselves," Maggie said when Raine and Beau reached their sides. The redheaded Maggie looked gorgeous in a purple silk Renaissance gown, the daring décolleté and corset-style belt rendering her even sexier than usual. "Great Goddess, is this good! You must try the marigold custard Nimue made." The striking redhead took another bite of the confection, as ecstasy shown on her face.

Raine smiled. "I will do that." She wandered over to the long food table, which, in reality, was two picnic tables pushed together and covered with green cloths. "It's difficult to choose." But this Sister loved salads, so she began there, helping herself to several selections from the Keystone Coven's offerings.

Beau and Thaddeus, on the other hand, were heartily enjoying Ian's chicken and herb stew. After a moment, Raine came up for air, asking her cousin and sister of the moon in a whisper, "Well?"

Maggie never kissed to tell. "Well what?" She raised a perfectly arched brow, turning from Raine to gaze into the *Beltane* fire, her Mona-Lisa smile curving her full lips.

Raine could only assume that the highly sexed Scorpio couple had found their own *Beltane* bliss within the shelter of the forest. As

Raine looked keenly into Maggie's eyes, she saw the Old Ways dancing with bright attendance– and knew the answer to her query.

Maggie and her beloved had ducked into the forest about the same time Raine and Beau had left the festival.

The night was superb. Through the leafy canopy of trees, the moon romantically cloaked the lovers with sporadic splashes of light and shadow, like exquisite black lace, giving greater scope to the imagination.

"Listen," Thaddeus whispered, "hear the sound of that little stream? Soothing, isn't it?"

More interested in amorous pursuits, Maggie returned, her voice low and throaty, "You have such power over me, you know." She sent him one of her smoky looks.

"Are you certain it is not the other way around?" He began peeling off her clothing, slowly, as if they had the whole night ahead of them.

As always, he was struck by her great beauty– her rich red, wavy hair that touched her round, white shoulders; her glittering feline eyes; her model's face, and voluptuous, hour-glass figure.

When his mouth covered hers, he pressed her against a tree, his tongue igniting the *Beltane* fires in them both.

Their kisses were always like confidences, attracting more and more; and this night, in Tara's sweet-smelling woods, it was nearly impossible to stop.

"You are a force of Nature, Maggie," he rasped into her ear, his breath growing shorter, his mouth dropping to the swell of her breasts. "I want to absorb you, every fragment of you, into my very soul."

"When I'm with you," she whispered, "I'm *deliriously* happy."

He skimmed down her body to his knees before her, gazing up at his goddess, his love– his Maggie.

"Maggie," he whispered then.

And later– "I adore you."

In the moon glow through the lacy covering of trees, her cat eyes flashed. "Show me," she purred. "*Show me.*"

His answer was to attentively cover her with caresses and kisses, omitting no single portion of her exquisite body.

From their first kiss well over a year ago, this very thorough professor had shown his lady an adroit skill in the art of love, and never did he fail to enflame her. Her hungry body threw itself into the *Beltane* experience with a witch's total abandon, and the pleasure they both experienced that enchanting night was greater than anything either had ever known.

"Maggie!" he cried out anew, as jointly they soared on wings of ecstasy to the great highland of the gods.

***

"Mmmmm, this is to die for! Who made this broccoli salad?" Raine savored the forkful she had popped into her mouth.

"I did," High Priestess Robin O'Malley (Athena) answered. This striking redhead resembled actress Nicole Kidman.

"It's one of her best creations," petite, brunette Brigid Hanlon (Autumn) and blonde, plump Deirdre Walsh (Luna) happily chorused. Each of the sisters held a plate with various samplings from the food table.

Deirdre, especially, appeared to be enjoying the array of pastries. "This ain't health food," the chubby sister laughed, "it is pure wicked-witch comfort food, and I'm going to enjoy myself tonight. *Beltane*'s all about satisfying the senses, isn't it?" she laughed again with a wave of a pudgy hand.

A thrill of happy giggles carried across the yard from the flower-decked swing, where several of the Coven sisters had grouped with their partners for turn-taking. A few sisters and brothers were jumping the Wishing Fire, though Raven had very nearly caught her long skirt aflame. Thank the great Goddess her husband had grabbed her, quickly rolling her in the damp grass. The incident had not, however, dampened the spirits of the lively Raven, who had merely laughed and invited her mate to join her.

Undine, true to her witch name, was making a wish at the fountain. Moonglow and Starlight, partners, in love and in their magick shop *Bewitched,* were lying on a blanket, peacefully gazing at the night sky. Nimue and her fiancé were toasting one another with glasses of Thaddeus' May Wine.

From the dark tree line, Aisling and Ian emerged, looking a tad disheveled. A few errant leaves clung to the back of Aisling's butter-yellow gown, and her hair looked a mite tousled. However, her cheeks were rosy, and her green eyes sparkled.

Ian walked briskly across the yard to join Beau and Thaddeus in a goblet of mead, whilst Aisling went to join Raine and Maggie at the refreshment table.

"Everyone seems to be having a merry old time of it," Raine quipped to no one in particular.

Robin (Athena) set her goblet of wine down on the nearby table. "You're about to delve into yet another mystery. Am I right?" The High Priestess stepped closer to Raine, her eyes fastening on the raven-haired Sister's face.

"We are. We've been asked to look into a cold case, an unsolved triple-murder from the early 1930s." Raine took a sip of her wine, holding the Priestess' steady gaze. She waited, sensing, *knowing*, that Robin had something of the utmost importance to share with her.

"This is such a *merry* fest that I hesitated telling you this tonight, but feel I *must*. In the days to come, take extra care to protect yourselves, my dear. The three of you will be in great danger, more sinister and menacing than you've ever encountered. Be watchful. Ever watchful."

Robin picked up Raine's left hand and turned it over. Then she removed the large, heavy silver ring she was wearing and, after placing it on Raine's palm, closed the Sister's hand over it, speaking slowly. "It's very old. I inherited it many years ago from a dear sister in Ireland. I was the maiden then, and I've worn it since. I am now the Mother; and, though it saddens me to part with this ring, I am gifting it to you, for you will soon need its *strong* energies. It is cast with spells for strength, courage, and strong protection, especially from evil entities. The blessings," she extended a graceful hand to touch the large aquamarine resting in Raine's palm, "enhance the stone's natural energies."

Raine was touched, and tears shimmered in her emerald eyes. "Are you certain, sister, that you want to part with this treasure? After all, it was a gift to you by someone who, obviously, loved you very much."

Robin smiled with remembering, tossing a glance at Maggie. "Her name was Maggie too, the sister who gifted me with this powerful ring. And she would approve what I am doing. You will need the ring's powers, and I think you know it's true. All I ask is that you treat it with love and respect. And, one day when you deem the time is right, pass it on to someone else in dire need of its energies." She smiled her lovely smile, the smile of the Goddess, and leaned over to bestow a kiss on Raine's cheek.

Raine, in turn, gave the High Priestess a hearty hug. "Thank you, sister, and blessings back at you three times three for all you've done for me! For *us*," she nodded to Maggie and Aisling, now beside her, who chimed in with thanks to Robin.

"I've already infused the ring with your names," she told the Sleuth Sisters. "And I've enhanced the blessings in it three times three for your special needs. Of course, I've smudged and recharged it often. All you need do is welcome it with a spell of your own making. It will serve you well."

Again the Sisters thanked the High Priestess.

"As always, we are indebted to the Keystone Coven for their kindness to us," Aisling stated with feeling.

"We admire the work you do," Robin replied, picking up her near-forgotten goblet from the table. She took a sip, her eyes again seeking those of the Sisters before her.

"What else do you wish ... *need* to tell us?" Maggie asked, apprehensive.

The merry sounds of the *Beltane* celebration seemed to hush, and for a long moment, no one spoke.

Finally, Robin set her goblet back on the table, and putting her arms around the three Sleuth Sisters, drew them close, saying, "Again, I entreat you to be vigilant. Don't take any unnecessary chances." Her voice lowered, and she spoke quietly and with careful choice of words. "Beware of one who'll be wearing an unusual piece of antique jewelry. For the life of me, I've not been able, thus far anyway, to conjure this ornament, so I can't tell you if it's a ring, pendant, or what; but perhaps– I hope and pray– you'll know it when you see it. Beware, Sisters, for the person wearing this thing will be *extremely* evil– *and dangerous*. Absolutely devoid of scruples, of a conscience."

The High Priestess' sapphire eyes sparked in the light from the *Beltane* fires, "Beware, dear Sisters– beware!"

Fixing her emerald gaze on the gifted ring, the large, glittering aquamarine surrounded by gargoyles carved in silver, Raine said, "Let's hope it won't be as bad as you think, and I won't have to release the flying monkeys." Raine nearly always depended on comic relief when troubles descended.

High Priestess Robin heaved an apprehensive sigh, as she picked up her goblet. "I think," she concluded, "you'll have to release them more than once in the days to come."

"Dance like the Maiden. Laugh like the Mother. Think like the Crone." ~ Anon

Chapter Three

"I fell in love with a Land Rover like this one a few years ago when I went on a camera safari in Kenya," Maggie conveyed to Kathy Wise, who was at her station behind the receptionist counter at the Auto Doctor's. "I love mine. She's a grand old crone with real character, though she's faithfully performed like a maiden. I've always surrounded her with a bubble of protection, but now she's in need of the Auto Doctor's magick."

Kathy glanced down at the paper in her hand. "Hmmm, a '79 109 station wagon V8. I think the Stage-1 V8 is rare here in the States."

"It is," Maggie answered. "I bought mine used; but the English gentleman who owned her, a fellow professor at the college, was a real homebody. He had her shipped here from the UK when he relocated to our area. Only drove round our little Hamlet, and he lived less than a half-mile from campus. He loved to walk. That was his preferred mode of transportation. He babied the Rover just as I do. So," Maggie gave her crystal laugh, "I call her 'Baby.'"

"You were speaking of Professor Leggitt?" Kathy slipped her pen behind her ear.

"The one and only," Maggie and Raine declared.

"Reggie passed away last year," Maggie said sadly.

"Nice fellow," Kathy remembered. She looked again at the paper she was holding, remarking in reference to Maggie's Land Rover. "Yeah, a grand old lady with a lot of get-up-and-go ... or she will be again when our guys get done with her. Do you need a loaner? This engine overhaul is going to take a week for certain; and I won't lie to you, we're so backed up that it might be a couple weeks before you get your baby back."

"Thank you, Kathy, but it's not necessary. Raine and I use her MG a lot this time of year, unless we've rough roads to cover. The Land Rover's basically our winter vehicle. We'll be fine."

"I didn't think you drove the MG," Kathy said.

Maggie laughed. "I don't. The only stick I can drive is my broom." Maggie reached into her purse for her sunglasses, looking up in a moment at Kathy Wise.

Known throughout the Hamlet as "Savvy Kathy," Wise was exactly as her surname proclaimed. She was a small, middle-aged woman with a big personality and a head full of know-how, knowledge and skills. The classic go-to gal, Kathy knew the answer to most questions, and she knew just about everyone in Haleigh's Hamlet. Her hair was super short, blonde-streaked and spiky, her clothing stylish. In summary, Kathy was streetwise, cute as a button, and someone the Sleuth Sisters always had an urge to hug.

Kathy leaned her elbows on the counter between them and pointed one perfectly lacquered nail at Maggie. "You got somethin' on your mind, don'tcha? Something you want to ask me. So go on–shoot!"

"We do want to ask you something," Raine blurted. "Do you recall ever hearing about the unsolved triple ax murders that took place in our Hamlet back in 1932? A woman by the name of Nellie Triggs, one of her two children, and her elderly mother. Nellie was killed in the kitchen, the others in their beds. The house, a small bungalow, was located on old Murphy Road, near the railroad tracks and the river. It was torn down not long after the murders."

Kathy frowned in an effort of recollection. "I remember my grandmother mentioning that local mystery a few times. Didn't the paper used to run the story every year at Hallowe'en, hoping someone might eventually come forward with information?"

"The *Hamlet Herald* ran the story annually for many years, around the middle of October when the murders had occurred. Columbus Day to be precise," Maggie corrected.

"But no one ever came forward. Am I remembering that correctly?" Kathy asked.

"You are," Raine replied. "No one ever came forward with one shred of information, and nary a clue ever surfaced, that we know of anyway. We were wondering if you can share with us any family stories about the murders. You know … stories passed down in your family. And if you know of any descendants of the protagonists still living in our area. By protagonists I mean Nellie, the people she worked for, suspects who were called in, law officers, *et cetera*."

"Also," Maggie interjected, "if you know anyone with whom the axed woman may have been close. We'd like to speak with descendants of Nellie Triggs' family, friends and associates, as well as descendants of anyone connected to the cold case."

"History homework, huh?" Kathy asked with a nod of understanding.

"Yes," answered the two history professors nearly simultaneously. Technically, it wasn't a lie.

Kathy inclined her head. "Well now, let me think. I don't recall my parents talking about this much. Can't think of anything right off the bat that they might have said, and my grandparents have been gone for some time now. She lowered her head and rubbed her fingers over her upper lip in a pensive gesture.

An instant later, Kathy's dark brown eyes widened. "I remember something my grandmother mentioned one or two times!"

The Sleuth Sisters sent her an encouraging look.

"Grandma always believed that Nellie Triggs and her family were attacked by one of the many hobos who used to hop the freight trains that came through here. You two know, this area was a railroad hub; and during the Depression, there was a constant flow of vagrants who got off and on the passing trains here in the Hamlet. The Triggs' home was very close to the tracks, as you pointed out. Hobos were continually seen down by the tracks and the river, camped out under the bridge, where they had fires going in the cold weather and where they divvied food and such. I guess they called those camps 'Hoovervilles' back then. Lots of homeless people during the Depression, ya know. But those camps around here, down by the tracks and the river, were filled with the rail-ridin' hobos of the era."

The Sisters bobbed their heads in accord. "Makes sense. One of them may have found his way to Nellie's door for a handout, and–" Raine stopped. "But why would a hobo go to a shack like Nellie's for a handout?"

"Because," Kathy returned, "so often it's those who hardly have anything who give the most."

"Another good point," Maggie cast into their boiling cauldron of notions.

"Hobos used to knock on doors for handouts all the time back then," Kathy went on. "And it was believed they left a mark, a symbol of sorts, that only other hobos would recognize, on the property where a house was a giving house. And Nellie–"

"Yes, she was said to have been kind-hearted," Raine interrupted, pacing a bit by now in thought as was her habit. "Our granny always said she knew our property was hobo-marked. Granny believed the symbol drawn was the primitive figure of a cat." She glanced up at Kathy, "Sorry, do go on."

"Well, Nellie Triggs just might have had a hobo mark somewhere on *her* property." Kathy straightened up. "Scenario!" she nearly shouted in a sudden burst of inspiration. "Hobo knocks on her door late at night, cold, wet, and hungry. She opens the door, and he steps inside out of the cold– I recall that my grandma said it was an unusually cold October the year of the ax murders. It even snowed.

"But getting back to my scenario, Nellie prepares him a sandwich or something to take with him, and he gets fresh with her. She fights him off, perhaps making a grab for the family ax– it would've been in the kitchen there somewhere– he wrestles it off her, panics and kills her. Then he has to kill the others in the house so they don't sic the cops on him. I mean there would've had to have been a ruckus by then, and the vagrant might not have known, for certain, the others in Nellie's family hadn't seen or heard anything that would incriminate him, so he axed *them* too." Kathy let out her breath.

"That's a damn good theory," the Sisters agreed in sync.

"The papers always said there was no sign of a break-in, so Nellie, or someone in that household, invited the killer inside. It could well have been your scenario." Raine ceased her pacing.

"Were fingerprint forensics used during the Depression era?" Kathy asked, resting her elbows again on the counter between them.

"Oh yes," the Sisters replied.

"The murder weapon was never found," Raine cited.

Kathy looked thoughtful. "You know there are several descendants still in this area of the tycoon industrialists who were part of the circle of bigwigs Nellie worked for. I just remembered she worked for the Fanes. You know, the family who owns the big mansion right outside of town, that huge castle-like place on top of Manor Hill, with the woods all around it?"

"Right," the Sisters echoed.

"Well, as I'm sure you know better than me, the Fanes had more money than God. Probably still do. Anyway, they moved in a circle of rich tycoons–" Kathy cut short the thought, adding, "In these parts, there was a millionaire or near-millionaire every few feet before the Great Depression. Again, I know I'm preachin' to the choir here, talkin' history to you two, but think about what I'm saying.

"All our big ole houses here in the Hamlet tell the tale, huh? When the Crash came, most of those wealthy families lost their shirts, but not the Fanes. It was always gossiped that they *made* money during the Depression." The receptionist narrowed her eyes, thinking. "I can recall my grandparents and my parents saying that all the Fanes were born with a suitcase in their hands. They're all globe-trotters. It's in their blood. The one who owns the house nowadays, Mada, is just like her ancestors in that respect– always on the go. She's a real free spirit, that one. I don't think she ever married. Holds all kinds of degrees, but she's down-to-earth … sorta like yourselves. Not so highfalutin that you can't talk to her, if you know what I mean? Mada's nice. I've enjoyed listening to her stories about all the places she's visited around the world. Interesting lady, very unique too."

"How so?" Raine shot back.

Kathy shrugged. "Nothing in particular."

"Please," Raine encouraged, "Describe her in your own words."

"Well, she's unique due to the adventurous life she leads, her many experiences, the clothes she wears. Mada's definitely got her own style. Always looks like she's on safari or something. Even her way of talking. All those things make her, I don't know, set-apart … *different*." Kathy pondered over the information she had summoned. "She doesn't look or sound like anyone else around here." She smiled. "Not even you. I suppose, when all is said and done, *everything* about Mada is unique."

Now it was Raine's turn to shrug, seemingly satisfied with Kathy's response to her question. "We knew that Adrian Fane, her great-grandfather, was an esteemed industrialist and philanthropist known and respected across the entire Pittsburgh area," Raine stated.

"During the Hamlet's heyday," Maggie supplied, "his assets included railroads, banks, coal and coke lands, as well as various real estate holdings across the globe. His dealings and great wealth prompted his penchant for travel. I guess he passed that pursuit down in his family."

"And," Raine broke in, rambling, as she sometimes did, "we knew that Mada holds doctorates in both archeology and anthropology, in addition to countless accolades for her books on her field studies, but we didn't realize that she comes back home to the Hamlet. We assumed she lives abroad. You mean she still owns the Fane property here?" The raven-haired Sister looked to Maggie. "We heard … oh, about a year or so ago that the place was purchased by someone who was going to turn it into a bed and breakfast."

"That was just one of our Hamlet's never-ending rumors," Kathy laughed. "Gossip is the one thing we'll never run short of around here."

"Yes, and small, mean minds do so love gossip," Maggie remarked. Realizing what she had just uttered, she quickly amended, "I meant to suggest that people have always looked for the dirt surrounding our unsolved triple-ax murders."

Raine was biting her lip, as if puzzling out something that had entered her fertile mind. "The old Fane place always looks boarded up from the road. I never notice any lights on up there. When did you last see Mada?"

Kathy thought for a lengthy moment, finally answering, "Mada's still the owner of Fane Manor, as far as I know. I don't think there are any other Fanes around here anymore, though Mada might have a cousin living in New Zealand." She stopped, reconsidering. "Come to think of it, I remember hearing her say once that she has several relatives living abroad, scattered all over the world.

"Old man Steward, *George*, is the caretaker up at the Manor," Kathy related. "He's a retired janitor from the school district and a widower. You know him; I'm sure. He lives in the carriage house apartment on the Fane estate. Mada travels most of the time, usually to out-of-the-way places most of us never heard of. She only comes home once or twice a year. Last time I ran into her was about six months ago. Bumped into her at The Gypsy Tearoom in town."

"Did–" But Raine's inquiry was cut off when Kathy's dark eyes snapped with a sudden notion, and she exclaimed, "*That's* who you need to talk to about all this– Eva Novak. You see, her great-grandmother was the lady who read tea leaves for Nellie Triggs. Eva's great-grandmother read palms too; and it was rumored, after the ax murders, that she had just done a reading for Nellie prior to the poor woman's demise. My granny told me that story. Yep, and I recall Grandma saying that Nellie was addicted to the Occult, always runnin' for a reading. But then again, fear was common in those lean days of the Great Depression, and Nellie 'n probably many others turned to all sorts of spiritual help."

Kathy paused for a thoughtful moment, seeming to make up her mind about something. "Since I know just about everyone in this town, tell you what. I'll make a list of folks you should talk to. You know what they say, in a small town like ours, everyone's got a big mouth and everybody's related. Anyway, I'll make up a list of people who would be descendants of anyone I think may have had some connection to the murdered Nellie Triggs. When I get it done– won't take me but a day or so– I'll toss it in the mail to you."

"That would be most helpful and sorely appreciated," Maggie answered, reaching for Kathy's hand.

Kathy pursed her little mouth a moment, saying, "I happened just now to think of something else my grandmother mentioned about those unsolved murders."

Instinctively, Raine and Maggie moved even closer to the counter that separated them from the receptionist.

"You're right, Maggie, people started diggin' for dirt after Nellie and her family were killed. A lot of rumors about the poor woman took flight. One of them was that she had a secret lover, secret because he was a married man. That would've been a real disgrace back then. Not that it wouldn't be today, but you know what I'm saying. Many people were brought in for questioning, but nothing ever really surfaced about this alleged married lover of hers. I'm remembering stories as we talk."

Kathy's dark-chocolate eyes again sparked with recall. "Ah! Somethin' else my grandma mentioned. Nellie's brother was a leading suspect, due to the fact that Nellie's little boy told the police his *uncle* was the one who attacked him and the rest of the family. That *boy* was the only one to survive the attack, the only eye-witness.

"It was rumored that Nellie's brother had a violent row with her and ended up killing her because he was afraid she was disgracing the family. And even though he had an air-tight alibi the night of the killings– he lived out-of-state, Maryland, I think– many people believed he was the killer. When the little boy– Billy, I think his name was– refused to go and live with his uncle afterwards, a lot of people were convinced that Nellie's brother was the guilty party.

"My grandma said that little kid stormed and screamed *bloody murder* when a judge tried to get him to go and live with his uncle in Maryland. *That* must've *really* made the uncle look guilty as sin to the law, but I guess there was never enough evidence," Kathy wavered, amending, "any real evidence to speak of against the man."

"Who did Nellie's little boy Billy go to live with? Do you know?" Maggie questioned.

"I don't know off the top of my head, but I do think I remember my grandma saying it was a distant cousin. I know it was someone here in the Hamlet." Kathy raised her eyes to look beyond the Sisters to the door, which had just opened. "I'll find out, and if that person has any descendants residing in our area."

The newly arrived customer came up to the counter then, and the Sisters knew that their time with Kathy had ended– for now, at least.

"We'd better let you get back to work," Maggie said, backing away from the counter to allow the gentleman, who needed to speak to the receptionist, room to do so. "Oh, before we go, I want to remind you to make sure they check the brakes and rotate the tires on my Land Rover."

"Will do!" Kathy said, taking a sheet of paper from the male customer's extended hand. "I'll get that list made up for you, and if I think of anything else, anything significant, I'll telephone you," she told the Sisters.

"*Please* do that," they chimed in unison. "Thank you!"

A few moments later, the Sisters were getting into Raine's MG TD, which she had parked in the lot, in front of the Auto Doctor's.

"The stories Kathy remembered having been passed down in her family match those that our own granny told us," Maggie commented, as she settled into the passenger seat. She adjusted her sunglasses. "Although Granny never mentioned a hobo theory, you must admit that Kathy's vagrant scenario is a good one."

"It is," Raine replied, plopping her purse in Maggie's lap, after having retrieved the ignition keys.

Ever since her fanciful childhood when she polished off Nancy Drew mysteries faster than her granny could supply them, the impressionable Raine planned on having a vintage roadster of her own one day. When she was ready for the purchase, she searched everywhere for just the right car, scanning the Internet and newspapers daily, round-about used-car dealerships weekly, but to no avail.

Then the clever young woman decided to *manifest* her goal MG, just as Maggie had manifested her Land Rover. She did research and got a clear vision of precisely what she wanted, intensifying the energy each and every time she visualized the 1953 model she desired. She was thoroughly and carefully specific with each and every detail, from the signature headlights to the wire-wheels, and she truly *believed.* Within a month, the MG of her dreams appeared in the classified ads of the *Hamlet Herald*– within the price range she had programmed into the spell.

The sports car's like-new red and black interior and grill were the Sisters' high school and college colors, and the pristine cream body was the perfect canvas for the wee magick wand Raine had detailed on the driver's door, with her initials in fancy script on the wand's grip. Dr. Raine McDonough, PhD, was resourceful as well as clever.

"This," she stated decisively, "is only Saturday morning, which means we have the whole rest of the weekend to do some serious sleuthing before we have to be back in our classrooms on Monday. So what's the plan?"

Maggie laughed. "Darlin', that's a no-brainer. Let's get ourselves over to The Gypsy Tearoom."

Raine's bejeweled hand paused at the keys, as she was about to turn on the ignition. "Weren't you supposed to meet Thaddeus for lunch today?"

Maggie extracted her smart phone from her designer bag. "Yes, but there's no reason why the three of us can't lunch at the Tearoom. I'll ring him now to meet us there. He won't mind. And you know Thaddeus. He'll be more than willing to contribute to our sleuthing." The redheaded Sister tossed a peek at the diamond and ruby watch she was sporting. "It's nearly 11:30. The Tearoom opens at 11:00. He should be finished grading papers by now. He can join us for lunch, and we can eat and talk to Eva in one stop. Brainstorm in between."

Raine gave Maggie's shoulder a knock. "Wiz-zard! That fits in nicely, and we could do with some help. It's a bit early for lunch, but we had to start out with our errands so early today that we hadn't time for breakfast. I'm starved."

Maggie sent her cousin and sister of the moon one of her pointed Maggie looks. "You're always starved."

Raine's sidelong glance was mischievous. "For one thing or another."

"Nothing wrong with passion," Maggie affirmed. "Passion is good. It's the witches' way."

With a sigh, Raine replied, "Beau has to work today, and tomorrow I just know he'll get a farm call or two. Is Thad free for the rest of the day? I'm thinking that we should stop in to talk with Chief Fitzpatrick after we leave the Tearoom. I'm hoping he'll let us peruse the old police files on our Hamlet's unsolved ax murders."

Maggie bobbed her head in reply, for Thaddeus had answered her speed dial. "Darlin', would you mind terribly if Raine joined us for lunch? We really need to do some substantial sleuthing this weekend, and we were wondering if you–" Maggie laughed, the sound evocative of wind chimes. She sent Raine a zesty thumbs-up, as she listened to the rest of her lover's comment. "Right. Raine and I are en route there as we speak. See you in a few!"

Chapter Four

The Gypsy Tearoom was empty when Raine, Maggie and Thaddeus entered. It was rather early for lunch, and they were happy the place wasn't busy, for they hoped to be able to speak privately with the owner Eva Novak.

The café's semi-dark interior greeted the arrivals, causing them to pause and let their eyes adjust to the dim lighting. It was bright outside, though a spring storm was forecasted for the day. As the three professors made their way to a booth, the soulful music of a Gypsy violin, from a collection the proprietress played when live entertainment was wanting, issued from a speaker on the wall.

The Gypsy Tearoom was a cozy place with romantic, flickering wall sconces and intimate seating. Located in the lowest level of what had once been the Hamlet's original armory– a 1907 fortress-like, red-brick structure built in the late Gothic Revival style– the comfy seating in the basement level began life as horse stalls.

The historic building was purchased by Eva Novak when the new armory was built several years earlier. During renovation, the roomy box stalls were transformed into private booths, ideal for the readings that Eva's clientele often asked for, along with their tea and scones. Like her ancestors, Eva read tarot cards, palms, and tea leaves.

The ground floor was the banquet hall, reserved for groups and events. Eva used the third floor for her private quarters. Her living room occupied one of the building's two brick turrets, her bedroom the other, making her feel, as she often said, like a queen in a castle tower.

Renovation of the old edifice had been as the definition of that word affirms – cleaning, repairing, and reviving with as little actual remodeling as possible, for Eva was determined to keep the historic building's integrity.

In the Tearoom, rustic, wood table-and-bench seating filled each horse-stall-turned-booth. The walls of each cubicle were covered with dark-red, tufted leather, against which the occupants could rest their backs. The booths' thick, padded walls provided added privacy as well. Each table was topped with a different stained-glass lamp, and on the opposite wall from the stalls was a magnificent stone fireplace. A few small, rustic tables and chairs, also Gothic in style, occupied the center of the room. The ceiling flaunted the original walnut beams, the walls the same rustic aged brick that was on the building's exterior. Sliding barn doors, with charming black hardware, separated the dining area from the kitchen.

No sooner had the Sisters and Thaddeus arrived, when Eva, in colorful Gypsy attire– long, bright, vari-colored skirt with off-the-shoulder blouse– appeared from the adjacent kitchen. "Welcome!" she sang. Smiling warmly, she made her sprightly way to their booth, and as the Sisters looked into Eva's honest face, they saw her honest heart.

"I haven't seen *you* for a while." The proprietress eyed the three college professors. "No offense, but you look a bit drained. Spring break over and the students back in the classrooms, eh?" Before they could answer, Eva exclaimed, "Let me bring you a pot of my special brew! It's on the house. It'll relax you and keep you calm for whatever you have to face."

Maggie and Raine exchanged looks.

Eva spun on her heel, and her large gold-hoop earrings winked in a beam of light from a flickering wall sconce, as she flew off to get the tea.

Leaning forward in her seat on the opposite side of the table from Maggie and Thaddeus, Raine whispered, "Great Goddess' nightgown! Do you suppose she sensed we'll be facing something dark and sinister before too long?"

"I wouldn't be surprised," Maggie answered. "Eva is a talented psychic."

Shortly, the kind woman returned with a tray holding the tea things– a large, steaming, floral china pot of what Eva called her "special brew," along with three matching eggshell-thin cups and saucers, spoons, linen napkins, and menus.

"No sugar, honey, cream, or lemon with my special brew. Just enjoy the aroma and flavor of the tea itself," Eva stated nicely.

The Sisters regarded the woman as she poured their sweet-smelling tea.

Though in her fifties, Eva Novak looked a good twenty years younger. Her hair was casual, short and wavy, brushed softly back from her face, an enchanting blonde mix of silver and gold. One little wisp of a curl fell forward to the center of her forehead. Her skin was what used to be called "peaches and cream," unlined and glowing with health and happiness. Eva's almond-shaped hazel eyes were the eyes of a leopard, knowing and exotic, reminding the Sisters of Sophia Loren. Like Loren's, Eva's figure was full-blown, though no one could call either goddess overweight. Rather, "voluptuous" was the word-choice most would use.

Eva had a soft voice and a natural-born womanliness that rendered her affable– both men and women liked "Sister Novak." In summary, Eva was warm-hearted, vivacious and witty. She made life a high joyous thing for anyone around her.

The Sleuth Sisters and Thaddeus sipped the delicious tea, and Eva handed each a menu, the cover of which bore a dreamy Gypsy likeness of the proprietress' great-grandmother. Anna was the woman who had started the Tearoom, many years before in a portion of her own home, a big, rambling old Hamlet house that was now a nursery school, a fact that would have pleased the children-loving Anna. Every time the Sisters looked at a Tearoom menu, they noted that Eva bore a strong resemblance to Anna's ethereal likeness.

Eva had been married four times. For some unknown reason, the woman had a penchant for the name "John," as well as for firemen. The Sisters didn't know whether the husbands' given names were each John, or if Eva just called each by her favorite name. All the Sisters knew is that all four of Eva's husbands had been called "John," and all four had been firemen. They knew for certain, too, that each husband had been, like Eva herself, Hungarian. Eva had been widowed twice and divorced twice. And never had anyone heard the woman speak unkindly of any one of her former mates. Indeed, when any one of her husbands was ever mentioned, Eva habitually pulled a paper towel from the bra of the low-cut Gypsy blouse or dress she was sporting to wipe tearful eyes. The Sisters had never known her not to be prepared with that towel. Eva was one-of-a-kind.

"Enjoy your tea while you look over the menu. Today's special is hearty ham and cheese scones, with my special honey butter, served with fresh fruit."

"You know what?" Raine replied, looking across the table at her companions, I think we'll all want the special."

Maggie and Thaddeus readily agreed, and Eva reclaimed the menus. "Coming right up!" She started to turn but waited, seeming to study her favorite customers; and clamping one hand on a rounded hip, prodded with zest, "So how do you like my special brew?"

Thaddeus began stroking his beard, a gesture indicative of his pensive mood. "Does it really do what you say, calm and strengthen the partaker for ... whatever? What's in it?" He remained thoughtful for a meditative moment, while–

Eva responded with her secretive smile. "A Gypsy never reveals everything. We like our secrets. The main herb is greenthread, as you find in Navajo tea. The Navajo have been brewing it in tea for centuries. Greenthread grows wild on their lands out West."

Dr. Weatherby patiently repeated his question. "But does it really center and calm the recipient for whatever he or she has to face in life?"

Eva smiled again, tilting her blonde head, the silver and gold threads of her soft hair shimmering, like spun gold in moon glow, under the flickering candle sconces. "I got so tired of answering that misgiving with my standard reply, 'Tea time will tell,' that I named my special brew just that–'Tea-Time-Will-Tell.'"

"Will it calm nausea and dizziness too?" Thaddeus asked in a half-serious tone.

"Yes!" Eva answered without hesitation. "That's one of the many things it does." Noting the looks on the professors' faces, she laughed, "Not to worry, dear patrons, everything in my tea is perfectly legal." With that, she headed for the kitchen to prepare their order.

Outside, the forecasted downpour was starting to blow in, as rain pelted the small leaded-diamond windows across the room from where they sat. The Farmers' Almanac that Raine and Maggie always kept on hand in Tara's kitchen predicted an especially wet spring, and thus far, it was coming to pass. Thunder and lightning rumbled and flashed close by, as Raine, Maggie and Thaddeus continued sipping Eva's witchy brew, relaxing in the tranquility of their private booth.

After several minutes of quiet, Dr. Weatherby said, "I don't think I'm imagining it, but this tea *is* calming. I feel as though I've had a nice relaxing glass of wine. Ah yes, *exceedingly* relaxing." He began anew to stroke his van dyke mustache and beard. Then in an enthusiastic whisper he expressed to the Sisters, "Eva's special brew just may be the answer to our time-travel difficulty. We don't know yet if it'll eliminate our nausea and dizziness when we land in a different era, but *it's certainly worth a try.* We should each drink a mug of this," he raised his cup in a toasting gesture, "right before our next time trek. Let's ask to purchase some before we leave."

The Sisters could only nod in response, for a beaming Eva was bustling toward them, carrying their order on a large silver tray.

Later, when Eva returned to their booth to see if everything was satisfactory, Raine asked her to join them for a few moments. The storm was raging toward tempest heights; and thus far, no one else had come into the Tearoom. Rain and wind thundered against the windows, as though something evil was seeking to get inside.

"Sit here, next to me," Raine invited, patting the seat and moving over to make room for their hostess.

"Eva, do you recall any stories, remembrances passed down in your family, about the unsolved triple ax murders that occurred in our Hamlet back in 1932?" Maggie opened without preamble.

Eva tilted her blonde head in a thoughtful gesture. "Some," she replied succinctly. She looked directly across the table, locking eyes with Maggie. "I don't know if you're aware of it, but my great-grandmother was the murdered woman's psychic. Nellie had become *deeply* interested in the Occult, and she often visited my great-grandmother Anna for readings. That bloody episode in the history of our sleepy little village was … well, so unusual, so dreadful, and so wickedly mysterious– a messy, malicious maze that was never untangled. My guess is that *most* folks around here could tell you stories about it that've been passed down in their families."

The proprietress tapped her lips with her index finger in reflection. "I recall one story in particular," Eva began, inducing her listeners to pause in their eating. "Mama Anna–" she broke off, adding, "That's what we Hungarians use for Nana or Grandma." Eva had pronounced the word "Mama" as "Momo."

"Mama Anna," Eva continued, "did an in-depth tarot reading for Nellie Triggs shortly before the murders. I remember that Mama Anna's daughter, my own grandmother Franciska– we all called her Mama Franci– always said that never did Mama Anna break client privilege with Nellie, or anyone else for that matter. Our family never even knew what she told the police when they sounded her out. I mean *if* she actually told them anything. The only way her daughter, my Mama Franci, knew anything about that fateful reading is because she was loitering outside the parlor when Nellie was in the house for what turned out to be her last visit, and she overheard a couple things."

"What things?" Raine blurted, twisting partway round on the bench to face Eva, who was sitting next to her. The raven-haired Sister took a long pull of her tea.

"Mama Franci was just a child then, about six, I think. Anyway, she was eavesdropping, you see, and she heard Nellie say over and over again– "I'm afraid, so *very* afraid."

Eva gave a brisk nod in response to the looks on her guests' faces. "And I recollect too that my Mama Franci said she would always remember Nellie's face when she arrived at the house that night, as well as when she left, because it was burned in her memory forever. White as a sheet that poor woman was– *as if she'd seen a ghost.*"

Maggie shook her head sadly. "'Poor woman' is right. I wonder who or what she was afraid of? If only we knew the answer to that question! Was it the reading itself that she feared, or was it a person?" The redheaded Sister speared a plump strawberry with her fork and slipped it into her mouth.

Eva ducked her head, answering, "Whatever the answer, Nellie and my Mama Anna took it to their graves, each of them."

Raine adjusted herself on the seat. "Do you remember anything else, any other tidbits of information passed down in your family? It doesn't matter how trifling or insignificant you might think it."

Eva wrinkled her brow. "I haven't thought about this for a long time, many years in fact. The local newspaper stopped running the story like it used to. Memory's not what it was, you know." She closed her eyes, deep in thought.

Directly, Eva's heavily-outlined eyes flew open wide, and she exclaimed, "Yes, I remember Mama Franci saying that she'd heard the words 'Death card' uttered by her mother during Nellie's card reading!"

Outside, the storm hit its peak, as loud thunder rolled in, and lightning flashed.

"That, as you know, doesn't always portend a literal death," Maggie said almost to herself. "I wonder if that was what put such fear into Nel–" She cut off, finishing, "but you mentioned that Nellie *arrived* for the reading white as a ghost, so likely it was *not* the reading itself that walloped her with fear."

"A logical supposition," Raine murmured.

- 84 -

"And," Maggie went on to Eva, "your ancestor would've most certainly explained that the Death card in Tarot most often refers to some sort of change or transformation, though often through strong force."

Raine made a deep sound of agreement. "Uh-huh, a sweeping change … a parting of the ways. However, the image of Death charging across a field on his spectral steed would strike fear in the heart of almost anyone. I mean humans naturally fear the unknown, and Death is the greatest unknown."

"Well, whatever it was that made that Nellie woman go white, it must have come like a thunderbolt to her." Eva frowned as a new thought entered her mind. In a moment, she lit up with another memory. "I just thought of something else that Mama Franci told us kids about Nellie."

Again the three professors paused in their eating.

"Nellie," Eva recounted, "had worked at the Hamlet Sports Wear. You three know the place I'm talking about. The old factory that used to be over on the West Side. They tore it down; oh, it's years ago now. The story goes that Nellie worked there until the place shut down during the Depression. Since she was the sole supporter of her family, of her two kids and her elderly mother, she had to keep working, so she sought employment elsewhere, finally landing a job managing the antique shop in town for the wealthy Fanes. *Enchanting Things*, I think it was called.

"Anyhow, I recall Mama Franci saying that Nellie had become *dis*enchanted working for the Fanes; but she desperately needed that job, so she stayed on with them. You know better than I, as history professors, that was the age of soup kitchens and Hoovervilles. People had to take what work they could get. If they were lucky enough to get work at all."

Thaddeus, who was filing everything that Eva was saying into his eidetic memory bank, asked suddenly, "What do you mean by *disenchanted*?"

Eva pursed her lips. "*Uncomfortable* I think is what my grandmother meant, though I can't say for sure."

The Sisters flung one another a look, with Raine posing the begging question, "Can you elaborate on that? The Fanes, after all, were leading citizens of the entire Pittsburgh area."

Eva gave a slight shrug. "I can't really. I admit that I honestly don't know what my Mama Franci meant."

Maggie poked at another piece of fruit. "Do you know if Nellie worked for the Fanes in any other capacity besides the antique shop?"

A brief silence followed before Eva answered. "Once again, I can't say for certain, but I think, as I mentioned earlier, she *managed* that shop for them. They traveled a lot, you see. And I recall hearing that Nellie took in laundry and ironing to supplement what she made at the shop, so perhaps she did the Fanes' laundry, in addition to running their antique store. Either Nellie or her elderly mother did a bit of stitching … *sewing*. Probably clothing repairs, alterations and the like, so maybe she did that for the Fanes too. I really don't know. I know Nellie traded favors with my Mama Anna for a reading now and again."

Raine pushed her plate aside after having polished off her fruit. "Have you ever heard the rumor that Nellie had a secret lover, a *married* lover?" She took up her napkin and dabbed the corners of her mouth.

The Sisters were glad to see that rain still pelted the two leaded-diamond windows, and in the distance, a roll of thunder could be heard. The storm was keeping anyone else from coming into the Tearoom.

"Hmmmm, a secret lover?" Eva pondered. "You know," she pronounced after a moment, "I *do* recall hearing that."

"From family stories?" Maggie queried, pushing her own empty plate aside.

"Yes," Eva stated, "and from other folks too. I think the police were after finding this phantom lover, but they never did. Not that I know of anyway."

"Do you know the names of Nellie's two suitors that the police *did* interrogate?" Thaddeus asked. He too had finished his fruit. He poured the last of the tea into their cups, sharing it between the three of them, as he waited for the proprietress to conjure the sought-after names.

"I'm not a hundred percent sure I'm remembering their given names correctly. As I said, it's been a while since I even thought about this tragedy; but I think I'm right when I tell you that Nellie's boyfriends were Biff Valentine and Jasper Swain. If you know the story of our Hamlet's ax murders, it's kinda hard to forget those two names. In addition to Nellie's brother, they were the *top* suspects."

Eva peered around the end of the booth to the door. She thought she heard someone come in.

A lady with a little girl had entered the Tearoom, prompting the proprietress to stand. "Customers," she mouthed in a whisper. "I hope I've helped you. I'm aware of the remarkable things you do, helping those in need and aiding the police with so many baffling cases. I'll never forget how you solved that shocking missing-child case a few years back, and how you solved the nearly three-hundred-year secret of our Hamlet's mysterious hermit."

"You've definitely been a help to us," the Sisters answered in unison. "May we talk to you again about this?"

"Of course," Eva said, signaling to the newly arrived guests to be seated. "I'll be over in a bit with the dessert cart and more tea." The proprietress took a step, then spun back round to say with ardent breath, "I hope you solve this long-time mystery, too, for our dear Hamlet."

Later, after another cup of Eva's delicious tea and a sampling of her berry tarts, Maggie said to Raine, "Thaddeus and I will follow you to the police station in his car. We know we can also count on Chief Fitzpatrick to aid us in any way he can."

"Good man, Fitzpatrick," Raine replied, standing to follow her companions to the Tearoom exit, where they waved goodbye to Eva Novak, busy now with lunchtime patrons.

"I hope we can count on this tea," Thaddeus said, extending the purchased package of Eva's special brew to Maggie, "to ease our tempestuous expeditions to other epochs."

"Time will tell," Raine quipped.

Outside, Maggie said, "I can't help but be haunted by Nellie's words– **haunted**. '*I'm afraid, so very afraid.*'"

Raine's hand shot out to grasp Maggie's arm. "I know," she huffed out a breath. "My keen Irish feeling is that axed Nellie is guiding us to speak with certain people. She *wants* us to solve this mystery so that she can finally rest in peace."

***

The Hamlet's police station dominated the block where it was located. Castle-like, the grey stone building was of the Gothic Revival architecture so popular at the turn of the twentieth century when Haleigh's Hamlet was enjoying its heyday; for then, the village was populated with several of the leading industrialists who helped transform America from an agricultural nation to a booming industrial one.

As soon as Raine, Maggie and Thaddeus entered the station, Chief Fitzpatrick, who was standing at the outer desk, talking to one of his junior officers, strode briskly forward to greet them. "Well, well," he bellowed, "what brings you down here today? Not trouble, I hope." The big, affable man shook hands with Dr. Weatherby, before extending his arms to encompass both Sisters and give them a joint bear hug.

Fitzpatrick was a burly fellow with a thick crop of snowy white hair and a high color to his fair Irish complexion.

"May we take a few minutes of your time, Chief?" Raine asked. "We really need your assistance."

"Let's go into my office," he answered, ushering his visitors ahead of him with a magnanimous sweep of his arm.

"So that's what we know thus far, which really isn't a whole lot," Maggie concluded from her seat across the desk from the chief, who, leaning back in his chair, was mulling over what his visitors just shared with him. After telling Fitzpatrick about their encounter with the mysterious woman on the train from Salem, the Sisters revealed what they had been ferreting out about the Hamlet's unsolved triple ax murders.

The more direct Raine probed, "Chief, we were wondering if you'd permit us to study any old files you might still have here on that cold case." She sent him her beguiling smile, the dimple making its appearance in her cheek.

"That's no problem," Fitzpatrick replied without pause. "I've learned to trust you Sleuth Sisters and your tight circle of associates. I appreciate your crime-solving contributions here in the Hamlet and elsewhere." He rubbed the side of his ruddy face with the back of one hand. "I've never looked into it, but we must still have a file, or files, on that case."

The chief's blue eyes locked with his visitors. "No such thing as a closed unsolved murder case, you know. No statute of limitations on murder. Though *I've* never seen a file on the case," he chortled– "way before my time– anything we have on it would be in the basement where we keep old files. Come on down with me. There might be a ton of stuff on that particular case, and you can each carry something. We'll bring the works up here to my office and lay the files out on that long table back there," he gestured toward the rear of the room, where you can pull up chairs and take as much time as you need, today and in days to come."

Fitzpatrick stood. "Follow me."

After flicking on the light at the top of the stairs, the chief cautioned, "Have a care. These steps are narrow and steep." He started down, leading the way, the flashlight he grabbed at the top of the stairs augmenting the indistinct lighting.

As they descended, Raine, Maggie and Thaddeus were met with a slightly musty odor and the soft hum of the dehumidifier they spotted in the large basement room they entered. Tall, metal file cabinets lined every wall.

Straightaway, the chief, light in hand, began moving toward what he believed might be the cabinet holding files from the 1930s. "Thank God we've never really had a lot of crime around here. The Hamlet's always been a pretty safe place to live." His flashlight scanned the years marked on the front of the cabinets. "Ah!" he exclaimed of a sudden. "Here we go. It should be in this one."

Yanking open a heavy drawer from the top of the cabinet where he'd stopped, the chief started rooting through the files. "Here," he said, handing the light to Dr. Weatherby, "hold this while I dig through these."

Thaddeus obliged, scanning the light to keep up with Fitzpatrick's busy, thick fingers.

Several moments later, they struck pay dirt, with the chief booming, "Eureka!" He extracted several files, double checking to make certain he'd pulled every folder connected to the Hamlet's unsolved ax murders. Then, handing each of his companions something to carry, they all headed back up to his private office.

Raine set the folder she had been leafing through back down on the table in front of her. She stretched, yawned, and glanced at her watch, an enchanting piece of gold jewelry with moon, stars, and faerie charms encrusted with tiny, glittering pavé diamonds. It was going on seven o'clock, and she was hungry. Turning toward Maggie and Thaddeus, she announced, "I'm starving. Let's call it a day, go get something to eat and discuss what we've gleaned thus far."

Her companions readily agreed, and the three of them began neatening the folders and separating them into what they had read and what they had not yet examined.

"Chief," Raine and Maggie began in sync, "may we return after school tomorrow to continue our perusal of these files?"

"Sure. I'll leave everything on this table for you," Fitzpatrick replied, "until you crack this hard-shelled crime– and I have all the confidence in the world that you will."

The Sisters nodded, with the absent-minded Thaddeus feeling in the pocket of his blazer for his smart phone. "Maggie, grab my phone, will you? I must've left it on the table there among the files."

In spite of Dr. Weatherby's photographic mind, Maggie had asked him to use his phone to capture, with the chief's consent, a few of the pages. Maggie always liked to have what she called "extra insurance."

When the redheaded Sister located the phone, her eyes lighted on something in that particular file. She picked it up, sharply drawing in her breath.

Great Goddess! she nearly cried out. Her stomach plummeted, and her hands flew to her open mouth.

Chapter Five

At the entrance to the tree-lined path that led to Aisling and Ian's place, the wooden sign creaked on its heavy chain, as it swung from its pole in the gusty wind. The placard's words– *The Black Cat Detective Agency*– were barely discernible in the gloaming of that misty, stormy night.

Below the curved Gothic lettering, was mounted the sooty, arched figure of a fierce-looking, ebony cat. As Dr. Weatherby's vintage Studebaker entered the lane, the dazzle of its headlights seemed to momentarily enliven the cat's golden eyes, making them glow. Though that always happened when entering Aisling's driveway during hours of darkness, it was, nonetheless, each time startling.

From the Hamlet's police station, the three professors had made one stop, to drop off Raine's MG at Tara. Now, both Maggie and Raine were passengers in Thaddeus' 1950, maroon, bullet-nose Studebaker. The vintage car resembled a missile, and that perchance was why Dr. Weatherby habitually urged his students, prior to weekends and holidays, to be careful in their "missiles."

Like a monstrous night creature, the heavy vehicle's tires made crunching sounds on the gravel, as the threesome motored up the narrow, twisting drive to the stone house that served as home and business for Aisling and her husband Ian. Aisling inherited the charming property, along with the means to start the agency, from Granny McDonough, who had purchased it for Grandad McDonough as a hunting lodge, hoping that it would be a pleasant distraction from the relentless work he heaped upon himself.

"It was nice of Aisling and Ian to invite us to supper tonight," Thaddeus remarked, as he guided the car to a stop in front of the rustic, woodsy home.

"Aisling told me on the phone when I called her from the station that supper'll be what she and Ian call an 'ad-lib meal,'" Raine replied. "But they're excited to hear what we garnered about the ax murders, after poring over those police files today."

The raven-haired Sister emphasized her next words with a slight wave of hand. "Aisling said it was *destined* that we meet tonight. Ian got a great deal on filet mignons at the market today. He plans to toss them on the grill when we get there. She's made a big healthy salad. Port and sorbet for dessert."

"Sounds good to me!" Thaddeus, an avid steak fan, commented, as he switched off the ignition. He looked to Maggie. "Are you feeling all right, luv?"

The red-haired Sister shuddered out an audible breath. "I just can't get those dreadful police photos of the axed victims out of my mind." She gave a little shiver, as Thaddeus helped her from the vehicle.

"They *were* gruesome," Raine agreed, stepping out of the car. "But a good dinner and some wine will fix you right up, Mags. Everything is beginning to fall into place for us with this case. Tonight's the perfect time to brainstorm with our two expert gumshoes! I just wish Beau, Hugh and Betty were joining us."

On cue in direct response to the Sister's desire, headlights shone in the lane, as another vehicle made its gravel-crunching way up the drive to the house.

"Is that who I hope it is?" Raine asked eagerly.

"Sure is," Maggie answered. "Aisling wanted to surprise you. Beau's free tonight. She invited our sleuthing set right after she spoke with you."

"Wiz-zard!" Raine exclaimed, using her favorite expletive.

***

It had been a simple but most satisfying meal. And now, in the Gwynn's rustic living room, as the port flowed, so did the conversation.

"Merry Fay was very proud of her twice-baked potatoes," Maggie remarked, settling herself on the couch next to Thaddeus. She crossed her shapely legs, encased in sheer black stockings, and smoothed the skirt of her black dress with its witchy stand-up collar. "I think that child's going to take after you, Ian, in the kitchen."

"I hope she does," Aisling replied. "I never enjoyed cooking, though I sometimes serve as Ian's sous chef."

"No problem," Ian grinned. "You've got so many other talents." He slipped an arm along the couch-top behind his wife and dove in for a kiss. They were seated on the long, leather sofa next to Maggie and Thaddeus. Facing them, Betty and Hugh were ensconced in the smaller love seat, and on the fur rug before the cheery fire, Raine and Beau settled in for a productive evening of symposium sleuthing.

"Where *is* Merry Fay?" Raine asked, glancing round the spacious, wood-paneled room.

"We trotted her off to her room. She's happily curled up with Merlin, watching TV," Aisling answered. "Ian and I asked her not to disturb us this evening while we brainstorm. We don't want her to hear about the grisly murders."

"Good," Raine and Maggie replied at once.

"She told Ian and me that she and Merlin chatted with faeries today, when they were out in the flower garden," Aisling commented with a pleased grin. "Children see magick because they look for it."

"True!" Raine giggled. "*We* always did."

"What do you mean *did*?" Maggie laughed. "Magick is all around us. All we have to do is *believe*."

"You know," Raine said in a wistful tone, "Merlin is, more and more, the spittin' image of Granny's old Myrrdyn!"

"Well, he *is* a direct descendant!" Aisling retorted. "Ian refers to him as an 'undercover agent for the Blues,' seein' as we've noticed over the years how much he shares my husband's enthusiasm for old-timey, bluesy-blues music."

"Oh yeah," Ian cut in, "and he has his special favorites– Bessie Smith's 'Empty Bed Blues'; Louis Armstrong's 'Chimes Blues'; though, by far and true to his nickname, he delights in Tina Turner's rendition of 'Undercover Agent for the Blues.'"

"'Course he does," Raine quipped, "he's a *cool* cat!" She reached for some almonds from the bowl on the coffee table.

Nuts, crackers, grapes, and a cheese board, graced with baby Swiss, sharp Cheddar, and a savory Port Salut, topped the coffee table with the port.

Maggie took a deep breath. "Aisling's house always smells … *peaceful*. I'm not really sure that a house can *waft* peace and goodwill?" Maggie laughed. "But I do know this– there's always been an atmosphere of harmony and love here. I sense it each and every time I enter your home." She raised her wineglass to Aisling and Ian, "The very stuff of magick."

The couple smiled. "Thank you, Maggie."

"I'm chomping at the bit to get to our current mystery," Betty said, leaning forward and rubbing her hands together, causing her huge charm bracelet to jingle. Betty could never contain herself when a good whodunit loomed before them.

"Yes, tell us what you gleaned today," Hugh pled. "We're all ears."

"Before we went to the police station to dig into the old files connected to the ax murders," Raine began, "we spoke with Kathy Wise at the Auto Doctor's, as Hugh had suggested. Then we lunched at The Gypsy Tearoom so we could talk with Eva Novak." She sat up to arrange herself in lotus position– Raine believed it helped her think clearer– smoothing her long, black, handkerchief-hem tunic over the knees of her leggings.

The Goth gal, Maggie, and Thaddeus took nearly an hour to relate what they had reaped from both Kathy Wise and Eva Novak, with Maggie concluding, "I couldn't help but think of Nellie's haunting words, '*I am afraid, so very afraid,*' when I saw those gruesome police photos of the axed victims."

Hugh turned Maggie's remarks over in his sleuthing mind, finally huffing into his cavalry mustache, as he stretched his long legs out in front of him. "Kathy's hobo theory isn't bad. Not bad at all."

"And I agree with you," Betty gestured to Raine and Maggie, "If, as Eva said, Nellie arrived for the reading at Eva's great-granny's house white as a sheet, then it was *not* the reading that frightened her, but something or someone that figured into her life before she ever heard the ominous words– *Death card.*"

"So Nellie became uncomfortable working for the wealthy Fanes, did she?" Ian ruminated over his cheese and wine. "That might prove significant."

"Now tell us what you discovered, thus far, in the old police files," Aisling urged. The former police detective turned toward Maggie, and their McDonough eyes met over the rims of their wineglasses.

"Whoever wielded that ax did it with great power and violence," Maggie asserted. "Nellie's face and head had been *severely* hacked. Her collar bone was nearly severed, and her arm was broken, though the broken arm could have been due to the fall from the kitchen window into the alley. Raine and I think she was attempting to escape and run for help. Nonetheless, in our experience, and the chief concurred with us on this, as we think *you* will," the red-haired Sister's emerald gaze swept their set of sleuths, "one motive especially seems to incite such ferocity."

"Revenge!" Aisling, Ian, Hugh and Betty answered in unison, with Beau nodding in agreement.

"*Revenge*," Raine and Maggie repeated with quiet force.

Hugh leaned forward, to the coffee table, for a cracker and a sliver of white cheddar. He munched broodingly for a few seconds before saying, "You need a list of descendants of anyone connected to this case, so–"

"Kathy Wise is making up such a list for us, and we started our own today at the police station, once we began digging into the files," Raine interjected. She grabbed a handful of nuts to share with Beau, who was lying next to her on the hearth rug, his head propped up by a couple of orange throw pillows.

"The three top suspects," the raven-haired Sister continued, "were Nellie's two suitors and her brother, since her son Billy, who survived the attack, was adamant that his *uncle* had wielded the ax."

"However, each of those men had an alibi. Or so it was said. We always heard, and the *Hamlet Herald* continually stated that the alibis of the three top suspects were *air-tight*; but we discovered today in the police files that the *suitors*, anyway, each had a window of opportunity," Thaddeus revealed. He took a swallow of his port. "You tell them about the suitors, Raine. You're the best narrator."

Raine set her glass down on a small side table. "Biff Valentine, the suitor with whom Nellie broke up, shortly before the murders, had a history of violence, *especially when he drank*. Seems he liked to carry a flask of bathtub gin around with him when he was off duty from his work. The police files stated that he had been arrested twice, once in Maryland, where he was from, and another time here for altercations that led to exchange of blows– those with men. To top the lot, three former girlfriends had filed complaints about him prior to the ax murders of Nellie and her family."

"What did he do for a living? Do you know if he had a job during the period when the ax murders were perpetrated?" Betty queried, reaching for a handful of almonds.

"Valentine worked as a guard for the railroad, and he resided at a place called the 'Emerald House,' a boarding house located down by the station and populated by railroad workers. It was torn down decades ago." Raine took a breath, pressing on, "The police files contained statements by several people who had witnessed Biff manhandling Nellie in the parking lot of the Café Crawford just two days before the murders. He told the police, when they brought him in for questioning, that he had done nothing but grab her arm. But he admitted to police he had a tendency to get," she gestured imaginary quote marks, "'**riled**,' he called it, when he took a drink. And the witnesses with whom the police spoke affirmed it was considerably more than grabbing her arm. One witness said that Biff was jerking Nellie around and was ready to backhand her across the face, when a gentleman in the area intervened."

Aisling reached forward for a slice of Port Salut. "Did you ferret out what the argument between him and Nellie had been about?"

Maggie gave a quick nod. "Apparently, she'd broken off with him, and he could not accept it. Witnesses heard him demanding to know why, *why* she did not want to see him again. That type of man, and I use the term loosely, can never see the fault with themselves. Witnesses also said that Biff spewed out the name of Nellie's other known suitor, Jasper Swain, along with this juicy tidbit of information– Biff called Swain a 'whorin' womanizer.'"

Raine inclined her head, picking up the story. "When the police grilled Valentine– and it was several times that he was brought in for questioning– he admitted Nellie had broken up with him. He owned up to having been jealous, but he swore he never hurt her or her family. He avowed over and again his innocence, stating that the incident with Nellie on the Café Crawford's parking lot was the last time he saw her.

"Biff admitted to the police that she refused to see him when he went to her house the day after the parking-lot incident to apologize. The police report said her mother answered the door and related to him that Nellie did not want to ever see or speak to him again, that he had publically humiliated her, and that she was done with him for good." Raine took a sip of her wine, her emerald gaze sweeping the sleuthing set for their reactions.

"The 'if-I-can't-have-her-nobody-can' motive is an especially strong one. In *a* word, *revenge*," Hugh reflected. "And those police-file photos sure look as if the killing ax was wielded for revenge!"

"What was Valentine's alibi when the murders took place?" Ian asked, picking up a small bunch of grapes from the platter on the coffee table. He sat back to listen and consider what Raine was about to disclose.

"He said the night of the tragedy, he spent the entire evening at the boarding house, and the police files showed he had several people collaborate his story. He told police that after supper at the Emerald House, he and several other boarders moseyed into the community room, where they listened to the radio for a while– the news followed by *Amos 'n Andy*– then sat talking and smoking till he said he went to his room around eleven o'clock to bed." Raine paused here for emphasis.

"The police asked him if he went out after that. He answered *he did not*, that if he *had*, the boarders still in the community room would have seen or heard him leave the house, since he had to pass *by* that room to exit the building. The landlady always kept the Emerald House's backdoor securely locked. But police noted that Valentine's room was on the first floor in the back of the house. He could well have slipped out of the building through his bedroom window onto the dark backyard, cut across an alley and made his quick way to Nellie's bungalow only a couple of blocks distant." Again Raine waited a beat.

"The window of opportunity," Hugh quipped, nodding his silver head.

"Indeed," Aisling concurred. "So what about Nellie's other suitor, the Swain fellow?"

"Jasper Swain," Raine resumed her account, "was a salesman. Sold beauty products to beauty shops round about the area. He did like women, as his rival Biff Valentine had so crudely stated; but, then again, he was always around women. Women were his customers, and he flirted to get them to buy his products. Whereas Biff Valentine was a rough-tough macho man, Jasper Swain was a dandy.

"A couple of weeks prior to the murders, Swain had proposed to Nellie Triggs; and when she turned him down, he took the ring back to the jeweler's. He bought it on time, he told the police, and he said there was no sense in paying for something he might never need, so he took it back, informing the jeweler that if his lady-love changed her mind, he'd come back for *it*, or another ring, later.

"The night of the murders," Raine swept on, "Swain told police he'd made himself something to eat at his home, a house he'd recently inherited from his mother, who passed away the previous winter. He then ambled down to the Stardust Hall, to watch the dance marathon that had begun the previous weekend. There were three couples remaining, he told police, and two of those couples were friends of his, so he wanted to attend. He related that, not long after he got to the dance hall, he spied an old flame; and he eventually ended up sitting with her to watch the dancing. He said they left together later to walk to an all-night diner, the Lamppost, for burgers. After the burgers, they shared a piece of pie, and he walked his ex-girlfriend to her door, a mere two streets up from his house."

"The murders happened around midnight," Ian said. "What's Swain's timeline?"

"Here's *his* window of opportunity," Raine began. "Swain told police he was not wearing a watch, that it was at the jeweler's for repair." Raine cast a glance round the room. "By the bye, when the police followed up on his statement, it was true. Swain told police that when he felt tired of watching the dance marathon, he suggested to the lady– and the lady was an easy-to-remember buxom blonde– that they go for a burger, and again, that part of his story checked out with the woman he was with **and** the waitress at the Lamppost diner– **but** the lady friend couldn't tell police the exact time they left the dance hall, the diner, or her front porch, though the waitress thought the couple had left the diner around eleven-forty-five."

"What about when Swain returned to his house?" Hugh probed. "What did he tell police was the time when he got home that night?"

"He told the police he was dog-tired," Raine replied. "He said he had to set out early in the morning, on the road in sales, and so he headed straight for his bedroom, removed his clothes, and flopped down on the bed. He added that he reached over and set the alarm clock, but did not look at the clock's face. He had done it so many times, he could do it in the dark. He did *not* switch on a light."

"Convenient," Betty remarked, looking over at Hugh, whose only response was to snort into his mustache. "What about Nellie's neighbors?" Betty asked, turning again to face Raine. "Did you read anything in the police files about what they might've had to say about the murders?"

Raine nodded, but Maggie answered, since the former was taking a sip of her wine.

"The police reports confirmed what we'd gathered on our own. None of the neighbors saw or heard anything unusual. Remember, we told you the Moretti family lived *right next door*, and they all claimed they had never seen any 'hanky-panky' over at Nellie's place. We did get to read their statements. Louis, the father of the boy who discovered Nellie's mangled body in the alley behind her house, the morning after the murders, told the authorities that she appeared to be ladylike in every way– dress, manner, and speech– that she worked hard to bring up her children properly and to care for her elderly mother. Neither Mr. Moretti nor his wife Rosa had ever seen, they assured police, anything questionable at Nellie's. They *swore* they hadn't seen or heard anything unusual the night of the murders."

"We did note," Thaddeus interjected, "that the police harbored some *doubt* about the Morettis' statements. There was a note in one of the files that stated, and I quote, 'Louis and Rosa Moretti acted as though they might have been withholding information. There looked to be some fear on their parts when speaking with the police.'"

"You know," Maggie answered, stretching catlike next to Thaddeus on the couch. "Immigrants were often fearful of anyone in uniform. It may be that they were keeping nothing back, that they carried their fear of uniforms with them from the old country, and that is all their reticence was. Or," she sucked in her full lower lip, "they spoke broken English and were fearful of saying something that might be misunderstood, perhaps something that might inadvertently hurt Nellie, whom, it seemed, they truly liked."

"I agree with Mags," Raine said with sudden ardor. "Their children's statements to the police were identical, as if rehearsed. Thus, the parents may've had them memorize what to tell the authorities, rather than risk their kids saying something that might've hurt Nellie."

"What Maggie and Raine said carries a lot of truth," Thaddeus pronounced, but let us not rule out that the Moretti family might've seen something that filled them with fear, in addition to the discovery of Nellie's body, I mean."

"Thaddeus is right," Aisling added. "Let's not rule out anything at this point." The blonde Sister glanced down at her notebook, where she had jotted a few comments. "Did you find anything, any mention at all, about Nellie's alleged secret lover, thus far, in your perusal of the police files?"

Maggie and Raine turned to face one another. "Yes," they chorused to their coterie.

"But nothing significant," Raine amended. "Only that several people interviewed had mentioned it was *rumored* Nellie had a secret lover; and the consensus was, because this *liaison* was so secret, it might be a married man." Raine furrowed her brow. "Apparently no one had ever seen Nellie with anyone in a compromising situation–"

"Then what made people suspect she *had* a secret lover?" Betty interposed. She toyed with the turquoise fetish charms on her huge silver bracelet, a sure sign she was in deep thought.

Raine took a quick sip of wine and set the goblet down on the small low table next to her. "Seems a rumor quickly spread through the Hamlet about Nellie: Given that she'd never accepted a marriage proposal– and good-looking woman that she was, she'd had *a few* since her husband's passing– she must've had a secret lover. You know how rumors get started. The subsequent chatter– and apparently, there was *considerable* whispered speculation among the villagers– was that the phantom lover was secret because he was a *married* man.

"Nellie's namesake and great niece told us on the train that after the murders, gossip ran *rampant* about Nellie. One person interviewed even told police that Nellie was always seen posting letters, parcels, *et cetera*; soooo," the raven-haired Sister rolled her glittering green eyes, "that individual stated, in the report, Nellie must've had a secret lover who resided outside the Hamlet."

"Didn't she *manage* the antique store for the Fanes?" Ian asked, rushing on to answer his own query. "She just might have been posting packages and correspondence connected to that business and her job?"

Aisling bobbed her blonde head. "Makes sense."

Raine and Maggie once again shot fleeting looks at one another.

"It does make sense," Raine replied, "but my witch's intuition is telling me there just might've *been* a secret lover in poor Nellie Triggs' life."

"Hmm," Maggie concurred. "The intriguing phrase has popped up a lot since we began looking into this cold case. I think, too, there might've been a hot fire behind that smoke screen."

Now it was Aisling's turn to exchange looks with her husband.

"To be honest, we have a feeling there was a secret lover too," Ian revealed.

"But why would–" Beau was forestalled when Ian anticipated his thought.

"Why would she have an affair?" the private eye put to the entire gathering. "Why would any woman choose to have an affair? Humdrum existence. She feels trapped, bored, powerless, and lonely. Aisling and I have been detectives a long time now; so believe me when I tell you that some people treat love like a game. They play, and when they get bored, they cheat."

"You know what they say," Raine interjected, "the cure for boredom is curiosity. Nellie may have been curious about someone, someone interesting and, I don't know… *mysterious* … **taboo**, who happened to be married, and *voila!"*

"You say the cure for boredom is curiosity," Beau joked. "So what's the cure for curiosity?"

Raine laughed. "Oh, there is no cure for that!"

"Like Raine, I have a keen witch's feeling that Nellie was a dreamer, and she daydreamed a lot, as lonely, but hopeful, people do. That, I feel, is what got her involved with her secret, married lover," Maggie deduced.

"But Nellie had several suitors! Why choose to have an affair with a *married* man?" Betty exclaimed of a sudden.

"We must always keep in mind that intuition isn't hard evidence," Aisling chided.

Too bad it isn't enough, Raine sent Maggie. *I know what I know! So do I*, Maggie shot back.

"Though **our** intuition–" Aisling was musing, not paying mind to her fellow sisters of the moon. She broke off abruptly, continuing, "We don't know for certain that Nellie's secret lover, *if* he existed, *was* a *married* man." She thought for a meditative moment, finally adding, "Perhaps he was someone of a different race. Society wasn't accepting of inter-racial relationships back then. Or perhaps he was someone a lot younger than she.

"Perhaps," Aisling nearly shouted, "her secret lover was a woman! That surely wouldn't have been accepted in the 1930s! Think about it. Beautiful young woman who rejects one male suitor after another. Kind of unusual for the era, especially in light of the fact that during the Depression, this is a woman trying to bring up two children and care for an elderly parent on only what she could earn. Or … *or* perhaps Nellie's lover was someone who had done something that landed him in prison. **Yes**," she slapped a hand down on her knee, "there was a lot of *crime* during the Great Depression! Her lover could've been someone in prison or on the lam!" She took a breath, concluding, "Other than being a *married* man, Nellie's secret lover just might have been someone who would *not* have been *accepted* by her family or 1932 society at large."

Hugh snapped his fingers, blurting, "And perhaps, just perhaps, her brother found out about this embarrassing affair, and he fought with Nellie about it which resulted in–" now *he* broke off, saying almost to himself, "No, Nellie's brother is the one top suspect with an unshakable air-tight alibi."

"I wonder," Maggie murmured, as she ruminated over what Hugh had planted in her mind. She glanced up at the others in the room. "I wonder just *how* air-tight and unshakable Nellie's brother's alibi really was?"

Chapter Six

That spring was the wettest the Hamlet had ever known. After *Beltane*, it rained all through May with only about three days of sunshine the entire month. Thunderstorms were nearly a daily occurrence, leaving the Hamlet enchantingly opalescent. Lucent drops fell from the white and purple lilacs. The leaves of the village trees and ubiquitous woods looked positively polished, and the green, lush grass smelled sweet. Apple blossoms misted the charged, cleansed air with white and soft pink; but apple blossoms have a short stay, and the thunderstorms were hard on them.

As the year before, there were many chilly days that spring– "sweater days" Raine and Maggie called them– as if, two years in a row, Old Man Winter refused to relinquish his tenacious hold. And then, finally, it was June.

The Hamlet's wealth of rambler roses, one of the village's many charming features, burst out to cling to the picture-postcard white picket fences and the grey stone walls of Haleigh College. All over Haleigh's Hamlet, they bloomed on lattices and gazebos, on archways, patios, on the castle-like mansions, and in the old-fashioned gardens– ruby red, blush pink, cheery yellow, and with the purity and innocence of ivory. Everywhere was the delightful scent of those Victorian roses the Hamlet was known for.

Raine and Maggie's Tara was enhanced by a riot of roses, as well as by large, grape-like clusters of purple wisteria that cascaded from its lattices– the roses in the backyard, the wisteria on the sides and front of the stately old manse, with morning glories and clematis splashing color and clinging prettily to the trellises on the neat, brick garage. Tall amethyst and pink phlox graced the backyard flower beds near the faerie font, along with vibrant iris and monk's hood.

Though June with its gifts of beauty– and for Raine and Maggie, freedom from their teaching duties– had definitely made an impression, the rain and the storms continued, quiet to boisterous.

It was during one of those intense June thunderstorms when Raine, who happened to be passing through Tara's living room, paused to answer the ringing telephone. Suddenly, what looked like a ball of fire shot through the room, just two feet from where she stood, seeming to explode on the brick hearth! To declare that the Sister was electrified would be an understatement.

Some minutes later, she announced to Maggie, who came running downstairs when she heard Raine scream, "This reminds me, in some ways, of our weather last year, when we vanquished the ancient *Macbeth* curse from Whispering Shades." The Goth gal shook her head with the memory of the terrifying battle they had fought in their theatre. "When I think of what last year's unusual weather heralded, I can't help feeling that this year's, too, might well be a bad omen." She tossed back the Irish whiskey that Maggie handed her.

"In light of what Granny and High Priestess Robin both told us, I'd say your sentiment is spot-on," Maggie quipped. "By the way, who was on the phone?" The red-haired Sister sat at the antique oak table in the kitchen, to nurse a drink of her own. Raine's scream had rather unnerved her.

"Hugh," Raine answered, standing and starting for the refrigerator. She poured herself a glass of soda to chase the strong whiskey, then she re-joined Maggie at the kitchen table. "He's down with a sinus infection, and he asked if we'd mind taking Nero and Wolfe for a long walk in the woods once this storm front has passed through. "I told him we'd come over for the dogs in a bit." She sprang up again to peer out the window. "It's clearing up now."

"Great Goddess, I can't recall a more rainy spring! Not even last year's was this wet," Maggie cried, rising to follow Raine to the backdoor. "I wonder if it'll mean a drought later this summer?" The redheaded Sister quickly reversed her thinking, not wanting to program anything negative.

It was a good thing Raine could communicate as effectively as she could with animals, for the big, strong German shepherd brothers were raring to go when she and Maggie set out, from Hugh and Beau's place, on the path that led into the woods.

At the tree line, she knelt in the grass before the shepherd siblings, letting them lick her face. Then she pinned them with her big-cat eyes. *Settle down now, boys!* Raine told them telepathically. *Maggie and I plan on letting you run when we get deep into the woods. I want your word, both of you, that you'll mind me today. I am taking you out as a favor to Hugh, and I promised to bring you back to him safe and sound after our outing. Do I make myself clear?*

The canine pair, their heads inclined as they absorbed Raine's message, barked in unison.

OK, the brunette Sister answered, sending the communication to the dogs. *I'm trusting that you'll keep your word. And I'm asking that you be especially good for me and Maggie today. We're deep into another mystery, and we want to mull it over as we walk; it helps us think. So we don't want you to be out of our sight. Understand?*

We do! the pair barked again. *But c'mon, enough of this talk. Let's go!*

"Now that finals are over, and we're free from our teaching duties– Levitation, end-of-term can be overwhelming sometimes!– we can dedicate our full attention to our current mystery." Raine unhooked the dogs from their leashes to allow them freedom to run. As she did, she sent them a reminder about staying close. *One more thing, boys. When you hear me whistle, you come. Are we clear?*

Clear! the dogs barked in quick response.

Draping the leashes round her neck, Raine asked, "Did you return Nellie's phone call? I tried calling her last night but couldn't reach her, and she didn't have a recorder on."

Maggie gave a nod. "I touched base with train Nellie this morning while you were showering. I told her that we'd meet with her at some point but not yet, that we were still in the process of fact-gathering." She took a great gulp of air. "The air smells so fresh and clean, doesn't it? While we walk, let's review our latest findings from the police files," Maggie suggested.

As they tramped along the sodden wooded path, their feet made shushing sounds on the layers of leafy forest debris. While above, in the tree branches, birds were happily singing their *après*-storm songs of serenity.

"Great Goddess, this ground is soggy!" Maggie remarked. "I'm glad I wore these old boots."

Both Sisters sported jeans, long-sleeve tees, and paddock boots. They had switched shoes for boots in their stable, a short walk from the rear of their house, before collecting the dogs from Hugh.

"Nellie's brother, Clyde Hardiman, appears to have been a control freak," the willful, free-spirited Raine stated with a cutting edge to her voice. "The police file I read yesterday led me to believe that he was estranged from his sister when she was killed. Clyde told police he had not been in contact with Nellie for months, and he readily admitted that he'd been upset with her for, and I quote, '… straying onto a dark path.'"

"'A dark path,'" Maggie repeated pensively. "I wonder if by that he meant the Occult?" She glanced over at Raine, walking next to her on the wooded trail. It was nearing noon, and the sun, making its appearance after the rain, danced light patterns, through the leafy canopy of trees, onto their faces and shoulders.

"He could've meant the Occult," Raine answered.

"Perhaps Clyde was one who felt strongly against anything that *smacked* of the paranormal," Maggie said, slapping a mosquito away from her face. "You know how closed-minded some muggles can be, darlin'. Remember that music box that belonged to a witch from over in Perryville. When the sister passed on, her family, who never had anything to do with her or the Craft, sold all her things to an antique shop. Long story short, Roxanne What's-Her-Face from the Hamlet here unwittingly purchased the enchanted item; then called us in frantic desperation to come and get it because she said it was *witched*, turning on every day at exactly four o'clock all by itself."

"Hecate yes!" Raine quipped. "How could I forget? The crazy muggle acted as though the thing were possessed by a demon, when the good, deceased sister had only liked to listen to the sweet sound of the music box whilst taking her afternoon tea!"

"But getting back to Nellie," Maggie said, "keep in mind what Eva Novak told us– Nellie had become more and more desperate for her great-granny Anna's readings. Eva told me on the phone today that Anna warned Nellie time and time again not to use readings as a crutch, but her words landed on deaf ears."

"Hmmm," Raine concurred, "Nellie's brother's negative attitude toward her could well have been due to her interest in the Occult. Or it could have been that he learned of her *liaison* with a man he judged unsuitable, *objectionable*, for his younger sister, and that subsequently turned him against her."

"Or a combination therein," Maggie added. "Whatever it was that alienated Nellie and her brother Clyde, it caused an argument between them here in the Hamlet about six months prior to the murders."

"Right," Raine agreed. "And *that*, Clyde told police, was the last time he saw his sister alive. The two were seen and heard arguing on the railroad-station platform before he boarded the train home to

Cumberland, Maryland, the day after her twenty-eighth birthday in April. Likely he was visiting his sister for her birthday."

Maggie toyed with the large African pendant she was wearing, acquired years before during a camera safari. The necklace had belonged to a Masai chief, and it always helped her to commune with Nature.

The Sisters continued walking through the deep woods. Here, the trees grew very close together, and it was dim and shadowy. They trod upon broken twigs, last year's leaves and, here and there, the green stubble of a young fern, or the shoots of a wild geranium soon to blossom.

"Today this path reminds me of a Grimm's Faerie Tale, where the innocents are led into the evil witch's lair." Maggie shook off the chill she was feeling. "Let's go over the comments from the police files that revealed what witnesses heard Nellie and her brother fling at one another on the B&O Railroad-station platform."

Raine gave an agreeing nod. "Two witnesses heard Clyde say, 'I promised Dad the night he died that I'd look out for you and Mother, Nellie, but you aren't making it easy for me!' The same witnesses heard Nellie retort, 'I never asked you to stick your nose into my affairs, Clyde! And I'd just as soon you stayed away, if you can't let me live my own life!'"

"Then," Maggie went on, "there's our *newest* clue, the letter that Savvy Kathy dropped off to us last night, the letter found in an old recipe book that she inherited from her grandmother. This missive was written by Clyde's wife to her old friend and former neighbor here in the Hamlet. Kathy said she never realized that her great-grandmother and the murdered woman's sister-in-law had been close friends."

"Lucky for us Kathy opened that timeworn cookbook to look for her granny's recipe for old-fashioned strawberry cobbler! She said she never really had time to bake, but she'd gotten roped into making something for the strawberry fest at her church. Think about it! What were the odds of Kathy opening an old cookbook passed down in her family, a book she'd never even bothered to leaf through previously?! And what do you know? She finds a noteworthy letter from axed Nellie's brother's wife tucked between the pages!" Raine sent another telepathic message to Nero and Wolfe, telling them not to stray far.

A blackbird called a clear, cool note from a branch above a thin, running stream; and after a moment, he had answer from his fellow hidden in the trees behind the Sisters.

"That letter was destined for *our* use in solving this case," Maggie answered. "No question about it!"

"I think so too. So let's analyze the contents," Raine said, extracting the letter from the breast pocket of her shirt. "The date at the top of the page is faded but still legible– October 13, 1932, the day after the Hamlet's murders when Clyde's sister Nellie and her family were axed.

"I'm certain news of the murders had not yet reached Clyde and his wife Irene when she sat down to scribble this correspondence. Note," Raine slanted the aged, brownish paper for Maggie to see, "Irene penned the words 'Early Morning' at the top of the page under the date. She began with the usual greetings then wrote that her husband had recently purchased a new Ford V-8 roadster. She said his doing so angered her 'to no end' because he never talked it over with her."

Raine's eyes lowered to the letter, as she read, 'He simply went out and spent $500 on a new car, part of which was my inheritance from my recently departed Aunt Pearl! I never have a say in anything, and doggone it anyway, doesn't he realize we're in the midst of a depression! I thought we were just fine taking the train for distant travel and making use of trolley and shoe leather for getting around locally. You recall, I am certain, how, when we lived next door to you in the Hamlet, I used to cry on your shoulder about Clyde's high-handedness. Well things have not changed! But I'll tell you this, old friend, I am getting fed up, and for the past week, my bossy husband has been sleeping on the couch downstairs in the parlor!'

"Note too, Mags, that Irene underscored that last bit about Clyde sleeping downstairs on the couch. The remainder of the correspondence includes a couple of promised recipes, so that explains why Kathy came across the letter in an old cookbook." Raine carefully refolded the missive that Savvy Kathy had loaned them, returning it to her pocket.

Maggie paused on the path. "But is there enough in the letter to give Nellie's brother the window of opportunity in his so-called airtight alibi? Thus far, in the police files, we haven't come across the mention of Kathy's great-grandmother or this letter. I've a feeling that Kathy's great-granny didn't think anything in this communication *relevant* to the unsolved Hamlet murders, so she never turned it over to the authorities."

"Yes," Raine mused, "and likely, very, very likely, neither Clyde nor his wife Irene related to police that he was sleeping on the couch and not in their bedroom. That would have been *too* personal to divulge."

"Uh-huh," Maggie agreed. "Irene wouldn't have felt that personal tidbit of info was in any way relative to the murders, so she never mentioned it to police. And it wouldn't have been anything that macho-man Clyde would've readily proclaimed, to other men especially."

The pair started walking again.

"This mystery is as twisted and snarled as the buried roots of these trees. And just as liable to trip us up." After a few more steps, Raine ventured, "There are, I think, *two* significant bits of information in this letter." She patted the chest pocket of her tee, where she'd slipped the missive. "The fact that Clyde had a new Ford V-8 and the fact that he was sleeping downstairs on the couch in the parlor and not with his wife. He could have driven the seventy-odd miles from Cumberland, Maryland, here to the Hamlet and, after arguing anew with his sister, killed her in a rage, then, in blind panic, axed the witnesses to that rage.

"It's very possible," Raine reasoned further, "that after an evening of card playing the night of the murders, Irene went up to bed, tired, fell fast asleep and didn't even know that her husband left the house and drove to the Hamlet and back. Likely, she'd closed the door of the bedroom to him. What I mean is, with the bedroom door closed, she might've been less apt to hear him leave the house. And I bet you she closed and locked her bedroom door to him, as angry as she was with her husband. In the morning, she found him on the couch, and assumed he'd been there all night."

Maggie bobbed her head, imaging the scenario Raine was painting. "The police thought the murders occurred around midnight, **but** the coroner could have been off an hour or two in his approximation of the time of death. Forensic science then was not nearly what it is today."

"Sure, the coroner could well have been off as to the time of death," Raine answered. "I'm not saying for certain that Nellie's brother Clyde wielded that ax, but his new Ford V-8 coupled with the fact that he was sleeping downstairs on the couch … well, now we've given the third of our top three suspects that all-important window of opportunity. And let's not forget that the only eye-witness, Nellie's son Billy, was *positive– adamant–* that the killer was his uncle."

Raine chortled, suddenly remembering a piece of history. "You know that new 1932 flathead V-8 engine was a 'dandy,' to quote another man named Clyde who came to depend on it for his line of work! In fact, a letter survives at the Henry Ford Museum in Dearborn, Michigan, penned by Clyde Barrow, of Bonnie and Clyde infamy, to Mr. Ford himself. It read– and I memorized it, for it made me laugh– 'Dear Sir: While I still have got breath in my lungs, I will tell you what a dandy car you make. I have drove Fords exclusively when I could get away with one. For sustained speed and freedom from trouble the Ford has got every other car skinned. And even if my business hasn't been strictly legal, it don't hurt anything to tell you what a fine car you got in the V-8. Yours truly, Clyde Champion Barrow.'"

"What did Clyde Hardiman do for a living, do we know?" Maggie queried.

"He was a mechanic at a garage in Cumberland, as well as a self-employed welder. Did repairs on farm equipment and such." Raine stopped on the path, looking quickly round for the dogs. **"Nero! Wolfe!"** she shouted.

Both Sisters remained quiet, listening, but no answering barks did they hear.

Again Raine called for the sibling shepherds. And again silence answered, except for the sounds of the birds and the wind in the surrounding trees. She cocked her dark head, listening intently. *Be there voices in the wind– voices that bespeak of something grisly and terrifying?*

Raine was a multi-gifted witch, and she sensed keenly that something momentous was about to occur. Beau always teased her that she must have been a druid in a former life, because, on more than one occasion, she'd heard voices in the wind– whispering to her through the trees.

Wind-listening is an ancient form of divination. On a windy day, Raine liked to go, alone, deep into Tara's woods, stretch out on the forest floor on her back, close her eyes and feel Earth Mother beneath her. Then, when in complete harmony with her surroundings, she would listen keenly to the wind rustling through the leafy trees, listen to the voices, whispering messages– just as they were doing now.

The Goth gal started to voice her concern to Maggie, but decided against it, opting instead to call anew for the dogs. Putting thumb and forefinger to her mouth, she gave a piercingly loud whistle.

In jig-time, the dogs, tongues lolling, came running toward them.

Raine bent to caress the excited shepherds. "Good boys!" she praised, giving them each an admiring pat. "Now stay close to us."

The dogs let out a unified bark in response, as they bustled along the path ahead of the Sisters.

"A few moments ago," Raine began, tossing a look at Maggie, "I felt that something of great magnitude was about to happen."

"You mean something connected to our current case?"

"Of course to our current case!" Raine rounded, continuing up the wooded path in a reflective hush before finally saying, "I keep going back to something Eva shared with us, about Nellie becoming disenchanted with the Fanes."

"*Uncomfortable.* Isn't that what she said?" Maggie pulled a couple of hard cinnamon candies from her pocket, offering one to Raine, who shook her dark head.

"We'd be wise to remember," Maggie cautioned, "that observation did not originate with Eva's great-grandmother Anna, who knew Nellie personally, but rather with Anna's daughter Franci– Eva's grandmother– who passed that comment down in the family, gleaned when Franci was but a child. Or garnered from hearsay later."

Changing her mind, Raine pinched the candy from Maggie's hand and popped it into her mouth. "Hmmm," she mused, "it was what a *child* overheard. And that, contrary to what you just said, might make it *more* credible. Children's testimony, as over the years, you, Aisling, and I have discovered, is actually trustworthy." She paused for a moment, adding, "When they're not showing off."

"I was thinking," the redheaded Sister drawled, "that Nellie surely valued her job, especially in that era when work was so scarce, but the job *itself* could've made her feel uncomfortable. Her uneasy feeling might not have had anything to do with the Fanes themselves. So many others here in the Hamlet and elsewhere would have been struggling to find even *odd* jobs to feed their families. I mean how much business could that antique shop Nellie managed for the Fanes have had during the height of the Great Depression?"

"An excellent point!" Raine exclaimed, patting Maggie on the shoulder. "She might have felt a bit uncomfortable that she enjoyed such a situation, though she likely didn't earn much at the job, if she had to augment it by taking in laundry and ironing," she rambled; "but when so many others stood in bread lines … yeah, probably there was some jealousy from those others, and –" She let the sentence go unfinished, posing another point at issue. "But if, *if*, she had become disenchanted … ." Her attention switched to Nero and Wolfe, who had begun digging furiously into what looked like a muddy dip in the forest floor.

"What are they digging up?" she said more to herself than Maggie. She walked briskly up the path, the few feet to the dogs. Both were fanatically burrowing through muddy forest debris, with Wolfe, in doggie delight, snatching up a bone.

"So you've uncovered a long-dead wild animal, have you? *Wonderful.*" Raine peered closer at the shepherd's unearthed treasure; and as she did, the wind whispered again its chilling message, though the meaning was ghostly unfathomable.

Of a sudden, Nero's frenzied paws revealed what very much looked to be a human skull, which set both dogs to barking wildly.

Leave those bones alone, boys! the raven-haired Sister shouted telepathically to her furry wards. She slapped her leg, commanding, **"Come here, both of you! Now!"** To Maggie, who had come up behind her, she called, "Mags, get on the phone and ring up Chief Fitzpatrick. **Hurry!**"

Whilst the dogs stared up at Raine–

Maggie looked past her sister of the moon to the bones, the skull's open jaw reverberating in her head as the sinister silent scream of one of their earlier mysteries. "Great Goddess' nightgown!" She speed-dialed the chief, handing Raine the phone, her widened eyes yet on that riveting skull.

The brunette Sister spoke clearly but rapidly when Fitzpatrick answered. "A skull," she replied to his query about the unearthed bones, "and what might be a femur. They look human," the archaeology professor stated, "but, at this point–"

"I'll call the coroner, and we'll meet you there," the chief interposed. Where exactly did you say you are?"

Raine rattled off their location.

"*Stay* there and make sure no one disturbs those bones! I'm on my way!"

It was then Raine noticed that the large aquamarine ring, gifted to her by the Keystone Coven's High Priestess, had begun to feel exceedingly warm on her finger. When she looked down at her hand– the ring's protective gargoyles appeared to come to life!

"Where there's a witch, there's a way!"
                                    ~ Every Witch Who Ever Was

Chapter Seven

The following day, Raine, Maggie, and Aisling waited behind the yellow police tape, next to Chief Fitzpatrick and the Braddock County Coroner, as the forensic team, swarming over Haleigh's Wood, finished up their excavation.

The sun had set, and the light was fading. The chief hadn't wanted to start digging the previous afternoon only to have to stop due to lack of daylight. Thus, he'd ordered the site "taped off" with a police guard overnight and excavation beginning early in the morning.

Maggie leaned over to whisper into Raine's ear, "Despite the chief's efforts to keep a lid on this, it hasn't taken the press long to make an appearance, has it?"

"Never does." The raven-haired Sister twisted partway round, hoping the reporter and cameraman wouldn't recognize them.

At the moment, the journalist pair were making their hurried way from their van, the side of which read: "WIIP– ALLEGHENY COUNTY NEWS CENTER– PITTSBURGH'S MOST ACCURATE NEWS."

"Take heart," Maggie breathed, poking Raine in the ribs. "It's Molly Wiggin. At least she's nice, and she has integrity."

"I had a hunch I'd find you three here," the pretty blonde reporter announced pleasantly as she neared the police tape, the cameraman in her wake. "I heard you were the ones who discovered the bones here in the woods."

The Sisters exchanged looks.

"Who told you that?!" Raine questioned, ebony eyebrows raised in surprise.

Molly laughed. "I never divulge my sources." She sent her cameraman an eye-contact signal, extending the microphone toward the Sisters, who were still standing close together on the opposite side of the yellow warning tape from the television reporter.

Raine leaned a tad closer to the mic. "Actually, Maggie and I discovered the bones yesterday while we were walking our friend and neighbor's two dogs. The heavy rains and erosion had brought a buried bone to the surface, and the dogs started a frenzied excavation, resulting in the unearthing of what looked to us like a human skull. We immediately telephoned our Hamlet police chief, who in turn rang our Braddock County Coroner, and that's all there is to tell for now."

Molly gave a signaling nod, as she looked into the camera. "We're coming to you live from a forensic dig site at Haleigh's Hamlet, Braddock County. I'm speaking with Aisling McDonough-Gwynn, a former Pittsburgh detective turned private eye and her cousins, Doctors Raine and Maggie McDonough, professors of history and archeology at Haleigh College here in the normally sleepy little village of Haleigh's Hamlet."

The reporter tipped toward Maggie. "It was only a few months ago when I last interviewed you … 'Sleuth Sisters,' as you've come to be called far and wide, for your part in solving a nearly three-hundred-year-old mystery involving a Colonial hermit of Haleigh's Hamlet. And that mystery, too, was ensnared with unearthed bones."

Molly sent the Sisters a genuine smile. "You've been making quite a name for yourselves as super-sleuths! In fact, I'd go so far as to say you three are 'mystery magnets.' Mysteries seem to fall into your laps no matter where you go!"

Again the magickal trio traded quick looks.

"It seems that way to us too," Raine quipped.

"With your backgrounds, you," Molly gestured to Raine and Maggie, "immediately noted that the bones the dogs dug up were human. Is that right?"

"I wouldn't say *immediately*," Maggie replied. "The dogs first uncovered what looked like a femur … thigh bone; but, honestly, our first reaction was that the bone was from a long-dead wild animal of some kind."

"But when the dogs' frantic digging revealed a skull," Raine interjected, "then we immediately telephoned our chief of police."

"It looks as though," Molly's sharp eyes scanned the situation on the business side of the police tape as the investigating team was completing its work, "forensics is winding up their excavation. "How many bodies did they unearth? And do you think–"

"Not things we are at liberty to discuss," Aisling interposed with the authority of her former police status. "You'll have to put any other questions forward to our chief here." She looked to Fitzpatrick, who had stepped up to speak to the reporter.

Molly shifted the mic to accommodate the burly, uniformed police chief. "Chief Fitzpatrick, I *will* put that question to you. How many bodies did your team uncover today here in Haleigh's Wood?"

"Three," came the chief's pithy response. When, after a beat, he volunteered nothing more, Molly shot him another query.

"Do you think these bones are as old as the skeleton unearthed last fall here in the historic Hamlet? If I recall that skeleton dated back to Colonial times and the French and Indian War era. Or will you declare this a crime scene?"

The chief flung a glance at the coroner. "Let's just say these bones have been in the ground a long time. There's no need for the public to be alarmed."

Molly shoved the mic under the elegant coroner's aquiline nose. "Can you comment, Dr. Wight?"

Dr. Benjamin Wight was a tall, fastidious man in his mid-fifties with slightly wavy, black hair frosted heavily with grey. His eyes, too, were the color of steel, and though he looked like he strode straight out of the silky pages of *Gentlemen's Quarterly*, it was steel he was made of. In brief, Dr. Wight did everything as meticulously and as accurately as humanly possible– perfection was his life's credo.

"I'll merely reiterate what Chief Fitzpatrick has just stated. There is no need for the public to be alarmed. These bones *have* been in the ground a long time. I'll say no more until I complete my investigation." Wight smiled benignly. "I can't produce all the answers in an hour or less, as those magician medical examiners on the television dramas do."

Molly Wiggin turned her head to face the camera. "We'll keep you posted as we get more information on this story. For now, you heard it first at WIIP, Pittsburgh's most *accurate* news station!" Then with a wave of hand at the cameraman, she concluded, "That's a wrap!"

Molly tilted her blonde head and stared for a weighty moment at the Sisters. "I remember the first time I interviewed you ... about five years ago when you solved a missing-person's case in nearby Avalon. Then when you unraveled that baffling missing-child crime the following year in White Oak. A colleague of mine interviewed you when you cracked those nasty murders here in Haleigh's Hamlet last fall. Then I interviewed you again last winter when you solved that Colonial skeleton mystery. I've always liked you three, and I greatly admire what you do." She patted Raine's, the nearest Sister's, shoulder. Good luck on this one, ladies, and I hope I'll be covering the story when you solve it."

No sooner had the news crew departed, when the forensic team ended their work, with the head of the unit declaring to the chief and the coroner, "If there were any other bones in there, they've gone to dust."

Dr. Wight nodded in a satisfied manner to the team leader. "Get those bones back to our lab, so we can see what we've got. Good work!" he acknowledged in a louder voice to the blue-jacketed unit as they made their way out of the forest to their marked vans.

Then, turning to the Sisters, the coroner said, "Several months ago, Dr. Raine McDonough made a comment to me in regard to the skeleton unearthed when a local family was having a swimming pool put in. 'If only those old bones could talk, tell their story.'" Dr. Wight brought the tips of his long, slim fingers together, as if in prayer. "As you know, I was a forensic anthropologist for several years at the University of Pittsburgh before I came here to serve in the position of Braddock County Coroner, so bones *do* speak to me, often loudly and clearly; and those particular bones are more than ready to tell me their story." He started away, turning after a couple of soggy steps to add, "I'll be in touch."

During the next several days, Raine and Maggie had little time to dwell on their shocking discovery in Haleigh's Wood, for they quickly submerged themselves in their own research.

Five days hence, the pair were en route to the Braddock County Coroner's office and laboratory. Conveniently, the complex was only a twenty-minute drive from Tara, the Sisters' home; and because it was a weekday, traffic was light.

"It was good of Chief Fitzpatrick to invite us to meet with him and Dr. Wight!" Raine exclaimed.

"So what's the plan for today?" The gorgeous redhead turned to study Raine's profile, as the latter expertly shifted gears to maneuver her vintage MG into the passing lane. The firm set of her cousin's jaw told Maggie that Raine was laboring under some agitation of mind.

Keeping her eyes on the road, Raine answered, "Mags, after we're all done at the coroner's, let's begin interviewing the descendants of those who were connected to our 1932 ax murders.

I've two people scheduled for today, with a lunch break between, so you and I can do a bit of brainstorming, in addition to touching base with Eva Novak at the Tearoom."

Maggie thought a moment, answering, "We should have begun conducting those interviews three weeks ago, but our end-of-term duties at the college took everything we had. Now that we're free for the summer ... yes, let's begin straightaway with those inquiries."

Raine flipped on her turn signal to return to the right lane. "We only just completed the addresses and phone numbers last night to our list of descendants' names, so we've not been wasting time. Thank God most of these folks still have landline phones in their homes. Makes it so much easier to set up interviews."

Maggie smartly bobbed her head, saying, "Sure does. So you telephoned the two people we're to speak with today? They know to expect us?"

"Yes," the raven-haired Sister replied. "Henry Moretti, a descendant of axed Nellie's next-door neighbors and Beatrice Hart, a descendant of Nellie's cousins who took Nellie's little boy Billy into their home after he was orphaned and traumatized by the ax murders. I didn't go into detail about what we wanted to discuss with them, only that we want to speak with them about a bit of Hamlet history. I explained that since they and their families have resided here for so many decades, yada, yada, yada."

"Good. We'll work our way down that list of descendants with firm focus now," Maggie replied. "We're bound to gather some helpful pieces of information. We must harvest as much info as we can, from a variety of sources; glean as many clues as possible before we make use of Athena, our crystal ball, and our Time-Key."

"Exactly!" Raine agreed. "To gain greater success, we must do as much leg work and dot-connecting as possible before we utilize our magickal tools. We know from experience, preparation and groundwork are just as important as magickal devices to achieve our goals." She pulled into an empty space near the main entrance to the Braddock County Coroner's Office and Forensic Laboratory.

"I can't wait to learn what Dr. Wight has to tell us!" Maggie removed her outsized sunglasses and slipped them into her designer bag. Turning toward her cousin and sister of the moon, she needlessly voiced the question, "Ready?"

"More than ready," Raine answered, raising her own sunglasses to the top of her glossy black head. "Let's go!"

When Raine and Maggie were escorted by an assistant to the laboratory, they saw immediately that the blue-uniformed Chief Fitzpatrick was already there, standing on the opposite side of a long, steel lab table from Coroner Dr. Wight, who was wearing a pristine white lab coat and surgical gloves.

"Ah, here they are now!" Chief Fitzpatrick thundered, as he looked up to see the Sisters coming through the door. "Will Aisling be here soon?" he asked, looking beyond Raine and Maggie to the hallway.

"No, Chief," Raine said somewhat apologetically. "She and Ian had to go into Pittsburgh this morning for a case they're working on."

"Well, we're glad you two could make it. We've learned, over the years, to trust and count on your mixed-bag of extra-sensory gifts." The chief reached out a great paw of a hand to pump the much smaller ones of Raine and Maggie.

"It's good to see you again," Dr. Wight echoed in his refined manner. He glanced down at the trio of skeletons on the long laboratory table between them, sending the Sisters the eerie sensation that he was introducing them to the spooky specimens.

"Have the bones spoken to you, Ben?" Raine asked, her tone brimming over with curiosity.

Wight looked up, his intense grey eyes locking with Raine's glittering emerald ones. "Oh yes, Dr. McDonough, they've spoken to me loudly and quite clearly, as a matter of fact. I can safely state today, after careful examination and analysis of the unearthed skeletons you discovered in Haleigh's Wood, that these bones have been in the ground since the early 1930s."

Raine's eyes slid to Maggie's, with the chief speaking out in a slightly too-loud voice that seemed to echo in the vast chamber.

"How exactly, Doc, did you determine that?"

"We've been blessed with a bit of luck. Doubtless by accident, while bending forward, whoever buried these fellows dropped a couple of coins into the graves– coins dating to the 1920s and '30s. The more recent coin gave me the *terminus ad quem*." Noting the confused look on the chief's broad, ruddy face, the coroner explained, "*Terminus ad quem* is the final limiting point in time. For us here and now– the latest date these individuals could have been buried."

"And that *terminus ad quem* was?" Raine asked anxiously, feeling the chief's confusion.

"It was 1932," Wight replied.

Fleeting, though consequential, looks traveled between the Sisters.

"Another clue that these individuals died in the 1930s are the teeth, which I'll discuss in full a bit later. However, I want to state now that the teeth of all three skeletons look as though they've never been treated with fluoride. Fluoride wasn't used in water until the 1940s. And," Dr. Wight said with gusto, pointing to the second skeleton on the long table, "here's another bit of luck. To further anchor the time of burial to the 1930s, this individual had a filling in one tooth. Chemical analysis revealed that the amount of mercury present in that filling was two-thirds the metallic material present in the filling. That's a lot of mercury relative to the tin and silver. The 66:33 ratio, to make a long story short, is indicative of the 1930s."

"OK, then go ahead and share with us what else your forensic investigation has revealed," the chief charged with a bit of impatience. "And let's begin with what you like to call the 'Big Four.'"

"Age, sex, race, and height," Dr. Wight recited. "I'll start with age. For adult age determination, we rely first upon the pubic symphysis, where the two halves of the pelvis meet in the front," he indicated on the nearest skeleton, "and the auricular surface, where the sacrum– the tailbone, in layman's terms– joins with the pelvis. The sternal end of the clavicle is fused in all three skeletons; thus, these people were definitely all over twenty-five.

"The teeth provided the same answer. Teeth that looked to be in poor condition for all three individuals, but, as I said, I'll discuss that shortly. All the teeth were permanent, root tips complete in wisdom teeth, dental wear supporting evidence that this person," he pointed to the first skeleton, "was in his thirties. And those two," he indicated the other two skeletons, "were middle aged.

"After the age of thirty, bones become more porous." Wight inclined his head. "There are increases in little arthritic projections, work-related injuries, *et cetera*. I determined by the signs of degeneration that these bones," he again indicated Skeleton One, "belonged to a person in his early to mid-thirties, what we in my field would classify as an 'early middle adult.' And those two skeletons," he gestured toward Skeletons Two and Three, "belonged to persons in their late forties or early fifties– 'later middle adults,' both. There's more pitting in their bones, and that indicates more age.

"I used multiple age indicators to get a composite for the age of each skeleton, but I won't weary you with all the Phase info. Suffice it to say that the Suchey-Brooks Method, which analyzes the pubic symphysis, is the most reliable, *and* there's no damage to bone material.

"These bony ridges– associated with muscle markings– on all three skeletons' wrist bones," Wight went on, indicating, on the first skeleton, the area to which he was referring, "convey that all three of these men worked with their hands. The older skeletons," he waved a gloved hand toward Skeletons Two and Three, "show a high degree of arthritis in the elbow, shoulder, and clavicular joints. I would say that all three individuals have done some heavy lifting in their lifetimes. The older two show *a lot* of osteoarthritis in the spines, with some Schmorl's nodes in the lower thoracic and lumbar vertebrae."

Before the chief could ask, the coroner, noticing Fitzpatrick's muddled expression, translated, "Those are depressions on the superior and inferior surfaces of the vertebral bodies, caused by the compression of the intervertebral disc into the bone." Still noting the chief's confusion, Wight divulged, "These individuals were not professionals. They've done heavy work in their day, and the teeth and bones of all three indicate varying degrees of malnutrition, so very likely these were vagrants, Depression-era hobos, if you will."

"Many vagrants passed through here on freight trains during the Depression era," Raine interjected. "Haleigh's Hamlet was, in the old days, a railroad hub."

Dr. Wight gave a brisk nod in Raine's direction. "The teeth of all three individuals indicate poor overall oral health. There's a high number of dental caries, aka cavities; high amounts of calculus– tartar; and periodontal disease, indicated with resorption of alveolar bone," he pointed to the correct area of the skull, the portion of the jaw where the teeth are housed. "Too," the coroner elaborated, "there's a high incidence of ante-mortem tooth loss– that is lost teeth before death, especially with the molars. The teeth of all three," he made a derogatory gesture, "are stained by smoking.

"There was," Wight expounded further, "evidence of periostitis on the bones of each skeleton. All three individuals showing both active, at the time of death, and healed periostitis. This is the result of stress, which, I am certain, a vagrant lifestyle would invoke. Stress manifests as small, pinprick-like holes on the shafts of long bones, most especially on the tibia … see here," he indicated on the second skeleton. "If active, the holes have sharp margins," he pointed out. "The holes' edges round off … as they are here, and smooth over as they heal."

The tall coroner drew in a breath, continuing, "As you might recall from our unearthed female skeleton last year, the most reliable skeletal area for determining sex is the pelvic girdle. The female pelvis is shaped differently to accommodate the needs of childbearing, though the *skull* is also a good indicator of gender. And if you recall too, men have bigger skulls," Wight stated. "Female skulls are smaller, more delicate, usually. In fact, we can get about an eighty-five percent probability on sex from the skull alone. These three skeletons are most definitely *male*.

"And," the coroner glanced up at his listeners, "based on the maxilla … *jaw* and other characteristics of the skull– *Caucasian*.

"The tall, narrow anterior nasal aperture– the nose hole– and pinched nasal bridge are the most telling for Caucasians. Those of European descent have a simplified cranial suture pattern." The coroner indicated the jiggly lines of the first skeleton's skull. "*And* Caucasians tend to have a high, rounded skull, with sloping orbits, as all three of these skeletons clearly have.

"The soil where these three skeletons were uncovered," Wight pressed on, "was not quite as neutral as the wind-blown topsoil of our unearthed female skeleton last year, but we've also been lucky as far as pH– it wasn't that much different from our earlier skeleton. Disintegration of materials depends on the pH of the soil. Acidic soil tends to dissolve even bones over time, but the soil where these three fellows were found has a pH of nearly 7; so the soil was nearly neutral. And, as far as animal damage, there's virtually none. The skull of this one skeleton was unattached, but other than that, animal damage was minimal.

"These skeletons were originally buried in somewhat shallow graves, the one with detached skull about three feet down, the other two about four feet."

The coroner paused for a moment to again take a breath. "Now," he said of a sudden, "when we calculate stature, we provide a target and a range. We typically use the length of the femur and plug it into an equation to determine how tall a person was. These men were all three of medium height. As you know, we did not find any belt buckles, or any other fragments of clothing, shoes, belts– and there was good draining soil there, albeit due to the unusually heavy rains and erosion of late–" He broke off, saying, " I'll explain further in a few moments, but I feel strongly that these three men were buried without any clothing whatsoever.

"Presently, we're working on facial reconstruction," Wight looked to Fitzpatrick, "and I'll get those to you, Chief, upon completion. Give us a couple weeks, at least, on that. We want to do the best possible job we can for you, and you know me– I am always thorough."

A few moments of intense silence ensued– like the throbbing stillness after the cutting off of a high note in music held too long.

"So is there anything more you can share with us today?" Raine asked, sensing that there most definitely was, that the drama-loving coroner had saved the most significant information for last.

Dr. Wight scanned the three people before him, his unyielding regard holding his audience spellbound. "There's more than meets the eye, the untrained eye, here."

I wonder ... mused the Sisters.

"Well, spit it out, Ben!" Fitzpatrick nearly roared. The chief wasn't always tolerant of the coroner's dramatics. "Can you tell us how these three men died? Was there foul play, d'ya think?"

Unruffled, Dr. Wight continued with his usual precision. "I'll try and make what I mean clear. I checked carefully for signs of trauma, and to be sure, there are some, which I'll get to in a moment. There're no bullet holes, but– and this is a big but– I'm convinced that *each* of these men– *each*– was stabbed through the heart. Note," he pointed to the nearest skeleton with a gloved finger, "that the sternum, this elongated bone shaped like a capital T, appears to be scraped, slivered, by what was likely a knife or dagger of some sort."

The coroner moved down the long metal table to the second skeleton. "Same thing here. Note the sternum," he pointed to the place where the bone appeared shaved, after which, he progressed the few steps to the end of the table. "Ditto here," he indicated the third skeleton's sternum. "Makes me think too that the same person perpetrated these stabbings. There's a definite pattern, as you can see for yourselves."

"So what *are* you saying?" The chief nearly shouted. "You've something in mind."

"I believe these three men were all killed in some sort of ritual murder." The coroner locked eyes with the Sisters. "My educated guess is that these three people were stabbed through the heart, very possibly by the same person."

Very possibly, the Sisters reasoned to themselves and telepathically to each other.

"See," Wight was saying, "there are no parry … *defense* wounds on the hands or forearms. None on the feet or legs either, in case the victims were lying down when attacked; so I'm thinking," he jerked his head toward the table of skeletons, "these men were restrained in some way while they were killed." He cocked his head. "Buried nude in the woods, all three close to one another. Think about it. Burials with no coffins, and absolutely nothing interred with the deceased, no shred of any clothing in good-draining, neutral soil?"

Wight raised an arched, dark brow. "This all translates *sinister* to me. *Most sinister.* As bizarre as this may sound to you, my gut tells me these men were victims of some sort of grisly ritual involving," the coroner stopped dead, pronouncing in an especially low tone, "*human sacrifice.*"

The Sisters traded pointed looks, with Maggie musing aloud, "Vagrants would make the perfect victims for ritual killers. No one would report them missing."

"Hell and damnation, Ben, what you're proposing is pure assumption!" the chief thundered, "not to mention far-fetched!"

The coroner, cool and ever confident, remarked. "At first blush perhaps, but–"

The chief guffawed. "These fellas could've been part of a Depression Hooverville and died from malnutrition and the elements in those woods, in the cold of winter, and their bodies buried by others in the camp. You said yourself that we had plenty of vagrants around here during the Depression, and those camps, Hoovervilles, were scattered throughout our area and just about everywhere else across the country back then." Fitzpatrick looked thoughtful. "Maybe other vagrants, in the Haleigh's Wood camp, who buried these fellas, stripped them of their clothing for the simple reason that they needed the clothing for themselves. Could well be there was nothing sinister at all about their deaths!"

Dr. Wight shook his head. "Lest you forget the three slivered sternums. In ritual killings, the stabbings would usually be from a knife held high and plunged into the chest where the killer best believed the heart to be. It would be hard and fast and most likely would hit bone, sternum, or rib. The larger the knife, the more bone damage, and most sacrificial knives are reasonably large."

The coroner's steely regard shifted to the triad of spine-chilling, open-jaw skeletons. "Those fellows are screaming to be heard." He shook his head somberly, and his patrician face went grave. "No, Chief, your scenario is *not* what my intuition, together with my examination and analysis, is telling me."

Dr. Wight fixed his penetrating silvery gaze on the Sisters. "*You* know better than most that instinct should not be denied. You know, and *well*, I might add, that ghastly things happen every day– even in usually quiet little towns like Haleigh's Hamlet. As hard as it is to believe, things like human sacrifices still go on in this world. Why, just last week, I read in the paper that ..."

But the rest of Wight's thought was lost on the Sisters when Maggie sent Raine a telepathic message: *I'd wager there's a connection to our Hamlet's 1932 triple ax murders!*

Raine answered her sister of the moon with a subtle nod. *You and I both know that there're no coincidences, no accidents in life. Everything happens for a reason. Fate led us to those bones to help us get to the bottom of our Hamlet's unsolved ax murders.*

The raven-haired Sister felt herself trembling on the precipice of discovery. *Oh yes, I think there's most definitely a connection between those skeletons and our ax murders! And if my surmise is correct ...*

Chapter Eight

En route from the coroner's lab to Henry Moretti's home, the Sisters were deep in discussion over what Dr. Wight had shared with them and Chief Fitzpatrick.

"It all made sense," Raine stated. She checked her mirrors, then swung into the passing lane to overtake a slow-moving station wagon that looked as if it should be put out of its misery.

"Except for how, during the Depression era, our Hamlet was the setting for bizarre ritualistic killings without any shred of it ever surfacing until now, decades later." Maggie glanced over at Raine, whose only response was to shrug.

"It could explain why nary a clue was ever uncovered in regard to the unsolved triple ax murders of the same era. I mean," Raine rationalized in hurried statements, the words tumbling out, one over the other, "there must be a connection. We both sense strongly that there *is* a connection, and you know what I think? I think no one ever came forward with information about the ax murders, even though the *Hamlet Herald* ran the story every October to aid the police in seeking out clues, because whoever had info on the ax murders also knew about the ritual murders, and they were too damn scared to come forth. *Fear.* That's the answer why no one ever came forth with info about the ax murders. And not just ordinary fear– **terror!***"

"But the paper ran the story for years," Maggie countered. "Why didn't anyone come forth years later?"

"Maggie," Raine rasped, gripping the MG's steering wheel as the realization leaped upon her– suddenly, alarmingly, and without warning, like the attack of a savage beast– *"that fear, the terror, still exists!"*

Fifteen minutes later, the Sisters pulled up to Henry Moretti's neat ranch home, which was located on the opposite side of the Hamlet from their Tara. The small yard was immaculately groomed, with multi-colored petunias lining both sides of the brick walk that led to the front entrance.

After sounding the bell, the Sisters waited only a few moments before Mr. Moretti answered the door. "Come in! Come in!" he enthused. "It's been a while since anybody visited me. An old man gets lonely. And today, two very pretty ladies come calling." With old-world charm, he gallantly ushered the Sisters inside to his homey living room, where he indicated they sit on the sofa upholstered with a pastoral tapestry design.

"Thank you for inviting us into your home, Mr. Moretti," Raine opened, touching his arm. "In years past, we looked forward to your music at the various high-school programs and parade days." She looked to Maggie.

"It's a pleasure seeing you again, though we must confess," Maggie voiced, recognizing that Raine was asking her to explain their visit, "this is not exactly a social call. We were hoping to jog your memory about something connected to Hamlet history."

Henry Moretti sighed, misunderstanding the Sisters' objective. "Sometimes I miss the old days. It's been several years since I orchestrated a music program at the school. I volunteered to do them after I retired, but it finally got to be too much for me." With a smile then, he said, "Before you try and jog an old man's memory, may I offer you some wine? I haven't made my own for a couple years now, but I still have a few bottles left. It's good red wine. Will you take a glass with me? My doctor tells me a glass a day is good for me."

The Sisters could see that the elderly gentleman was hoping they would join him for a bit of refreshment; and thus, Maggie answered, after a nod from Raine, "We should *love* to join you in a glass of wine. Thank you."

A few minutes later, Henry returned to the parlor, carrying a tray upon which stood a carafe of red wine with three small wineglasses. "Here we go." He poured, handing each Sister a pretty, etched goblet of the clear, ruby liquid. Then he raised his glass, saying, "*Salute!*"

Raising their goblets, the Sisters repeated the traditional Italian toast.

Henry sat down, and in that moment, the Sisters studied him, for it had been several years since they'd seen the former high school band director.

Moretti's thick, wavy, nut-brown hair had gone snowy, and his face had become somewhat weathered, due, they were sure, to his love of working outside in his garden. Henry was not a tall man; in fact, he was rather short of stature, a fact made more pronounced since he retired and his girth had broadened considerably. His pleasant face always seemed to display a smile; and when he spoke, his voice boomed like the percussion section of his former band. This last, the Sisters decided, was due to two reasons– Henry was losing his hearing, and he was, by nature, a most jovial fellow.

"Henry, your wine is delightful," the Sisters chorused.

Moretti looked pleased. "Thank you," he beamed, proudly lifting his wineglass to the shaft of sunlight streaming through the picture window. "Crystal clear, isn't it? Glows like expensive ruby. My sons tell me I should take an interest in making my wine again. They would do most of the work, but," he shrugged, "after my wife passed away, I lost interest in so many things. I still plant and cultivate my garden, though I end up giving most of it away nowadays. My Fiorella isn't here to cook me her delicious, old-fashioned Italian meals."

Henry looked past the Sisters to the portrait of his deceased wife on the wall. His shoulders sagged. "Yes, so much of the glow of life has faded for me without my Fiorella. You know what her name meant?" A trace of a smile and he answered without waiting for the Sisters to respond. "Little Flower." His soft brown eyes suddenly shone with tears. "She was so like a little flower."

"She was beautiful. You must have loved her very much," Maggie pronounced softly in a wistful tone.

"We are so sorry for your loss, Mr. Moretti," Raine added.

Shortly Henry brightened, bringing his hands together. "Now, let's not be sad. Not today. It's a happy day when I get visitors. What was it you wanted to discuss with me? You were vague over the phone when we talked."

Raine set her goblet down on a coaster she spied on the end table next to her. After clearing her throat, she asked, "Henry, you were only four when your older brother, Orlando, discovered Nellie Triggs' body in the alley behind your childhood home on Murphy Road; so probably you don't remember too much about the murders. But as history professors interested in our Hamlet's past, we hope you might share with us any stories passed down in your family about the unsolved ax murders."

"Can you do that?" Maggie prompted kindly. She looked closely at the elderly man, thinking, as she did, that he certainly didn't look like he was eighty-seven years old. *Mid or late seventies,* she decided, *but certainly not eighty-seven. And his mind seems sharp.*

"Professors," Henry began, "I doubt I'll be able to tell you anything you don't already know." He took a drink of his wine and settled back in the easy chair, into which he had lowered his ample girth earlier.

After a pensive moment, the old man laughed. "I remember the neighborhood kids were all scared to death to go down the alley in the dark, where Nellie's body was found. Not me! I'd do it every time on a nickel dare." He let out a breath. "In those long-ago days, a nickel bought a big bag of candy!"

"I don't suppose you remember Nellie at all, or do you?" Raine asked, pulling a notebook and pen from her bag.

Henry tilted his head with its thick, wavy, white hair. "Not really, no, but I can tell you both my parents thought the world of her and her kids. They liked her mother too." He shook his head. "Terrible what happened to them. Terrible! And we never knew why. My parents could never understand how something so ..." he groped for a word, settling on, "*awful* could happen to such nice people."

"Did your parents ever say who *they* suspected might've wielded the killing ax?" Maggie ventured, taking a sip of Henry's ruby-red elixir. She crossed her legs and settled back, leaving the note-taking to Raine.

Henry did not immediately answer. In fact, he took so long to respond, the Sisters thought he had chosen not to. Finally he said, "If they did, they kept their opinion to themselves ... you know, between the two of them. To tell you the truth, they never wanted to talk about the murders. I suppose they didn't want us kids to grow up frightened."

"Is there *anything* you can tell us, Henry? No matter how trifling you might think it," Raine beseeched, leaning forward on the couch. "This mystery has always intrigued us." It was only a wee white lie, and one the Goth gal could utter without guilt.

The old gentleman took another sip of his wine, visibly reaching back in memory as he did so. "I remember the first Hallowe'en, a couple weeks after the killings. My two brothers and I shared a bedroom, understand, and that room looked out onto what had been the Triggs bungalow. The little house was boarded up, dark and empty after the murders; but that Hallowe'en night, while lying in bed, my brothers and I saw someone prowling around in the yard over there. The next thing I knew we spotted a light inside.

Someone was moving through the house with a flashlight, or it might've been a lantern."

Henry drained his wineglass and set it down on the end table next to his easy chair. "The reason this is so vivid of a memory for one so young is that my brothers *shot* out of bed and crouched down below the window sill, peering out and whispering that the 'murder house'– that's what we called it– was *haunted*. Word spread. The kids all prattled on after that about ghosts and how the Triggs house was haunted by the spirits of those who were axed there."

Henry inclined his head, pursing his mouth. "There were other break-ins besides that one, as the ghost stories about the place got bigger and taller, and evermore gruesome. Consequently, no one wanted to live in that house, and eventually it was torn down."

"Hmmm," Raine mused, "I wonder if the murderer came back to find something he thought might incriminate him, or–" She interrupted herself to ask abruptly, "Henry, I don't suppose you recall what the prowler looked like? I mean, I realize that it was dark and a long time ago, but can you remember anything you or your brothers might have gleaned from catching sight of the murder-house prowler that Hallowe'en night?"

Henry nodded, as if he had just come to a decision. "Most of the time, my memory is as shadowy as that long-ago Hallowe'en night, but I can recollect my older brother Orlando saying that the prowler looked like Billy's Uncle Clyde. I mean the intruder wore a fedora like Billy's uncle always wore. Orlando said he recognized that hat, the way Billy's uncle wore it– slouched down over his face."

"Did you boys tell your parents about this, and did they report it to the police?" Maggie inquired.

Henry shook his head. "When we told them, they told us that we must've been dreaming, having a nightmare about the murders, and to forget about it and not say anything to anyone about what we *thought* we saw." He wrinkled his brow. "They were trying, I am certain, to protect us kids. You know, not to suffer trauma, nightmares, and bantering from other kids, I suppose."

Maggie fired Raine a look, resulting in the latter's next question to their host.

"Mr. Moretti, did you kids ever feel as if your parents were hiding something?" The impetuous Raine regretted the way she had worded the query as soon as it left her mouth, for she could instantly tell that it struck a sour note with the former band director.

"What are you trying to say?" he asked, alarm darkening his face and the timbre of his voice.

"I'm not saying anything, Mr. Moretti, I'm merely asking if you can recall any family memories … stories that might show that perhaps your parents were frightened of something, or someone, and that fear kept them from revealing everything to the police." Raine jotted the words *Prowler, Fedora, Hallowe'en Night* in her notebook. She also dashed off the phrase *Fedora slouched over face like Billy's Uncle Clyde wore his fedora.*

Meanwhile, Henry was definitely looking offended, his arms crossed over his barrel chest. Presently, he drew himself up. "I am certain my parents would have told the police everything they could." His voice carried his affront, along with a hint of anger. "They were hard-working, decent people, who never broke a law, of God's or man's, in their lives." The old man stood, and the Sisters knew they had overstayed their welcome.

"Don't beat yourself up for being too impulsive in the way you worded that crucial question, darlin'," Maggie said, glancing over at Raine, who was sitting stiffly behind the wheel of the MG. "I think we both observed that what the police suspected about Henry's parents could very possibly be true. They harbored a real fear, and not just the fear of a murderer on the loose. It was something more, and I think Henry knows it."

"I really like Henry; I hope he isn't upset with us," Raine shook her head ruefully. She reached up to adjust her sunglasses. "Though the way we smoothed it over, he–"

"Henry's not the type to remain upset with anyone for long," Maggie interposed. "The next time we see him, he'll grace us with his million-dollar smile. You'll see."

Raine was unusually silent for a while and drove without speaking.

Maggie glanced over after a few minutes to say, "C'mon now, cheer up!"

"I'm glad that Beatrice Hart rang my cell to ask that her interview be scheduled earlier. It'll be better to speak with her first, then finish at the Tearoom for a late lunch." Raine slowed on the shady, tree-lined street, so that she and Maggie could better see the house numbers.

"There!" Maggie cried. "Number 724. Little white Cape Cod with black shutters and black and white roof. That's it."

Raine eased the MG to the curb and switched off the ignition key. "Let's go. And this time, I'll try not to be so impetuous."

Maggie patted her cousin and sister of the moon on the shoulder, as the pair walked the few steps to the cottage's glossy black door with its brass ship-wheel doorknocker. The redheaded Sister rapped, and within moments, the door opened to reveal a matronly woman with a pleasant face and salt-and-pepper hair done up in a loose bun.

"Doctors McDonough?" she asked with a welcoming smile.

"Yes," the Sisters chorused.

"Do come in," Beatrice said kindly. "I'm glad you could come earlier. My niece telephoned to ask if I'd go shopping with her later."

"So you're saying that what we've uncovered in our research is true. Billy Triggs was deathly afraid of his Uncle Clyde?"

Beatrice's eyes widened with surprise. "Oh my yes! My grandmother, who raised Billy after the murders, and my mother always maintained that the boy was *petrified* of his uncle."

Raine leaned forward in the overstuffed chair where she was sitting in Beatrice's sunny parlor. "What stories do *you* recall about the murders, Beatrice?"

"And anything you can share with us about Billy and his relationship with his uncle, please do," Maggie urged from her chair opposite Raine.

Beatrice Hart was a retired elementary-school teacher, a spinster in her seventies, who lived alone. She was warm, friendly, and appreciative of the Sleuth Sisters' reputation for solving mysteries and performing good works about the entire southwestern Pennsylvania area.

"I can tell you truthfully," she began with slow, precise words uttered from the rocking chair across the room, "that my family believed Clyde Hardiman committed those heinous crimes. We never believed he set out … *planned* to kill Nellie and her family, no; but that he lost his famous temper with his sister, whom he always endeavored to control."

Beatrice wagged her head from side to side in a gesture of disapproval. "Oh, if he were here, Clyde would tell you that he was only looking out for his younger sister, a widow with two children to care for. He'd say, too, that he was looking out for his widowed mother, who, of course, was living with Nellie; but he was a disagreeable sort, a control freak, as the modern saying goes."

"I wonder," Maggie mused, "if Clyde Hardiman ever helped his sister care for her wards, monetarily, I mean. After all, as you said, Nellie's widowed elderly mother was *his* mother too."

"Don't quote me," Beatrice answered, "for I only have a vague memory from family talk on this; but I think he did, in the beginning, after Nellie's husband first passed away. However, if I recall what my family said about the matter, Nellie stopped accepting financial help from her brother so that he would stop bossing her. *No pay, no say.* I think when she started managing the antique store for the wealthy Mrs. Fane, that helped to free her some from her domineering brother. Nellie and Clyde's father didn't leave their mother with much when he passed. After the father died, the mother went to live with Nellie, because she got on with Nellie much easier than she did with Clyde. Nellie and Clyde were sister and brother; but, from what I recall from family talk, as different as night and day."

"Do you know if Billy ever made peace with his uncle?" Maggie asked.

Beatrice gave a snort. "*That* I can answer without any qualms whatsoever. I know for certain that he did **not**," Beatrice stated firmly. "For several years, at Christmas time and around Billy's birthday in the spring, Clyde would try and visit Billy at my grandmother's house here in the Hamlet. He'd show up at the house with presents, but Billy would get so worked up, *hysterical*, that my grandparents asked Clyde never to come up here anymore."

"Did Clyde honor that wish?" Raine brushed a wisp of ebony hair from her eye.

"Yes," Beatrice nodded, "for years he did. But when the war came– World War II– and Billy enlisted, Clyde showed up at my grandparents' home to wish his nephew well. But Billy was having none of it. He refused to the end to speak with his uncle. I say 'to the end' because, as you probably know, Billy was killed during the war in Italy."

"This may seem like a strange question, Miss Hart, but do you know if Clyde Hardiman often wore a fedora?" Raine asked after a pensive moment.

Beatrice thought for several seconds, saying, "Let's see if there's a photograph of the man in the old family album I have. It belonged to my grandparents. There'll be photos of Billy too." She rose. "And can I bring you something to drink? Tea? Coffee?"

"No thank you," the Sisters replied in sync.

"We'll be going for a late lunch in a few minutes," Raine added.

"Be right back," Beatrice pronounced, as she withdrew from the room.

Within a couple of minutes, the former school teacher re-entered the parlor with an old-fashioned, black photo album. "Let's all sit on the couch," she directed. I'll sit between you, and we'll all be able to see the photographs."

The three women moved to the long, tan divan in front of the unlit, river-stone fireplace.

"Now," Beatrice said, settling down with the tufted album on her lap and opening it, "let's see if I can locate a photo of Clyde.

She began turning the pages. "Here's a nice likeness of Billy," she declared. "He must've been about twelve in this picture, so this would've been taken about three years after the murders."

The Sisters scrutinized the preteen's image. The boy bore a lost, melancholy air that gave him the appearance of a little old man.

"He looks so sad," Maggie said softly.

"He was," Beatrice replied. "My family always said that he never recovered from the trauma he'd suffered."

"Understandable," Raine interjected. "Who's *this* person, do you know?" the Sister asked, indicating, with pointer finger, a young girl kneeling with Billy on the grass, where they were embracing a medium-sized dog that looked to be a shepherd mix.

Beatrice regarded the image, answering, "That's our cousin Mabel. She and Billy are playing with Billy's dog–" She struggled with Time, giving, after a few reflective moments, Time the victory. "Can't recall the dog's name. I do remember that Billy hadn't wanted a pet, but my grandfather thought it would do him good."

"Did it, do you know?" Raine queried, looking up from the photo album at their hostess.

"Yes, I believe it did, but it never altered the fact that Billy was a loner," Beatrice stated ardently.

"As Billy got older, did he have a sweetheart?" Maggie inquired in her soft voice.

"Billy was always afraid to get close to anyone. Afraid he'd give his heart, only to lose it. No, never a sweetheart, never a best friend, always a loner. Ah!" Beatrice exclaimed of a sudden. "Now I remember. Billy's dog's name was Pal. It was Billy's only friend. When that dog died, Billy was devastated. They had been together about sixteen years. It was soon after Pal died that Billy enlisted."

Beatrice turned her head to look at one Sister, then the other. "You know, of course, that our Billy was decorated. He threw himself on a German grenade to save his buddies." She shook her head sorrowfully. "He must have finally bonded with his brotherhood of soldiers, and perhaps he felt he had to prove something, prove himself. I don't know. A psychology professor once told me that Billy had long suffered from survivor's guilt."

"What a sad story is Billy's," Raine said, staring down at the boy's black-and-white image, to that long-ago moment, frozen in time, in which he was embracing his sole friend– a dog named Pal.

Maggie was quiet, lost in her own thoughts, and she appeared to be puzzling over something.

Miss Hart slowly turned the pages, going backward in the album, her action bringing forth a sharp exclamation. "Here's a picture of Clyde! I went a few pages back, because I knew if he was in this album, it would be *before* the ax murders and not after. "That's him!" she pointed.

When the Sisters fixed their eyes to the page, they saw that the man in the old photograph was sporting a fedora– and it was slouched over his eyes.

No sooner had the Sisters reached The Gypsy Tearoom, when Eva, with both hands extended, came rushing forward to greet them. "You must be psychic," she said, amending with a laugh, "well, of course you are! I was just about to telephone you. Mada Fane is back in town!"

Chapter Nine

"Bless my wand!" Raine exclaimed as she munched happily. "These sandwiches are to die for! Great choice to order the English sampler plate to share, Mags."

Maggie gave an enthusiastic nod. "My favorite is the goat cheese and watercress, but I love the curry chicken salad too."

"This is smoked salmon on pumpernickel–" Raine made a sound of delight– "Mmm, **mmm!**" She took a swallow of her tea. "I'm longing to see what Eva has for dessert today! I was starved, but now, let's–" Her words were again interrupted, this time by the sound of her cell that she had programmed with the bewitching music of Rowena of the Glen. She dipped a hand into her bag for her phone. "Dr. McDonough," her deep voice rumbled.

Raine listened for a few moments whilst the caller spoke into her ear, finally answering, "Yes, we can do that." She checked her watch. "Six will be fine. No worries; we'll find it. See you then."

"Who was that?" Maggie asked, wiping crumbs from a corner of her mouth.

"Josie Means, our next interviewee," Raine said, returning the smart phone to her purse, which was next to her on the bench-like seat in one of The Gypsy Tearoom's padded booths. "She wanted to know if we could come over at six tonight rather than tomorrow afternoon; and, as you heard, I agreed. I was thinking we could see if Aisling might be able to accompany us."

"We're on a roll, so why stop?" Maggie gave her crystal laugh. "That will clear the afternoon tomorrow for a nice long interview with Mada Fane, if she'll agree to it."

"She'll agree," Eva declared as she approached the Sisters' booth. "I already paved the way for you. She's fine with that. Actually, she's expecting you to telephone her this evening to set the time for a visit with her tomorrow afternoon. I hope you don't mind that I took the liberty of speaking in your behalf?" Eva dropped down on the bench next to Maggie.

"Not at all!" the Sisters chorused, with Raine adding that she always wanted to see inside the magnificent Fane Manor.

"We'll call her this evening and set a time in stone for tomorrow then," Maggie concluded.

"Thank you, Eva," the Sisters replied.

"Have you remembered anything else about Nellie or the triple ax murders that you might share with us?" Raine asked, picking up her last sandwich, a creamy, dreamy caviar egg salad on ultra-thin rye. "Oh Eva, these sandwiches are scrumptious!"

The proprietress looked ever so pleased, raising her hands in an overt gesture of delight. "Thank you, my darlings! Wait till you see what I have for dessert today!"

"We most certainly will be having dessert," Maggie effervesced.

"Good, I'll think about what you asked me, as I prepare the dessert cart," Eva said. She rose and headed for the kitchen.

"Ring Aisling and see if she can accompany us this evening to Josie Means' place," Maggie suggested. "Tell her we can pick her up, or she can meet us there, whichever she'd prefer."

Raine poured herself another cup of the green tea they ordered, then speed-dialed the blonde with the wand, sipping the hot drink as she waited for her sister of the moon to pick up.

After Aisling answered, it was quickly decided that she would meet Raine and Maggie at the address the raven-haired Sister provided for Josie Means' place.

When Eva returned with the dessert cart, Raine and Maggie had a difficult, albeit mouth-watering, time deciding. After several moments of deliberation, Raine selected an English Trifle, saying, "Did you know that George Washington preferred this to all other desserts?"

"I didn't know that," Eva replied; "but now that I do, I must remember to whip up this dessert for my customers on his birthday each year."

Maggie finally chose a Boccone Dolce, asserting after the first bite of the Sweet Mouthful that the combination of strawberries, chocolate and meringue was enough to send her right out of this world!

Raine giggled, quipping that she never thought she'd hear Maggie McDonough say that about anything other than sex.

Maggie laughed, as she refilled her tea cup from the fresh pot Eva had brought with the desserts.

The proprietress returned to the Sisters' booth after they had polished off their sweets, sitting down once again next to Maggie. "Finally getting a break," she whispered, blowing out a breath. "I think you'll really like Mada. Especially since her field of study is similar to your own. Rather than history and archaeology, Mada holds doctorates in anthropology and archaeology. She knew who you were when I talked to her, and in fact, she seemed quite taken by all your accomplishments. Oh," Eva snapped her ringed fingers, "she mentioned that she met Dr. Yore, joint head of your college's archaeology and anthropology departments, one or two times in the past, at some function or other. I can't recall now."

Eva adjusted herself on the bench. Today, she was wearing a long blue and white striped skirt with a low-cut, white peasant blouse that she wore off the shoulders. As she talked in her animated manner, her rings and large gold-hoop earrings gleamed in the flickering light from the candle-like wall sconces.

"Anyway, Mada's really looking forward to meeting you, all three of you Sleuth Sisters, in person. She said she's heard so much about you." Eva leaned forward. "She called you 'superstars,' from her own hometown, she's never had an opportunity to meet. So I told her you'd telephone her this evening and set up a time, and that's when she piped up with, 'Why not tomorrow afternoon? I'd love to have them join me for tea tomorrow at the Manor.'"

"Sounds good," Raine said, dabbing her mouth with her napkin. "We'll certainly take her up on that invitation to meet with her tomorrow."

"How old is Mada now, would you say?" Maggie asked.

"Oh, she's got to be in her, I don't know, early fifties maybe," Eva answered after a short pause.

"What does she look like?" Raine asked, curious. "I can't recall her image, though I know I've seen it several times in her books. Of course, people don't always look like their photographs."

Eva squinted, thoughtful for a moment. "I think she looks a lot like Bette Midler. The way the actress looks today… you know, with short, honey-blonde hair, casual and wavy, brushed back from the face, kinda like I wear my hair, though hers is a darker blonde. Oh, and she's got a really beautiful complexion– glowing. That's why I guess I hesitated with her age when you asked me. Mada has beautiful skin."

The proprietress thought for a protracted moment, attempting to summon an image of the woman they were discussing in her mind's eye. "Medium height, medium build. Kinda busty. *Relaxed*," Eva uttered abruptly. "That's a word I could use when describing Mada Fane. Relaxed and casual in dress, manner– everything. She knows who she is, but she doesn't put on airs; though, of course, she could. You'd never know she was wealthy. Old money, though, is like that, I've noticed. It's the *nouveau riche* who grate on my nerves. Mada is a no-frills kinda gal. Not a lot of makeup or jewels either. Her look, every time I've seen her, has been casual and natural. And she's got an easy-to-be-around manner that you'll like."

A fleeting silence ensued with the Sisters sipping their tea in thought, until Eva blurted, "So, you haven't mentioned a word about it, but did you notice my new sign when you came in?"

Bringing her bejeweled hands together, Raine exclaimed, "I saw! I saw!" as she conjured the placard depicting a sexy Gypsy woman lounging with a steaming cup of tea on a glowing crescent moon that proclaimed in lipstick-red script– *The Gypsy Tearoom.*

Eva's face went positively white, and her green-gold leopard eyes widened considerably, whilst she clutched the edge of the table. "Forgive me, but your words just stirred a deeply buried memory, Raine. I *do* remember something more about Nellie. About that last time she visited my great-grandmother, Anna, for a reading. If you recall, I told you that Anna's daughter, my grandma Franci, was only a child of six then, but she was what they call a *precocious* child. She had listened in to a portion of Nellie's reading that night, to what turned out to be Nellie's *final* reading from Anna. Mama Franci–" Eva stopped herself, going off on a tangent, "and, at this moment, I can see my grandmother clearly, in my mind's eye. I can see her face and the turmoil in her eyes as, years later, she repeated the words that Nellie had screamed that telling night– **'I saw! I saw!!'** It was after that, then, that Mama Franci said Nellie declared, 'I am afraid. I'm so *very* afraid!'"

Eva leaned in again, her eyes wide, reaching to grasp each of the Sisters' hands. "Listen to me," she interrupted their tumbled thoughts with an urgency on her soft voice. "You are in danger. Or you will be. Everywhere you go, look over your shoulders. Trust no one. Suspect everyone."

"First Granny warns us that we're in extreme danger and now Eva," Maggie reminded Raine later that evening.

"*Déjà vu,*" Raine stated. "I mean we're nearly always in jeopardy when we're on a case. It goes with the territory. *Forewarned, however, is forearmed.* Right now, let's focus on our next interviewee. My research told me that Josie Means is rather a loner."

"She's a writer," Maggie shrugged. "They're often loners. How else can they write?"

The Sisters were parked in front of Josie Means' home on a pretty, shaded lane not far from Tara. Josie's house was a tiny Craftsman-style home, so sated with charm and fantasy that it looked right out of the pages of a Grimm's faerie book.

"Josie's certainly not part of the old guard of elderly Hamlet ladies," Raine took a breath, hurrying on, "of those descended from the," she gestured quote marks, "*best* families, who belong to the elite clubs and auxiliaries, attend church every Sunday, and know intimately all the ramifications of the county kith and kin."

Maggie was so conditioned to Raine's rhetoric that, at times, she tuned her out, though not this time. "I read in one of her rare interviews that Josie doesn't even like to do book talks and signings. 'Authors,' she said, 'should be read and not seen.' What time do you have?" the redheaded Sister asked.

"Ten till six," Raine answered with a glance to her watch.

Less than a minute later, Aisling eased her SUV to the curb behind Raine's MG. The blonde Sister signaled in the mirror to Raine and Maggie, prompting the former to return the gesture.

Once the Sisters rang the bell, it was opened within seconds by the lady of the house. That is, it was opened a crack.

Josie Means peered through the chink in the door with, exception of Dr. Weatherby's, the bluest eyes the Sisters ever recalled seeing in anyone's head. "Just let me nab my two cats, and I'll let you in. Hold on!"

The door clicked shut.

The Sisters could hear her enticing the cats to another room. Then they heard hurried footsteps coming toward the entrance. At once, the arched door opened wide, and Josie invited them in.

"Please remove your shoes," their hostess asked mildly. "I hope you don't mind, but I never wear shoes in the house. And it's been so muddy due to all this rain we've been having."

The Sisters started removing their shoes to leave at the door, on a mat in the foyer. At that juncture, they scanned the woman before them.

Josie Means was no longer young, and her face held a mild, worried expression, which might have been focus or deliberation.

On closer inspection, she looked to be in her early sixties, though the magickal trio reckoned she was somewhat older. Her thick, straight grey hair was not the more common salt-and-pepper variety, but rather the solid, smoky-grey hue of a Russian Blue cat. She wore it chin length, turned under, in what used to be called a "page boy," and held back from her face with a blue velvet headband. Miss Means was slender with an artsy taste in clothing that became her author's status. The gauzy, asymmetrical blue top and long skirt she was wearing today deepened her eyes to sapphire, eyes that smiled at the Sisters, who could not help smiling back.

"Sorry about having to close the door in your faces like that. But you see, I have two Abyssinians, Abigail and Abner. I don't know if you're familiar with the breed, but Abyssinians are Olympic sprinters and climbers. They're super curious, and they never shut up. At any rate, I have to be watchful when anyone comes calling." She frowned. "As soon as a door opens, their unified goal is to dart through it! They're rascals, to say the least. But I wouldn't part with them for the world.

"Won't you sit down and make yourselves comfortable?" Josie gestured toward the quaint parlor, which, on one side of the small foyer where they stood, was more like a library, so bursting was it with books.

The Sisters sat together on the sofa, across from an old-fashioned, brown leather Morris chair that Josie chose for herself. That is, she started to lower herself into the chair, when she straightened.

"May I offer you something?" their hostess asked, her blue eyes still smiling.

"No thank you," the threesome chimed.

From the next room, the Sisters could hear the loud cat wails that told them the Abbys were not at all used to being ignored.

"You can let them out," Raine ventured. "We love animals, and I, especially, have a way with them."

Josie looked unconvinced, and for a moment the Sisters thought she might demur. "My cats are little devils," she stated firmly. "I don't want them," her eyes swept the black clothing each Sister was sporting, "climbing all over you."

"They'll be fine," Raine promised. "No outfit is complete without a few cat hairs. And it'll be so much better for us to talk … and hear one another," she finished over the loud caterwauling.

Josie rose and opened the door that led into the kitchen. As soon as she did, the energetic Abbys came dashing out, the ruddy-colored duo taking a flying leap to land smack on Raine, who squealed with delight, then quickly used her witchy gift to send the pair a telepathic message to– *Settle down!*

"My, you must have a great rapport with cats!" Josie exclaimed, astonished that her fur babies, as she often called them, calmed almost instantly. At the moment, they were both snuggled up with Raine, one on her lap, the other next to her on the sofa, with front paws possessively positioned on that Sister's knees. The fact that both cats were staring adoringly at the Goth gal utterly amazed Josie, who was want to tell folks that Abbys were one-person cats, and that one person in *her* Abbys' lives was *she*.

Raine laughed low in her throat, stroking her feline admirers as she answered, "I have a gift for communicating with animals, and they always seem to like me."

Now it was Josie's turn to laugh. "I wish you could tell them to stop climbing up my new drapes! Ornery little imps! They're forever climbing up something, or knocking over something. And they refuse to listen to me. I've had cats all my life, but these two ... are in a class by themselves!" she finished, her tone snatching the feline pair's attention as two little heads turned in sync toward their owner.

Raine lifted an ebony brow, then steadily fixed her glittering emerald gaze on the cats. *You heard what your mistress just said.* She glanced over at the living-room drapes– midnight-blue velvet with a lighter blue, fringed valance. *Those drapes look to be expensive. I'll see to it your climbing urges are satisfied, if you stop tormenting Josie with your shenanigans. What say you to that? Huh?*

The Abbys inclined their little heads at once, shooting the Sister a quick, appraising look, their mouths opening to give their unified response. *What do you mean you'll satisfy our climbing urges?*

Raine dimpled. *Pay attention and you'll find out, my fine furry friends!*

"Josie, may I call you that?"

The author nodded, as mesmerized by the Sister's telepathic abilities as were the cats.

"These two Abyssinians really need to climb, but they'd be willing to lay off your drapes if you'd get them a nice, big kitty gym.

I've seen them online, in pet stores, and cat magazines. There would be all sorts of climbing opportunities and kitty challenges in one of those contraptions that would satisfy their needs and desires." Raine lowered her eyes to the purring pair who had befriended her.

Do you promise to behave if your mistress gets you your very own kitty gym?" She sent them an image of one that had popped into her head.

Abigail and Abner looked at one another, then sent Raine their joint reply– *Agreed, but tell her not to dally. We want it without delay! Josie has a maddening habit of putting things off.*

The raven-haired Sister held the feisty felines with her witchy stare. *You must understand that it's going to take several days for your grand new toy to arrive after your mistress orders it. However, I expect you to keep your word– no more climbing drapes and no more knocking things over.*

Raine shifted her regard to their hostess. "If you promise to get the kitty gym right away, they will stop causing havoc." The Sister ducked her glossy dark head a wee bit. "They said you have a habit of putting things off, but I heartily appeal to you not to delay this purchase. I really believe they will keep their word and behave themselves much better for you."

Josie's eyes grew as large as the proverbial saucers. "They told you that?!"

"They did," Raine answered. "Trust me on this, please, and once it's delivered, don't hide it away. Put their gym here in the main part of the house, preferably in front of a big window that looks out onto the street. They sell all sorts, and you'll find one that won't clash with your décor; I'm certain."

After a magickal moment, Raine added, "This will make it so much easier for you to write. They resent the fact that when you write, you ignore them, but a kitty gym would keep them entertained enough so that you can write in peace."

Josie shook her head. "Ignore them when I write they said? Sounds like my ex-husband." She noted the look on the Sisters' faces, or she imagined she did. "No, I'm not an old maid, like so many in this town think. I returned, **years** ago, to my maiden name– not that I ever really took his name– I wasn't going to put his name on my published works; that's for certain."

In a blink, the author shifted her ground, regaining her humor to remark, "If I hadn't heard so much about you three, I would say this cat conversation is one of the craziest things I've ever experienced. However," she exhaled noisily, "my intuition, as well as your reputation, tell me otherwise, so I *will* opt for the kitty gym, and yes, right away."

"Now," the practical Aisling sighed too, "let's get to why we came over here today."

"As you know," Raine began, "Maggie," she looked to that Sister, "and I teach history at Haleigh College. Of late, we've become deeply engrossed in researching a few of our local moguls, including your grandfather, J.D. Means."

"Would you be so kind as to enlighten us even further on your illustrious ancestor?" Maggie continued, petting the cats as she waited for Josie to respond.

"I included a lengthy segment about my grandfather in my history work *Chronicles of Braddock County,*" Josie replied, gesturing with a wave of an elegant hand toward a wall lined with shelves stuffed with books.

"We have that book," Maggie stated, tossing a peek at Raine.

"We've referred to it often in our classrooms," the professor Sisters concluded with enthusiasm."

"A well-researched, well-crafted work," Maggie put in. "But share with us a few *personal* stories about your grandfather," the red-haired Sister implored. "We're interviewing several descendants of our local industrialists, and most certainly your grandfather occupies a spot at the top of the list. We always say in our classrooms that he was unique for his era."

Josie gave a little chortle. "Oh, he was unique all right. As you know, his was a dog-eat-dog era. There weren't a lot of regulations in business and banking like we have today, which, as I'm certain you know too, was a big reason the stock market crashed in 1929."

Josie settled herself more comfortably in her chair, crossing her legs at the ankles. "During the coal and coke boom, my grandfather made his fortune buying and selling coal lands." The author made a derisive sound, fairly flowing into excited speech. "You say the word 'coke' nowadays, and young people think you mean *dope!* I know *you* teach some local history, but don't grade-school and high-school teachers talk about our rich local history anymore?!"

Raine couldn't help but chortle, "All history is local. Think about it."

Oblivious, the author surged on, "I can't tell you how many young people ask me, at book talks, to explain what I mean by 'coke'! 'It's a by-product of coal,' I say, 'used to make steel!'" She wrinkled her small nose. "I don't like to do book talks. Used to have to, but not anymore." Her expression softened, and she quickly lowered her voice, "Forgive me. I didn't mean to unload on you.

"To hark back to my grandfather and his story, I must tell you that he was a good person, not in any way *ruthless* like so many of his contemporaries. A few of those contemporaries were ruthless in business but caring husbands and fathers at home. My grandfather was a caring person everywhere."

Again, Josie's face changed, this time to mirror the sadness she was feeling. "It was his downfall."

The Sisters traded looks, with history professors Raine and Maggie putting on knowing faces.

"Grandad," Josie went on, "was never involved in actual coal mining operations; rather, he was a sort of coal broker. And in a sense, everyone benefited: my grandfather and his associates, the steel companies, because they needed large and dependable supplies of coal and coke for steel making, and the farmers and other land owners who sold mineral rights but retained surface rights.

"During the Roaring Twenties, my grandfather also made money by advising other people how to put their money to work for them. And as a result," she smiled, and her sapphire eyes twinkled a little, "J.D. Means became known as 'Jim Dandy, the Millionaire-Maker.' As I am also certain you are aware, we had, during that boom era, a millionaire or a near-millionaire every few feet throughout the Hamlet coking basin and our Braddock County."

"We most assuredly did," Raine concurred. She glanced down to see Josie's two cats totally relaxed, their slanted eyes half-closed, their purring a comforting sound.

"The decade of the 1920s was the height of my grandfather's success," Josie continued. "He worked his way up the ladder at his father's bank, inheriting the bank and its presidency upon his father's death. Quickly did he establish himself as a man of integrity, and many people invested their savings in his bank. In turn, Grandad channeled those funds into his coal-land interests.

"A friendly atmosphere prevailed at my grandfather's bank, and he extended the same folksy attitude toward small depositors as he did toward high-rolling speculators. Nearly everyone called him

'J.D.,' 'Jim,' or even 'Jim Dandy;'" Josie gave a little laugh, "though the 'D' actually stood for Dalton, which was his mother's maiden name.

"Although he became a successful banker, Grandad's fortune was created from the 'black diamonds' known as coal, not really from banking *per se*. His father, Jonathan, had the foresight, prior to World War I, to quietly purchase coal lands as cheaply as he could get them. J.D. followed suit, finally owning virtually every important coal tract in the tri-county area. Later, he sold some of those lands for a very nice profit.

"In 1927, the banner year, Grandad's First National Bank led thousands of banks nation-wide, including metropolitan giants, for surplus and profits in proportion to capital. The bank proudly advertised itself as: 'First in the City; First in the County; First in the State; First in the United States.' *It was not an empty boast.*"

"On a personal note, what was your grandfather like?" Aisling asked, waiting with pen poised above her trusty notebook.

"On a personal note?" Josie gave an unguarded smile. "Grandad was a likable chap, very personable, as I said, rather handsome, though portly, with great charisma, and remarkable mathematic ability. He could breeze through long columns of numbers, adding, subtracting, multiplying or dividing the figures in his head like a computer, and it is recorded by several sources, that his memory was phenomenal.

"After the Stock Market Crash of 1929, and by 1932, my grandfather incurred serious financial problems. A big land deal with Adrian Fane fell through after a bad beginning–" Josie stopped herself abruptly. Her face took suddenly a rather grim line, and something flickered in her brilliant blue eyes, something that the Sisters could not quite decipher.

The author gave the impression that she was fumbling for the words to complete the sentence she had begun several moments earlier. Finally, after a lengthy, somewhat awkward, pause, she said, "My grandfather held out for the amount of money he wanted for coal lands Fane wished to purchase from him. Though Grandad was far from greedy, he could, at times, be stubborn about money."

"And as a result, a rumor quickly spread that your grandfather's bank was in trouble; an investigator was sent in, and soon depositors at the bank started a run that some, yet today, believe was *staged*," Raine supplied, pulled from one of her history lessons.

"Do *you* believe the run on my grandfather's bank was staged?" Josie asked, her eyes searching the Sisters' intent faces.

"Yes," the two history professors answered without hesitation.

Josie nodded, the gesture subtle, barely noticeable. "Grandad, being a man of integrity, assured depositors they would be paid 100 cents on the dollar, and that promise was very nearly fulfilled, though unsecured creditors received far less. Fast-forwarding a bit, within days, my grandfather's bank shut its doors– for good."

The author took on a far-away look as again she quoted from her book in a rather absent voice, as though she were transporting herself into the scene she had written, "'It was an unusually cold September day as, what local newspapers called "curiosity seekers," their faces registering their emotions, shouted, cried, and spat curses in the pouring rain outside the locked doors of the First National at Unionville, the Braddock County seat. Police officers, billy clubs in hand, stood ready in case of trouble.' I stated in my book, it was the month 'everything changed. Vivid expectations were dashed, and the future itself seemed to lie in those damp, shattered shards.'"

Josie took a breath, continuing, "The bleak tidings summoned to Unionville a reporter from the *New York Tribune*. When he arrived at the bank, the journalist found, working there alone, steady, sensible Edgar Hixon, the bank cashier and Grandad's longtime friend and associate. 'I have gathered the impression that, far from panicked, Mr. Means is reacting rather well to the distressing turn of events. Is that so?' the city-slicker scribe prodded.

"Old Mr. Hixon declined a direct response. 'You'll have to determine that for yourself.'"

The author inclined her head, "The reporter was eager to see the spectacular estate, Oakmont, where my grandparents resided; he felt he had nothing to lose by going there for his interview.

"When the newsman reached Oakmont, he found Grandad far from tongue-tied. 'I've been a worker all my life. I am a worker now,' he told the rubbernecking reporter. 'I am going to work this thing through all right. Just wait and see!'

"The journalist fired back with: 'What prospects do you have, man? Your bank just failed, and you're in debt up to your neck!'

"The invincible J.D. Means drew himself up and lifted a rather surprised brow, answering boldly, 'I have the land! I have the coal!'"

Josie pulled in a long, deep breath, letting it out slowly. "Creditors, however, began to get edgy, and writs descended on Grandad like an angry swarm of killer bees– some fifteen hundred against him and his associates and about 700 against him personally.

"On October 1, 1932, Braddock County Sheriff Martin Keefer took three hours to read those writs aloud, the names crashing against my stoic grandfather, who sat upright in a chair at Oakmont, where the lethal roll call tolled like a requiem bell.

"The strain became unbearable for one coke company superintendent who was a trustee for the fortune of his grandchildren. When his money seemed lost in the general collapse, he went looking for my grandfather with a loaded gun. Not finding him, the desperate man went off and shot himself. Stacks of hostile mail appeared weekly at the Oakmont mansion, telling Grandad his house would be bombed, and threatening him and my grandmother with death. I remember from family stories that it was a very frightening time.

"Needless to say, Adrian Fane, without bending or breaking so much as one law, got quick hold of all my grandfather's coal lands. Some might say all's fair in love and war, and pre-income-tax-era business." Again something flickered in Josie's eyes. "In tandem, Grandad's loyalty in the coke region plummeted fast." The author's brows rose. "But his past was quite blameless.

"You are aware, I am certain, at the time of my grandfather's troubles, there had been a drop off in steel production that filtered down to the demand for coal and coke. However, with the winds of war beginning once again to howl across Europe, the demand for steel would soon escalate– once again, there would be an insatiable call for coal and coke to make the steel that would churn out the vast weapons of war.

"If only my grandad could've held on, even for a year or so, he very likely would *not* have lost his fortune. Instead, a merciless Fate threw him into a maelstrom– and the destructive gale swept his affluence completely away."

Josie sighed heavily, resuming after a musing moment, "My hopeful grandfather was aboard ship bound for Europe to ask his sister, who was married to a well-heeled English lord, for a loan of money so that he *could* hang on, but he mysteriously disappeared from that ship. I mean *literally disappeared*. Of course, everyone thought he committed suicide, jumped overboard in the dark of night in total despair. But my family never believed that was the case."

With shades of her forefather, the author drew herself up straighter in her chair. "J.D. Means was *not* a quitter, not the type of man to commit suicide. His disappearance shocked a great many people."

The author inclined her head, fumbling for a mental image of her ancestor. "If you'd known my grandfather, you'd have been surprised at his dying of anything!"

Raine was all ears. "Do you think it was a conspiracy? My family always believed the bank run was staged, and I think I can venture an educated guess who and what was behind the ploy to ruin your grandfather financially to get hold of valuable coal lands."

For a protracted moment, Josie did not respond, and again something flickered in her eyes. It was there for mere seconds, but there was no mistaking it– *it was fear. Stark fear.*

As though by a magick sponge, suddenly all emotion was wiped away, and ignoring Raine's question, Josie chose to answer in a whole different vein. "We do have to look hard at the one fact so many have pointed out over the years: My grandfather was critically overextended. He treated his bank as a storehouse for credit, ever-abundant and ever-available. Yet, J.D. Means was not a greedy man; his sin was not avarice. When the bank failed, Grandad still owned those thousands of acres of coal lands, but converting them into cash would take time, time he did not have. His personal fortune was estimated at $85 million– *on paper*. A fortune he amassed in about a decade, I might add."

Josie smiled then, a sad little smile. "As I keened in my book, 'After twenty-five years of glory, at age sixty-six, coal baron, bank president, and civic leader J.D. Means slid down the slippery financial slope from unbelievable wealth to abject bankruptcy. Hundreds of his friends and associates went with him, drawing a black curtain of woe over the county he so loved. Certainly our area would come to know future economic crunches, but that first big bite on the heels of the Stock Market Crash was, by far, the worst, choking most of the region.'"

"Josie," Maggie tried again, sending a warning to Raine with her eyes, "at the risk of being a tad pushy, I feel as though you had started to tell us something a few moments ago, but you stopped yourself." She brought her hands together to tap her mouth with her pointer fingers. With pleading eyes, she asked, "Is it possible you're *afraid* to tell us everything you know about your grandfather's story?"

"Whatever you say will stay within these walls; we assure you," Aisling said kindly.

"I've said too much already," the author muttered under her breath.

The Sisters looked dissatisfied.

"You know our reputation. Know then that you can trust us," Raine encouraged. "If you're afraid of something or someone, hadn't you better tell us what it is? We can *help* you."

Josie swallowed hard and shook her head, sitting as still and stoic as the Sisters had envisioned her grandfather sitting when he was hit with those crippling writs. The author's expression was nothing short of wooden.

Raine sent Maggie the thought: *She looks as if she was taught to sit very straight as a child, and not to loll. She's always done so. Even now. And I can't read a thing from her mind or expression.*

Maggie came back with: *Uh-huh, masklike. She'd make a nifty poker player.*

Finally, Aisling leaned forward, and lowering her voice, she said, "Look, we're going to level with you. The reason we're garnering all we can from descendants of anyone living here at the time of our Hamlet's triple ax murders is because some information has recently come to light that we believe–"

"The skeletons you discovered in the woods!" Josie's eyes widened in sheer terror, as the color fled from her face, and it puckered in anxiety. One slender hand was gripping the arm of her chair tensely.

The Sisters exchanged quick looks.

"Please help us," Maggie pled. "Don't you want closure for your grandfather? We don't think he committed suicide either. We never did. We want you to help us give him closure, as well as some others whose spirits we are certain are not at rest."

Raine tried again too. "We sense that several mysteries from that ill-omened year of 1932 are connected. *Please*, you can *trust* us."

But Josie remained motionless, her expression stoic, though her watchful eyes told the tale.

"I've been a detective for many years," Aisling stated quietly; and, together, we sense that you know something significant you're afraid to share with us." The blonde Sister leaned toward the author, adding in a beseeching tone, "*Help* us. Help put your grandfather's spirit to rest. ***Please tell us what you know.***"

Josie got to her feet, a bit unsteadily. She reached out and grasped the back of her chair for support, then took a tentative step and stopped, standing there a moment, swaying on her feet and looking ghastly.

The Sisters rose too, rushing forward to their hostess' aid. "Are you all right?" they asked, concerned.

Waving aside their help, the author swept a wisp of hair back from her forehead and moved a bit uneasily toward the door, as if to escort her visitors out. Her face lost even more of its color, though her voice was still smooth. "I'll tell you one more thing, and then you have to leave. What I know is that you're opening a Pandora's box of intrigue and evil. *That's* what I know!"

Chapter Ten

"I think it's time for a brainstorming session with our special sleuthing set," Raine announced, when the Sisters had exited Josie's house and walked to their cars, at the curb in front of the faerie-tale home.

"Not yet," Maggie countered. "Let's save that for the weekend. By then we'll have completed our interviews."

"How many more do you have?" Aisling asked, fishing in her purse for her keys.

"Four," Raine and Maggie supplied.

"Tea with Mada Fane tomorrow afternoon," Raine replied. "We just spoke to her on the phone a couple hours ago. The subsequent day is our meeting with a direct descendant of Clyde Hardiman, axed Nellie's brother; and then, at the end of the week, our last two interviews with descendants of Nellie's two suitors."

"Maggie's right. Get those interviews done; touch base with the chief for further news on those skeletons, and then let's schedule our brainstorming session for Saturday or Sunday." Aisling checked her phone for text messages. "Oooooooh, must get home. Ian's made Merry Fay her dinner, and he has a nice candle-lit supper ready for him and me."

The blonde Sister leaned toward her cousins and sisters of the moon to give each a hug. "Watch your backs. I've a witch's, as well as a seasoned detective's, gut-feeling that whatever or whoever the people you've spoken with are afraid of, that fear– and the source of that fear– is still very much alive. It's an ever-present shadow, a very dark and sinister shadow."

The Goth gal nodded. "And my feeling is that several are aware of this shadow. We'll let you know how things shape."

Raine and Maggie watched Aisling drive away, thinking that her closing sentiment matched theirs exactly.

"I'm hungry, aren't you?" Raine asked, glancing at her watch.

"I could eat something," Maggie answered, opening the door on the MG's passenger side.

"Let's stop at Sal-San-Tries and pick up something as take-out. We'll have more privacy at home, where the two of us can do a bit of problem-solving and sorting out while we eat." Raine slid into the driver's seat and, fishing out her key, started the ignition. The vintage sportscar roared to life and vanished in a cloud of smoke.

Around the Hamlet's picturesque gazebo, the tree-shaded park benches, town center, were occupied by the village old-timers– some smoking their pipes, some whittling and talking, others listening with acknowledging nods, as they habitually solved the world's problems. These fellows claimed those seats during the warm season. When Old Man Winter blew his frosty breath, the motley crew routinely abandoned the park benches for the wooden chairs that encircled the cozy, warm stove at Sal-San-Tries café-deli.

Quaint, Victorian-style shops, with matching green-striped canopies, formed a charming circle around the lacy, white gazebo; and big baskets of colorful live flowers hung from the Hamlet's pretty Victorian streetlamps.

When Raine and Maggie got out of the MG, at a space in front of Sal-San-Tries, the pair sent a friendly wave to the bench sitters, joined today by the Hamlet's bag lady Old Milly, who sometimes entered into their lively discussions. The group paused to return the wave. Just as everyone in Haleigh's Hamlet had known Granny McDonough, everyone knew the Sleuth Sisters, or as some called them, the "McDonough Girls." For the most part, Haleigh's Hamlet was a friendly place.

A mélange of delicious aromas greeted the magickal duo as they entered the café-deli, the bell on the door chiming their entry.

Small, round tables occupied more than half of the café, with the deli near the entrance. The Sisters covered the short distance to the large glass cooler and counter, glancing around for the owner.

In a trice, Sophie Miller came bouncing through the red-plaid curtains that separated the main part of the café from the kitchen and storeroom.

"Hi!" the rosy-cheeked young woman greeted with her winning smile. "I was in the back, baking pies." She wiped her hands on her apron. "What can I get you today?"

Raine and Maggie returned the smile. They could hardly recall a time when Sophie wasn't in a good mood. Or a time when the café owner wasn't sporting her bouncy, strawberry-blonde ponytail.

Everything about Sophie was bouncy. Today, over the white tee and jeans she was wearing, her bright pink apron, sprinkled with dark-red cherries, matched the ribbon tied round her ponytail.

Sophie habitually coordinated her hand-sewn bibbed-aprons with her hair ribbons, and they always celebrated the season. As it did the Sleuth Sisters, Savvy Kathy, and Eva Novak, the Hamlet considered Miss Sophie one of its personalities.

Sal-San-Tries' proprietress wasn't what the fashion experts would call "slender," but she wasn't chubby either. Sophie was average height with a heightened cheerleader personality that never failed to cheer her customers.

"What's the special today?" Raine queried, studying the choices in the cooler.

"I'm plumb out of a couple of 'em, but I could whip you up two of my great tuna melts. My special tuna salad with sharp cheddar and fresh tomato grilled on my homemade multi-grain bread. That comes with my house chips and a big deli pickle," Sophie smiled, "*two* each for you guys. I know how much you love the pickles."

"Sounds good!" Raine replied, getting an enthusiastic nod from Maggie.

"Is this to go?" Sophie asked, already starting to build the sandwiches.

"Yes," Maggie answered. "And what do you have for dessert today?"

Sophie tightened her glossy mouth, her eyes narrowing a bit in thought. "Pies aren't ready yet, but I have a few of my famous poppy seed cakes left. They're fresh. Just baked them this morning."

"Perfect! Give us what you have left," Raine directed with gusto. "Can't pass those babies up. They're our favorite."

Sophie's azure gaze traveled down Raine's slim figure in the sleeveless, black linen dress she was wearing. "Honey, I don't know how you do it!" she threw up her hands. "You have such a ravenous appetite, and yet you stay so slender."

Raine leaned over the counter to whisper into Sophie's ear, "*Magick*."

"It must be!" Sophie laughed. "You usually eat more than two men, I swear."

Raine touched a finger to the gold, diamond-encrusted magick-wand brooch on her lapel. It was her signature piece of jewelry. She designed it and had her jeweler craft it to remind her of her life's credo: *Thoughts are magick wands, powerful enough to make anything happen– anything we choose.*

As Sophie continued putting together the Sisters' order, Raine asked, "Sophie, do you recall ever hearing about our Hamlet's unsolved triple ax murders?"

"Sure," the café owner nodded, causing her high, silky ponytail to bob about. She laid the cheese atop the tuna-spread bread slices. "I mean, what Hamlet resident hasn't heard of those grisly– *mysterious*– murders?! Happened during the Depression years, right?"

Maggie came quickly back with, "That's right. Were any stories passed down in your family in regard to those murders? Your family's one of our Hamlet's founding families, so they were living here way before 1932."

"Let me think a moment," Sophie said, after placing the tuna melts on the grill. "Why do you ask? Delving into another mystery, huh?" In that split second and before the Sisters could reply, Sophie dropped the knife she was holding, her eyes widening in what could only be called "fear."

"The unearthed skeletons! D-do you think–" she fumbled for both the knife and for words, and the Sisters could not help noting that her face had gone a sickening green. "Do you think our Hamlet's unsolved ax murders are connected to those skeletons you discovered in Haleigh's Wood?!"

"I might put those same questions to you. 'Do you think the skeletons are connected to the ax murders?' and 'Why do you ask?'" Raine retorted, though not unkindly.

Twenty minutes later, Raine and Maggie were back in the MG, with their food order, and headed home to Tara.

"I'm beginning to get the feeling," Raine began, "that everyone in our Hamlet with whom we've talked knows something we don't. It's not only a strange feeling, it's one I'm not accustomed to– and I sure as hell don't like it!!"

"One thing's certain. I never saw the bright and breezy Sophie so shaken, have you?" Maggie asked, turning to look at Raine, who was behind the wheel.

"Can't say I ever did. I've seen her rattled one or two times about something or other in the past, but not frightened like that." Raine shook her head in a perplexed manner. "Well, at least, before she scuttled back to the kitchen, she let slip, then finally shared with us a family story about two of her Depression-era ancestors who, it sounded to me anyway, were a couple bad apples on the otherwise unspoiled family tree."

"Ye-s-s," Maggie mused, "the Miller brothers. Twins, who, after losing their fortunes when J.D. Means' bank failed, resorted to rum-running from Canada across Lake Erie. I seem to recall reading about that pair, but I never associated them with the sweet Sophie. Miller is, after all, a common surname."

"Y—yes, I remember reading about them too. Three, four years ago, I think it was, though I forget *why* I was reading about them. Their rum-running boat was powered by a supercharged engine, a Rolls Royce Merlin." Raine began muttering to herself, "The Merlin *transformed* the P-51 Mustang in World War II."

"What did you say?" Maggie asked, confused.

"I remember why I stumbled on an Internet article about the Miller boys. I'd been researching World War II fighter planes. But getting back to the Millers, the twins were tough, became evermore ruthless, and–" The sentence went unfinished as Raine chewed her lower lip, pulling what she could from memory. "Suffice it to say, those two were real badasses. Anyone who opposed them, if I recollect correctly from what I read, had a way of disappearing, though nothing could ever be proven."

"What ever happened to the Millers? How did they end up?" Maggie asked, staring for a moment out the window at the sign that marked their long driveway, the wooded lane that led to their Tara. Though the end-of-day light was nearly gone, the sign, with its glow-in-the-dark paint was still visible– *Witch-Way.*

A few years before, two of their more adventuresome students had fastened it to a stately oak tree at the entrance to their lane, and since the Sisters took a fancy to the winsome placard, it remained.

"I think the notorious Miller brothers were finally killed– authorities couldn't catch 'em, so surprised them– on their souped-up boat in a shoot-out with the Coast Guard. We'll look it up after we eat."

When Raine and Maggie arrived home at Tara, they found Hannah Gilbert just preparing to leave after a long day of cleaning.

The Sleuth Sisters' devoted housekeeper bobbled across the clean kitchen floor on bright purple sneakers that matched her colorful personality.

"Evenin', chicadees!" she sang out, and though her voice and manner were brass– her heart, as the Sisters always said, was pure gold.

"Twenty-four karat," Raine liked to add.

Despite her penchant for gossip, along with a tendency to be a mite bossy, Hannah was a nurturing soul. She took good care of the Sleuth Sisters and Tara, scrubbing and polishing the old house with almost religious fervor, and she regularly looked after Aisling's little girl, Merry Fay.

"I'm afraid you're working too late and too hard, Hannah. We appreciate all you do for us, but we don't want you to overdo," Maggie chided, giving the loyal maid a warm hug.

Raine kissed Hannah's cheek, asking if she'd like to take a couple of Sophie's poppy seed cakes home.

Hannah lit up. "Is the Pope Catholic?! As for workin' late, I started late today, and I wanted to finish the upstairs rooms. The house is tidy and sparklin' clean, so see if you kin keep it that way." She plopped the evening paper down on the kitchen table, as the Sisters were unpacking their food. "What's the word on those skeletons you two discovered in the woods? The paper doesn't say much about it."

Maggie put four of the little cakes into a plastic container and snapped on the lid. "I always tell you to toss these things out; but, you're right, Hannah, they do come in handy." The redheaded Sister handed the container to the older woman. "Enjoy. Nothing new on the skeletons. It's too early to say what is really what yet."

"Hmmm," Hannah brooded, scratching her grey head. "I just wonder … ." Her words dropped off, as she leaned an ample hip against the sky-blue kitchen wall, in reflection. "There were some pretty shady goin's-on around here back then, during the Depression years. I remember my granny telling us kids stories about all sorts of bad things. Scary things too. Hobos livin' down by the river and the tracks, and even in abandoned coke ovens; rum-runners and bootleggers usin' the Laurel Caverns up the mountain for storin' their booze stashes smuggled in through Canada; illegal numbers rackets, prostitution rings. All sorts!"

Interested, Raine paused in her tea preparation, and Hannah lifted the kettle from her to begin making the Sisters' favorite imported tea to go with their light supper. "I can do th–"

"Ya know," the motherly housekeeper went on, ignoring Raine's protest, "the Depression-era crime around here shot outta control when ole Jim Dandy's bank failed; and, to boot, that happened not long after the Stock Market Crash! A lot of folks in these parts lost everything when that bank failed. They didn't know which way to turn! So some turned to crime. I remember my folks sayin' the police didn't know which way to turn either. And to tell you the truth, I don't think the police know which way to turn now, when it comes to these skeletons that you two discovered. I just bet you–"

Raine nearly dropped the napkin holder she was about to set on the table. "Which way to turn!" she echoed nearly to herself. "That's it, Hannah!" she erupted loudly. "You might have just hit on a valuable clue!"

By nine that evening, while waiting for Beau to join her at Tara, Raine was becoming more and more submerged in 1932 research on her computer. One surprise after another pulled her deeper and deeper into the Hamlet's Depression years.

Maggie had gone off with Thaddeus, who told her he had a surprise to show her.

***

"Can't you at least tell me where we're going?" the redheaded Sister asked, staring at the professor's profile in the reflected light from an on-coming vehicle.

"If I did *that*, it wouldn't be a surprise, now would it?" Thaddeus answered, not taking his eyes from the narrow, one-lane country road onto which they had turned. "I can tell you this– you'll *like* it."

"I will, will I?" Maggie joked. "C'mon now, give me a hint." When he didn't respond, she lowered her voice to a sexy level. "Just one little hint."

"No hints. Correct me if I'm wrong, but I thought you loved a good mystery, Maggie McDonough," he chortled.

"We certainly seem to be off the beaten path," she uttered almost to herself, as they bumped along the narrow, winding trace. "I don't think I've ever been on this road before … that is, if indeed, one can call this a road. Good thing we're in my Rover." She peered intently out the front windshield. They were deep in the woods, on a remote back road somewhere high in the mountains above Haleigh's Hamlet. That much she knew even in the dark.

"Pretty soon, I'm going to have to ask you to put that blindfold on that you'll find in the glove compartment," he said. "Get it out."

"Blindfold?!"

The professor slowed the vehicle, his eyes searching the narrow road for a place to pull off. "Get the blindfold out now, Maggie, and I'll stop and put it on you," he stated mysteriously, his twinkling eyes holding hers.

Maggie's heart began to beat excitedly, as she imagined all sorts of reasons why her inventive lover would want to blindfold her. With those stimulating thoughts in mind, she did as he asked, saying, "OK, I have it."

Thaddeus rolled the Land Rover to a stop and put it in park. He leaned over and, taking the blindfold from Maggie's hands, very slowly and deliberately secured it over her eyes. He drew her close, tracing her glossy mouth with a finger, then running the finger in a feather touch along her full lower lip. He kissed her deeply, touching and caressing her until she moaned with pleasure and her soul sang.

"Please," she whispered.

"Please?" he questioned with a touch of humor. "Please what?"

"Love me," she purred softly.

"I do love you, as you will soon see. Have a little patience, my dear. Good things come to those who wait; don't you know that?" he chortled low in his throat, sliding over and putting the Land Rover back in gear. "Keep your hands away from that blindfold. We'll be arriving at our destination soon, and then, *au bon moment, I* shall remove it."

Maggie could feel the car moving again, slowly, as her heart continued to beat wildly.

Within a couple of minutes, the Rover came to an abrupt stop, and Thaddeus switched off the ignition. Again, he leaned toward her, kissing her lips, her neck, and breathing into her ear, while he touched and fondled her, sending wave after wave of pleasure coursing through her.

"Now," the methodical professor uttered, checking that her blindfold was still secure. "Do not move. I will come to your side of the car and lead you to where we are going."

Maggie could not speak, breathless as she was. She waited until her beloved opened the passenger door. Taking her hand, the good Dr. Weatherby led her outside into the cool mountain atmosphere. Sucking in a deep lungful of the refreshing air, she released it slowly. An owl hooted, and the not-too-distant cry of a bobcat reached their ears. Owl was one of Maggie's animal totems, and its presence always meant something good was soon to unfold in her life.

Thank you, brother, she whispered.

The soft, green vintage dress she was wearing fluttered sensually against her skin in the refreshing breeze, as, together, she and Thaddeus started slowly forward, her hand in his. Nearby, the red-haired Sister could hear what sounded like wind chimes on the summer eve's gentle breath. She listened harder, sensing there was a stream close by.

Squeezing her lover's hand, she stopped to listen again. Yes, she could clearly hear the tranquil sound of rippling water now.

She felt him move his hands to the blindfold, untie it, and gently pull it away.

"Open your eyes," he commanded.

Maggie's breath caught as she clapped a hand to her mouth. "Ooooooh!" she exclaimed. It was all she could manage. Her cheeks were faintly flushed, and her emerald eyes glittered with delight.

There, in a clearing within the thick forest, surrounded by a rustic, Colonial-style rail fence, was the most darling log cabin, its windows glowing golden, through which she could see pristine, white crisscross curtains. Suspended from several of the trees, under which the gloaming played light and shadow, she spotted the wind chimes– in a variety of sizes and designs. Some were golden moons and silvery stars, others bright butterflies, still others multihued birds.

"I thought it would be nice to have a place here in the mountains to get away from it all," he said quietly. "So I bought it." Again, he took her hand to lead her the rest of the way up the flagstone walk to the front porch. There, he pointed to the rustic plaque on the log wall next to the entrance. "What do you think?" He unlocked and opened the door. "If you don't like it, we can always change it."

"Wood Haven," Maggie pronounced, savoring the name of the retreat on her lips. "I like it." Then, turning to Thaddeus, she asked, "When did you do this, darlin'?"

"I've been thinking about doing it for a long time, and when this property became available, I jumped on it. We closed a few days ago. It's completely furnished, but as I said, we can always change things to suit our tastes." He swept her up and carried her over the threshold, setting her down inside.

Maggie stood, looking about. In the glow of a pair of lit, stained-glass lamps that topped log end tables on either side of a saddle-brown leather couch, her eyes began taking it all in– the huge fieldstone fireplace, the rustic beamed ceiling and stout log walls. A pair of antique snowshoes embellished the wall opposite the hearth. A third wall was lined with shelves holding a colorful collection of books interspersed with various, small antique items. A leaded-diamond window on the back wall looked out onto the wooded stream that tumbled merrily over the river rocks in a mini-waterfall.

"Ooooh!" Maggie exclaimed anew, her feline eyes sparkling. "Where did you find that?!" She was pointing to the unique, glass-top coffee table, the base of which was a life-size sculpture of a mountain lion. "It's so life-like!" She turned to Thaddeus. "Cougar is my chief animal totem, you know."

"I do know, and that's why I purchased that table. The only piece of furniture the former owners took with them was the split-log coffee table. While searching online for a replacement, I came across this, crafted by a local artisan. How propitious was that? I thought it would please you. I hope I was right."

He was rewarded by the look of pure joy on her face.

She pressed quick happy kisses against his bearded cheek. "You were totally right. I love it! Darlin', one of the things I absolutely adore about you is that you are so *sentimental*."

"Incurably."

"I hope so." She laid a whisper of a kiss on his lips, then cast another swift look around. "I see that the cabin has electricity, but what about water?" she asked, peering into the adjacent kitchen.

"It has both, and a rather nice bathroom too. C'mon," he tugged on her hand, "let me show you around. Pointing above them, he said, "Loft bedroom. Cozy, isn't it?"

Maggie could see that it was. The large bed was covered with an eye-catching patchwork quilt in deep, rich colors. There was a half-moon window in the loft, and a nice-size antique dresser. Wooden pegs on the loft's log walls replaced the need for a closet.

"The cabin has good heat and even air-conditioning. What it doesn't have is phone or Internet service, and when we come here, we're shutting our cell phones *off*," he commanded. "This place was designed as a getaway retreat, and I plan to keep it that way. It'll be nice to have a place we can escape to. C'mon, I'm anxious for you to see everything."

The living room opened into the small, but functional, kitchen with its handcrafted table, complete with two log chairs. The split-log tabletop was covered with a pretty, embroidered, sky-blue runner upon which stood a darker blue kerosene lamp. Both the living room and the kitchen ceilings held antler chandeliers, the smaller one in the kitchen. What looked like a new stainless steel refrigerator and deep farm sink won squeals of approval from the redheaded Sister, as did the Victorian-style stove, similar to the one at Tara, albeit this one was pearl grey. Another window, with white, crisscross curtains, looked out onto the forest stream. On the grey soapstone kitchen counter awaited champagne flutes and an ice bucket on a silver tray.

"Champagne's in the fridge, cooling," Thaddeus announced. "And I stocked up on food, so we can have a tasty snack later and a gourmet breakfast in the morning."

"You dear, sweet man!" Maggie whispered as emotion filled her essence. "Show me the rest of the cabin. It seems to have lots of storage space. Where's the bathroom?" she asked, glancing quickly about.

Thaddeus led her back toward the living room, where, near the ladder that led to the sleeping loft, he opened a door to reveal the bath. "What do you think of the place thus far?"

Maggie smiled her Mona-Lisa smile. "It's not a question of thinking." She threw her arms around his neck again and kissed him. "It is a question of," her hand rushed to her heart, "*feeling*, and my feeling is– *this* is the most darling log dwelling I've ever seen! I don't want to change a thing!"

When Thaddeus flicked the light switch, Maggie noted that the log walls in the bath supported a pair of candle-like wall sconces that flickered to mimic actual candlelight. As in the other rooms, an antler chandelier provided the main lighting, though at present, none of the chandeliers were turned on. Tonight, Thaddeus preferred the softer lighting of the lamps and flickering sconces.

The bathroom was actually the most breathtaking space. A thick tree stump served as the base for the sink, above which hung, on the log wall, a one-of-a-kind, oval, pine-cone-framed mirror. The roomy, jetted Jacuzzi tub, in front of the large bathroom window, was faced by logs, rendering everything in perfect harmony with their forest setting. Unlit candles surrounded the tub, and the relaxing scent of lavender lingered pleasantly on the air.

"I love this bathroom!" Maggie exclaimed. "How wonderful it will be to soak while gazing out onto the water and the woods!"

"Later," the professor declared, "we'll do it together." He kissed her mouth, his lips traveling to her ear, where he delivered his lusty intentions in a hot whisper.

Maggie returned his kiss– eagerly.

"First," he chucked her under the chin, "let's go back into the living room for a glass of champagne, shall we? I remembered to bring some of our favorite CDs, so we can relax and listen to music."

Less than an hour later, Maggie and Thaddeus were enjoying their second glass of the bubbly in the hot tub. The bathroom candle wall-sconces flickered charmingly in the semi-dark room, the only other illumination the now-lit scented candles that encircled the whirlpool. But the best shimmer was outside in the deep, surrounding forest.

Before they removed their clothing and stepped into the Jacuzzi, Thaddeus had flicked a switch that sent magick to the woods– where dozens of tiny, white and gold lights– created, in their window-view, their very own enchanted forest.

In addition, the wind picked up just enough for the numerous chimes to serenade the couple with delightful, faerie-like music.

"There's something magickal about making love in water," Maggie breathed. She stroked his van dyke, "Maybe it's because we're water signs, Scorpios both." She sighed again at the intensity of the soothing, warm jets on her back, reaching for his hand. Smiling at him from beneath her lashes, she sent him a silent *I love you*. "If only ..."

"Only what?" He brushed a kiss on her temple.

"There could be an invention that bottled up a memory, like perfume. And it never faded. Never grew stale. And then, when one wanted it, the bottle could be uncorked, the memory unleashed, and it would be like living it all over again."

"Maggie, my Maggie," the professor drawled. "You are a poet in a world that is still learning the alphabet." He kissed her again. "Tonight was quite nice, wasn't it?" he smiled warmly down at her.

"Hmmmmmm, it's like we're inside a big, bubbling cauldron that serves the Goddess." She closed her eyes and felt his warm breath at her ear, as he posed the question she knew he wanted to ask.

"Ooooooh yes," she whispered in return. "Let's do it all."

His eyes were full of a fire Maggie had never before seen. "Our love does serve the Goddess, Maggie. Don't you know that?" He slid slippery, magickal hands along her sides, cupping her breasts, his thumbs massaging, before lowering his mouth to first one, then the other.

Maggie reclined her head and ran her hands over the back of his neck and head. "Hmmmmmm," she moaned, eager for more.

She did not hold back her groans as he lifted her backside. In a moment, they moved in unbroken perfection.

Oh, how she enjoyed their lovemaking. The pace her lover set seemed near-impossible to sustain, but Maggie knew not to underestimate her professor. He had stamina and strength like no other lover she had ever experienced– and Maggie had had many lovers. But tonight, oh tonight, he was proving himself beyond belief.

"Ooooooooh, Dr. Weatherby," she arched against him to draw him deeper inside her. "I love it when you're naughty! Hmmm … yes! Don't stop!"

Sensing her near end, he brought his mouth down on hers, as they swirled together, and she felt as though she were drowning in him, the man she had come to revere as so much more than a lover– before he again plunged her over the edge with rippling waves of pleasure.

***

Earlier, when Beau arrived at Tara, Raine was waiting for him, in anticipation of a significant dose of forest delight of their own making.

Several years prior, the Goth gal had commissioned, from a renowned San Francisco artisan, a mystical forest-bed. The sketch she presented him to create what became her bedroom suite, she had drawn from a vision.

The bed's legs were ultra-stout tree trunks complete with roots, while the head and foot boards were lacy networks of entwining limbs and gnarled branches. A matching tree-trunk nightstand and rustic, log-and-limb bench at the foot of the bed rendered a woodsy result that was positively bewitching.

The forest-bed ensemble, stained and shellacked a rich, glowing mahogany, blended nicely with the raven-haired Sister's other bedroom furniture, the heavy, antique rosewood pieces, inherited from Granny McDonough.

Under the mattress of her unique bed, Raine had tucked a special talisman infused with blessings of ultra-strong protection.

In concert with the Enchanted-Forest wallpaper (purchased years earlier in the Witch City of Salem) and the leafy Greenman-of-the-Woodlands collection of wall-tapestry, bedspread, and drapes, Raine's spacious, high-ceilinged bedchamber, especially in the glow of the lit green-marble fireplace, made her feel close to nature and the great Goddess. It was, she often said, "… like being in the great green-cathedral depths of a magickal forest." Raine had chosen the Greenman motif because he was the protector of the green world– as well as the symbolic reminder of the unity of male and female.

Passion is to witches as honey is to bears.

When the heavy drapes were open on the tall, leaded-glass windows in Raine's bedroom, the view of the violet-hued mountains, coupled with the nearer, mysterious tangle of inky-green woods, put the Sister in the magick and security of a faerie circle.

Another curious thing was that the glass in the diamond-paned windows was so old and so thick and wavy that looking through them was like gazing into a dream.

A cool breeze wafted the night-time music of the adjacent forest into the bedchamber. It was a damp, cool summer's eve, so Raine had asked Beau to light a fire. The crackling, dancing flames cast magickal shadows on the ceiling, the walls, and across the king-size forest-bed.

Lying on the bed in each other's arms, their lips were inches apart, and when he rolled her on her back, and his mouth came down on hers, his kiss was soft but insistent. Raine's bejeweled fingers curled round Beau's thick, ebony hair, gripping him, as the kiss deepened, and his large, strong hands traveled over her lithe body.

Tracing a finger along the Sister's full lips, he whispered, "You have witchcraft in your eyes, your lips. Do you know how much I enjoy kissing that pouty mouth of yours?" he asked. "Raven hair and ruby lips, sparks fly from your fingertips," he crooned from "Witchy Woman."

Raine laughed deep in her throat. "These little hands *have* performed magick."

He seized one of her hands, studying it for a moment. "Such small, graceful hands with such delicate fingers," he said quietly. "They belie the power they hold." He kissed the hand, his mustache teasing, as his mouth glided to the sensitive skin on the inside of her wrist.

After several moments, he paused, lifting his gaze, his dark-blue eyes holding her green ones. "You've got something on your mind. What is it?"

"I want you to make me forget about everything tonight. My head has been spinning with this mystery– the skeletons, if and how they are connected to our Hamlet's unsolved triple ax murders..." her tip-tilted emerald eyes narrowed a bit, "the secrets coveted by the descendants we've questioned–" her eyes widened again. "Make me forget all of it just for tonight, Beau."

His response was to kiss her again, continuing all the while to caress her.

Pulling back, he slid a hand along the gentle curve of her face. "I love how your eyes darken when you're aroused."

"Oh, baby, I am soo ready for you." Raine raised up a bit to whisper in his ear.

He lifted an ebony brow, then began an earnest exploration of her body, doing everything he knew she liked.

"Don't be a tease, big boy," Raine rumbled deep in her throat after several minutes had passed. "I've thought about this all day, and I want you now," she rasped.

"Why you little witch!" he tormented. "I think you'd better tell me again what it is you want exactly." He lowered himself to her, kissing her lips, her face and neck, as she again breathed her desires into his ear, ending her demands with a flick of her tongue.

He gave her his sexy grin. "I love it when you're wickedly witchy, and I see that tonight you're packin' an extra-measure of wicked witch."

Raine thrust her hips upward, using her hands to push him off her. Catlike, she stretched, her eyes glittering, as her hand lowered to her belly and slowly traveled south. "And I intend to get even more wicked," she drawled.

"You sexy little witch," he groaned, reaching out a hand to massage her breast.

"Ooooooooooooh, yessssssss ..." she screamed in an elongated sigh, "that's exactly what I am, and that's why you love me. I think you're enjoying this even more than I am." Her eyes were half-closed, and a half-smile curved her glossy, red lips. "I'm even more ready now, Beau," she purred, "are you?"

He reached down and yanked her toward him, her long legs wrapping round him and gripping his hips. Then he lifted her tight, little tush and pushed himself into her.

"Beau," she squealed, "tell me what *you* want!"

"I want *you*, little witch. I've always wanted you, from the first moment I saw you years ago. I want you every day, every way I can have you." He pushed harder. "And I mean to make you mine!"

"Then take me, take me harder and deeper and stronger than ever you have!"

He reached up to brush her wispy ebony bangs from her eye, and she saw, in a flash, as she had in the past– via the Sight and what she had come to believe was former-life memory– the entwined blue serpents of Avalon, symbolizing wisdom and power, that braceleted his wrist. As they had on previous occasions, the serpents seemed to writhe, and when they did, she felt something beyond description flood her entire essence. It was at once unsettling– and unbearably exciting.

"Take me, Beau ... *ravish* me!"

He did not disappoint, and it wasn't long before Raine screamed his name in ecstasy, "Beau! Beau, you're magick ... *magick!*"

"Yes," he answered with an especially strong thrust, echoing her earlier response to him, his low, resonant voice seeming to come from a distant time and place, "that's exactly what I am, and it is why I will soon make you completely mine– *forever*."

Chapter Eleven

Whilst the Sisters motored up the lane that wound its sinuous way through the woods to the top of Manor Hill, three pairs of McDonough eyes gazed in the direction of the eminent Fane mansion. As they drew closer, the great house took shape before them, dark and surprisingly sinister. The trees and shrubbery were badly in need of trimming, and the whole property gave the impression of neglect.

"Looks like the kind of place Dracula would choose for a residence," Raine quipped.

"Oh now, Tara would look like that too," Maggie countered, "if we traveled for most of the year. Very possibly old Mr. Steward, Mada's caretaker, can't handle it all anymore, especially with the relentless rain we've been experiencing this spring and summer. *Our* yard boy told us just last week that he's so far behind, due to all the rain, he won't be getting to our hedges for another week or so, and they sure need attention."

"Other than the overgrown vegetation, I don't think Fane Manor looks that bad," Aisling said. "It's the kind of place that would grow on you."

"Oh, I think something would grow on us, if we lived there. Well," Raine relented after a pensive moment, "the turrets are awe-inspiring. And that blue slate roof likely cost more than our Tara."

"You'd look spooky too, Sister, if you were over a hundred years old," Aisling joked, sending Raine a grin in the rear view mirror. Maggie shared the front seat of Aisling's black SUV with the blonde Sister. Raine was in the back.

Finding that she was free for a few hours today, the blonde with the wand had offered to pick Raine and Maggie up at Tara, then drive the three of them to Mada Fane's for the scheduled interview. As they continued on, up the lane to the house, Aisling stole a glance out the vehicle's side window to catch sight of an old gravestone in the woods. "I think one of the Fane ancestors is actually buried on this property."

"Great-Aunt Merry McDonough is over a hundred, and she doesn't look at all spooky," Raine retorted to Aisling's quip.

"Mada's expecting us at four for tea," Maggie reminded, glancing at her watch. "We're about five minutes early, but I don't think she'll mind."

***

At about the same time as the Sisters were arriving at Fane Manor, train Nellie was standing before her bathroom mirror, preparing to brush her teeth. She had taken the day off from the small publishing house that employed her to get caught up with some editing chores in the solitude of her home. After working for hours without a break, she decided to get dressed and go out for a breath of air and a bite to eat.

Just as she brought the toothbrush to her mouth, the bathroom mirror filled with a swirling white mist. Taken aback, the stunned woman dropped the toothbrush in the sink, drawing in her breath. Rapidly, the bloody image of her ancestor, the axed Nellie Triggs, took shape within the swirl, staring with sad eyes at her great-niece from that glass portal to the Other Side.

Alarmed and horrified, train Nellie could not move as she stared at the grisly figure in the mirror. The face, head and collar bone were severely hacked and covered with gore, but there was no doubt in train Nellie's mind who the ghost was. She remembered that an uncle told her, years before, that he had seen an apparition of axed Nellie, but *she* never expected to! Nothing like this had *ever* happened to her!

Now, as she stood, immobile, before the mirror, it was as though she were trapped in an eerie nightmare, and her legs and feet had turned to lead. She tried to open her mouth to form the words, "What do you want?" But like her feet, her lips would not respond.

However, the apparition seemed to catch her thought, for in the next instant, the ghostly image vanished, leaving behind, in its stead, a message. It manifested, one letter at a time, printed via an invisible ghostly finger, backwards on the fogged mirror. Nonetheless, its meaning was clear– "Help me!"

***

Fane Manor's heavy, ornate door creaked opened to reveal the mistress of the Manor– a medium-build woman with short, honey-blonde hair and eyes of a vague color, neither green, nor blue, nor grey, but rather, a mélange of all three. "Do come in," she said in a pleasant voice.

"I hope we're not disturbing you and intruding on your work. Our request was rather short notice," Maggie said.

"Bosh, not at all! My privilege and my pleasure." Mada reached both her hands out to the Sisters. "My invitation was rather short notice. I'm glad you could come. I rattle round this big old house like a lost soul, but I have to come home once in a while to check on things."

The Sisters entered the manse, looking about with unabashed interest, as they stepped into the grand foyer with its high, ornate ceiling and huge, baroque brass and crystal chandelier.

In those few moments, the Sisters eyed their hostess attentively, with eager curiosity. She was wearing a shin-length, khaki safari dress, the short sleeves rolled up even shorter. Her feet were shod in soft, black leather ballet slippers. As Eva had mentioned, Mada appeared to be wearing no makeup other than a touch of lipstick, and her nearly perfect skin was radiant.

"Our friend, Eva Novak, was right," Raine blurted. "You *do* resemble Bette Midler!"

The welcoming woman before them gave a short laugh, inclining her blonde head. "Not, I hope, the way she looked in *Hocus Pocus!*"

"One of our favorite films," Raine returned with a grin, "but the answer to your query is 'Most certainly not.' In fact, I meant it as a compliment."

"I'm certain you did, dear," Mada replied in a warm tone. "But the resemblance ends there. Don't ask me to sing anything for you. I can't carry a tune in a basket," she laughed again.

The Sisters introduced themselves properly, after which Mada said, "I apologize for the exterior of the Manor. The old place probably looked like a haunted house to you as you were driving up. Mr. Steward just can't keep up like he used to, and what with all this rain. The poor old thing keeps insisting it's not too much for him, but I told him this week I'm going to hire a service to take care of all the cutting and trimming from now on. He can stay on as caretaker for the house only, at the same wage."

The very next second, the older woman's face showed concerned. "Oh dear me! I'm so sorry to keep you standing here. Please come this way. I've prepared the library for our tea." She gestured with sweeping motion for the Sisters to enter the spacious area to their left.

"What a fascinating room!" Maggie exclaimed.

Now that they were inside, the Sisters couldn't help but be charmed with the stately home and its mistress.

"Thank you," Mada was saying in response to Maggie's compliment. "I travel so much that I have Mr. Steward cover all the furniture with sheets. Nowadays, when I'm here, I just leave most of the rooms that way. Sign of getting older, I guess. It's just too much trouble to uncover all the furniture in the rooms I don't even use. But the library is one of the rooms I always use. "Do sit down and make yourselves comfortable." She indicated the couch and overstuffed chairs, positioned in front of a yawning, black-marble fireplace, unlit on such a warm summer's day as this one.

Dozens of leather-bound books lined the walls, along with what the Sisters were sure were valuable oil paintings of various places in the world. There was a sliding library ladder, and old-fashioned torchiere lamps stood next to the room's overstuffed chairs. In the center of the high, baroque ceiling was a large plaster medallion, busy with scrolls that swirled and looped to resemble four capital-letter Ps connected in the center with a fancy star-burst. However, the Sisters soon noted that the most interesting items in the room were the curiosities and souvenirs from all the exotic places in the world Mada and her family had visited and explored.

It was obvious by her expression that Mada was pleased with their reaction to her library. It was apparent, too, that this was her favorite room in the sumptuous residence. Her face beamed, as she brought her hands together in delight, "You know what happens, don't you, in these grand old houses at four o'clock? *Tea!* And it almost makes the property taxes worth it. *Almost*," she winked.

"We thoroughly enjoy our teatimes too," Raine concurred. "Every day, no matter what we have going on. There's nothing nicer than returning home to a tray of readied, waiting tea things."

"If you'll excuse me, I won't be long." As Mada started from the room, the Sisters asked, nearly simultaneously, "May we help?"

"No need," the older woman replied with a smile, "I have everything ready. I'll bring it all in on a teacart. Make yourselves comfortable. Look around, if you wish."

All three of the Sisters took advantage of their hostess' invitation to peruse the bookshelves and curiosities about the room, exchanging looks over some of the items in Mada's varied– and what they immediately deemed *valuable*– collection, items from the Mayan, Aztec, Egyptian, Celtic, and Native American cultures, particularly the Pawnee.

Raine sent Maggie the extrasensory message: *Some of these things must be worth a king's ransom!*

If they're real, Maggie shot back, peering closer at the artifacts. *And they do look to be genuine.*

My educated guess, or witchy gut, is telling me that they are, Raine returned.

Several moments later, Maggie stopped short in her tracks when she noticed, in a sealed glass case in a far corner of the library– a shrunken head. "Do you suppose *that's* real?" she whispered to Raine, who was standing next to her perusing a book on the Jivaro Indians of the Amazon.

I don't know, Raine answered telepathically; for, at that express moment, Mada re-entered the room, pushing an Italian inlay teacart toward them, laden with all the things one could imagine for a most delectable teatime.

"Ah," Mada observed, "I see you have an interest in the Jivaro headhunters. A *fascinating* culture. I've conducted several field studies among the Jivaro." She locked the cart's wheels. "I'm cognizant of the fact that your parents are celebrated archaeologists–and I must confess they're the main reason I was so eager to meet you. Have they ever done field work on the Jivaro?"

"Only *our* parents are archaeologists," Raine replied, indicating herself and Maggie. "And, in answer to your question, yes, they've studied the Jivaro, as well as other Shuar Indians of the upper Amazon." She glanced over at the blonde Sister, remarking, "Aisling's parents were in law-enforcement, as were she and her husband before they opened their own detective agency."

Mada began pouring the tea. "I see. Archaeologists, detectives, historians," she looked to the Sisters, "they all connect the dots, don't they?"

"We say that all the time!" Raine and Maggie chorused.

"You seem to know something about us," Aisling said, accepting a cup of tea from their hostess.

Mada gave an assenting nod. "Our mutual friend Eva told me a bit about you. As I said," she handed Maggie a filled cup, "I admire your parents' many contributions to archaeology." She handed a steaming cup of the fragrant tea to Raine. "We're not going to be formal, my dears. Just help yourselves to whatever you want in your tea, so you can enjoy it just as you like it. And don't be shy about taking whatever you wish from the cart to accompany it. If you don't eat it, it will go to waste. I'm not much for sweets. Everything's fresh from the deli this morning." The older woman flashed them a winning smile. "I've never been devoted to the home duties of a domestic woman."

A silver tray of dainty sandwiches, along with a triple-tiered platter of scones, muffins, and a large square of rich plum cake shared space atop the teacart with the four-o'clock beverage, sugar, cream, lemon wedges, butter, jams, dessert plates, silverware, and napkins. The Sisters noted that the antique china was egg-shell thin and hand-painted from Bavaria, and the tea service and flatware were sterling.

"What a treat!" Raine squealed in delight, resisting the childlike urge to clap hands. Mada's afternoon tea reminded her of both Granny's and Great-Aunt Merry McDonough's.

The Sisters helped themselves from the teacart before returning to the long, brown leather sofa, where the three of them sat, resting their plates before them on the massive, rose-marble coffee table.

Mada took a seat opposite them, in a matching leather chair positioned next to a small table and lamp.

"We feel at a bit of a disadvantage," Aisling began. "Why don't you tell us a little about yourself? Based on your collection of books and curiosities alone, you must live an exciting life."

"I do *that*." Mada observed the magickal threesome over the brim of her delicate teacup for a musing moment before answering. "I was born with the proverbial silver spoon in my mouth, and truth is, I wouldn't have to work; but, the further truth is, I **want** to. I must, you see. I can't stop working, for I absolutely *love* what I do."

"And that is what exactly?" Aisling prompted kindly.

Mada laughed heartily. "What a leading question! Yes, I can see that you're a good detective, my dear. Like Raine and Maggie's parents, I conduct field studies all over the world. In some of the world's most remote areas. Doctorates in both archaeology and anthropology. I lecture and I write. I never married, never had children, not even a pet. *No time*." She shrugged. "Life's a trade-off."

The academic's faintly bitter smile hinted that there had been a love of her life, at some point, someone whose memory was registered, *secreted*, in her heart.

"I presume you're cognizant of the fact that I've written several books on my studies and findings." Mada's eyes were searching. "I was wondering if your parents," she regarded Raine and Maggie, "ever mentioned my work? I very much admire theirs."

"Yes," Maggie and Raine answered in sync, with Raine continuing, "they've mentioned your work several times, relating on more than one occasion how impressed they are with what you've achieved, are achieving, along your chosen path."

"*We* are familiar with your books as well," Maggie added. "And we've referred to them, from time to time, in our classrooms. Your excavations, study and analysis of the Plains Indians, such as the Pawnee … *impressive*, to say the least."

"You flatter me, but thank you. Probably sounded like I was fishing. Honestly, I wasn't. There are so many legends yet to explore, so many mysteries just waiting to–" Mada tilted her head, as though puzzling over something, and her face took on a bemused air. "Oh yes," she said in sudden realization, "Eva did say you teach *both* archaeology and history."

Dr. Fane took a sip of tea. "I met the joint head of Haleigh College's archaeology and anthropology departments ... oh, several years ago now. Dr. Yore, isn't it?" She picked up an egg salad sandwich to take a dainty bite.

"That's correct. Dr. Yore," Raine and Maggie replied.

"She's rather a quaint figure, isn't she?" Mada asked, taking another sip of her tea. "Not waiting for a response, she rushed on, "Does she still sport those long capes and that staff?"

"Yes," the professor Sisters smiled, "she does."

"Makes me think of Dr. Mead." She cocked her head in reflection. "I met Margaret Mead at Columbia, back in the early seventies it was. I was with my father. A captivating woman, and a great teacher. She convinced me to go straight through for both my doctorates."

Mada set her teacup down on the stand next to her. "You said your parents *did* conduct field study among the Jivaro?"

"They did, several years ago when they were still working at the Smithsonian," Maggie replied. She drank some tea. "I must ask you, Dr. Fane—"

"Please, dear, call me 'Mada.' As I said, no need for formalities. You want to know if, in my objects garnered for remembrance and study, the shrunken head is real. Am I right?"

Maggie gave a quick nod, crossing her legs and smoothing the skirt of the vintage navy-blue and white dotted-Swiss dress she was wearing.

"Real, yes. And quite old, from the early 1900s. It was part of my great-grandparents' collection. I inherited a good many things from them." She paused, as though recalling a family memory, her eyes sweeping the room, as a faint smile curved her lips. "I know I should sell this old place, but it's difficult to part with so many memories. God knows I don't need the money. Really, I should donate this house and the acreage around it to the Hamlet for whatever the town deems best for its use. I think it would make a fine school, a private school. Or perhaps I'll just donate the entire property– land, house, and most of the furnishings to Haleigh College. That appeals to me. *It does*," she beamed as if with sudden solution.

"That would be quite generous," Raine and Maggie echoed Aisling's thought.

Mada lifted her shoulders, spreading her hands, palms up. "My family carries a reputation for being generous. Several philanthropists in the family, you know, with each generation. I don't want to be lacking in my responsibilities to uphold our name. I think when one is blessed with great wealth, one ought to put back into the system. It's always been the Fane philosophy."

"Have you any relatives remaining in this area?" Aisling asked of a sudden.

Something flickered in Mada's eyes, something that the Sisters recognized as fear, though it was there for a mere second, peering out quickly then retreating to the deep recesses of mind and heart.

"No!" Dr. Fane's voice promptly tempered. "No family around here. Not anymore. Any relatives I have reside abroad," the older woman replied dryly.

"Oh, yes, I do recall hearing something about that," Maggie stated. "Are you close with them?"

Mada swallowed, lowering her eyes for a moment before answering. "Not really. I don't have time for family gatherings. My work demands my full attention; or, at least, I give the work my full attention." She raised a hand to flick back a wisp of honey-blonde hair from her forehead, and that's when the Sisters noticed the large, ornate ring she was wearing.

"I can't help admiring your ring," Raine said. "It's very unusual."

Mada glanced at her hand bearing the large ring with its ebony stone set in heavy, ornate silver. "It's quite old." She chortled, her gaze again drifting over the room, "Like everything here. Something else I inherited from my great-grandmother. The stone is black tourmaline."

"Ancient magicians relied on black tourmaline for protection," Aisling declared.

"Yes," Raine averred. "It's a premier talisman for protection."

"Among other strong properties," Maggie added.

"If you believe in that sort of thing," Mada countered, lifting her teacup to her lips.

"Don't you?" Maggie asked, raising a brow. "As a renowned anthropologist *and* archaeologist, I'd wager you do–"

"I'm busted," Mada cut in with a delightful laugh. "You got me on that one. I *do* believe that real magick exists." She stood and picked up the teapot, refilling her guests' cups, then her own, before returning the engraved silver vessel to the cart.

Raine regarded her for those few moments, saying nothing more. The look was speculative, and the Sister's attention was riveted. "I suppose you *can't help believing*."

Mada gave a little chuckle, as though remembering a private joke. "Oh yes, *real* magick does exist," she pronounced softly, bobbing her blonde head slowly. "What I can't help from doing is returning to what we were talking about earlier. I could speak for hours on the Jivaro and their Amazon home. And speaking of magick, *there* be magick." She closed her eyes for a few seconds, saying, "It's a *mystic* land of deep forests pitted with lagoons and laced by lazy rivers– a vast green marshland where the sun only *attempts* to shine. The Amazon forest possesses such *power* and watchfulness– like the ever-present witch-doctor among his native flock."

Mada stared moodily off into space, as though recalling a particular incident of her field studies. "Unknowable," she muttered almost to herself, "the Jivaro and the region itself– each a mystery forever.

"*True*," she nodded to the Sisters, "the region of the upper Amazon, the goal of *countless* quests, will forever remain a mystery, as will the Jivaro themselves, their faces painted with magickal symbols. *Forever and ever a mystery*."

The scholarly woman leaned forward, her elbows on her knees, and it was evident she was enjoying herself, for she sensed that she held her audience in rapt concentration. "The Jivaro are such *free* spirits, you know. *Wonderfully* free! The only authoritative voice they obey is the power of the witch-doctor, who, as I said, is ever-present among them." A sudden thought struck her, interrupting her words. "I had– and this was a so-called educated person– ask me once at one of my lectures, what I thought of the savages of the Amazon. The Jivaro are not savages!

"There are no such things as savages! All peoples are civilized. True, some, like the Jivaro, may stand low on the scale of civilization, but they have their place there." Mada cocked her blonde head. "Those," she made imaginary quote marks with her fingers, "*savages* have many admirable traits. I admire, for instance, how free they are from the tyranny of time. They wake with the hum and buzz of insects, they eat and sleep when they feel the need.

They are not dictated to by time, as we are, and time has had no real effect on them."

"What say you about their cruelty, Dr. Fane?" Maggie queried.

Mada turned a startled face toward that Sister. "The Jivaro don't have atomic bombs that can destroy the planet X-times over. They are no crueler than we. I wouldn't say they are crueler than other tribes, as many have labeled them. Rather, I would say they are less compromising than their neighbors. They've made no concessions, refusing, time and again, to betray their proud past."

"Ah," said Maggie, making a tactful sound and digesting the details of Mada's absorbing account, "the Jivaro seem to have captured both your admiration and your respect."

Mada did not answer. She was staring in front of her at nothing. Finally, the lauded academic returned her regard to the Sisters. "One must experience their culture, *any* culture, first hand. If that is not possible, then the trick is not to judge. I tell my audiences that they should take a step back, with a deep breath, and actually look at something with a different perspective. But most people won't do that. Hah!" she exclaimed abruptly, "lest *I* judge!"

Dr. Fane's expression softened. "I often close my lectures with this: We can't sit still and let life lap around us. We have to *plunge* into it! The whole point of life is to experience a little of everything; and," she smiled, picking up her teacup and lifting it in a toasting motion, "I think life's better when there're a few surprises tossed into the mix." She set her cup in its saucer with an almost satisfied sigh.

The Sisters weren't sure what she meant by that last; but before they could ask, Mada, having settled back in her chair, posed a question of her own. "Now," she said, folding her hands in her lap, "suppose you tell me the *real* reason for your visit here to Fane Manor. If I can help you in any way, I surely will. I am quite cognizant of your good works. Works I heartily approve of, by the way. And mind, I don't dispense my approval too readily, but I do take my various hats off to you three."

Mada looked keenly at the Sisters for a long, studying moment. "I was just thinking that it's a good thing you're on the right side of the law. You'd be holy terrors if you weren't!" she laughed.

Over the brims of their teacups, the Sisters swapped glances.

"The reason for our visit," Aisling began in a professional tone, "is to ask if you'd be willing to share with us any stories passed down in your family in regard to the unsolved triple ax murders that took place in our Hamlet back in 1932." The blonde Sister bent forward and, reaching inside her bag, extracted a pen and small notepad.

Mada looked thoughtful for a moment before answering. "Whew," she blew out her breath, "that was *way* before my time, but it's family stories you're after and not memories. I'd be most willing to share such stories with you; but I can't think of any right off the bat, as the saying goes. I may need a little time." She tapped a finger to her temple. "I've got a lot of material stored up here, ladies. And sometimes, nowadays, I need a little time to search through the files," she grinned.

"Perhaps we can help to jar your memory," Maggie said kindly. "We know that the woman who was axed, along with her children and elderly mother, worked for your great-grandparents. Her name was Nellie Triggs, if that helps you."

Mada's expression revealed that the name unlocked something in her mind's vast vault of information. "That name *has* triggered several things. I recall my grandparents and later my parents verbalizing about those murders, how they were a shock to the whole community. My grandparents," she furrowed her brow, "yes, yes, I recall they remembered their parents saying that no one could imagine why anyone would've wanted to harm that good woman and her household. I can recall once– oh, I was just a youngster– when the local newspaper rehashed the entire account. This, of course, would've been years after the murders occurred. I heard my grandparents and my parents discussing it, and the one thing that leaps to my mind is how much my great-grandparents appreciated Nellie Triggs. I believe they put her in charge of their antique and curiosity shop. They traveled a lot, and they needed a shop manager they could wholly trust. They trusted her, and they liked her very much. That I recall vividly from family discussion about the murders."

Raine's cell phone sounded with the music of Rowena of the Glen's *Book of Shadows* echoing numinously in the high-ceilinged library. She immediately snatched the phone from her purse, speaking to the caller in a low voice before looking up at Mada. "Excuse me," the raven-haired Sister said, sliding out of her chair and coming quickly to her feet, "May I take this call out in the foyer? It's rather important."

"Of course," Mada replied. Then, turning toward the two remaining Sisters, she asked, "I know you've a reputation for solving mysteries; but, if I may ask, why are you delving into such a cold case?" In a flash, her face changed again, and the flicker of fear the Sisters had caught earlier returned now, peering from the older woman's eyes and rendering her speechless for a protracted moment. "The skeletons!" She nearly jumped out of her chair. "You think those skeletons are a possible connection to the Hamlet's unsolved ax murders!"

The Sisters exchanged quick looks, with Aisling answering, "It's too early to tell, but we are looking for a connection, yes."

Mada let out a held-in breath, but the fear in her eyes lingered.

The Sisters pretended not to notice her manner, how quiet it had become, with her sudden reluctance to speak further about the ax murders.

"Surely there is no connection," Mada said after a long pause in the conversation. "Think about it. This was, for many decades in the past, a busy railroad hub, and during those lean years of the Great Depression, many vagrants rode the rails through this area, searching for work, hoping for it, since this area was steeped in industry. Perhaps–"

"We know where you're going with this," Aisling interjected. "Vagrants camped out in Hoovervilles. Those who passed away in those camps– the unearthed skeletons– were buried by others in the cam–"

"Those who were *murdered* in the camps buried by whoever killed them for whatever they could get hands on– a couple of dollars, pennies even, warm clothing, shoes." Mada sat back in her chair, concluding, "That makes more sense to me than the unearthed skeletons somehow connected to the ax murders."

"Certainly your scenario is something to consider, as we're connecting the mystifying dots," Aisling said with conviction.

"So many people around here lost everything during those hungry years," Mada said adamantly, "and when people are hungry, and their families, their *children*, are hungry, they'll do things they normally wouldn't do. Just about anything, in fact, including murder. That's what I think. If you'll permit me an educated deduction– and I've been studying human behavior longer than I care to mention– those skeletons are not connected to the ax murders. If forensics show that those individuals were murdered, then it was by other vagrants for what they could get from the victims, as I said, money, clothing, a piece of jewelry or anything they could sell for food."

"We have not established, or mentioned, that the skeletons were vagrants," Aisling said point-blank.

Mada cocked her head, "I read in the paper that they were, and though I don't put much stock in the media, I would have to say it makes the most sense, given that the paper also stated that no one was ever reported missing in the Hamlet then, except–" The scholarly woman stopped short, saying, "Something just popped into my mind. Have you interviewed a descendant of one of the Hamlet's historic figures, J.D. Means? There is a descendant of his still living in town. I just ran into her the other day, at the Tearoom actually." She pursed her lips. "But I can't think of her name right now."

"Josie," Raine supplied, reentering the library from the hall. "That's who just rang me on the phone. She wants to talk with us again," she delivered to her two cousins and sisters of the moon, "*tomorrow* evening."

Mada cleared her throat. "Please don't think that I was *disparaging* your theory," her expression and tone were apologetic, "that the Hamlet's unsolved ax murders and the skeletons have some connection. Truly, I was not. I am cognizant of your abilities as super-sleuths. I was only attempting to lend a bit of help. As an anthropologist, I have studied human behavior all over the globe for most of my life, and I can tell you this– the world over, desperate people will resort to desperate actions. When people are starving and cold *and afraid*, when their *children* are starving, they will resort to just about anything– and that 'anything' includes murder."

"Levitation, Dr. Fane," Raine blurted, "you mean to say that nobody's incapable of murder?!"

Mada tilted her blonde head. "I have often wondered."

The Sisters traded quick glances, with Maggie replying, "In a way, we're all like the moon. We all have a dark side. I think each of us is–"

"Oh, I know what you're thinking!" Mada exclaimed. "We're all capable of killing when it comes to self-defense, but *murder*, murder is something else again. With all due respect, ladies, *think*. What I'm really talking about here is– *survival*. And isn't that a form of self-defense, self-preservation?"

With a bit of a flourish, Mada drained her teacup and set it down on the end table next to her chair. "Talking about this has released another memory for me. Discussion always frees memories, doesn't it? I remember my grandparents saying, when I was a child, how worrisome it was for my great-grandparents during the Depression years. Adrian Fane, my great-grandfather, had a true gift for making money, a sixth sense, if you will, about it all. Oh, he might've done a few things that would be harshly judged today, but he was no worse than his contemporaries in that pre-income-tax era when whatever you could make was yours to keep. Regulations were virtually non-existent in business, banking, and in the stock market. My great-grandfather and his colleagues were all ruthless entrepreneurs, fiercely competitive every one of them. Adrian was not unique in that. How he was unique, as I said, was the sixth sense he had for making money– and keeping it.

"Not long before the Stock Market Crash, he had a bad feeling, and he pulled all his money out of the market. During the Depression, he actually *made* money by investing in real estate and liquor. He scarfed up oil and other shares cheap, and I think," she inclined her head in a pensive gesture, "yes, he even invested in a new thing called 'supermarkets.' So there he was, he and my great-grandmother Elsa living in this magnificent house while so many were homeless, out-of-work, and hungry.

"Though he and my great-grandmother gave a lot of money to numerous charities, it was still pretty disquieting for them at that time. Those Hoovervilles and hobo encampments drew a lot of rough characters, so you can imagine and comprehend, I am certain, my great-grandparents' concerns. We all know how much crime escalated during the Great Depression."

Mada smiled then, a warm smile that came across as genuine. "That's all I was attempting to do. You must forgive me. I am so used to lecturing, that I seem to do it all the time now, and I can get emotional when I lecture. But I shouldn't be lecturing you, my guests. Forgive me, please."

"No offense taken," Aisling replied, looking up from her notepad.

Mada gave a little nod. "I trust I've been of service to you."

"You've given us a lot to think about; that's for certain," Raine replied.

Mada thought for a moment, adding, "When old Jim Dandy's bank failed at the county seat, in the wake of the market crash, that really caused crime around here to run rampant, as I'm certain you history professors know quite well. My great-grandparents weren't the only ones who feared for their lives. If I recollect rightly, J.D. Means feared for his life from a large number of people around here who lost everything when his bank went under. They blamed him personally, and several of them actually threatened to kill him.

"Well, history is not my forte, as it is yours, so I'll say no more about that, or I'll be lecturing again, and this time, preachin' to the converted," she laughed. "I will say this, though, it's good that you're garnering as many facts as you can before rushing to judgement. Shows how professional you three gals are."

A half-hour later, the Sisters were comparing notes on Mada Fane, as Aisling headed the large, black SUV down the hill and away from the imposing mansion.

Looking out the vehicle's rear window for a last look at the Manor, Raine said, "There's no doubt in my mind that something or someone frightens her. And it seems to me, the first sign of that fear became visible when we asked her if she had any other relatives still residing here in the Hamlet."

"Hmm," Aisling mused, "and even more pronounced when you mentioned her relatives living abroad. I wonder if she's afraid of one or more of her family members?"

"That could very well be it! I think she's hiding something; and except for Eva and Kathy, so, it seems, is everyone else with whom we've spoken," Maggie added.

"That's precisely what I'm thinking," Aisling rejoined.

"And I think I love a good mystery," Raine quipped, as her smart phone sounded with Rowena of the Glen's song *The Creature*. She fished in her bag and answered the call, her deep voice rumbling, "Dr. McDonough here." After listening for a few seconds, her tip-tilted, emerald eyes grew large, and her jaw visibly dropped. **"What?!** Do you mean– What *do* you mean?!" She listened again. "Sure thing. Yes, yes, yes, I know the area. Give me the address."

"Who was that?!" Aisling and Maggie questioned as soon as Raine ended the call.

"Train Nellie. She just had a horrifying visit from her ancestor. Axed Nellie left her a chilling message on the bathroom mirror." Raine returned the phone to her purse. "Our present-day Nellie is

- 184 -

pretty shaken up. She asked if we could come right over." The Sister spouted the address.

"On our way!" Aisling voiced with fervor.

"Every good and valuable thing you do in life makes your world a better place to be." ~ The Sleuth Sisters

Chapter Twelve

A few minutes sufficed to hasten the Sisters, via Aisling's SUV, to train Nellie's not-too-distant home. En route, the Sisters decided that they should conduct a séance.

"We don't want you to be afraid," Aisling told train Nellie, whose qualms the magickal trio could easily read. "We won't let anything bad happen. Anyone filled with fear, skepsis, or any disrespect for the spirits and spirit world will jinx a successful séance.

"We know you aren't a skeptic, not after what you just witnessed in your mirror, and we know you aren't the type of person to disrespect the spirit world, but fear is the greatest of all the negatives, and there is *no* place for it when opening a portal to the Other Side. We don't want to draw anything dark with our conjuring," the blonde with the wand concluded.

"I understand," Nellie answered.

"Are all our cell phones turned off?" asked Aisling.

The others answered affirmatively, and Nellie moved to make sure the door was closed and locked.

Satisfied, the Sisters set about to prepare a sacred space in train Nellie's spic-and-span kitchen, so they could summon axed Nellie. Like Raine and Maggie, Aisling always carried a witch kit in the trunk of her vehicle. The kit contained white sage for smudging/cleansing; candles of various colors, depending on the spell or situation at hand; a wand; a large container of sea salt; a portable altar; *Book of Shadows*; and various other witch tools and necessities, such as a fire-starter, etc.

Aisling chose the kitchen for the séance due to the room's round table that would comfortably accommodate all four women. A round or oval table was the best for a séance. Nellie provided a clean, snowy-white tablecloth. The Sisters preferred to use a white or light blue tablecloth during a séance. It was a simple matter of preference, but they believed either of those colors aided in attracting only friendly spirits.

Raine lit three white sage-bundles that she placed in freshly scrubbed Pyrex dishes. In an instant, the air filled with the sweet, pungent aroma of the sage's good smoking essence. Maggie drew from Aisling's witch kit, three large feathers; and the Sisters began walking through train Nellie's small house, room by room—there were only six— wafting the smoke from the burning sage with the feathers whilst chanting, "We cleanse this home completely free of all evil and all negativity!"

After a few moments, they commanded Nellie to chant with them, as they continued on, each Sister smudging two rooms, with Nellie accompanying Aisling: "We cleanse this area completely free of all evil and all negativity!"

In every room, the Sisters feather-fanned the cleansing sage smoke, chanting their spell, walking slowly and deliberately, deosil— clockwise— making certain to fully smudge Nellie's home, every nook and cranny, letting the pungent smoke glide over everything, everywhere.

Once all the rooms were smudged, and the women were all back in the kitchen, Aisling, with her wand, drew a circle of protection.

In unison, the three Sisters began again to chant: "Wind spirit! Fire in all its brightness! The sea in all its deepness! Earth, rocks, in all their firmness! All these elements we now place, by God-Goddess' almighty strength and grace, between ourselves and the powers of darkness! So mote it be! Blessed be!" This, while Raine and Maggie gave the kitchen an extra smudging with the good white sage.

When that was accomplished, the magical threesome decided on an additional action— a "just-in-case," as Granny used to call it. After setting her still-smoking sage on the kitchen table, Raine concluded the cleansing ritual by sprinkling saltwater, with a hand-held sprinkler, widdershins— counterclockwise— around their kitchen circle, then walked her smoking smudge-bundle deosil— clockwise. *That*, the Sisters hoped, would have cleansed the area of any lingering negativity.

To prevent the smoke from choking them during the séance, they placed the still-burning smudge-bundles at different locations around the kitchen. Aisling drew a cone of dragon's blood incense from her kit and, touching her fire-starter to it, set it in a Pyrex dish on the kitchen counter.

Finally, Maggie dimmed the overhead kitchen light, as Aisling lit a large, white beeswax candle that she set in the center of the round table. The Sisters chanted a strong incantation of protection, ending with the petition, "God-Goddess between us and all harm!"

After a brief pause, Aisling cleared her throat, and, giving Raine and Maggie a signaling nod, the four women clasped hands round the table. "Nellie Triggs," the blonde Sister cried out, "we respectfully ask that you join us this evening!"

A weighty moment passed in silence.

Aisling gave another nod to her fellow sisters of the moon, and the three chanted, using the invocation taught them by Granny McDonough: "In peace and love, and by the Supreme Majesty of the God-Goddess, we evoke and conjure thee, Nellie Triggs! Come hither and join us! Come ye forth; we conjure thee, Nellie Triggs! Come ye forth!"

"Focus and believe," Aisling commanded. "Clear your minds of all doubt and negative thoughts. Be not afraid. Think loving thoughts. Nellie, you think about how much you love and respect your great-aunt, and how you want to help give her closure to rest in eternal peace."

"Nellie Triggs," the Sisters evoked again, "we ask that you honor us with your presence!"

Suddenly the candle in the center of the table began to flicker wildly.

"Nellie, are you here with us now?" Aisling, who was acting as the medium, questioned. "If you are here, give us a sign, please."

Again, the candle flame began to flicker wildly.

"Nellie, we want to help you. It is why we are gathered here this evening. Tell us what you want, please. Tell us whatever you want us to know; we entreat you." Aisling closed her eyes for a petitionary moment, then opened them, repeating the request.

The overhead kitchen light blinked off and on, and again the candle on the table shimmered frantically, this time nearly going out.

Aisling squeezed train Nellie's hand, sensing that she was becoming frightened. "Nellie, tell us what you want, please," the blonde Sister beseeched. "We gathered here to help you. We are trying to find out who did the evil thing to you and your family. We want to give you closure, so that you can rest in peace. What were you trying to tell your great-niece Nellie?"

With the door and window shut tight, a cold wind breezed over the women, as they continued to hold hands around the table. The kitchen soon became icy cold on a mid-summer's eve.

"She's going to tell us who the murderer is," Aisling whispered, squeezing again Nellie's hand. "I sense–"

Of a sudden, the blonde Sister's lithe body tightened, and she became more alert, her keen McDonough senses working at full-tilt. "Another spirit has entered our space. And it is not a good one," she whispered. "Spirit, who are you?!" she demanded in a loud, strong voice.

The glacial wind blew over the women again, this time with an evil laugh carried on its chill breath.

"Be gone!" the Sisters demanded loudly and firmly. "You were not invited here! You are *not* wanted here! Be gone with you! We cast you out in the name of the God-Goddess! In the name of all that is good and holy, in the name of Archangel Michael who holds the great sword of Light! **Be gone!**"

"This is an extremely *hostile* entity, ladies," Aisling stated quietly. "We must end the séance now and–" The blonde Sister broke off, indicating with a jerk of her head and the shift of her eyes to the far wall– where a large, sinister, black shadow had surfaced. The shadow appeared to be that of a man– a man wearing a fedora! It moved slowly toward the table where the women sat.

"Granny McDonough!" the Sisters called out with the sacred Power of Three. "Granny, we call on you to help us cast the evil from this space!"

Aisling could strongly sense train Nellie's rapidly escalating fear, as the woman screeched out a loud lament, and that fear was serving to make the tense situation even worse. It was breaking down their protective bubble of Light and opening the door even wider to the evil presence!

With a firm nod to her fellow sisters, and, at once, with force, Aisling led them in Granny McDonough's vanquishing chant anew: "Be thee gone, unwanted spirit! We cast you out in the name of the God-Goddess and their army of archangels, especially Archangel Michael! We cast thee out in the name of all that is good and clean and holy! **Be you gone!** You are not invited here!"

In tenacious response, the black shadow advanced closer. Accompanied by a disgusting, gagging odor, the foul odor of excrement, the entity hurled the filthiest of obscenities at them in a snarling, unearthly voice that sounded as if it came straight from the deepest pits of Hell.

How?! Raine and Maggie questioned, firing off to one another the following quick messages:

How could this evil entity have entered our sacred space after all the precautions we took?

It must be shockingly strong, the worst class of shadow entities!

These spirits are highly intelligent, capable of working powerful magick, and extremely devious.

Not only are they capable of psychic attacks, but physical ones as well!

Beware! But we mustn't alarm train Nellie!

Having picked up bits and pieces of Raine's and Maggie's thoughts, Aisling, her lips moving in a protective chant, squeezed train Nellie's hand; with the other, she squeezed Maggie's; and Maggie, in turn, squeezed Raine's, who pressed Nellie's other hand.

The raven-haired Sister was glad she was wearing the shielding aquamarine ring with which the High Priestess had gifted her at *Beltane*. All three Sisters were wearing their protective talismans; though, had they known, they would have carried with them their ancient stones, etched with images of the wild boar. The powerful stones were presented to them, this past spring, by High Priestess Violet of Orkney.

The wild boar glorified the McDonough coat of arms, and it was one of the Sisters' chief animal totems. Thus, Aisling chose to call upon this powerful icon as well, for the strength and courage it would provide them!

"I call upon Wild Boar, McDonough totem and companion of the warrior! Grant us courage and strength, via the grace of the God-Goddess, to carry on this fight to trounce evil!" Aisling repeated the plea twice more, with Raine and Maggie joining in. The Sisters understood that thrice was a charm, delivered each time with ever more confidence and energy.

The shadow-spirit was not vanquished yet; but due to the Sisters' joint powers, which the evil thing clearly sensed, it approached cagily.

When the dark force was nearly upon them, in one last defensive burst of the Power-of-Three energy, they chanted en force, their voices loud and strong– **"Granny McDonough! McDonough Wild Boar! Athena, Goddess of Wisdom and War! Come ye now to the fore! Spirits of Air, Earth, Fire and Sea, set us of this evil free!"**

The sinister shadow juddered to a dead stop; and, to the Sisters, it looked as if it recoiled, its eerie snarl and gagging stench hanging on the air.

With the warrior strength of their Irish granny and the Goddess of Wisdom and War, with the tenacity, courage and fighting spirit of the courageous McDonough Wild Boar, the Sisters bellowed in unison– **"Angels and Guardians of this spell, drive this evil back to Hell!"**

They had called upon Goddess Athena the previous year, when they needed to rid their theatre of evil; and now, they prayed their granny's vanquishing chant would again work its mighty, evil-effacing magick.

"Angels and Guardians of this spell, drive this evil back to Hell!"

Suddenly, with the full force of the Sisters' strong magick upon it, the uninvited entity again unleashed its revolting stench, the shadow whirling into an evil black mist that loomed dangerously above them.

"Angels and Guardians of this spell, drive this evil back to Hell!!"

Quick as an imp, a demonic face appeared within the murky vapor, its snarling features plunging toward the Sisters with an unearthly, spine-tingling shriek, the mouth open to reveal the terrifying fangs of a ferocious wild beast! The Sisters could smell its rotten breath, just as they felt the burning heat of its presence.

Nellie lost the grim struggle to control herself, letting out a loud scream– a scream that electrified Aisling.

"Hold!" the senior Sister commanded. **"HOLD!! Fear cannot defeat the McDonough Boar! The Boar embodies ancient primal POWER– and victory! The Boar fears not. The Boar does not retreat!! Hold, Sisters! HOLD!!"**

Unmoving, the stalwart Sisters, resonating with Aisling's firm command, could sense victory, for the malevolent specter, the split second before making contact with them, again abruptly shrank back with a bloodcurdling shriek.

Granny McDonough's spell was working!

"Be you gone, foul spirit! And never return! Be gone!!" the Sisters shouted, whilst Aisling waved her wand in a powerful vanquishing gesture: **"Magick of night! Magick of day! We banish all evil and harm away! Listen and hear the Call of Three! As we will it, so mote it be! SO MOTE IT BE!"**

With a final, horrifying screech, the evil suddenly vanished, for the present anyway, as the brave Sisters breathed a unified sigh of relief.

When Aisling looked at train Nellie, she saw, in the soft light, a ghostly pale woman, stiff as the proverbial board, but otherwise unharmed. The senior Sister knew to allow her to return to normal on her own.

Between two fingers, Aisling snuffed out the candle, then she turned up the overhead light. Suddenly, both Raine and Aisling noticed that Maggie looked to be in a trance, her eyes were glazed over, as she stared, unseeing, as stiff as train Nellie and unmoving in her chair.

"Do *not* touch her!" Aisling commanded loudly, throwing her arm in front of a swooping Raine. "Let her return to us on her own. If we allow that, she just might have a message for us from axed Nellie. I recognize the signs."

Catching Aisling's eye, Raine questioned, aloud this time, though keeping her voice to a whisper, "How did the uninvited entity get in? We took all the proper precautions, and–"

Train Nellie's face went even whiter as she stirred for the first time, attempting to shake herself free of the harrowing experience. She licked her dry lips and breathed in a shuddering voice, "It might be my fault."

The still-shaken woman sucked in a long breath of air, letting it out slowly, and her voice trembled as she went on. "After I received that message from my aunt in the mirror, and I got hold of myself, I dug out the old Ouija board I'd purchased at an antique shop in Salem. I bought it when I was attending that writers' conference in Boston, the one from which I was returning when I met you on the train. I'd toyed with the board on the trip, and it gave me the creeps. When I got home, I stashed the thing in the back of a closet." Catching Raine and Aisling's expressions, she finished in a whimpering tone, "But after my aunt's appearance in my bathroom mirror, I tried to contact her for more information."

"Levitation!" Raine cried out with her quick McDonough temper. "Why didn't you tell us that?!" The hot blood was pounding in her ears. "You didn't protect yourself, I'm guessing, and," her ebony brows flew together, "do you know how *dangerous* that is?! Do you?! We could have all been harmed, even physically!"

Aisling took firm hold of Raine's arm. "Settle down, Sister." To train Nellie, she said, "You should have told us. Raine's right. Using an instrument of magick to open a portal to the Other Side without knowing how to protect yourself is downright foolhardy and reckless. As Raine said– *dangerous*. I want you to give us that board before we leave this house. Have you any other such tools of magick?"

Train Nellie shook her head miserably. "No," she uttered in a weak voice. "I'm *so* sorry. *Extremely sorry*. I didn't realize." Her tears, very near the surface, glistened in her eyes, and she gave a sudden, quick shiver. "The whole thing is such a horrible, *dreadful* nightmare!"

"It's OK," Aisling softened, reaching a hand out to Nellie. "We've vanquished the evil, and we learned that there *is* an evil entity who, I think," she received a like-minded nod from Raine, "just might be the murderer on the prowl. The fact that–" she stopped short, when Maggie shifted in her chair, a moan escaping her lips.

Aisling and Raine stood on either side of Maggie, who remained upright in the kitchen chair at the table, unmoving though her emerald eyes looked normal now. "Maggie, are you all right?" the Sisters resounded.

Maggie bobbed her head but remained seated and still.

"Maggie, have you received a message from axed Nellie?" the blonde Sister asked softly.

"Athena," Maggie uttered. She shook her head, as if to clear it, blowing out her breath. Tilting her fiery red head from side to side, the Sister loosened her stiff neck. Then she stood and stretched in her feline manner, the color returning to her face.

"What does she mean?" train Nellie asked, nervously wringing her hands, concern and confusion mirrored on her features. "Is she referring to the chant you used to vanquish the evil spirit?" She blinked back tears, and the Sisters noted that her hands were shaking.

"No," Raine and Aisling answered together, their identical McDonough eyes locking.

"She's referring to our crystal ball," Raine whispered to Aisling, who nodded her agreement, her emerald eyes narrowing with determination.

"That was just about the most challenging séance we ever conducted," Maggie affirmed, completely herself now. "I had a vision of both Granny and Auntie Merry. They were holding our crystal ball Athena, extending it to me, as if telling me it was time to consult it."

Her sisters of the moon each put their arms around the striking redhead, drawing, in a twinkling, train Nellie, too, into their circle of love and protection.

"Good job, all of you," the senior Sister stated with pride. "You all showed real courage tonight! When someone surrenders to something evil, it hurts the whole world." Aisling smiled warmly on the other women, who returned the gesture. Even Nellie managed a brave smile, as the love vibration flowed round their enfolding circle to rejuvenate each of them. It was an *empowering* sensation.

"Let us not neglect to thank and to end our ritual in the proper way," the blonde with the wand reminded. "We'll need to smudge this room and the entire house again before we leave," she charged.

Without further delay, the Sisters thanked the God-Goddess for protecting them and aiding them in their work. They thanked their angel and spirit guides, principally Archangel Michael, their Granny McDonough and Auntie Merry, the Goddess Athena, as well as the McDonough Wild Boar. And they thanked axed Nellie Triggs' spirit for attempting to communicate with them. They then opened the circle and released all energies.

Nearly an hour later, en route to Raine and Maggie's Tara, Aisling advised they wait till the following day, when they would be fresh, to consult Great-Aunt Merry's crystal ball Athena.

"*Tempus fugit*," the blonde Sister mumbled, stifling a yawn. "It's getting late, and I really need to get home to Ian and Merry Fay," she added. "We do *not* want to handle that ball after what we've just been through anyway. I'll be free all day tomorrow, and the three of us will try our hands at consulting our crystal seer. It will be the first time without Auntie Merry's guidance; but I believe, *united*, we can do it. And I want you both to think the same way," the senior Sister encouraged. "Tomorrow, don't do anything with Athena but cleanse her, as per Auntie's instruction, and I'll join you at Tara in the morning. I'll ring you when I'm en route."

"Remember," Maggie reminded, "we have to meet with Dale Hardiman, the direct descendant of axed Nellie's brother Clyde tomorrow too, and then, tomorrow evening, with Josie Means again. She said she's ready to share something of great significance with us."

"We'll fit it all in. I want to take advantage of my free day to join forces with you. It's not often I have the whole day off," Aisling interposed.

Raine and Maggie swapped glances, with Raine saying, "Tomorrow should be a very *interesting* day!"

Maggie threw back her head and laughed her crystal laugh. "Great Goddess' nightgown, darlin', what would you call today?!"

Chapter Thirteen

Tara's attic room was taking on the pleasing mingled aromas of burning white sage and dragon's blood incense. Having smudged their sacred space, the three Sleuth Sisters seated themselves about a small round table from which they had temporarily removed a lamp. Now, the lit lamp rested on a trunk positioned behind the large, amethyst crystal ball that their Great-Aunt Merry had christened "Athena."

"Auntie told us that we must always remember to address her by her name," Raine began, looking across the table at Aisling. "Maggie and I gave her a nice cleansing just before you got here. As per Auntie's instructions, we bathed her with a soft cloth in bottled tepid water and a mild, good-smelling dishwashing soap."

"Good," Aisling replied, "you must keep her clean physically. It will cleanse her energies as well." The senior Sister placed her hands lovingly on each side of the ball, whilst she talked quietly. "Before we begin to program her for *our* special needs, we'll also have to smudge her with good white sage *before* and *after* our session today, as Auntie taught. In fact, we will need to smudge her with each use, so no negative energies will ever do her *or us* any harm.

"Now," Aisling sighed, conjuring the day just this past spring, with their beloved Auntie Merry at the Witch City of Salem, "when we *actually* begin, the leader will do some talking, while the others remain silent and focused. It's a difficult discipline to master, talking and focusing when scrying. Auntie has been doing it for many decades, so it was no problem for her." Aisling looked thoughtful. "I'm thinking *Maggie* should be the one to lead this scrying session rather than me? She is the most gifted with a crystal ball. More than you and I," she said to Raine.

"Yes," Aisling decided. "*You* lead us, Maggie. **You** had the vision of Auntie and Granny handing you the ball. And none of us can deny the power of a vision. Have you and Raine read over Auntie's *Book of Shadows*, to refresh all the steps, all the DOs and DON'Ts?"

Raine and Maggie answered in sync, "We have, Sister."

"I believe we should all three come in physical contact with Athena," Aisling said. "Remember how Auntie continued to stroke the ball before using it? She did that in order to energize the crystal and strengthen her psychic bond with it. We need to do it too– the three of us together."

For several moments, simultaneously, the Sisters caressed the large, amethyst crystal ball, gently passing their hands over the lovely purple surface. Athena was so large, this action was effortlessly feasible.

Finally, Maggie reached deep into the pocket of her long, black ritual robe for the Lemuria oil she had put there earlier. Glancing at Aisling, she held the vial out to receive an assenting nod from the firstborn Sister.

The redheaded Sister dabbed a bit of the oil on the third-eye area of her forehead, passing the ampoule round, so that Aisling and Raine could do the same. At that, Maggie began a deep breathing pattern, allowing all the stress and negative energies to flow completely out of her body as she exhaled. Her two sisters of the moon followed suit, breathing deeply, each at her own rhythm, as each meditated: *Healing energies in ... negative energies out. Healing energies in ... negative energies out. Healing energies in ... negative energies out.*

There was a silence whilst the magickal threesome applied themselves to their task. It was at this juncture when Raine remembered feeling, last spring at Auntie's Salem cottage, like a child waiting, with bated breath, for the white rabbit to be whisked from the depths of a wizard's enchanted top hat.

After several minutes, Maggie opened her eyes and began focusing on an area of the ball that she felt expressly drawn to. "Focus," she pronounced in her silky voice, "focus on an area of Athena's crystal depths that draws each of you in."

Several quiet, peaceful moments passed, after which Maggie began to chant softly, "Athena, as we go into a trance/ Bestow on us the magick glance/ Take us back in time today/ Reveal what happened come what may/ To the night, many years past, when Nellie Triggs and her family were axed/ Take us to their little shack, for all the images and the clack/ For long-kept secrets to be unlocked/ Within the hours of the clock/ That you have chosen for us to learn/ *The truth!/* For *that*, we now return!"

As the huge crystal ball's powerful energy commenced to flow around the seated, black-robed Sisters, their vibratory levels rose to harmonize with the antique crystal sphere to make the needed psychic connection.

The very special magick was working! All three Sisters could feel it!

Within a few minutes, each witch began to experience a strange tingling sensation. Maggie and Aisling felt a rush of heat, whilst Raine felt suddenly cooler. Each was adjusting to the ball's vibration– each in her own way.

"Remember, expectation is *not* helpful," Maggie pronounced softly, thus far keeping within the trance. "Clear away any and all expectations. We will see what Athena wants us to see– nothing more, nothing less.

"Let us allow our minds to become as clear as the crystal. *Relax,* relax and stare into the ball's deep crystal cavern. Do not look away; hold your gazes, Sisters. Auntie counseled us that sometimes this takes what seems like forever, other times not."

Keeping their regards on the ball, not batting an eye or moving an inch, the Sisters smiled as, inside the big crystal ball's mystical amethyst depths, a ghostly mist began to form.

"Ahhhh, our connection with Athena has been made," Maggie drawled softly. "The door is opening. Keep still, and keep your focus. Calm and centered … yes … yes. *Calm and centered.* Let Athena's mists draw us in. That's it," she crooned. "Good. *Very, very good.*"

The ethereal mist swirled inside the amethyst ball, slowly at first, then faster, then slowly again, before the crystal began to clear.

"Now, my dear sisters of the moon," Maggie droned serenely, "let us allow ourselves to drift. Yes, drift inside Athena's crystal cave, for like Merlin's, it will show only the truth and all truth. Soon now, the light and sound images, indestructible and eternal to this Universe, will reveal to us the truth that we seek."

As the mists cleared, Maggie recalled something significant about which their auntie had warned them. She cautioned softly, "Remain calm, and do not break the trance with emotions. We might see and hear what we do not expect. Often, this is what happens. Again, I forewarn– do *not* anticipate, Sisters. Remember, Auntie advised us to never expect *anything*, but simply to let Athena take us where she will, in order to show us the truth.

"Do not try and make sense of anything until everything has completely faded away, for attempting to sort out what we see will lead to the breaking of concentration along with our spell and bond today with Athena." Maggie's full lips were open slightly, as she sighed softly.

"Sisters, do not permit yourselves to become excited or anxious. Keep your emotions in check. Simply *allow* the scenes to flow, one into the next. We will know when Athena's magickal movie has ended. We will just *know*, for everything will fade, dissipate and dissolve." Maggie drew in a breath, slowly releasing it, as she kept her focus and her gaze.

Suddenly, an image of a humble, old-fashioned kitchen took distinct form inside the ball. It was night, but a small wall sconce provided ample light for the Sisters to see that the room was empty.

As Auntie had informed them, the magickal trio was drawn deeper inside the huge ball's crystal cavern, there to witness exactly what had unfolded that deadly night, in 1932, when Nellie Triggs and her family were savagely axed.

Irrespective of Auntie Merry's caveat, her nieces grew evermore eager, so much so they could scarcely draw breath. The kitchen image inside the ball fluttered, nearly disappearing, as the Sisters struggled to control their emotions.

Forthwith, all three witches heard a distinct knock sound at Nellie's kitchen door. An elongated shadow of a man wearing a fedora wavered on the pale-yellow wall, as the dark figure peered into Nellie's kitchen window, where the yellow dotted-Swiss curtain was tied back.

I feel like someone peeking through the keyhole of a locked door, Raine told herself. Now she gazed at that "door" with heightened wonder.

Indeed, both she and Maggie were so excited, they jointly drew in their breaths, their over-zealous feelings causing the image to swiftly evaporate before them.

Aisling gave a groan. "Perhaps we can get it back. Don't panic, Sisters."

But it was no use.

No matter how hard they tried to relax and focus, to gaze without expectation into Athena's amethyst depths, all that returned was the swirling smoky haze. It was as if Athena, too, were breathing out, releasing her breath– and with it, the witches' stirred emotions.

However, to the Sisters' succor, from the ball's eddying mist emerged a familiar face– a beloved face, who smiled at them to deliver comforting words.

"You know now that you *can* do it, my dear girls," Auntie Merry spoke kindly. "But you are *trying* too hard. You did very well for the first time working with Athena– *very well*. Aisling, you were wise to appoint Maggie to lead." Merry grinned. "Her super-sensual nature is purrrrrr-fect for directing your scrying sessions. That's enough for today, my dears. Conclude your ritual, following the proper steps, and give it another go on the morrow. Put Athena completely out of mind till then." She inclined her snowy white head to one side, lending her the appearance of an amiable cockatoo. "I have a keen Irish feeling, as *you* ofttimes say, that you'll experience even greater success come the new day. So mote it be, my darlings! Blessed be!"

And as rapidly as Auntie's benevolent image had appeared, it seemed to fragment, snap, and vanish!

"Blessed be!" the Sisters exclaimed, then they stroked the large amethyst ball, jointly thanking the God-Goddess for helping them via their beautiful crystal oracle.

The disappointed, but curiously happy, witches finished by smudging Athena with more of their white sage. Covering the crystal ball with a black velvet cloth and settling her comfortably back inside her protective case, Raine returned Athena to the wooden cabinet, that they kept locked at all times, in their sacred attic space.

Athena was, not only to be kept cleansed and covered, but she was to be stored in a *dark* place, where no sunlight could lessen her ability to perform and no other hands would ever handle her but the Sisters'.

"Now blink," Maggie suggested. "Blink your eyes several times and breathe deeply, so that we can allow our minds to return to the physical plane. A cold glass of water and a light snack will help to ground us, as we gradually reconnect to the Earth's energies."

"We know that well from our Time-Key travels," Raine stated with a sigh. "After all, this, too, is time-trekking."

Aisling exhaled slowly and stretched, "Don't feel bad, Sisters. Crystal ball gazing … scrying of all sorts takes a lot of practice and patience. Maggie, you did a first-rate job." The blonde Sister cast a gentle glance to Raine, "She does it better than we do. But, in time, we'll all three become more adapt and skilled with Athena. Auntie told us to be patient with her when she bequeathed her to us. She asked only that we treat her with the utmost respect; and she, in turn, will serve us well in the good works we attempt to do."

"It was so sweet of Auntie to manifest to us," Raine sang, as she skipped down the attic steps with Maggie and Aisling en route to Tara's kitchen for their refreshment.

"Yes, we must telephone her tomorrow," Maggie replied.

"I prefer the Athena way!" Raine giggled. "**Hec**-a-te yes, it's quite better than Skype!"

Once the Sisters grounded themselves with water and a snack, they galvanized into action again. The interview scheduled with Dale Hardiman, the great-grandson of axed Nellie's brother, the fedora-sporting Clyde Hardiman, was something they were very much looking forward to– especially after the séance the evening before and their session with Athena that morning.

When Aisling pulled up in front of the address to which her GPS had directed her, the Sisters gazed out the window at the neat row of English Tudor-style townhouses. Tudor Gardens was located outside of town, about halfway between Haleigh's Hamlet and the Braddock County seat of Unionville. "This is it," the blonde with the wand announced needlessly. "Number Three. We're right on time, so let's make haste. We don't know how long this meeting will take, and we don't want to be late for our interview with Josie later on."

After Raine rang the doorbell, she whispered, "My witch's intuition is telling me–" The raven-haired Sister quieted abruptly, as–

The door was flung open by a grey-haired man who stood six feet tall and bulked large. Glaring down at the Sisters and wearing what looked to be a permanent scowl, he asked in a most unwelcoming fashion, "Are you those McDonough cousins from the Hamlet?" As though judging a cattle show, he ran bloodshot eyes over the threesome, his look appraising, inquisitive– and most unpleasant.

"We are," Aisling replied flatly to his query. "We have an appointment to speak with Dale Hardiman."

"You're lookin' at him," the man growled, moving only slightly to let the ladies pass inside. "Well, come on in, and let's get this over with." His tone was anything but encouraging.

Detecting the foul cocktail of alcohol, cigarettes, and halitosis on the man's breath, the Sisters entered his living room, which, contrary to the townhouse's attractive exterior, was as unsavory as he.

Piles of magazines and newspapers cluttered the space, as well as used coffee mugs, dirty glasses, discarded soda cans, fast-food containers and pizza boxes. All about, ashtrays overfull with smelly cigarette butts, added to the clutter. The mess didn't seem at all to bother or embarrass their host, as he brusquely indicated the sofa, saying, "Sit down, if you can find an empty space." There was none.

Raine sent Maggie the telepathic message: *If it's true that cleanliness is next to godliness, we're in for a hell of a time!*

Aisling picked up a large pile of newspapers and set them on the floor. Raine and Maggie followed suit, finally ridding the sofa of clutter. Hardiman had flopped down in the only chair devoid of muddle, which happened to be facing the couch where the Sisters now sat.

"Now suppose you tell me why you're bent on digging up my family's dirt after all these years?" the obnoxious man asked point blank, smoothing an errant lock of greasy hair back from his broad face.

"Digging up dirt is hardly our goal with this investigation, Mr. Hardiman; I assure you," Aisling answered, unruffled.

"Then what is your goal, blondie?" he rounded in an angry tone. "To embarrass my family again, after people here have finally started to forget about the friggin' ax murders?" He reached in the breast pocket of his stained polo shirt for a cigarette, lit it and began puffing away, blowing a raspy stream of smoke toward the Sisters, who were trying not to react negatively.

Raine's Irish, however, was beginning to boil, as Maggie could readily tell by the heightened color in her cheeks.

"Now look here, sir!" the Goth gal exclaimed. With her keen sense of smell, she was snatching the whiskey on his breath from where she sat.

Maggie quickly reached behind her cousin to pinch her firm tush, which caused the raven-haired Sister to emit a tiny squeal before she quieted.

The redheaded Sister smiled sweetly. "What she meant to say is that we were approached by a relative of yours, Nellie Triggs, to look into this cold case for the purpose of giving her great-aunt Nellie closure, so she can finally rest in peace. We–"

"Nellie, eh?! I might-a known! She's every bit as screwy as her aunt was! No common sense, no sense about anything! Man-crazy too, a real jezebel! Gallivanting around with every Tom, Dick, and Harry! That's what got her great-aunt killed, and it's what's gonna cause that little bitch to end badly too!"

"Really, Mr. Hardiman! I don't think that's a very nice way to refer to members of your own family, especially since you were concerned, just a few moments ago, that *we* might embarrass your family with our investigation." Aisling pulled a small notebook and a pen from her bag, which she had set on the floor at her feet.

"Come now, Mr. Hardiman," Raine interjected, having gained control of herself, "you've no reason to take on that attitude. No one knows who committed those ax murders and *why* they were done. We're after the truth, and we need your help in getting to it."

The revolting man made a grunting sound of disapproval. "I suppose nothin' I say will stop you from dredging up the whole mess again, so spit out what you came to ask me and get out. I like my privacy, but it's folks like you who never allow people like me to enjoy it." Setting the cigarette in a smelly, overflowing ashtray on the table next to him, Hardiman yanked a dirty-looking handkerchief from his pants pocket and noisily blew his nose.

"What we came to ask you, Mr. Hardiman," Aisling began coolly, "is if you have any family stories you'd be willing to share with us, to help us uncover the facts in this long-running mystery. The truth come what may, for the truth will be the *only* thing that will stifle the speculation and the hearsay about this case and put it, along with poor axed Nellie, to rest once and for all."

Hardiman filled his lungs with smoke, momentarily considering Aisling's request, as his face went scarlet. "You want the truth, girlie? I'll give it to you with both barrels!" the unpleasant man retorted, stopping to draw in a deep breath before he went ranting on. "Nellie Triggs was a cheap little tease who played around once too often and with one too many guys. She got what she asked for! And she brought shame and a load of smut down on our good name, for generations, with her blasted murder. Everyone blamed her brother, my great-grandfather; but, if you ask me— and that's pretty much what you're here for, isn't it?— Clyde didn't kill Nellie and the others in her house. It was one of Nellie's boyfriends who flailed that ax. Who else would've had a strong enough motive? A brother doesn't wield an ax in revenge against his own sister! It was a jealous, cast-off lover who took that ax to Nellie! Revenge, jealousy and hate are pretty strong reasons for murder, don't you agree?" he pointed a somewhat shaky finger at the Sisters, ending by waving aside any further queries with the age-old gesture of exasperation.

It was at that moment that the magickal three noticed the unusual ring he was wearing. It was quite large with a deep red stone in a heavy, gold, ornate setting.

Not affected by the man's attempt at bluster, Aisling remarked, "That's a very unique ring you're wearing. May I see it?"

Hardiman's red face went purple. "Are you here to discuss jewelry or the ax murders? I can see why people call you the Snoop Sisters!"

Maggie realized her mouth was open and closed it quickly.

Meanwhile, struggling anew to control her temper, Raine twisted the talismanic ring on her finger, gifted to her at *Beltane* by the High Priestess of Keystone Coven. Her emerald glance lowered to its large, glittering aquamarine surrounded by gargoyles carved in heavy silver. *Don't make me release the flying monkeys, mister*! Aloud, she said, "Folks routinely refer to us as the **Sleuth** Sisters."

"Whatever!" Hardiman rose, taking a final drag from his cigarette before flicking it into the fireplace. "The ax murders aren't any of your business!" he shouted, pointing a pudgy finger at the Sisters. "You're not in law enforcement! None of this is your concern!" His gaze, at that moment, landed smack on Raine, who responded to his angry expression with a face that the Hamlet would have duly labeled the "McDonough stare."

"Do I look concerned?" she returned in a controlled, flat tone, her witchy stare rendering the man bewildered for a moment. *What I am is tempted, mighty tempted to–* but her thought was interrupted when the odious man went off again.

"I wish you hadn't decided to dredge all this up." Hardiman hitched up his trousers which were slipping down his fat rump. "I was so relieved when the blasted Hamlet newspaper– *The stupid rag!*– stopped printing the story year after year; and now, just when people have forgotten about it all, *you* have to start everybody talking again! Damn the paper– and damn *you! Who th' devil do you think you are anyway?!"* He drove one clenched hand into the palm of the other. "You've upset me enough. Now get the hell out of my place, and don't trouble me again!"

As the Sisters piled into Aisling's vehicle, Raine joked, "That went well." She had succeeded in maintaining a smoldering silence; and now, her anger having faded, she heaved a sigh of annoyance. "I don't intend to let that boorish muggle ruin my day. He's the type who's always on the warpath about something or other."

"I'm proud of you, Sister! For a minute there, I was afraid he was going to have to answer to an angry witch," Aisling voiced, her tone teasing.

The raven-haired Sister dimpled, as her green eyes glittered. "He came friggin' close, and his answer would've been, *"Ribbit."* She glimpsed her watch. "Let's go get something to eat where we can brainstorm a bit before we have to be at Josie's."

"Yes," Maggie concurred, "let's. It's been a funny sort of day, and I'm dying for a bracing cup of tea! Ooh," she shook herself in disgust, "what a dreadful ... *horrid* man! If he possessed even a nodding acquaintance with psychology, he'd–" she stopped, exasperated. "Oh, I shan't talk about it." She slipped on her outsized sunglasses and buckled up.

"Tiresome," the cooler Aisling nodded, as she put the black SUV in gear and pulled away from the curb. "Did you notice how angry he became when I asked to see his ring?"

"We sure did," Raine and Maggie answered.

Clues and motives appear to be lying thicker and thicker on the ground around us, Aisling told herself. *If his ancestor Clyde Hardiman was anything like him ...*

As the SUV passed in front of the townhouse, Raine and Maggie noted the glaring red face in Number Three's window, glowering at them through a slit in the drapes. The man's expression was murderous. As they looked back at him suspiciously–

Aisling asked, "What do you feel like? Tearoom or deli?"

Raine and Maggie looked to one another, then Maggie said, "Let's go to Sal-San-Tries. It'll be quicker, and we'll have more time to talk. Didn't you say you want to put a few questions to Sophie about her ancestors, the evil twins?"

Aisling shook her silky, silvery-blonde head. "I do, but let's refrain from calling them that, shall we? I think we've caught enough abuse for one day, don't you?"

***

"Oh, please don't ask me anything about those two devils!" Sophie wailed, as she served them their egg salad, avocado, and watercress sandwiches. "I think I'd do anything to keep people from discovering their foul deeds!" She set a colossal bowl of her homemade potato chips on the table for them to share. "I'd be happy to discuss my *Colonial* ancestors with you," the deli-owner smiled. "I'm proud of them— as you know, they were one of our Hamlet's first families."

"Sophie, you know we don't spread gossip, so rest assured we won't be telling tales round about regarding the Miller twins," Raine said, as she reached for a chip to plunge into the homemade sour-cream-onion-and-chive dip Sophie placed on the table to accompany the chips.

"We're just trying to gather all the facts we can about our Hamlet and its people during the era of the unsolved ax murders," Aisling explained. "Mmm, great sandwich, Sophie," she remarked, after taking a bite. She brushed crumbs from her black cotton top and capris.

"And anyway," Maggie added, "every family tree has a couple bad apples, horse thieves or something. Lends color. Perfection can be quite boring, you know." Maggie had a penchant for color, as her clothing bespoke. Today's outfit was a vintage Forties' summer tea dress with spatters of turquoise, red and black against a beige cotton backdrop.

"*Bad* apples?" Sophie curled her lip. "I think most people would say the Miller twins were downright *rotten* apples. It's embarrassing to admit they're ancestors of mine," the café proprietress lamented in a confidential whisper, though no one else was anywhere near the Sisters' table, which was situated in the rear of the deli, off to itself in a quiet corner. "The only good thing I could probably say about the disreputable duo is that they weren't prejudiced."

"What makes you say that?" Aisling queried, curious. She picked up her iced tea and took a sip, then reached for the huge deli pickle that always accompanied Sophie's gourmet sandwiches.

"Because," Sophie grimaced, "they hated everyone equally. Though I'd have to say they had an *especial hatred* for J.D. Means, blaming him *personally* for the loss of their money. You know, when Mean's bank failed."

"Yes," Maggie lit up, hoping to spark a bit of info from the café owner. "I've touched on that in my classroom. It was even thought the twins killed J.D. when he disappeared from that ship bound for Europe, murdered him and tossed his body overboard. I never believed jolly ole 'Jim Dandy, the Millionaire-Maker,' killed himself, did you?"

Sophie swallowed, a surge of color flushing her face. "As an officer and long-time member of our historical society, I would have to say 'No.' *But* it doesn't mean the Miller twins killed him! I mean, after all, hundreds of people blamed J.D. for losing their money when his bank went under, and quite a few threatened to kill him."

"That's true," Maggie agreed. She reached for her sandwich and took a bite, chewing pensively. *Clues, clues, and more clues*, she thought. *My head is spinning!*

"Look, I said the twins *hated* him. I *didn't* say they murdered him." The café owner regarded the Sisters sharply. "You haven't talked to anyone who told you that the twins actually killed J.D., have you?"

"No," the Sisters chorused.

Sophie released her held-in breath. "Like I said," she reminded, "the twins hated everybody. Heck, I think they even hated one another!"

"What makes you say that?" Aisling asked, tilting her blonde head to study Sophie's flushed face. "You mean they distrusted each other, as partners in crime usually do."

Picking up Aisling's vibe, Raine and Maggie tuned in to Sophie's sensations.

"The Miller twins both courted Nellie Triggs!" Raine erupted, louder than she meant to.

A surge of customer laughter prompted Sophie to glance quickly around. It was a bit early for her supper crowd. Only one other table was occupied– teens who appeared oblivious to the Sisters and Sophie, engrossed, as they were, in their own banter. "Yes," she finally responded to Raine's outburst. "They were both sweet on Nellie, as people used to say back then."

"Do you know how long that was? How long the Miller twins courted Nellie, and how long before the ax murders took place?" Maggie asked, setting her sandwich back on its plate and swiping crumbs from the full skirt of her colorful cotton tea dress.

"I don't know," Sophie said, clearing her throat. "I only know that the twins each courted her *before* they embarked on their life of crime, so it couldn't have been too close to the date of the murders."

"I wonder why Nellie broke off with them?" Raine said so softly that it was as if she were speaking to herself.

Sophie shook her head, causing her high, strawberry-blonde ponytail to bob. "I couldn't say why they stopped keeping company with her. Lordy, I mean only the twins and Nellie could tell us that!"

"I wonder, too, why there's nothing about the Millers being brought in for questioning in the police records. Nellie's other boyfriends were interrogated," Raine mused.

Sophie shrugged.

"Oh, of course," Raine said, slapping the palm of a hand to her forehead, "the twins would've been on the lam from the law by then!"

"To repeat," Sophie answered, leaning toward the Sisters and again lowering her voice to a whisper, "I'd do anything to keep the Miller twins' outlaw escapades from being publically thrashed out, so I am begging you– please don't broadcast this stuff to the Hamlet." She screwed her expressive face again into a grimace. "I know the 1930s is practically ancient history, but no one would want it publicized that people like those twins existed in their family. No one!"

"As Raine said, we're not gossips," Aisling said evenly. "We only want to get to the bottom of our Hamlet's unsolved ax murders."

Sophie nodded, chewing her lower lip. "Do you still think the ax murders are connected to the skeletons you found in Haleigh's Wood?"

"We don't know that yet," Aisling replied noncommittally, "but we're going to find out!" she added with aplomb.

Raine and Maggie exchanged the brainwave– *And sooner than we think.*

***

The Sisters were only a few minutes early for their evening rendezvous with Josie Means, when they pulled up to her faerie-tale home on its quiet, tree-lined Hamlet street. Since the house was only a few blocks from Tara, they had stopped at home first to freshen up.

The sun had set, but it wasn't quite dusk. As they alighted from Aisling's SUV and walked up to Josie's front door, they speculated over what it was that she sounded so desperate to share with them when she'd telephoned them the day before.

"I wonder if Josie's Abyssinians have settled down?" Maggie asked, glancing at Raine, who was pressing a finger to the doorbell.

"I'd wager they have," Raine replied with a grin, intensifying the dimple in her cheek. She adjusted the belt, hand-painted with gold runic designs, on the black flax dress she was wearing. "I can't wait to hear what Josie has to tell us!" She shifted her weight to her other foot.

The Sisters waited at Josie's door for several minutes.

"Ring again," Aisling said. "She may be upstairs working on a manuscript."

Raine sounded the bell again, but still the author did not answer the door.

About the same time, Maggie wandered over to the window and, cupping her hands round her face, peered closely inside. "Great Goddess!" she exclaimed in a loud, shrill voice, her mouth falling open.

Raine and Aisling dashed to her side to gaze into the same window, their hands cupped round their faces. What they saw startled them.

Josie, wearing a nightgown, her feet bare, was lying in a pool of water on the living-room's hardwood floor. Shards from a broken vase and a vintage glass-shade lamp were scattered around her, as was the spilled-out bouquet of tall, multicolored gladiolas.

"Call 911!" Aisling directed, as she fished her cell from her purse to ring Chief Fitzpatrick. Her powerful witch's intuition was telling her to get him on the horn straightaway.

Maggie put in the emergency call, after which Raine asked, "Should we try and get in? I have a lock pick in my purse." During their years of sleuthing, Raine had become an expert "cat burglar," and those occasions in the past, when she made use of the skill, had served the Sisters well.

"Ambulance will be here in jig-time," Maggie interjected, returning her phone to her straw bag.

"No," Aisling answered Raine, reaching for that Sister's arm, "don't break in. We don't want to disturb anything. I have a feeling this just might turn out to be a crime scene."

"What do you suppose happened?" Maggie pondered. "Could've been a heart attack. Perhaps," she peered again into the window, "Josie grasped for the table, as she was falling, and knocked the lamp and vase over."

At that point, the Sisters heard the screaming siren of the ambulance fast approaching.

"Let's go out to the curb and flag them down!" Aisling exclaimed.

When the paramedics determined that Josie was dead from electrocution, the chief, who arrived on the scene a few seconds behind the ambulance, rang the coroner.

"So what do you make of this, ladies?" Fitzpatrick put to the Sisters. Since he was off-duty when Aisling rang him, the chief was in mufti.

"Obviously, that large vase of gladiolas was somehow knocked over and crashed to the hardwood floor, breaking, and spilling the water. Somehow that glass lamp," Aisling pointed to the shards of glass near the body, "fell to the floor too, and when it did, it broke the lightbulb. See," she pointed, "the filament is in the water. Josie must've heard the crashes from her bedroom last night, got out of bed and rushed downstairs here in her bare feet, stepped into the water, and– that lamp must have been on; could've been a night lamp she kept on. Anyway, she ran down to see what the ruckus was, and when she stepped into the water, she was electrocuted. This is an old house; it didn't kick the breaker."

The chief tightened his mouth and gave an abrupt nod. "That's how I see it too, Aisling."

Maggie wandered over to Raine's side, "Well, so much for those Abbys keeping their word to behave themselves," she whispered. "They must've knocked the large vase of flowers and the lamp over. It's the only explanation."

"No," Raine shook her head. "I don't believe they did this. And it is *not* the only explanation."

"Cruelty, wickedness, and hate are not the greatest forces in the Universe because there is nothing eternal in them. Only *love* is eternal." ~ The Sleuth Sisters

Chapter Fourteen

Sharply turning his head, the white-haired Fitzpatrick asked, "Do you have a hunch about something, gal?!" With his handkerchief, he switched on yet another light.

"Ooooooh ye–ah," Raine replied, suddenly remembering that her familiar, Black Jack O'Lantern, had told her that a pair of red cats would figure into their current mystery. "I have a hunch. But first I need to talk to Josie's cats!" She looked round the living room and adjoining dining area. There was no sign of the Abyssinian pair.

When she didn't find the missing felines in the kitchen, Raine walked back into the living room to speak with Maggie, Aisling, and the chief, who were now joined by a junior officer and the coroner, Dr. Benjamin Wight.

"I'm going to nip upstairs to find those cats," Raine announced, after a perfunctory greeting to the new arrivals. "The ambulance siren and our voices, strange to them, have frightened the poor babies into hiding. I'll be down directly; and not to worry, Chief, I won't disturb or touch anything." Raine pulled a couple of tissues from her bag, before heading upstairs.

Within fifteen minutes, the raven-haired Sister returned, and her fellow sisters of the moon could instantly tell that she had been successful in her mission. "The cats did *not* knock the vase or the lamp over. They were sleeping on Josie's bed with her last night when they heard the crashes. They leaped up and crept downstairs, ahead of their mistress, to see an intruder here in the living room."

"Man or woman?" Aisling interposed.

"They couldn't tell. The intruder was wearing pants and a beaked hat is all I could get from them. Anyway, the cats, creeping along the floor and keeping to the shadows watched the invader break the light bulb with his or her booted-foot, then plug the felled lamp into the wall-socket behind the drape. They told me–"

"Dr. McDonough," the fastidious coroner firmly interposed, "with all due respect, for I do appreciate your diverse sleuthing skills, but you don't really expect us to believe that the dead woman's cats communicated with you about what happened here, do you?!"

Chief Fitzpatrick held up a broad, stubby hand. "Ben, I know it sounds preposterous, but I also know that this woman can effectively communicate with animals. Trust me on this; I *know* it. Let's hear her out!"

"Tell you what," Raine said, wheeling round and pointing, behind her, at the drapes. "How about we check behind that curtain for clues."

The chief, giving a brusque nod, turned to his junior, "Give me your flashlight." He took it, then proceeded to the heavy, midnight-blue velvet drapes. Carefully, he pushed back the thick fabric to see the wall-socket in the dark paneling where the fallen lamp was still plugged. Aiming his light, he looked closely at the floor. "Hello! What's this?" Bending, he retrieved a small chunk of mud that, by the look of it, he could tell had fallen from the deep tread of a pair of shoes or boots.

"What did you find, Chief?" Raine requested in an anxious voice.

"Looks like your conversation with the victim's felines paid off. Someone was standing behind this drape all right." He held up the piece of mud. "Of course, we don't know how long this chunk of mud's been here." Fitzpatrick glanced around. "There're no footprints visible. There's only *this*– this one isolated fragment of caked earth."

"We just interviewed Josie a couple days ago, and when we did, she asked us to remove our shoes," Maggie stated. "She flat out told us that *no one* wears shoes in her house."

"Hmmm." The chief mulled over Maggie's words. "You know, I just happened to think– those cats are lucky they didn't get zapped too."

"Oh, they sensed the intruder was dangerous, and they kept away from him, in addition to which they didn't want to step into all that water," Raine reckoned. "Cats aren't exactly fond of water."

"The water," Aisling mused aloud. "If this was a murder, and I feel that it was, how could the murderer be certain there would be a large vase of tall flowers here to knock over, unless," she deliberated, "*unless* the killer brought those flowers into this house himself."

Raine lit up like a Midsummer's Night's fire ritual. "I need to converse with those cats again!" And out of the living room she hastened. The others could hear her sprinting up the stairs to the second floor.

"Let's search everywhere for forced entry," the chief told his junior. "Mind you don't contaminate anything. You check the front door, and I'll check the backdoor in the kitchen over there." Fitzpatrick strode into the kitchen, where he examined the door and the window. After several minutes, he concluded, "I can't find any evidence of forced entry there."

"And if no one broke in during the night, then this was most likely an unfortunate accident," the coroner reasoned, folding his arms against his chest. "Accidents happen so easily, even to the most sensible and careful people. And most accidents happen at home."

"Well," Raine replied, re-entering the room. "I had a hunch, and when I get a hunch, I am usually right." She looked to Fitzpatrick. "You're familiar with my hunches, Chief. This is not the scene of an accident, but a crime scene. Murder pure and simple, though murder," she rambled, "isn't pure, nor is it particularly simple."

"What else did you find out from those cats?" Aisling asked, getting a bit impatient.

The coroner groaned.

Not letting Dr. Wight's skepticism affect her, Raine calmly answered Aisling's query. "They said someone delivered those flowers yesterday, late in the afternoon. I found out, the general time of day, since it was shortly before Josie sat down to her supper. The cats always get a share of her meal, you see, if it's something they like. And," she digressed, "it *was* something they liked. Tuna, so they rememb–" Noticing the look on Aisling's face, Raine hurried on, "And get this– the person who delivered the flowers was the *same* person the cats spied in this room last night!"

"There's no card anywhere with those flowers," Fitzpatrick mumbled to himself. "And I'd bet my pension that after I check with the florists around the area, I'll find that no deliveries were made to this address yesterday."

"The killer posing as the floral delivery person probably told Josie the flowers were from an admirer, a fan of her writings, who wished to remain anonymous, or some such," Raine remarked. "And those flowers," she pointed to the spilled-out gladiolas on the living-room's hardwood floor, "could've come from any one of a score of flower gardens in our bloomin' Hamlet. Pun intended."

The junior reentered the living room, announcing, "No forced entry around the front, Chief."

"Do a careful search all over the house, all the windows, the basement– everywhere." The chief rubbed the back of his hand over the evening stubble on his cheek, as he became broody, saying to himself, "The intruder could've used a lock pick. Would've been pretty easy to do for someone who knows how. There're no deadbolts on the victim's doors."

In the meantime, Raine was checking the backdoor. Without touching it, she was carefully examining the lock with a small magnifying glass she'd pulled from her purse. "Chief, come here. I've found something."

When Fitzpatrick joined her, she said, "Have a look." She handed him the magnifier. "Do you see that substance stuck to the lock?"

The burly man looked closely at the area she was indicating. "Y– yes, I do. What do you suppose it is?"

"The sticky residue left behind by a strong tape. Someone put a piece of tape– could've been duct tape– on this lock, so when Josie closed the door, it wouldn't lock, but she wouldn't have known that it hadn't locked." Raine chewed her lower lip, deep in thought. "Likely Josie, a woman living alone, always kept the door set for Lock. But when the murderer, posing as the floral delivery person, put a piece of tape *over* the lock; and then subsequently she closed the door after him when he left, Josie thought her door was locked as always, when, in fact, it was *not*."

"Question," the meticulous coroner interjected. "How would the murderer, posing as a floral delivery person, have put tape on the lock without the victim having been aware of the action?"

"Good question," Aisling replied. "My guess is that Josie took the flowers from the delivery person– we know she never permitted people with shoes to walk around in her home– and so, she padded into the living room to place the vase of flowers where she wanted it– there on the table," she gestured, "asking the delivery person to wait for a tip."

Both the chief and the coroner gave evidence, by their expressions, that this was a feasible scenario, since it was tradition in the Hamlet to tip delivery people.

"Ooooh, yes, the more I think about this, the more convinced I am that Josie took the vase of flowers from the delivery person, not wanting him to tramp through her house with shoes on," Aisling pondered aloud. "And I'd bet big bucks the delivery person told her to make sure and give those flowers more water, *so the big, tall vase would be full.* That's also common practice– for floral delivery personnel to remind recipients to give newly delivered flowers and plants water, since they usually don't have much water in them in transit."

No one spoke or moved for several moments. Finally, Raine snapped her fingers, nearly shouting, "Hold on! I need to speak with those cats once more. They're upstairs under the bed, still shaken up. Be right back!"

"Well," Maggie asked as soon as Raine came downstairs, "did the cats see the delivery person put tape on the door?"

"One did. Abner definitely remembered the floral delivery person putting something on the door after Josie took the vase of flowers to the living room. Abigail had followed her into the living room, and Josie gave her strict orders to leave the vase alone. Abner said that whatever the delivery person put on the door was ripped from a roll." Raine caught Aisling's eye. "Your hunch about a tip was right, Sister. Both Abner and Abigail remember their mistress going upstairs for her purse and then giving something to the flower person."

"That would've been ample time for the murderer to put tape on that lock," Maggie stated. "Not to mention case the living room– easy to eyeball from where he stood in the kitchen– for a lamp to use in the evil plan to murder Josie last night."

"Needless to say," Raine added, "once Josie was dead, the killer peeled off the planted tape, and pulling the door after him, allowed it to lock once again. *Voilà,* no evidence of a break-in!"

The tall, elegant coroner shook his head, again addressing the raven-haired Sister, "Even if you *are* communicating with the victim's cats, Dr. McDonough, you know you ladies can't use any of this twaddle in a court of law."

Raine huffed. "We are *quite* aware of that, Dr. Wight. This does, however, give us direction. Now we must connect the dots and get the proof."

"And, rest assured," the chief added in his booming voice, "they will!"

"Why would anyone want to harm this sweet old lady?" Aisling asked, not really expecting an answer, though in a moment, she answered the query herself. "Someone wanted to keep her from sharing that significant bit of information with us. That's why she's dead! No sign of a robbery, is there, Chief?"

"Doesn't look like it, but," he looked sharply at Raine, "did you ask those cats if the intruder took anything from this house last night?"

"I did," Raine replied. "Sorry, I should have mentioned that. The cats said the intruder took something that looked like a large book from a table here in Josie's parlor last night. No jewelry or money, or anything I could determine from them of value was filched."

"You say the victim had some important info to disclose to you," Fitzpatrick asked the Sisters. "In regard to the unearthed skeletons, the unsolved ax murders, what?"

"Yes," the Sisters chimed in unison, with Maggie concluding, "in regard to *both*. That is, that's what we think."

"Well, whatever that elusive evidence was, Josie Means will be taking it with her to her grave," the chief muttered. "Are you making any progress, ladies? Connecting the skeletons and the ax murders?"

"We think so," Aisling said. "I'm wondering if the 'large book' the cats told Raine the murderer lifted was a file of some sort? Or a manuscript? After all, Josie was an author."

"Could've been either. Either would make sense," Fitzpatrick replied. "Who all knew you were coming here to speak with Miss Means tonight?" he asked with sudden expectation.

The Sisters thought for a protracted moment, with Raine answering, "Mada Fane knew. We mentioned that we would be speaking with Josie; but, of course, we most certainly did *not* divulge that Josie would be sharing a significant piece of information with us."

"Do you think Mada Fane had any reason to stop Miss Means from speaking with you?" the coroner queried.

"I shouldn't think so," Raine replied.

"In fact," Maggie concurred, "I seem to recall that she *suggested* we speak with Josie."

A light went on in Raine's head. "Sophie Miller, the café owner in town, might've known we were coming over here to speak with Josie. I think she overheard us say we had an appointment to speak with Miss Means; but, again, she couldn't have known that Josie intended to share a weighty piece of info with us, although she's been acting a tad dodgy of late. But–"

"*But* we don't know if *Josie* herself told anyone," Aisling stated. "Though I rather doubt that she did."

"One thing's for sure– something's mighty fishy here," Maggie expressed with somber face and tone.

"Ye– ah, red herring fishy," the chief agreed, rubbing the back of one large hand against his bristly cheek.

Silence followed, as everyone delved into their own thoughts.

Finally, Raine asked, "What's going to happen to Josie's cats? We can't leave them here with no one to care for them."

"Does Miss Means have kinfolk in the Hamlet?" the chief questioned.

Raine shook her head. "I really don't think so. When we were ferreting out descendants of folks who lived here at the time of the ax murders, we found no other descendants of banker J.D. Means." She looked to Maggie for approval, sending her a thought. "Maggie and I could take them home with us, Chief."

"That's a good idea," the robust Fitzpatrick answered. "For now anyway, do that."

***

The following day dawned bright and sunny, one of the few days that spring and summer when the Hamlet did not get soaked with showers. Raine and Maggie rose early to prepare for their final two interviews with whom the Sisters were calling "descendants of the ax-murder protagonists." Today's meetings would be with Jake Swain and Harry Valentine, the great-grandsons of Nellie Triggs' principal suitors at the time of the ax murders.

"Aisling won't be able to accompany us today. She and Ian are swamped at The Black Cat, with a full day of detective work of their own." Raine glanced at the antique railroad clock on the kitchen wall and poured herself another cup of get-up-and-go from the coffee pot.

"Once we complete these last two interviews, the three of us will have another go with Athena, then we'll gather our sleuthing set for what will hopefully be a productive brainstorming session," Maggie proposed, as the pair was finishing their toast and coffee at Tara's claw-footed kitchen table.

"I was thinking the exact same thing," Raine concurred. "I'm glad we scheduled these two interviews last. In addition to Nellie's brother Clyde, her suitors Swain and Valentine were the top suspects." She stifled a yawn. "Our brainstorming sessions … you know, the rehashing and sorting through of gathered data and clues, always help to make things clear if we draw a blank, or–"

"What were you researching this morning on the computer?" Maggie interposed, watching her cousin and sister of the moon over the rim of her coffee cup. "I got up to go to the bathroom, and saw you lost in investigation before the computer screen. It wasn't even six yet."

Again Raine checked the time. "It's too deep to get into now. I'll tell you on the way to our hair appointment. You'll be a bit shocked at what I discovered this morning. I had a dream, and we both know that dreams are messages. Granny came to me in the dream, and she was holding a passport."

The Goth gal's tip-tilted emerald eyes darted to the clock. "I'll fill you in en route. C'mon, let's hurry. We've got a full day ahead of us. If we get to the beauty shop early, maybe Belle can take us a bit earlier. Anyway, *she's* another good source for Hamlet stories. Barbers and beauticians are like bartenders; they rake in a wealth of data."

"True," Maggie said, rising and taking her cup and plate to the sink.

***

"Honey, how old do you think I am?!" Belle Christie exclaimed, as she began to shampoo Raine's hair.

"Of course I realize our Hamlet's triple ax murders were way before your time, but you must've heard patrons commenting, over the years, on the unsolved mystery. I mean, the paper used to run the story every October, hoping someone would eventually come forth with information." Raine opened her eyes to regard Belle, who was standing above her at the shampoo sink, lathering her short, raven locks.

The Sisters were usually Belle's first clients of the day, and today was no exception.

Their community theatre's makeup and hair artist and Haleigh Hamlet's most popular beautician was a middle-aged, petite lady with platinum-blonde hair cut in a bob that framed a pleasant face.

Now, that face imaged the hairdresser's pensive state. "Let me think a minute." Belle's strong fingers massaged the shampoo through Raine's hair and scalp. Due to the Sisters' inspiration, Belle used nothing but organic products in her shop.

"It's been several years since the paper quit running that story, hasn't it?" Not waiting for an answer, Belle rushed on, "I don't get the *Hamlet Herald* anymore. No need. I hear all the news from my patrons. That's how I find out who died, who had a baby, who's getting married, *et cetera*. You wouldn't believe all what I hear. But, I make it a practice to see no evil, hear no evil, and certainly not to speak any evil."

"The paper stopped running the story about the ax murders fifteen or twenty years ago," Maggie chimed in from her seat in the adjoining waiting area, where she was leafing through a fashion magazine.

"Belle, your family resided in the Hamlet during the Depression years. Do you have any stories you could share with us about those unsolved murders? Stories passed down in your family or stories you've reaped from patrons over the years?" Raine asked, as the beautician began rinsing her hair.

"Well, now that I know what you're after, I do have a story I could tell you." Belle poured a measure of cream rinse on Raine's head and began massaging it through the ebony hair. "My great-grandmother went to school with the axed woman. What was her name? I can't recall it at the moment."

"Nellie Triggs," Maggie supplied without looking up. She continued flipping through the pages of the thick magazine.

"Yes, that's it!" Belle exclaimed. "Anyway, they had been good friends all through school, and even after they graduated from high school. When Nellie's husband was wounded in the war– let's see, that would've been World War I– my great-grandmother, or so my family always believed, was a comfort to her. Like I said, they had been great friends since childhood. You can sit up now," Belle instructed.

The petite, shapely beautician began to towel dry Raine's wet hair. "After Nellie's husband died, my ancestor was still her best friend, until Nellie Triggs started working for the wealthy Fanes. Then they drifted apart. I remember a few of my older relatives saying that working for the Fanes changed Nellie."

"Changed her how?" Raine asked.

Belle paused in her task to tilt her head and shrug. "Don't rightly know. Oh, I don't mean she changed from good to bad, or anything like that. I think I recall that, according to our family's tale, she was just too busy to laze about with my great-grandmother anymore. After all, she had her elderly mother, her kids, and her job workin' for the Fanes, which took a lot of her time."

"Is that all you remember from the story?" Maggie prompted gently.

Belle picked up a large, wide-tooth comb and began slowly dragging it through Raine's black hair, as if contemplating what the redheaded Sister had asked. "I haven't thought about or talked about this for a *long* time, ladies, and my memory is not as good as it was when I was younger. When you start down the backside of fifty, you'll see what I mean." Belle began sectioning off Raine's hair for a trim. "Say, are you determined to solve that spooky old Hamlet mystery? I guess if anyone can, it would be you McDonough girls."

"We're giving it the good ole college try," Raine answered with her dimpled grin.

All of a sudden, Belle stopped what she was about, and her china-blue eyes widened like the proverbial saucers. "Hey, you don't think the ax murders have anything to do with those skeletons you discovered in Haleigh's Wood, do you?!"

Raine and Maggie exchanged quick glances, for Belle's face looked as if she had suddenly seen a ghost.

"Please think hard, Belle," Maggie implored, looking up now from her magazine. "Do you recall anything else passed down in your family about the ax murders? You might be sharing something, something you might not even think meaningful, that could help us, especially since your ancestor was a close friend of the murdered woman."

"Well, let me think–" Belle looked as though there was something else she recalled, but she hesitated, and for several seconds no one spoke.

The Sisters had noted the hesitation in the beautician's voice, but for the moment, they did not press the point.

Finally, Belle cleared her throat. "Look, you both know how I hate to gossip. And, for all I know this could be just that– tittle-tattle– passed down in my family. I was always taught never to speak ill of the dead. But, if this will help you– I know what good you've always done– then OK. But do keep in mind it just might be pure hearsay and nothing more."

The Sisters responded with encouraging nods.

Belle shifted her weight and leaned a hip against her station, where she momentarily placed the styling scissors she'd been holding. "My family always believed that Nellie had a secret lover, someone who– and this bit probably is hearsay– was married. They always said, too, her secret lover was a prominent person in the area; and you know, as history profs, that our Hamlet, our whole area, was home to a lot of wealthy people back then. Anyway, the story was that Nellie had found a 'sugar daddy.' That's what people used to call a fella like that– a man someone like Nellie might latch onto."

"What do you mean by 'someone like Nellie,'" Raine interposed.

Belle looked as if she had said quite enough, and she reached over to retrieve her scissors, quickly pausing them in mid-air to remark, "You see, my folks thought Nellie was the sort of woman who lived for others. Even her photograph– I remember the photo– the one they used to run in the paper; it depicted a woman, a pretty woman, with a hunted, or perhaps the word is *haunted* look. You know what I'm saying," the beautician gave a nod of emphasis; "she lived for her kids, for her elderly mother, but when it came to the secret lover she was said to have taken up with, my family thought she went a little crazy."

Raine gave a terse nod, pursing her lips in thought. *I wonder if "crazy" could've meant Nellie had taken up with someone outside the law? She could've fallen for a fella with heavy pockets outside the law– like a bootlegger.* Aloud, she said, more to herself than to Belle, "We all of us have our particular devil who rides us and torments us, and we must give battle in the end."

Belle went on as if she hadn't heard Raine's aside. "Hmm, perhaps that's what my relations meant when they said Nellie had changed. It wasn't working for the Fanes that changed her, but the guy she'd fallen for. I don't know, but she must've really fallen hard. Or perhaps she knew what the sugar daddy could do for her kids, for her ailing mother. Story was that Nellie enraged one of her … *visible* boyfriends. When she cast off the two guys who were openly pursuing her around the time of the murders, simply put, it ticked one of them off to the point of a jealous rage."

Belle hesitated, reflective, then added, "Nellie was a real beauty. Several men were after her. I remember my family saying that, over the years, it became a Hamlet contest as to who would finally win the elusive Nellie Triggs."

Not the first time we've heard most of this, Raine fired off to Maggie.

The redheaded Sister speeded her sister of the moon the telepathic reply: *And **that** makes me think the info has credence.*

Unmindful of the Sisters' psychic communication, Belle bit her lip, and the Sisters noted real fear in her eyes. *"Please* don't repeat what I've said to you, because there are people living here in the Hamlet related to the folks in the saga of our ax murders. Oh yeah," Belle reiterated in a low tone, "make no mistake. They're still around."

Less than two hours later, Raine and Maggie were sitting on a leather couch in Jake Swain's rustic den, staring at his wall of animal trophies, the sight of which incensed the Sisters, who were struggling with their feelings about the robust, blond man they had just begun to interview.

"Shall we come to the point, ladies?!" Swain nearly shouted from the leather chair across from them. "I know what you're driving at, and it's *preposterous*! I don't understand why you're so determined to prove my great-grandfather murdered that woman! Your manner tells me you're flat dedicated to that mission, and I want you to know that I highly resent it!" The man spoke with a haughtiness that was almost as disgusting as the trophy bragging he had spewed, upon showing the Sisters into his den.

Raine's eyes snapped, and a hot color rose to her cheeks. "We are not dedicated to proving your ancestor guilty," she spat tartly. "We're dedicated to the truth. We want to solve this Hamlet mystery, as we've solved others. We want the victims to rest in peace." She could feel Maggie stiffen beside her.

Jake Swain's wide, fleshy face reddened. "That's fine and dandy, but I can't allow you to say harsh things about–" He broke off, his tone taking on sharp indignation, "My great-grandfather Jasper was a hardworking man, as was my grandfather and my father after him," Swain swore with fervor. "He would not have murdered anyone!" he bellowed hotly.

"I don't recall either one of us," Maggie darted a glance at Raine, "saying that he did. But *someone* murdered that woman and her family, and–"

"Jasper wanted to *marry* Nellie Triggs," Swain professed aggressively. "He purchased an engagement ring for her, for Christ sake!"

"Yes, but she turned him down," Raine countered, having recovered her composure.

"She did," Jake admitted, "but as the police found out when they spoke to the jeweler, "my great-grandfather was not," he groped for a word, "*incensed* over it. Certainly he wasn't angry when he returned the ring to the store. The jeweler told the police that Jasper Swain related to him that Nellie needed time to think, that if, in the future, she gave him a different answer, he would return to the store to either re-purchase that ring or choose another. The jeweler, a credible person in the Hamlet, stated to the police it was his observation that my great-grandfather understood and accepted, *with grace* I might add, that Nellie needed more time."

Jake fixed his eyes on the Sisters, who, sitting directly across from him, were studying him closely. "Does that sound like a crazed ax murderer to you?!"

The Sisters declined to answer, causing Swain to gallop on, his anger quite unfounded.

"I resent all this very, very much!" he stormed. "That idiotic newspaper of ours used to get some sort of thrill dredging up this sick ax-murder mess every fall, and now you're picking up where the paper left off! Don't you see how this hurts people! Hurts their good names! But apparently, you don't care who you hurt. It's not just my family, you know. This crap hurts several others too, each and every time the blasted story is dug up! And for what?! Nothing good will ever come out of this, I tell you! **Nothing!**"

Raine raised her ebony brows, wanting to respond but holding her tongue.

"Newspapers are often sensational in their accounts, but hardly as accurate as one might wish. I mean most people know they can't believe everything they read in the papers," Maggie said, hoping to soothe the irascible man. The redheaded Sister displayed no outward reaction to the man's airy impertinence.

"Enough is enough!" Swain hollered at the top of his voice. "I don't know why the police don't close the book on this damn thing once and for all!"

"Because," Raine said in a calm, business-like tone, "there's no such thing as a closed unsolved murder case, Mr. Swain!"

He wagged his greying blond head, the too-long hair worn in an obvious comb-over to minimize the evidence of baldness. "Yes, yes, yes, I know, no statute of limitations on murder," he recited in an irritating timbre. "But it would seem to me that when a case is as cold as this one– Jesus, those murders happened back in 1932!– you'd think the police would be done with it, and let the people involved rest in peace!"

The Sisters exchanged telling looks with Maggie concluding, "There have been colder cases than this one solved. And as far as letting the people involved rest in peace, that, as we said, is exactly what we intend to do– solve the murders and give closure and peace to the victims."

"Then," Swain said, jumping to his feet to indicate the interview, as far as he was concerned, was over, "I suggest you stop pesterin' me with all these questions and interview Biff Valentine's descendant. Harry Valentine still lives in this blathering little burg!"

***

The first thing Raine and Maggie noticed when Harry Valentine opened the door to them was the large ring on his right hand. Mostly silver, the ring's gold square top was bordered by curious engraved symbols.

"Come in," the tall, neatly dressed man beckoned with a sweeping gesture of his hand. "I've read and heard so much about you."

"All good I hope," Raine pronounced pleasantly, as she and Maggie entered Valentine's old-fashioned parlor.

"All good," their host repeated with assurance.

"That's such an unusual ring," Raine remarked, attempting to get a closer look. "May I ask what the symbols represent?"

"You may," Harry answered without hesitation. "This is called a Kabbalah ring. The symbols are in Hebrew and signify protection against the evil eye. It is said that those wearing this talisman can ward off evil." His gaze dropped to the ring, which he twisted slightly on his finger to straighten. "It was a gift from my wife when we were abroad on our honeymoon," he thought for a moment, adding, "*many* years ago."

"Did she feel you need such protection?" Raine blurted, hoping her impetuous nature would not again bring negativity upon them.

This time, Harry did waver with his reply, and something stirred in his dark eyes, something that also wavered, for it was there but a fraction of a second, retreating behind Harry Valentine's well-mannered poise.

"Oh, I think all wives are protective of their husbands, aren't they?" he smiled. "Just as husbands are protective of their wives."

The Sisters pitched the thought to one another: *The ring's energy **is** protecting him– but against what exactly?*

"Do sit down." The charming man indicated a pair of rose-colored wing-back chairs positioned, at an angle, on either side of a rustic red-brick fireplace that was flanked by built-in shelves overflowing with books. The volumes did not confine themselves to the bookcases that reached to the ceiling. They were scattered about on tables, chairs, and even the floor. Yet there was no sense of disarray about them. Rather the Sisters sensed a sort of reverence for the books. A lively Degas print of ballet dancers, *en pointe pirouette*, graced the wall above the mantel, and an antique blue vase held a bouquet of colorful wild flowers.

This interview might just go better for us than the last couple. Raine sent the thought to Maggie. *Anyone who loves books this much **has** to have a good side.* Her discerning gaze glided over the parlor.

There was an old, quiet smell about the room, as though the air in it was little changed, for all the sweet scent brought to it over the spring and summer from the elaborate flower garden, which the Sisters could see through the window. Whatever air came into this room, from the garden, would lose its freshness, becoming part of the unchanging room itself, one with the slightly musty-smelling books, one with the dark paneling, one with the heavy draperies and antique furniture.

Glancing about, Raine sent the thought to Maggie: *This room has a sort of **ancient** smell, mossy, like one might experience in an old English abbey, where ivy takes hold and grows, clinging, upon the stones.*

Yes, the redheaded Sister returned, *it's a room for contemplation, a room for quiet meditation.*

"My, you've quite a library, Mr. Valentine! You must love to read," Maggie exclaimed, as she sat in one of the vivid rose-hued chairs.

Harry's eyes darted to the crammed shelves, lowering to a stack of leather-bound tomes. "A home without books is like a person without a soul. I have a nice first-edition collection, and I like to collect old and rare books." He smiled. "Our home has twin parlors. This is the one I use for our library. I always say there isn't a cup of tea large enough or a good book long enough to suit me. To start," he looked inquiringly at his visitors, "may I offer you tea? My wife is visiting her sister this week in Pittsburgh, but I'm pretty adept at making a good pot of tea, and placing the cookies she baked on a platter."

"That's very kind of you," Raine answered. "But we really want to get down to why we asked to speak with you."

"Of course," Harry replied, taking a seat opposite the Sisters in a somewhat worn, burgundy leather chair that the Sisters instantly felt was his favorite reading spot in the attractive, cozy atmosphere of the Victorian house.

"Before we begin, though, let me say you have a beautiful home, Mr. Valentine," Raine remarked, her gaze drifting anew to the window and the bright splashes of color in the flower garden beyond. She glanced over to see Maggie staring at the high, ornate ceiling from which was suspended a sumptuous antique chandelier with etched-glass globes.

The redheaded Sister sent Raine the thought, *Library's indeed impressive.*

"Thank you," Harry responded with a smile. "We like it." His eyes swept the room as the smile lingered on his countenance. "We've filled it with mementoes of our travels and our life together. The walls of this old house hold wonderful memories. My great-grandparents, my grandparents, my parents, and my wife and I have had many fantastic gatherings here. You know the third floor used to be a ballroom. Of course, my wife and I never used it for a ballroom, but back in the old days, when my great-grandparents built this house, they hosted many masquerade parties, what they called 'fancy-dress balls.' Those were all the rage back then."

Harry smiled again, remembering family stories, the Sisters supposed. "And so many holiday gatherings," he talked on. "There was always an excuse to throw a party in the old days. Especially was there a lot of merrymaking during the Roaring Twenties when this whole area was booming economically. If these old walls could talk!"

From somewhere in the house, a clock chimed. Harry seemed to catch himself, saying, "I didn't mean to rattle on like that. You've come here to interview me," he flipped a hand, palm up, extending it slightly toward the Sisters, "so do carry on."

"No problem. We've been interviewing several Hamlet residents whose families were living here during the years of the Great Depression," Raine declared.

"Mr. Valentine, we're researching our town's unsolved triple ax murders that took place in 1932." Maggie sensed that Harry already knew this was their reason for wishing to speak with him.

"Yes," he admitted, affirming her sentiment, "that's what I heard." After a brief pause, the amiable man added, "Heard too you think there's a connection to the skeletons you discovered in Haleigh's Wood."

"We think there might be," Raine replied, after exchanging a quick look with Maggie.

"I think you might be right," their host avowed, surprising them. "Don't know why or how, but I think you just might be right." He sat back in his chair, making himself comfortable, and it was at this point that the Sisters looked hard at the man before them.

Harry Valentine looked to be in his mid to late sixties with brown hair turned mostly grey. He was clean-shaven, rather handsome but not in the way most people would think of handsome. Harry possessed a pleasant blend of rugged masculinity polished by civility and poise.

"We're interested in this case both as sleuths and as history and archeology professors at the college," Maggie stated, hoping this would put their host at ease, though he very much appeared to be at ease.

"I'm certain you both know more about that case than I." He cocked his head. "I sincerely doubt that I could offer anything new," Harry said levelly. "I'm well aware of your reputation as super-sleuths."

"That's kind of you, but we were hoping that you would share with us any information– any *stories*– passed down in your family about the murders," Raine delivered, leaning forward to retrieve her notepad and pen from her bag, which she had set on the floor at her feet.

Harry raised his brows. "I'm certain you know that my great-grandfather, Biff Valentine, was one of the top three suspects in the ax murders." He let out a breath, adding, "And I'm sure, too, you know that many people around here, including the police, believed that *he* was our Hamlet's ax murderer. There just wasn't any real evidence to prove it. It was said that he had an air-tight alibi."

"Tell us truthfully, sir," Maggie asked in her soft way of speaking, "What do *you* think?"

Harry thought for a few seconds, replying, "There are times when I think my great-grandfather killed that woman and her family, because he had a history of losing his temper, with men and, I'm most sorry to relate, with women. But just because a man has a sharp temper doesn't necessarily mean he could do murder. *However*, those times, when my ancestor lost his famous, or I should say ***in***famous temper, were due to his over-indulgence in drink. On top of a hair-trigger temper, Biff Valentine liked his firewater. *And*, I might add, the moonshine and bathtub gin that people of the Prohibition era concocted was known, quite literally, as '*demon drink.*'

"As you history professors know better than I, the Depression era was a *violent* time, and crime was not exclusive to *our* county history by any stretch. People nation-wide sought release valves during the hard times of the Great Depression, in booze, women, the ponies, or, with a chance to change their fortunes, the forerunner to the State Lottery, the Numbers. Even when I was growing up, I remember folks talking daily about playing a number. Nearly everyone did it. There were even published 'dream books' to aid in the amusement of it. Mere pennies could be bet. The return was good, and there was no tax on the winnings!" he laughed.

Harry laid one long leg over the other at the knee. "Prohibition created a lot of the crime during the Depression era. Hell, the government should've known it wouldn't work! It didn't work in the Garden of Eden– Adam ate the apple!"

Harry talked on for several more minutes, whilst the Sisters continued to study him. It was quite evident that he was an avid reader. His impressive library was not just for show.

"… And hunger, in any era," he was saying, "makes people do things they wouldn't ordinarily do. Oh yeah, the Roaring Twenties and Dirty Thirties were wild and turbulent times for most of the country, and our triple ax murders were a horrific fraction of those times, as our ghosts could tell us."

"Ghosts?" Raine sat up, the word having perked her interest.

"Just a figure of speech," Harry chuckled.

Raine, however, had misgivings about that.

"What about family stories?" Maggie asked. "Have you any you'd be willing to share with us, about the ax murders?"

"You mean what my family's take on the whole thing was?" he asked.

"Yes," the Sisters chimed.

"To tell you the honest truth," Harry replied. "My folks were torn, but most of them believed Biff was the killer– because they *knew* Biff, knew what liquor did to him. Oh," he amended quickly, "I don't think anyone believed he *planned* on killing Nellie and her family. Only that he went to her house to get her to, at least, talk to him again, to forgive his embarrassing public display of anger and drunkenness a day or so earlier."

Harry tilted his greying head, fixing them with a particularly mesmerizing mien. "Don't you know? Biff, in his way, absolutely *adored* Nellie Triggs, one of the reasons I was once convinced *he* was her killer."

The Sisters sent the man before them a curious look.

"I think more often people kill those they love than those they hate. Possibly because only the people we love can make life unendurable. But all this doesn't help you much, does it?" he smiled. "Getting back to what I'd started to say a moment ago, I think Nellie was quite *thrilled* by Biff, at least at first. From what I could tell from my exploration over the years, both my great-grandfather and Nellie's other suitor, Jasper Swain, had a *power* over women. Glib characters, both, when it came to the fair sex. *Smooth and slippery*." He chortled. "Really, one could almost consider what they each uniquely possessed an *art*. The clever way they each had of treating Nellie made her feel like a queen, *I* think. It must've been exciting and romantic for her. As for my ancestor," again he looked off into the distance, "There's a fine line, or so they say, between love and hate."

Harry shifted in his chair. "You see, there had been an incident outside a café here in the Hamlet in which Biff grabbed Nellie and shook her, jerked her or something. I don't believe he hit her, though he may have. Someone, I think, intervened, but the public fiasco embarrassed the woman to tears, and she refused to see my great-grandfather ever again. He swore to the police and everyone, I suppose, who would lend him an ear, that he never saw Nellie Triggs subsequent to that. He told the story ever after that Nellie's mother turned him away at the door of their home, when he went there a day or so after his public show of anger to apologize and beg forgiveness from the woman he called his 'lady-love.'"

Harry tilted his head back in reflection. "Let's see, *that* would've been the *day* of the murders. But," he shook his head, "so often, *so often*, have I wondered if my ancestor returned to Nellie's house that fateful night of the murders, around midnight, rip-snortin' drunk and determined to *make* her forgive him and take him back.

"Perhaps he beat on the door, roaring for her to let him in. Perhaps then she opened the door, so he would stop making so much noise– noise that would wake the neighbors and bring her more public shame and humiliation. Suppose," his brown eyes held the Sisters, "after he got inside, he got into an argument with Nellie. It was common knowledge that Biff Valentine was not, in any way, a happy drunk. On the contrary, he packed a rep for being a *mean* drunk."

Again Harry shook his head, slowly from side to side, imaging the scenario across the movie screen of his mind. "Suppose Nellie reached for the ax– the Triggs bungalow was heated by a wood-burning stove. What I started to say is perhaps she grabbed for the ax to defend herself, because the unruly man was getting violent with her, and he wrested it from her and killed her in a jealous rage. Then he killed the others in the house because they were witnesses."

"We've pretty much thought the same thing," Raine admitted. "But, of course, that's not the *only* scenario we've imaged."

"That's only *my* imagined scenario," Harry clarified, "not a family consensus. Frankly, I had pretty much made up my mind, years ago, that my great-grandfather did the ax killings. He had that weakness of losing his temper when he drank. Most people can deal with one serious character flaw, but *two*? Obviously, Biff Valentine had another dangerous weakness– *jealousy*. It might've been more than he could handle." He looked hard at the Sisters. "You know, that might've been the straw that broke the camel's back. But now," he shook his head, "now that you've unearthed those skeletons from the same era, I have significant doubt my great-grandfather committed the triple ax murders. Now I am thinking there might have been a serial killer on the loose here in the Hamlet."

"Yes," Raine answered, "we're considering that."

"*If* the scenario you conjured a little bit ago is what happened, what do you suppose would have sparked Biff's killing rage once he was in Nellie's house?" Maggie asked, looking up from her notepad.

"*If?*" Harry locked eyes with the Sisters, answering their nods in a voice that bespoke significance, "Again, ladies, this is merely *my* speculation. But *if*– and now, as I said, that is a **bigger** *if* than in the past– the scenario I described did happen, then I think it would have been because Nellie finally admitted to my great-grandfather that there was someone else who occupied that special niche in her heart. Someone she had been in love with for some time. Someone she had been in love with *the whole time* she had allowed my obsessive ancestor to court her."

Harry lifted his head, and his soft eyes hardened. "***That***, ladies, would have been the straw that broke the camel's back."

***

"Whatdy'a think of Harry?" Raine asked from her position behind the wheel of the vintage MG. The pair was outside Harry Valentine's Queen Anne home, contemplating their next move. The raven-haired Sister turned the key, slipped on her sunglasses, and adjusted her mirrors.

"Can't make up my mind yet if his manner is polished or oily?" Maggie answered. "He kind of reminded me of my ex-husband, and that's interfered with my assessment of him. In fact, if Harry spoke with a charming Irish brogue, he'd almost pass for Rory McLaughlin."

"So that means you liked him," Raine prodded.

"Yes, I guess I did." Maggie gave a half-smile. "No one can help but like Rory, including me."

"Sooo, Harry collects old and rare books, does he? I noted a few on the Occult." Raine suddenly remembered something. "Didn't you mention once that your ex was a collector? What was *his* passion?"

"Horses and women," Maggie laughed.

"It amazes me how you always manage to remain friends with all your ex-lovers." Raine pursed her mouth. "About those books on the Occult ..."

The Sisters continued to exchange dialogue for the subsequent five minutes, after which Raine said, "Mags, there are two other aspects of this Valentine interview we'd better discuss now, whilst they're fresh on our minds. Did you notice …"

Nearly ten minutes after they had gotten into the MG, the Goth gal asked, "Where to now?"

Maggie was thinking. "I daresay we're getting closer and closer to connecting those confounded dots, darlin'. We must arrange to meet with our sleuthing set to brainstorm this weekend. But for right now, after what you told me you uncovered early this morning in your computer research, I say we hook up with Dr. Yore. Let's ring Liz to ask if she'd consent to meet us at Sal-San-Tries for a light meal."

"Sounds like a plan!" And putting the sports car in gear, Raine roared them away to their next destination.

Chapter Fifteen

The café deli's lunch crowd had thinned by the time Dr. Yore joined Raine and Maggie at their favorite table in the rear of the quaint establishment.

"Ah, here comes Dr. Yore now!" Raine said, setting her teacup down in its saucer and signaling to their fellow professor with a cheery wave.

The sixty-ish, Margaret Mead look-alike, flourishing one of her long identifying capes, swept purposefully toward the Sisters. Today, Dr. Elizabeth Yore's cloak was a mystical forest green. Holding her tall, forked staff, the joint head of Haleigh College's archaeology and anthropology departments resembled something betwixt and between an impish witch and a stern schoolmarm.

"Sorry I'm late; but when you rang, I was right in the middle of something. Never enough hours in a day. I got here as quickly as I could," the older woman explained, as her fingers sought to undo the ties at her neck.

"No problem, we haven't been waiting long," the magickal pair replied.

With an answering nod, Dr. Yore shucked her long cape, and the Sisters could see that it was a rain cloak, which prompted Maggie to comment that the morning sun certainly fooled them into thinking they were in for a dry day. The older woman placed her cape over the back of an empty chair and rested her staff in the corner, against the wall. "Reminds me of the year I spent in Scotland in my youth. '*Soft* weather,' they called it."

In jig-time, Sophie came hurrying to their table to take their orders. At once the Sisters, as well as Elizabeth Yore, noted the unusual necklace the proprietress was wearing– a large, primitive, oval clay pendant upon which was fired the pictograph of a hand.

"I've never seen you wear that before," Raine remarked. "It looks old."

"It is," Sophie answered, fingering the worn, brown leather thong that was holding the pendant. "My grandfather purchased it many years ago at a Native American powwow in upper state New York. It represents the Hand of God, and, shaman-blessed, it's for strength and protection. I don't think I've ever mentioned it, but I have some Iroquois blood. Seneca."

The Sisters looked to one another, exchanging the thought: *All of a sudden, everyone in our Hamlet is feeling the need for strong protection!*

The words of the Keystone Coven's High Priestess– *Beware of one who will be wearing an unusual piece of antique jewelry–* returned again to haunt them. The thought troubled the Sisters that this would include several people they had encountered in the past few days.

"Hello!" Sophie was saying, as she waved a hand before them. "Earth to Raine and Maggie! I asked if you guys would like to try my London grilled-cheese today."

"What is that exactly?" Dr. Yore questioned.

"Just the best grilled-cheese you'll ever experience," Sophie stated with aplomb. "Shredded Montgomery cheddar with onions, garlic and leeks packed tightly in my homemade sourdough bread. It's everything a sandwich should be– comforting, filling, and outrageously tasty!"

Favoring looks from her companions prompted Raine to exclaim, "Bring 'em on!"

"And a nice big pot of your green tea," Dr. Yore added, after checking with the Sisters on what they were drinking.

Sophie looked pleased. "The London grill comes with my old-fashioned German potato salad and, of course, the deli pickles you all love."

"Sounds wickedly decadent," Maggie jested with an approving nod and her crystal laugh.

Once the three professors were again alone, Elizabeth asked, "So what's this about? The skeletons you discovered in Haleigh's Wood, I assume."

"Yes, it's about that– and more, Liz," Maggie replied.

"What's the news on those skeletons?" Dr. Yore queried.

"Not much," the Sisters replied in sync.

"Nothing new since we first met with Chief Fitzpatrick and the coroner," Raine verified. "We just spoke with both of them again this morning. We're not at liberty to tell you everything at this point of the investigation, but we do know that those fellows, all three male, were buried in the early 1930s."

"And," Elizabeth pushed her short grey hair back from her cherubic face, as her blue eyes sparked, "you believe those skeletons are somehow connected to our Hamlet's unsolved ax murders."

"Gossip rides a fast horse in this town," Raine retorted *sotto voce*.

"True, but I've not heard any chatter," the older woman remarked. "I just know *you*."

Maggie smiled sweetly. "You know us pretty well then." Out of her peripheral vision, she caught sight of Sophie, headed for their table with the tea, and decided to wait to continue.

A few moments later, Maggie turned to Dr. Yore, "Your family didn't live around here during the Great Depression, and you're not originally from this area, so I don't know how much you know about our Hamlet's triple ax murders."

"I only know what I've read in the *Hamlet Herald*," Elizabeth replied, picking up the teapot to refill the Sisters' cups, then pour tea for herself. "Come to think of it, I've not seen anything in the paper about the ax murders for quite a few years now."

"The *Herald* stopped running the story between fifteen and twenty years ago. The recurrent story never brought forth as much as one shred of information on the grisly crimes. We've been interviewing as many descendants of the ax-murder protagonists as we could locate," Maggie said.

"You've met one of the people we interviewed," Raine stated. "Dr. Mada Fane."

Elizabeth Yore pursed her mouth as though giving careful consideration to the proffered name. "What do you think of her?" The older professor leaned back in her chair to savor her tea– and the response.

Dr. Yore's question had nudged the Sisters to exchange looks, seeking, as was their habit, each other's corresponding thought.

Predictably, it was the more loquacious Raine who answered. "She was warm and welcoming when we interviewed her at Fane Manor. We've always wanted to meet her, but we never before realized that she returns periodically to the old mansion. I mean the place always looks boarded up to us from down on the road." She thought for a moment, adding, "Unlike so many geniuses, Mada has a personable side that spins out to charming."

"Like Thaddeus," Maggie smiled to herself. Then turning back to Dr. Yore, she said, "You've met her. What do *you* think of her, Liz?"

"Like you, I've always been duly impressed with the woman's countless contributions to both archeology and anthropology. Her work … well," she shrugged, "what can I say? It's phenomenal." Elizabeth started to say something else, and then hesitated.

"Yes," the Sisters responded, "her work is rather exceptional." Raine locked eyes with Dr. Yore. "And?"

"And yes, I would have to agree– she *is* a genius, not to mention a prolific writer." Elizabeth paused in indecision, again tightening her mouth.

"**But?**" Raine and Maggie prodded in sync.

Elizabeth Yore raised a grey brow, reluctant to continue.

"What is it you're holding back, Lizzy?" Maggie prompted.

Dr. Yore pulled on her lower lip in thought, finally saying after a long moment, "When we met– oh, it was several years ago now, back in 2007, I believe– at an Archeological Institute of America conference in New York, I picked up what you young ladies would call a 'vibe.' I felt as though Dr. Fane was inwardly laughing at me, *mocking* me for," she broke off, groping for the right word, "oh, I don't know, *vaunting* my cape and staff, inwardly deriding me for a Margaret Mead imitator."

Elizabeth Yore took on a defensive demeanor, sitting up straighter in her chair. "I usually don't feel the need to justify myself at my age, but she made me feel as if I should– though, of course, I didn't," the vibrant instructor quickly put in.

The Sisters exchanged looks, for they had never heard their esteemed colleague stumble and ramble like this. For a few moments, Raine searched her essence for a tactful reply. Finding none, she remained silent, waiting for whatever else Dr. Yore might share with them.

"I adopted my style years ago, when I was a student at the University of Pennsylvania, and I was not trying to imitate anyone. My long capes, my staff," she raised her shoulders in another shrug, "they just feel *right* to me– *comfortable*. And I daresay, Dr. Fane has been the only individual in my life who has ever made me feel the need to explain them, though, of course, I didn't," Elizabeth repeated, more, the Sisters sensed keenly, for her own benefit than theirs.

After a weighty moment, the older professor softened her tone, adding, "I don't like to speak ill of such a fine academic as Dr. Fane. If the whole truth were to come out here, I'd confess that I am envious of her independence to live the life she wants to live. The woman is so wealthy, she's never had to trouble herself about making a living. She's free to travel to all the places that call to her, free to indulge in all the exciting field work and study that tickle her fancy, and she's free to write all those award-winning books. Her time's completely her own." She stopped herself, setting her cup firmly down in its saucer. "Truth is," she raised both her pointed grey brows, "I'm flat out *jealous*. And I was just being catty. So let's move on, shall we? What else did you wish to discuss with me today?"

"Here comes our food," Maggie breathed, eyeing the tempting fare on the tray Sophie was carrying to their table. "Let's wait till Sophie returns to the kitchen."

Several minutes later, Raine, who had telepathically received approval from her red-haired sister of the moon for what she was about to say, opened the discussion, leaning confidentially toward Elizabeth Yore, "Normally," she began in a whisper, "we would never do this, but we are going to take you into our confidence regarding one aspect of the unearthed skeletons."

"I assure you, fellow colleagues, I would never betray your confidence." Dr. Yore picked up her knife to cut her sandwich in half.

"We know that. It's why we're trusting you, for we want your thoughts on this," Maggie replied. "And I daresay it's right in line with your expertise."

The redheaded Sister looked to Raine, who launched into the coroner's discussion about the ritual killings. When she finished, all three professors sat back from the table for protracted consideration.

"If," Dr. Yore concluded, "Ben Wight has a feeling those individuals were stabbed in some sort of ritual killings, then *go* with that. He's the best in his field, and we're damn lucky to have him in our backwoods area of the commonwealth."

"I agree, Liz," Maggie nodded.

Raine made a little sound of agreement, as they all returned to their food.

For several moments no one spoke, until Dr. Yore said, "Like detective work, forensic anthropology depends on scholarship and training, experience– and intuition. As you can confirm, intuition plays *no* small part in either occupation."

Elizabeth picked up her sandwich and took a bite, chewing pleasurably for a few moments before speaking again. "From what you've told me, I agree with Ben's deductions." She picked up her tea and drained her cup.

The Sisters smiled in a satisfied way. They both liked Dr. Elizabeth Yore, and they trusted and valued her judgement.

"That's what we hoped to hear, Liz; for Ben's deductions made, *make*, perfect sense to us," Maggie replied.

"Perfect sense, yes," Dr. Yore repeated, "but the question begging is 'How are the alleged ritual killings connected to the ax murders?' The ax murders weren't ritual killings." She took a spoonful of the tangy potato salad. In a blink, her face lit up, and she exclaimed in an anxious whisper, "Unless–"

"Yes," the Sisters nodded emphatically, "*Unless* …"

***

"I want t' be in on yer brainstormin' session, missy!" the Sisters' poppet Cara demanded, as Raine was setting the hors d'oeuvres out on the long coffee table in Tara's parlor.

"And you shall," the raven-haired Sister replied, patting the ragdoll on her faded-yarn, mop-top head.

"Iffen you wudda invited me to sit in on yer crystal-ball scryin', you wudda had better success; I kin tell ya tat!" she chided via her Irish brogue with its shades of Colonial America.

"She may be right," Raine remarked to Maggie, who was bringing in a tray of crackers and cheese.

"Get outta **tat** garden, missy! I done tole ya and tole ya t' stop talkin' 'bout me as if I wasn't here," their poppet spat in a disapproving voice.

"Cara, you're a pistol. That's all I have to say." Raine arranged the food platters to look neater on the coffee table.

The little ragdoll leaned forward to glance out the window. "Bucketin' down out dere again. Win will yer sleuthin' set be arrivin'?"

"Any minute now." Maggie stepped to the window, cupped her hands and looked out.

"So at this point in time, you're absolutely *convinced* that the ax murders and the skeletons of Haleigh's Wood are connected, and you think author Josie Means' death is tied into all this too?" Hugh puzzled. He huffed into his mustache, then reached for his wineglass, taking a brooding sip.

"What makes you think that Josie's death is connected?" Betty's tone was merely inquiring and carried no disbelief. "Not that we can believe much of what we ever read in the *Hamlet Herald*, but the paper said she was electrocuted from a spilled vase and broken lamp." She scanned the coffee table's snack trays before choosing a whole-grain cracker and a slice of pepper jack cheese. "Made it sound, anyway, like it was an accident."

"And that's what we want people to think for now," Aisling answered. "OK," her vivid emerald eyes swept the coterie of sleuths in the room, "let me remind all of you of our covenant– *nothing ever leaves our circle.*"

Indeed, the Sisters' sleuthing set was seated in a circle, in the comfort and charm of Tara's Victorian parlor, Aisling and Ian on the long leather couch next to Maggie and Thaddeus. Opposite, on the smaller love seat, were Hugh and Betty; while, as was their habit, Raine and Beau were sprawled out on the floor, having copped the throw pillows from the couch.

Sitting up and setting her plate of food on the fireplace bricks next to her, Raine disclosed to their fellows the particulars of Josie's death.

"Have you any idea what she wanted to share with you?" Ian queried. He lifted his wine goblet from the coffee table to take a drink.

"Not with certainty, though we could make an educated guess," Maggie replied.

"Josie told me only that it was significant to our current investigation," Raine informed.

Beau and Thaddeus both focused their gazes on Maggie, with Beau asking, "So what's your guess?"

"Raine and I both think she wanted to reveal to us her family's consensus as to who killed her grandfather, J.D. Means. We feel strongly that she had a pretty good idea who murdered her historic ancestor. Josie was conducting her own research for years. Her killer, we think, is someone who did not want *us* to know who killed J.D., nor would Josie's killer have wanted to risk her putting that postulation– or perhaps the author had uncovered actual *proof*– in a book one day. After all, Josie was a good researcher, a respected author who wrote award-winning historic accounts, and she was a high-volume writer."

Raine fiddled with the angel sleeve of the long, black gauzy tunic she was wearing over black capri leggings. "We teach some local history each year, and neither of us ever believed that Jim Dandy Means killed himself. Suicide was contrary to everything we ever ferreted out about the stubborn, persevering man, not to mention that– and we recently found much evidence to support this– J.D. was a deeply spiritual person. Suicide?" she shook her head, "I think not. The 'Millionaire-Maker' was not, in any way, a quitter!"

"Quite right!" Maggie exclaimed with gusto. "Why would he have jumped from that ship bound for England? It makes no sense whatsoever. He was on his way to get money from his titled, wealthy sister who had agreed to bail him out of his troubles. The telegram she sent him to that effect still survives. Josie has it," she cocked her fiery-red head, "or at least she did. Since Josie's murder, we believe even stronger that J.D. was either pushed or thrown from that ship in the dark of night."

"And you're certain by now that *all* of this is tied together?" Hugh asked again.

"We are!" Raine and Maggie chorused.

"After spending the whole morning at the police station, going over the ax-murder police files for the third time, and after having completed our interviews with the descendants of the ax-murder protagonists, together with our own research, our witches' intuition, and our experience as sleuths and professors of history and archaeology, we've connected several of the elusive dots." Raine sucked in a long draft of air, blowing it out, before concluding, "We're close to identifying the ax murderer-slash-ritual-killer, as well as Josie Means' killer, who, we believe, is a descendant of the fore-mentioned murderer."

From her comfy position on Maggie's lap, Cara shot a directive to Raine, "Tell 'em what Hannah said t'other day tat made ya t'ink, missy!"

"Thanks, Cara," the raven-haired Sister replied. "When the news hit the paper about the unearthed skeletons we'd discovered in Haleigh's Wood, Hannah commented that, at the time of the ax murders, the police didn't know which way to turn. Then she repeated that they likely don't know which way to turn now. Anyway, her phrase *which way* made me think *w-i-t-c-h way*, though

I must reiterate, as I always do– and just maybe this will permeate the ethers and do some good– witches do not drink blood, harm or kill animals or humans, or worship the Devil!

"However, the ritual killer, Maggie, Aisling and I believe, was into the dark side of the Occult. As you all know from association with us," she lobbed a glance toward Maggie and Aisling, "with spellcasting, intent is everything, and the killer's intent was human sacrifice for big-time gain. I doubt it gets much darker than that." Raine paused to take a swallow of wine.

"We're clinging to the belief that there's an element of black magick about this *whole* business," Maggie reiterated.

"*Baa-ad* business, tat!" the poppet muttered.

Oblivious of Cara's utterance, Betty and Hugh shouted, "And the ritual killer axed Nellie Triggs because she accidently *saw*!"

"*Exactly*," Maggie replied. "Nellie must have stumbled onto a ritual murder in progress, was seen, and therefore had to be killed, her family too, in view of the fact that they were in the house when the murderer axed her."

"And whoever killed author Josie Means is a descendant of the ritual killer," Hugh reviewed aloud. "Which could mean the 1930s ritual-killing involved more than one person, that it was a secret society of some sort that– Great balls of fire!– *still* exists."

"Right again," Aisling remarked. "Raine, Maggie, and I are thinking there was a circle of close associates involved in the ritual killings, not just one person."

"Like a coven," Maggie interjected. "Though grammatically correct, I intensely dislike using that word here. I prefer, in regard to the ritual killers, using the phrase, as you did," she glanced at Hugh, "*secret society*– an oath-bound, arcane, esoteric society. We strongly believe there was a group of ritual killers, *thirteen*; twelve members with a leader." The redheaded Sister smoothed the skirt of her 1940s vintage dress. It bore a peacock design, the vibrant hues glorious with her dramatic coloring.

Betty's eyes opened wider than ever as the revelation impacted her, and she nearly dropped the finger sandwich she was holding. "You think that secret society, that evil cult is still in existence *here* in our Hamlet?!"

Without the slightest hesitation and in perfect harmony, the Sleuth Sisters answered, "We do."

"Though we very much doubt that *all* the members reside here. We're thinking they're scattered across the globe." Raine sipped her wine. "Pretty scary stuff, huh?"

"In such arcane, esoteric societies," Maggie added, "descendants usually follow in their ancestors' bloody footfalls."

"Yes," Raine coincided. "Usually each member's involvement goes back generations."

"You mentioned earlier that several of the people you interviewed wore an unusual piece of antique jewelry," Thaddeus reminded the coterie of sleuths.

"Yes," Raine replied, and she repeated the High Priestess of Keystone Coven's caveat to beware an individual wearing an unusual piece of antique jewelry. "But each piece of unusual jewelry we noted on the people we interviewed was different, one from the other. If the secret society of ritual killers wore an identifying piece of jewelry, we believe each member wore– would still wear– an *identical* piece of jewelry."

"Have you any idea which of the unusual-jewelry wearers is the ax-murder-ritual-killer descendant?" Thaddeus stroked his van dyke. "An individual who may just be a present-day member of this dark-arts society– and every bit as dangerous as his predecessors?"

"We're pretty sure," Raine and Maggie voiced in union.

"It's all getting clearer and clearer," Raine stated.

"Speaking of which," Maggie went on, "we must try again to consult our powerful crystal ball Athena. We hope to gain more insight, and we'll be grateful for anything Athena will reveal to us. Then, we'll make good use of our Time-Key."

Kitty, Kitty, Kitty! Cara summoned telepathically from Maggie's lap.

A moment of silence followed, whilst the Sisters paused to regard the Merlin cats. They had entered Tara's parlor to line up before Raine, where they sat to stare at her, their tip-tilted pumpkin-colored eyes fixed unwaveringly on her green ones.

"What are they saying?" Aisling and Maggie asked with eagerness bubbling on their voices.

"Ah, sure 'n aren't doz cats always upstagin' me!" Cara teased from her position on Maggie's lap.

Raine studied the three ebony felines, gazing silently into their eyes. After a long moment, she bit her lip, but said nothing.

"What did they tell you?!" Aisling demanded. She ran her palms over the fabric of her tight black jeans.

Reluctantly, Raine divulged the truth. "They say we'll soon be in great danger. We must remember to never let down our guard, and to have on our persons, always, our strongest protective talismans, including the ring from High Priestess Robin and our ancient, wild-boar stones bestowed on us by High Priestess Violet of Orkney."

"If you're determined to make use of your Time-Key to probe into the risky business of ritual killings and ax murders, then I insist you again take Thaddeus with you," Beau asserted. And the look he cast to Dr. Weatherby bordered on pleading. "That is, if he's willing."

"Count me in!" the professor exclaimed with fervor, a curious light kindling the vivid blue of his eyes.

"Brilliant!" Cara squealed, clapping her wee, mitten-shaped hands in glee.

Maggie hugged their poppet then leaned over to plant a kiss on her beloved's bearded cheek. "Thaddeus has been a great help to us in the past. I always feel safe in his presence– anywhere, any time."

"Thank you, my dear," the multi-talented genius replied. Always eager for another time-travel experience, he cast his request with unbridled enthusiasm, rubbing his hands together in anticipation, "When do we leave?"

The three Sisters swapped looks, with Raine replying, "We want to consult our crystal ball when we're fresh, so we'll wait to do that tomorrow."

"And that will drain us of a lot of energy, so we'll want to wait to use our Time-Key the subsequent day," Maggie reasoned. "Because we must be fresh for that too."

"Good thinking," Aisling remarked. The blonde with the wand felt for her talisman. "You know Merry Fay is the reason I don't accompany you. But, as always, I'll be with you to aid in your takeoff, Sisters, and I'll lend you my talisman so you will have as much of the Power of Three as possible." Aisling started to lift her sacred McDonough talisman over her head, being careful not to get the chain caught in her silky, silvery-blonde hair, when–

Raine rose briskly to her feet, **"No, Aisling, no!** The Merlin cats told me that we are *each* in jeopardy now, so you keep your talisman on at all times, until Mags and I absolutely need it for our time-trek, Sister! Then we'll give it back to you first thing upon our return."

The Goth gal began walking up and down, frowning. Pacing always helped her to think, and she was thinking now.

"Have you decided where your portal will be for this time-trek?" Aisling queried. She slipped the ancient talisman back over her head and under her black lace top, where it pulsed gently against her heart.

A reflective silence ensued, then Raine and Maggie recited from the thesis that gained them their doctorates, "As always the entry should match the targeted destination." The pair looked to one another, trading a thought.

"Though Nellie Triggs' bungalow on old Murphy Road is no longer standing, we do know just about where it once stood," Maggie ventured. She tapped her mouth with a finger, the nail glossy red to match her lips. "Right off the top of my head, that seems the most reasonable time-portal for this trek."

"I can supply you with an old map of the Hamlet," Betty, the former librarian, offered. "The one I'm thinking of would have what you need to pinpoint the exact spot where Nellie's house stood."

"We appreciate that, Betty." The practical Aisling considered for a moment, responding with a nod. "Depending, we could use Haleigh's Wood for the portal. That would be safer, I think, affording us the privacy we need, both for your send-off and your landing. Nowadays, there are homes all along Murphy Road."

"We'll know the right site when it's time for our departure," Raine advocated, sitting back down next to Beau. "But I'm liking Haleigh's Wood better every second. The woods are good cover for takeoff and landing. We never really know *how* we'll land."

"Right," Maggie reacted, looking to Thaddeus. "Raine and I have been thinking that it would probably be best to program our trip to commence a day *prior* to the ax murders, so that we can garner as much information as possible. After all, we want to find out *exactly* what Nellie saw that got her killed."

"I wholeheartedly agree," the professor said. "I'm certain we can tail her without being noticed."

"And our keen witches' intuition is telling us that whatever Nellie saw that ended up getting her killed, she witnessed shortly before she was axed. A day prior to the date of the ax murders just feels *right* to us. Thus, October 11, 1932, is the date we intend to program with our Time-Key," Maggie stated. "Of course, it all depends on what Athena reveals to us."

"You mean to say you'll be staying overnight in the Hamlet with an ax murderer and … *and* ritual killers on the rampage?!" Beau nearly shouted.

"Hardly staying *with* the ax murderer and ritual killers!" Raine quipped, lifting her little chin stubbornly.

"You know what I meant," Beau shot back.

"Since the Hamlet was a railroad hub, it hosted several hotels and boarding houses, so we'd have no trouble finding a nice place to stay," Raine teased. Noting that her other half was becoming stressed, she shifted gears, saying, "Oh for pity's sake, if all goes well, we'll have garnered all the facts we need to connect the remaining dots of this mystery shortly after midnight, and we'll zip back home straightaway."

"I have some period money, *coins*, that you're welcome to use," Hugh volunteered. "They're mostly from the 1920s. There might be a few from 1930 and '31. I'll check, and I'll drop the coins off to you in the morning."

"Older is fine, just so none of the money is *beyond* our target date," Maggie cautioned. "We appreciate your offer, Hugh, and we'll take you up on it."

"Regardless of whether our time-portal is going to be the site where Nellie's shack once stood or nearby Haleigh's Wood, we'd better take off in the dark of night," Raine remarked. She drew one of the Merlin cats into her lap and began stroking Black Jack O' Lantern's velvet fur, bringing forth his loud number-three purr.

"That's for certain," Maggie and Aisling agreed in response to a dark-of-night takeoff.

"We sure don't want an audience!" Aisling finished. "We must continue to guard and protect the secret of our Time-Key, so let's agree on Haleigh's Wood now."

Raine and Maggie both made sounds of agreement.

"Good, then *that's* settled," Aisling stated adamantly. "In just two days, the moon will be full, and that is the very best time for you to open the portal and enter the Tunnel of Time. Things are falling right into place, Sisters, a good sign that we've the Goddess' approval."

Beau started to interject one of his layered objections to the Sisters making use of their Time-Key when so much danger abounded; but, catching his eye, Thaddeus flung him a look that stopped his intervention. It suddenly occurred to the Sisters that Thaddeus and Beau had been doing some talking of late.

Raine fired the thought to Maggie: *I hope Thaddeus is putting Beau's mind at ease about our time-travel. Oh, were that the truth!*

"And this trip," the eager Dr. Weatherby was verbalizing with gusto, "our landing in another time and place should be eased, due to our friend Eva Novak's special Gypsy Tearoom brew."

"Tea-Time-Will-Tell!" Raine and Maggie chorused, their emerald eyes dancing with excitement.

***

Tara's sacred attic space swam in shadow, the only illumination a flickering candle of Goddess blue– that the Sisters lit to confer truth– and a miniature lamp behind the huge amethyst crystal ball known as "Athena."

With the necessary prelude for the all-important scrying session accomplished, Raine, Maggie and Aisling sat in chairs arranged in a close half-circle to the fore of the glowing crystal oracle. As before, the Sisters agreed that Maggie should lead in the scrying attempt.

Now, inside their strong circle of protection, with their poppet Cara sitting sassy and eager on her robed lap, Maggie began to gently work the spell.

Taking a deep breath and breathing in the pungent, sweet odor of burning white sage, the red-haired Sister closed her eyes to chant: "Athena, as we go into a trance/ Bestow on us the magick glance/ Take us back in time today/ Reveal what happened come what may/ Reveal to us what Nellie Triggs saw/ A sight that sent her a shocking fright/ A sight that got her killed forthright/ Then take us to her little shack for all the images and the clack/ Walk us through your crystal fields/ Whence long-kept secrets will be revealed/ Bestow on us all that we yearn/ Begin your magick for us to learn/ ***The truth!/*** For *that*, we now return!"

Maggie opened her eyes and began focusing on an area of the ball to which she felt expressly drawn. "Focus," she whispered in her honeyed voice, "focus on an area of Athena that calls to you, that will draw each of you into her crystal depths, into her crystal cave. Focus … *focus.*"

Several quiet, peaceful moments passed, after which Maggie began to softly chant anew.

As the vast crystal ball's powerful energy commenced to surge and swirl around the seated, black-robed Sisters, their vibratory levels rose to harmonize with their Auntie Merry's bequeathed crystal sphere; and soon, they began to make the needed psychic connection.

This time, the ancient magick was working even stronger! The Sisters could *feel* it! The very air they breathed was charged with energy, and the atmosphere seemed to crackle with Athena's transcendent power!

As each witch began to experience the now-familiar tingling sensation, each held to her focus, keeping her emotions under control. As before, Maggie and Aisling felt a rush of heat, whilst Raine felt suddenly cooler. Each was adjusting to the antique ball's vibration– each Sister in her own way.

"Expectation is *not* helpful," Maggie reminded softly, keeping within the trance. "Clear away any and all expectations. I can but ask for what we'd like to learn; nevertheless, we will see what Athena *wants* us to see– nothing more, nothing less."

"Now, Sisters, let us unclutter our minds to become as clear as the crystal before us. *Relax* … relax and stare into the ball's deep crystal cavern. Do not look away; hold your gazes. Auntie advised that sometimes this takes what seems like forever, other times not."

Keeping their regards on target, the Sisters noted that inside the great crystal ball's mystical, amethyst depths, a ghostly mist had begun to form.

"Our connection with Athena has been made," Maggie breathed. "The door is opening. Keep calm and still. Calm and centered. That's it, very good. *Calm and centered.* Let Athena's magickal mists draw us in. Yes, yes," she crooned. *"Very, very good."*

The ethereal mist swirled inside the amethyst ball, slowly at first, then faster, then slowly again, before the crystal began to clear. It all seemed to happen faster this time, and the Sisters took that for a good sign. Thus they carried on with more confidence than during their first session with Athena devoid of the powerful Salem witch, their great-aunt, Merry McDonough.

"Now, my dear sisters of the moon," Maggie droned serenely, "let us allow ourselves to drift. Yes, we shall all three drift in and through Athena's crystal cave, for like Merlin's, it will show only the truth. Soon now, light and sound images– indestructible and eternal to this Universe– will reveal to us the truth we seek."

As the mists cleared, Maggie softly cautioned, "Remain calm, and do not break the trance with emotions. We might see and hear what we do not expect. However, we need not expect at all, at all. We need only to relax and allow Athena to take us where she will. Always, then, she will show us the truth."

"Aye, she will t'at," Cara drawled quietly in her tiny voice whilst she swayed from side to side with the soft timbre of Maggie's voice.

"Do not try and make sense of anything until everything has completely faded away, for attempting to sort out *what* we see will lead to the breaking of concentration, along with our spell and bond today with Athena." Maggie's glossy full lips were open slightly as she sighed softly. "Keep your emotions in check. Simply allow the scenes to flow, one into the next."

"One inta da next," Cara echoed via her Irish brogue.

"We will know when Athena's magickal movie has ended. We will just *know*, for everything will fade, dissipate and dissolve." Maggie drew in a breath, slowly releasing it, as she kept her focus and her gaze.

Suddenly an image took form within the crystal ball.

Walking across a driveway, on which several late-twenties and early-thirties automobiles were parked, was a sad-eyed woman whom the Sisters immediately knew was Nellie Triggs. She was wearing a black beret and a belted, tan trench coat with the collar turned up. Knocking at what looked to be the backdoor of a large house, she called out, "Bessie! It's Nellie. Are you in there?"

When no one answered the door, Nellie opened it, and peering inside, she called out again, "Bessie! Are you here?"

As the Sisters watched Athena's magickal movie, Nellie entered the house's mudroom, moving quickly into the adjacent, neat and tidy kitchen with its tall, white cabinets. There, she waited, talking aloud to herself. "Bessie must be up on the third-floor, in the ballroom, serving the guests. Looks like a party here tonight." She took a quick look at the kitchen clock that the Sisters could see showed 5:15. "Might as well wait."

Pulling a chair out from the long, wooden table, Nellie was about to sit down to wait, for the person the Sisters surmised was the house maid, when, from the crystal ball, issued what sounded like the drone of chanting.

Within the ball, Nellie turned, to gingerly follow the sound into a hallway. She stopped short, glanced cautiously around, then ducked into a large room in which the Sisters noted shelves of books lining the walls. Just inside the door of the room, Nellie paused again.

The Sisters' gaze drifted along Nellie's line of vision– to one of the bookshelves, where leaping flames made it appear that the room had caught fire!

Slowly, step by step, Nellie inched toward the flames and the source of the chanting. At this point, the Sisters could see that the room was not on fire at all, but that the shelves slid back to reveal, behind, a secret room, where dozens of lit candles illuminated a circle of black-robed figures, thirteen in all.

With hoods up and heads bowed, their hands tucked inside the long, voluminous sleeves of their robes, the chanting figures circled a naked man strapped to a large, center table, around which were painted bizarre symbols. The man appeared to be drugged, for his open eyes looked glassy, his expression befuddled.

The Sisters observed Nellie creep a bit closer to the spot before the opened shelved wall, where she stood, frozen in time, watching, with horrified countenance.

Athena was providing the Sisters with the same ringside view as Nellie's. Of a sudden what looked to be the leader of the robed figures stepped forward. He raised his hand, chanting a strange language in an eldritch intonation that neither Nellie nor the Sisters understood. In his hand something glinted in the fire glow of the numerous lit candles.

Years of study, in both archaeology and history, told Raine and Maggie that the glinting object was an ancient ritual knife for human sacrifice. In the next moment, the leader plunged the knife through the bound victim's heart, bringing forth a loud litany of the strange words from the circle of dark figures.

Nellie's hand flew to cover her mouth, stifling a scream. She turned and fled back the way she had come, just as the backdoor opened and a robed figure entered the mudroom adjacent to the kitchen.

The Sisters struggled to remain calm and emotionless, watching, as, in the nick of time, Nellie slid into the pulled-out kitchen chair on pretense of being there the whole time.

"Oh," she exclaimed to the lone, robed figure, "I see the family is having a fancy-dress ball!" She rose and, with wide frightened eyes, began to inch toward the backdoor, "I don't want to intrude. I wanted to leave a message with the maid, but–" she stopped herself, adding in her haste to escape, "I'll come back another time!"

The Sisters watched as the sinister robed figure, the hood covering his head, followed the panicky Nellie with his eyes, as, casting a frightened glance over her shoulder, she darted out the door into the night.

Before them, the crystal ball began to fill with mist– grey, swirling mist, ghostly and effacing. Within a few moments, another scene manifested, as the Sisters continued to hold their gazes, along with a tight rein on their emotions.

Totally unexpected, and definitely not Nellie's shack that the Sisters requested, this scene gave the impression of a sumptuous bedchamber, in which a man and a woman were getting undressed. They were arguing. He was tall and dark with the sexy handsome face and physique of a film-star. She was petite and, though comely, possessed the sharp features of one who was conniving and crafty. Her platinum-blonde hair was finger-waved in the popular Jean Harlow coiffure of the day. She was smoking a cigarette in a long holder, and she appeared to be extremely agitated.

"We have no choice!" the woman shouted. She tossed the scarlet dress she had stripped off onto a chair and began pacing the floor in an ivory satin slip that clung to her lean, almost boyish, body, puffing all the while on the cigarette in its bejeweled holder. "We *have* to kill her! **She saw!** Emmerich said she was ghostly when he caught her in the kitchen. **You heard him! There was no question that she saw**!"

Having removed his shirt, the man dropped down onto a padded hassock, covering his face with his hands. His undershirt was sleeveless, and his suspenders hung down from his waist to the floor. "If only the damn fool had not left that panel open when he had to go outside. We should *not* have accepted him into our circle. He is weak. And now this!"

"Wait! Wa-a-a–it!" The blonde stopped pacing, spinning round to face the man. "In a way, this is perfect." Her face broke into a cunning smile that struck the Sisters as demonic, while a strange glint brightened the cold eyes. "Yes … yes, it's destiny! We could have a *double* sacrifice before everyone takes their leave tomorrow. *This has happened for a reason.* Don't you see?!"

Her eyes gleamed with appreciative malice. "We *need* to perform another ritual tomorrow." She put a hand to her hip, tilting her platinum head and puffing thoughtfully. "It's a sign of the times! These difficult times are calling for a double sacrifice this gathering! It's been shown to us– **we must kill her.** *A double sacrifice!"* she repeated, savoring the thought with an almost lusty glee. "It's the only way, the only way to reap gain in these trying times!"

The man shook his head, bent forward in the chair, his hands still covering his face.

The woman stood there, motionless, for several moments before exploding, **"What do you have against killing her!** *Unless,"* she rushed forward to stand directly in front of her fraught mate. Setting the cigarette-in-holder over an ashtray, she reached out, snatching, claw-like, at his hands to uncover his face. **"Look at me!** You look at me and tell me you're not in love with her!"

When no answer came forth, she shouted at the top of her voice, **"Are you in love with that sloe-eyed hussy?! I demand** to know why you object to killing her when our whole operation depends on it! **I have a right to know!!"**

The man looked up at the woman before him, saying nothing. He didn't have to. *She knew. She could read, as could the Sisters, what was in his heart.*

"I *see.*" The blonde blew out a breath. "It's what I've suspected. It's been *her* all along." She turned and again resumed her restless pacing, muttering under her breath. "That's why this has happened– to show me the truth." For a wild moment, she considered shooting her unfaithful husband. Then she stopped her pacing when a more enticing plan took form in her mind. "I will do what needs to be done myself."

Once more Athena filled with the swirling grey mist, as it erased the previous scene and began manifesting another. In a few moments, Athena's magickal mists pulled the Sisters into a small, dark, moon-lit shed. Tools hung on the walls and occupied places on the shelves. An old-fashioned lawn mower stood, like a sleepy, inept sentry, in a corner.

The same platinum-blonde woman burst into the shed. She was wearing a man's topcoat that she shucked off, tossing it onto a shadowed worktable. In the moonlight streaming through the shed's window, the Sisters watched her pull what looked like a man's change of clothing from a large hook on the wall– dark corduroy trousers, a plaid flannel shirt, and a shabby brown jacket and fedora.

The Sisters continued to stare into the ball as the woman swiftly donned what they took to be the gardener's clothing over her satin pajamas. Sitting on the shed's only chair, she pulled off her slippers and yanked on a pair of work books that she hastily laced up. Lastly, she returned to the workbench where she had flung the man's overcoat.

From one of the coat's deep pockets, she extracted an item that, at first, the Sisters could not identify. When the woman turned slightly, straightaway then, they saw, in a beam of moonlight, that it was a small revolver. Setting the gun on the workbench, the blonde quickly pulled on a pair of leather gloves, also drawn from one of the coat's pockets, working the fingers for a snug fit.

Picking up the gun, the woman expertly checked the chamber before tucking it into the pocket of her donned jacket. With a mumbled oath, she hurried out of the shed. Closing the door behind her, she melted into the night.

Mist began anew to fill and swirl throughout Athena's crystal cavern.

With bated breaths, the Sisters waited, motionless, holding their gazes steady on the huge crystal ball. After several seconds the ball cleared of any remaining mist. Maggie let out her breath, and Raine and Aisling knew that Athena's magickal movie had ended.

That evening, after Aisling departed Tara for her own home, Raine and Maggie decided to choose what they would wear for their imminent time-trek to 1932. They had closets full of vintage clothing, so shopping would not be necessary.

"If we have to stay overnight, we'll simply wash our undergarments out by hand," Maggie suggested, as the pair stood in Raine's bedroom, at her closet. "Whatever we choose to wear should be comfortable with comfy shoes. We never know how much walking we'll have to do. I don't know about you, but I don't fancy carting an overnight bag through the hurly-burly of the blustery Time-Tunnel. It would be downright dangerous and could knock one, *or all*, of us out! A purse is all I feel like managing, and it will be a soft shoulder bag."

"I agree," Raine remarked. "And don't forget we discovered, through our research, that it was unseasonably cold for October that year. It even snowed." She turned from Maggie to move into her closet, immediately drawing out a long, black, button-down wrap

skirt. "How's this, Mags?" she asked, extending, at arm's length, the wool garment toward her cousin and sister of the moon.
"Remember, I purchased this last year at The Time Traveler. Tristan told us that it was circa 1931, '32. I happened to think of that a little while ago. Destiny, huh?"

Maggie smiled at her in the mirror. "What will you wear with it?" She sat down on Raine's forest-bed.

"I was thinking a V-neck sweater set that I also bought at The Time Traveler. Wait," she said, slipping the skirt back into her closet, "let me show you." Raine opened the top drawer of her tall, massive armoire, from which she pulled the fore-mentioned sweaters, cardigan and pullover, a matching set in a soft baby-blue. "These are longer in length than most sweaters today," she indicated, holding them out for Maggie to see. "The sweaters, too, Tristan told me, are from the early thirties, though you'd never know it. They're in mint condition. Tris said they'd been stashed away in a cedar chest. What do you think?"

"I think that outfit will be perfect. Comfortable, warm and cozy, and it will look nice too." Maggie raised a hand, making a circle with thumb and pointer finger in the customary American "OK."

Raine snapped her fingers. "Mags, I think we should wear our long trench coats, like the one Nellie had on in Athena's magickal movie. We know they would be right in style, and that way, we'll blend in."

"Our long, black trench coats, with the liners in and the collars up," Maggie mused. "Yes," she laughed her crystal laugh, "I like it. Nancy Drew comin' through!"

"Whaddya say we sport our black berets too?" Raine questioned. "A hat will disguise my modern haircut." She tilted her head, studying Maggie's coiffure. "Your style is classic, so no problem." She placed the sweater set over the back of a chair. Turning, she ferreted out her long, black trench coat. It, as Maggie's, was belted like the one Nellie had worn. She reached for a hat box on a closet shelf and, opening it, drew out her outsized black beret, laying it over the sweaters.

"I've an idea!" Maggie exclaimed. "I remember Tristan telling us that hat brooches were all the rage then. Let's choose a couple of the brooches Granny left us, with energies appropriate to what we'll need on this mission. We'll secure one to each of our berets."

"Wizard idea, Mags!" Raine strode nimbly to the dresser, where she flipped open one of her many jewel cases. Studying the contents, she reached for a brooch comprised of a gold crescent moon overlaid with silver stars beset with clear, glittering rhinestones. "I think this one will be perfect for my beret, Mags. The trilogy of stars reminds me of the Power of Three, and the spell infused in this brooch is for great success. I recall that Granny had written in her *Book of Shadows* that whenever she really needed to succeed at something, she pinned on this brooch. Goddess knows that total success is our goal with each time-trek!"

"I think it's perfect too. Be sure to fasten it securely, darlin'." Maggie stood. "Come on, let's go to my room now, so you can help me choose my outfit. It's imperative that we blend in with the ladies of the era."

The Sisters moved to Maggie's bedroom. Quite as spacious as Raine's, the red-haired Sister's bedchamber, too, was graced with a large fireplace, though the marble here was dark red, the high-ceilinged room's color scheme garnet and gold, the fiery colors concordant with Maggie's coloring and passionate Scorpio nature.

"I was thinking about this snuggly, flannel shirtwaist dress," Maggie said, pulling the dark-green garment from her closet for Raine, who had flung herself across Maggie's huge French-Empire bed, to see. Holding it before her voluptuous frame, Maggie said, "This frock is shin-length on me, which is accurate for the Depression era. Historically speaking, hemlines go up and down with the economy," she laughed. "I love the scalloped hem on this dress, and the fabric's so soft and comfy, perfect for travel, perfect to blend in, and warm too. What say you?"

"Bless my wand! You know I love that dress. It's *my* color," Raine pouted, remembering how she tried to get Maggie to part with the frock, when they'd left The Time Traveler vintage clothing shop last December.

"It's your color, yes, but it's also one of *my* favorite colors," Maggie retorted. "And besides, it's not your size."

Raine stuck her tongue out at her cousin, rejoining with, "Not my fault you like your sweets!"

"I daresay, you can eat me under the table any day!" Maggie hung the dress on the closet door. "Shoes!" she blurted of a sudden. "You forgot shoes." She bent to retrieve a pair of vintage lace-up spectators, in soft black and green leather with thick, schoolmarm, two-inch heels. "Won't these be spot-on?"

"They will!" Raine replied, sitting up and crossing her legs in the lotus position she liked so well. "I didn't forget about shoes, Mags, I just forgot to show you. I'm wearing lace-up spectators too, a pair of vintage Red Cross shoes, a popular brand back then. Mine are pale blue and black. I found them at an online auction after purchasing that sweater set from Tristan. The baby-blue matches perfectly. And, of course, we'll each be sure to wear black stockings."

Maggie was only partially hearing what Raine was saying, for she was searching through one of her jewelry boxes for the exact right brooch for her hat. After only a few moments, she lifted an exquisite crescent moon, crafted in silver, the metal of the Goddess, and adorned with tiny rainbow moonstones. "This one," she announced, gliding it under Raine's regard. "This is the brooch I'll secure to my hat. Oh, ladies all wore hats back then," she added. "But," she tapped a bejeweled finger to her lips, "I think I shall wear a cloche hat. Yes, I have a beautiful green one trimmed in black grosgrain ribbon. The brooch will be cunning pinned to it!"

Raine thought for a moment, saying, "I know the hat you mean, and it will be the *pièce de résistance!* I'm not envious of the hat," she teased. "Though it is *my* color you'll be wearing, the cloche style does not suit me as it does you."

Maggie laughed breezily. She couldn't help it, for at that moment, Raine's face was unquestionably kittenish. She glanced at her watch. "Great Goddess, I promised to ring Thaddeus a half-hour ago. I want to remind him to pick up the 1930s suit, tie, topcoat and hat at Enchantments costume shop downtown tomorrow. I spoke to the manager, on the phone earlier, and thank the Goddess they have vintage men's clothing from that era in stock. As soon as I thought of it, I rang them to put those items aside for Thad in his size. I was afraid they were going to tell me they'd have to get those things from their Pittsburgh shop; and if we want to time-trek tomorrow evening, that just wouldn't do– to wait for items from Pittsburgh.

"I'll remind Thaddeus to try everything on," Maggie mused aloud. "He can wear that nerdy pair of oxford shoes he has; they will do just fine, and one of his own shirts. I thank my stars that he allows me to dress him nowadays. The only thing he still insists on is his signature, cherry-red bowtie; but on this trip, he'll wear the Thirties' wool tie from Enchantments."

The redheaded Sister started from the room, when Raine called out, "You make your call here in private, Mags, and I'll go downstairs and brew us some tea. Come down to the kitchen when you've rung off, and we'll ring Aisling, together, to finalize our plans for departure tomorrow night."

Chapter Sixteen

Haleigh's Wood was intensely dark and unusually grim when the three Sisters and Dr. Weatherby pulled up in Aisling's black SUV to the path entrance with which they were most familiar.

In the full moon's glimmering, the thick forest loomed before them. As night fell, the wind fluttered branches and undergrowth to create ghostly movements and deep shadows; and the strange sounds of owls and other night creatures punctuated the otherwise silence.

The darkness seemed to possess texture, thick and furred, like the pelt of a black panther. And this night it felt as dangerous. The darkness had dimension too, seeming so high and so wide that the arrivals felt immersed in it, engulfed by it. It was a breathing, dark, living thing, pulsing like a heart, and throbbing with secrets. And hidden in the dark– the eyes, the eyes of the forest and the eyes of a murderer from the past.

Always one to check the moon for visible omens, Raine opened the vehicle's door and stepped outside to look skyward. Through the tangle of trees, like a web of fine alençon lace, she could see the moon, huge and glowing silvery-white.

She gave a small sigh of relief. *No blood on the moon this night,* she told herself. *And thank the Goddess it's not a hot, muggy summer night, since we're dressed for a chilly October where we're going!* She stood perfectly still, letting whatever she was sensing seep into her essence. *There's something here,* she told herself, *something in these woods, waiting, waiting to show itself. I just hope whoever, or whatever it is, it's not here to jinx our mission!* Noticing Aisling staring at her, Raine sent her a weak smile.

The senior Sister had stopped first at Tara for Raine and Maggie, then at Dr. Weatherby's not-too-distant, neo-Gothic home, Joyous Garde. When the professor– tricked out for his 1932 time-trek– had come hurrying out to the curb, it occurred to Aisling and to Raine that they never did learn if the eccentric man named his home after the idealistic refuge of Guinevere and Lancelot or for John Steinbeck's sanctuary where he penned *East of Eden.* It was one of several mysteries yet to be answered about their brilliant cohort. Raine made a mental note to ask Maggie about Joyous Garde. One thing for sure was that Thaddeus was an enigma, and he could always be counted on, in times of need– and to surprise.

Whilst Aisling was getting her bag of magickal tools from the SUV, Raine, Maggie– carrying the poppet Cara– and Thaddeus, already out of the vehicle, began looking one another over to appraise their vintage attire.

"Thaddeus, you look positively *smooooth*. A real *pip*," Maggie pronounced, using the waggish speech of their targeted era. She stepped to his side to kiss his bearded cheek.

"*Och!*" Cara exclaimed, her little face pressed against Dr. Weatherby's chest, "Y're crushin' me, an' I kaint breathe!"

Maggie took a step back from her lover to tuck the magickal ragdoll's lower half into Aisling's large, canvas satchel. "You'll be more comfortable in there."

The professor's dark blue suit, in the dazzle from the lantern Aisling was holding, made his bright blue eyes look even bluer; and the square, padded shoulders of the suit jacket accentuated his own muscular form, creating a masculine V-physique that set his beloved's heart to racing. Over his arm, he carried a vintage trench coat of a taupe color.

"You ladies look swell in those black trench coats," he answered in tune with the dialogue of the Thirties. "The hats and the shoes are timely too. Very nice. Very nice, indeed."

"You all look your parts. C'mon," Aisling said in a slightly harried tone. "Let's get deep into the woods. "I don't want anyone to spy this light and get curious."

"Good t'inkin', blondie!" Cara quipped.

As they walked, keeping to the path, the redheaded Sister queried as she grasped Dr. Weatherby's hard-muscled arm, "Did you study that list of 1930s slang expressions I sent you this morning via your email?"

"They're all up here," Thaddeus replied, tapping his temple. "Filed and ready if we need them."

"I doubt we needed to trouble ourselves with the slang research, because Aisling's speech enchantment always works so well for us, but it never hurts to have backup. Raine and I jotted some of the expressions down in a little notebook that we're taking with us, along with a few notes from our research we may find useful. I even found a tiny, bejeweled pencil that belonged to Granny McDonough. It's from the Thirties. I remembered it this morning and popped it into my bag. Props and costumes, dialogue– they all help to keep us in character." Maggie reached into her black shoulder bag to draw out a folded slip of paper. "Let's make certain we have everything we need with us before we activate our Time-Key."

She opened the list to full-sheet and began reading, "Pepper spray, just in case. With our magickal powers and Thaddeus' black-belt karate, we'll be safe enough." *One of the things that make Thaddeus' karate so powerful is that it holds an even greater element of surprise. An attacker would never guess that my cerebral-looking professor is so skilled in the martial arts,* she told herself.

"Got it!" Raine answered, peering inside, at the pepper spray, then patting her black leather shoulder bag.

"Our small, travel *Book of Shadows*." Now it was Maggie who palmed her purse. "Got it!" Her eyes returned to the list, over which Aisling held the lit lantern. "A few can't-do-without toiletries." Again, she checked her purse.

"Right!" she and Raine echoed.

"Got my toothbrush," Dr. Weatherby remarked, thumping a hand to the breast pocket of his suit, "just in case we have to actually stay overnight."

"Oh, I think we'll polish off this case shortly after midnight," Raine replied. "That's when the police reports said that the ax murders took place."

"Darlin'," Maggie said, addressing Thaddeus, "are you wearing your contacts?"

"Yes," he replied. "And yes to the warning on your lips to keep my eyes tightly shut when we take off, so the wind in the Time-Tunnel won't dry and irritate my eyes."

"Okie-doke," Maggie rejoined, resorting once again to common Thirties' slang.

"Aisling," Raine asked, "did you remember to bring a thermos of Eva's special-brew tea? Sorry we had to ask you to bring it, but I couldn't find a thermos at Tara."

"Not to worry, it's in my bag. I'm glad you shared that discovery with me. Ian and I both enjoy it at the close of a long day." The blonde with the wand stopped, holding the lantern up and looking about the thick tangle of woods on either side of the path. "This is far enough. Let's get to it." She set the canvas bag down on a flat rock. Pulling a large thermos from the satchel, she opened it, and rummaging through the bag, drew out four plastic cups. After pouring the Tea-Time-Will-Tell for the time-travelers and herself, she said, "I think this calls for a special cheering cup. Thaddeus, would you like to propose a toast?"

Dr. Weatherby cocked his head and held up his pointer finger in a wordless plea for "One moment." He cleared his throat. "This is not my favorite *way* to travel, but it's, by *far*, pun intended, my *favorite* travel." With that, he raised his cup. "To the full success of our mission!"

"Hear! Hear!" the Sisters returned. **"So mote it be!"**

Everyone drank, and soon the cups were drained, as thoughts turned to their work at hand.

In the glow from the lantern, which Aisling had hung from a tree branch, Maggie's green eyes sparkled, and her laugh floated in the charged air for a second before she announced, "Now, before we take off, let's go over some important data. Thaddeus and I are a married couple, *Maggie and Thaddeus Weatherby*. Best to use our real names, as we've done on previous trips. OK," she went on, "Raine is my sister. Raine will be using her real name, and we all hail from Pittsburgh. We know the history of our commonwealth's Princess City well, so we'll have no difficulty answering any questions about it, should any be put to us."

"Good that we'll be from Pittsburgh," Dr. Weatherby approved, "in the event someone asks us something about our 1932 Hamlet of which we aren't cognizant."

"The fewer people you actually engage in conversation, the better," Aisling advised.

"That's our usual MO. Observe, listen and learn," Raine murmured, checking her face in the small compact-mirror she had pulled from her shoulder bag. The lion-faced compact had belonged to Granny McDonough. It had become a good-luck charm to the Sisters and served as added protection.

Raine and Maggie were wearing makeup in the fashion of the 1930s, which was a bit more subdued than the bold makeup of the Roaring Twenties. They decided to keep their usual eye makeup along with a well-blended cheek color that matched the crimson-red, matte lipstick that defined the natural outline of their lips. The cupid-bow mouth had vanished with the roar and the zaniness of the Twenties. Raine had nixed her habitual glittery black nail polish for the glossy crimson-red that both she and Maggie now displayed on oval-shaped, manicured nails.

"As before when you time-trekked," Aisling reminded, "we'll employ the same magickal method to deal with the era's speech."

After conferring several minutes with Raine and Maggie on the ritual they would be performing to witch their speech, the senior Sister continued, "Within our secret chant, we'll weave a spell that your speech will be heard by everyone you encounter as dialect familiar to them. The enchantment will work in the reverse as well, so that *everything* spoken to you and around you will sound … that is, will *translate* to your modern ears like our modern dialogue, slang, and patterns of speech."

"As I told you when you departed for Victorian Ireland, Shakespeare's England, the Pennsylvania frontier, and the remote Scottish Islands of Orkney, the enchantment is not perfect," Aisling added. "Some words and phrases may flee the charm, but as before, the spell *will* work." She gave a long sigh. "I think that just about covers it."

"Except for Cara," Maggie said, indicating their poppet, who, unusually quiet, was taking everything in.

"Leave her here with me," Aisling stated firmly.

"Yes," Maggie replied. "She just wanted to see us off and wish us well."

"*Och!*" the doll shrieked. "Sure 'n haven't I tole ya over an' yet again not t' talk 'bout me as if I hain't here!" She ducked her wee yarn-covered head. "Aye, I wanted t' be here f'r yer leave-takin'. Godspeed, me darlin's, and Goddess bless! This here's sumpin' from ye're granny." She brought her little mitt-hands to her face and blew a dramatic kiss. From the magickal poppet's smeared, crooked mouth came a rush of crystalline faerie dust, silver and gold and shimmering, that drifted to the time-trekkers and settled over them, brightening and polishing their white-gold auras of protection to a Divine brilliance.

In a rush of emotion, the Sisters and Thaddeus thanked the little doll, as Aisling reached toward her satchel to pat Cara on the head. Then the senior Sister pulled her black ritual robe out of her carry-all and slipped it on, over her ebony jeans and top.

Raine's fabulous emerald eyes swept the others, "Are we ready then?"

"More than ready!" Dr. Weatherby almost shouted, so eager was he to begin their passage. He pulled his vintage trench coat on, over his suit. Double-breasted with a wide, pointed collar, the trench was belted. In a few moments, Thaddeus had the coat buttoned and the belt secured round his trim waist.

"Sisters," Aisling commanded, "Thaddeus, let's spiritually and mentally prepare ourselves for your journey. If all goes as well as your previous time-travels, you'll be back in a literal flash, with no actual lapse in time, for we are mindful, as well as spiritually aware, that the past, present, and future are simultaneous. Let us proceed."

As Aisling delved into her satchel for her magickal tools, Raine caught her breath. A feeling of imminent danger skittered through her like an icy wind on a cold winter's day. "Maggie," she whispered, "do you feel it?"

Maggie stood perfectly still, rooted to the spot, scarcely breathing. "Yes," she returned in a whisper, "I do. And it's not just full-moon madness. We'll have to be especially vigilant."

We always are, Raine replied telepathically. She tilted her beret-covered head, her granny's brooch, with its silver spray of stars, glittered in the moon's rays, as she listened with a frown. For a fleeting moment, she thought she'd heard a voice, a woman's voice, warning them to be watchful.

Seemingly unaware of the exchange between Raine and Maggie or the plaintive voice on the wind, Dr. Weatherby's bright blue eyes reflected the excitement he was struggling to contain within his own simmering essence.

He always reminds me of an astronaut ready for launch, Aisling thought.

Maggie grasped Thaddeus' arm. "Raine and I sense that we–" She broke off, not wanting to alarm Aisling, who had started to speak and was fixing her with the riveting McDonough stare.

"Our chant will incorporate all the particulars. The date you've chosen to visit is Tuesday, 11 October 1932, the day before our Hamlet's unsolved triple ax murders. Though it is nearly midnight now, we'll program for the three of you to reach 1932 Haleigh's Wood at 4:00 p.m. Since where you're going will be October, it will be just turning dusk, and the woods will be dark enough for cover. Anyway, that should provide you with sufficient time to observe Nellie Triggs; see, for certain, whose house she was in about 5:15 when she witnessed the ritual murder; in addition to gathering the facts surrounding her demise and the attack on her family."

Aisling cleared her throat. "I strongly advise you to stage your return from Haleigh's Wood in the dark of night. If everything goes smoothly, when you do return to your own time, as I said and we all know from experience, not one minute will have passed since your departure. I'll be right here, waiting for you."

"Aye, an' I'll be here too!" Cara cut in with fervor.

Looking directly into the professor's eyes, Maggie spoke with the old-fashioned schoolmarm ring of authority she used when instructing her college students. "I know we've gone over this at the onset of each of our time-treks, and at this point in our relationship, I feel I hardly need to; but, nonetheless, I'm going to say this. When we arrive, you must not interfere with our plan. In every way, you will be, simply put, a *witness* to our endeavors– and a witness to history. And that is all. We must not, any of us, *in any way,* alter history."

"I quite understand," Dr. Weatherby assured his beloved, as eagerness exuded from every pore of his body.

Remembering how he had managed to twist and bend her rules during one of their time-treks, Maggie regarded the professor with her McDonough gaze, "Can we depend on your word, Thaddeus?" She touched his shoulder, "No tricks?"

"You can depend *fully* on my word," he answered firmly. "No tricks; I promise." And the look in his eyes told her he was sincere.

As was her habit, Raine was bracing herself for what she knew was about to take place. Pulling her scarf from around her neck, she placed it over her head and beret to double-knot it under her chin. Though she'd secured the black beret to her hair with a hatpin, she was taking no chances losing it with her granny's enchanted brooch in the blustery Tunnel of Time. She turned the collar of her black trench coat back up to send Maggie a look that transported her thought.

Taking her cue from Raine, Maggie did likewise with her neck-scarf, preparing herself for takeoff.

"Talismans at the ready!" Aisling commanded of a sudden. Reaching under the bodice of the ritual robe, the leggy blonde pulled her gem-encrusted amulet free from its resting place beneath the black knit top she was wearing. She lifted the heavy silver chain over her long, silky hair. The talisman's center-stone sapphire and scatter of tiny jewels glittered and sparked energy in the beam of moonlight that streamed through an opening in the tree cover.

Thus prompted, Raine and Maggie removed their amulets from around their necks. In addition, each wore a medieval ring of great significance. Hundreds of years old, the rings held strong arcane energies. Worn and dulled by Time, the rings' brass shafts bore faded secret symbols around the sides of the mounts that in each held a large blue moonstone. Already, the medieval rings were beginning to emit a shared bluish radiance, a glow that looked quite eerie in the forest's shadowy gloom.

While Dr. Weatherby watched, the Sleuth Sisters held out and fit together the three necklaces bequeathed to them years before by Granny McDonough, whose influential presence the magickal trio now keenly sensed. In each pair of Sisterly hands, the powerful talismans actually felt warm against the skin as they verily hummed with energy.

"Thaddeus and fellow sisters of the moon," Maggie enunciated in her mellifluous voice, "for the original definition of the word *talisman*, we must hark back to ancient times. Before it was known as a magickal symbol, *talisman* carried a far older meaning. From the Greek word *telesma,* meaning 'complete,' a talisman, in olden times, was any object that completed another– *and made it whole.* I say this to remind us, here present tonight in this wood, the green cathedral of the great Goddess– of the majestic Power of Three." Taking her beloved by the arm, she said, "You stand here, betwixt Raine and me."

The full moon, sliding from beneath a cloud, whence it had briefly cached itself, flashed a timely and quite dazzling blaze of light off the fitted talismanic pieces, as the Sleuth Sisters united their voices to invoke in perfect harmony, "With the Power of Three, we shall craft and be granted our plea! With the Power of Three, so mote it be! With the Power of Three, so blessed be!"

Holding her antique heirloom out to her cousins, Aisling said, "I want you to take this with you again. You'll most certainly require the energies of the third talisman."

"Sister!" Raine and Maggie protested, "that will leave you unprotected, and–"

"Keep your talisman with you this time," Raine insisted.

Aisling shook her head. "I'll have Cara with me."

"Aye, she will," the poppet put in.

"You must maintain, as much as possible, the sacred and supreme Power of Three," the blonde with the wand asserted.

Raine and Maggie hugged Aisling for a long, loving moment. Then Maggie slipped the senior Sister's amulet around her neck together with her own. Raine put her talisman on again, as Aisling reached into the large canvas bag she carried over her arm for the container of sea salt, a fire-starter, and a bundle of white sage that was handed to her by Cara.

With the salt, the senior Sister drew a circle of protection around the soon-to-be-traveling three people, whom, after her daughter Merry Fay and her husband Ian, she loved most in all the world. Flicking on the fire-starter, she lit the sage-bundle that she secured inside a safe Pyrex bowl. In an instant, the air around them filled with the sweet, pungent aroma of its good, smoking essence.

Walking a circle with the smoking smudge bundle deosil– clockwise– the blonde with the wand cleansed the area of negativity.

Finally, Aisling nodded to her sisters of the moon, as the powerful threesome chanted a strong incantation of protection, ending with the petition, "God-Goddess between us and all harm!"

As one, the Sisters again began to chant, "Wind spirit! Fire in all its brightness! The sea in all its deepness! Earth, rocks, in all their firmness! All these elements we now place, by God-Goddess' almighty strength and grace, between ourselves and the powers of darkness! So mote it be! Blessed be!"

Under the tree-hung lantern's golden rays of light, and with careful expression, the three Sisters and Thaddeus intoned aloud the ancient Gaelic words, the arcane phrases Raine and Maggie had, over the long years, so diligently ferreted out, the secret text neatly handwritten across their small *Book of Shadow*'s final pages– the powerful language that programmed and prompted their sacred travel through time.

As the ancient chant was in Old Irish, in order to get it letter-perfect each time, it was best for the Sisters to read the words from their *BOS,* though the chant had almost burned itself, by this point in time, into their collective memories. After his first spell-trek with Maggie and Raine, Thaddeus's eidetic mind had collected and stored the Time-Key, a fact that saved their lives on one, especially problematic, occasion in the past.

Their unified voices rising with each line in crescendo, the Sisters were closing the current segment of their ritual with the words, "To honor the Olde Ones in deed and name, let Love and Light be our guides again. These eight words the Witches' Rede fulfill– 'And harm ye none; do what ye will.' Now we say this spell is cast, bestow again the Secret we ask! **Energize the Time-Key!** So mote it be! Blessed be!"

In perfect stillness they waited.

Not a sound reached them. The night was totally hushed. The moon cast murky shadows through the canopy of trees to the forest floor, as the surrounding woods seemed to breathe a message that was just beyond hearing.

The Sisters and Dr. Weatherby knew from past experiences not to panic, and so they drew in their breaths and breathed out, centering themselves and maintaining the calm bestowed on them by Eva's tea.

As it had been with their previous time-treks, it was as though Time waited– as though something momentous were about to unfurl within their established circle.

"Let's recite the passage over," Aisling wisely proposed. "You have made your choice, and now you must focus! You've woven your intent within the ancient chant. You *will* arrive at your programmed destination. Put aside– each of you– any and all doubts, fears, and," fixing Thaddeus with her piercing McDonough gaze, "*impatience.* Free yourselves from all negativity– and allow the Great Secret to happen! Give yourselves up to it– for it *will* happen!"

Again, the Sisters and Thaddeus chanted the ancient evocation, hands raised in calling forth, with the Sisters, prompted by Aisling, adding at the end: **"Now is the time! This is the hour! Ours is the magick! Ours is the power!"**

The Sisters' ancient talismans radiated with heat and the super Power of Three against their skins, as the sparked energies swished and swirled around them. It was the way of strong magick, and thus it did not frighten them or their colleague the least bit.

For an evanescent moment, after concluding the repeated Time-Key chant, both Raine and Maggie thought they had caught sight, within the shadowy tangle of trees, of Nellie Triggs' ghost, her elusive words suppressed by the surrounding forest but captured and carried eerily on the wind.

"*Take heed!*" she wailed. "*Be wary!*"

In another moment, as in the tradition of ghosts, the vaporous form disappeared.

Raine and Maggie strained their eyes and ears, but there was nothing, only the woods, and, beyond that– the textured darkness.

"At last!" Thaddeus whispered suddenly.

There came, softly at first, then louder, an electrical crackling sound, as gleaming sparks and orbs of white light zigged and zagged above and around the human circle, rendering the moonlit, wooded scene, with its tree-shrouded night sky, ever more eerie.

Sliding in and out of clouds all evening, the elusive moon glided from behind its veil, and it was then Aisling took a step backward, outside the circle of time-travelers. Her long blonde hair, silvered even more by the moonlight, billowed wildly out behind her, as a terrific gust of wind swept across the area.

Otherworldly in its timbre, the wind carried on its breath the enchanted flutes of the mysterious race of people from Ireland's ancient past, the mystical *Tuatha De Danann*, from whom the Sisters had gained the coveted Time-Key.

From its supporting branch, the lantern began to swing precariously from side to side, causing the thick candle therein to flicker wildly.

When the mystic wind blew the lantern's sputtering candle out, Maggie grasped Dr. Weatherby's arm, gripping hard. "Steady on now, Thaddeus! You know what to expect!" she called over the din, as the ghostly gale tore at her long, black trench coat and her scalloped skirt beneath.

As always, the Sisters were impressed by Dr. Weatherby's show of courage. His upturned face looked calm, almost serene, and his eyes were closed. Securing his fedora tighter on his head, he shouted, "Let it happen!"

In a burst of light, a bevy of ethereal faces, skeletal figures, and vaporish human forms appeared in the rising, swirling mists, their gaunt arms open beseechingly. In a trice, the claw-like hands wrapped tightly round the time-trekker's ankles, heaving, with supernatural strength, Raine, Maggie, and Thaddeus toward the vortex of a pitch-black tunnel– a twister of helical wind that threatened to pull them into its infinite void with the force of a gigantic vacuum.

So strong was this gale, howling and whirling with accelerated ferocity, that the entire encircling woods seemed to scream and shriek. Not wanting to be separated, Raine, Maggie and Thaddeus held fast to one another, strengthening their power with the love they shared.

Simultaneously, just outside the circle and their established Doorway of Time, the senior Sleuth Sister stood her ground. With her long, blonde locks blowing violently about her upturned face, and her black robe billowing out from her tall, slender body, her arms shot skyward, as she sent the time-travelers an extra measure of protection, her chant carrying on the wind and swirling round them. Instantly did they feel its great power.

Aisling's courage and confidence never failed to infuse pluck and purpose into Maggie and Raine, and each locking hands with Dr. Weatherby, they raised their joined arms, the three of them repeating the last line of the arcane passage yet again.

A thick, vaporous cloud rose from the depths of the moist forest floor– that started quivering and rumbling beneath their feet. It was at this point, in the past, when a dreadful sensation of being suffocated had always threatened to overwhelm the time-travelers. But no such feeling menaced them this time. *It was definitely a good sign!*

While the air around them continued to swish and swirl like the mightiest of whirlpools, a loud crack of lightning, followed by a tremendous roll of thunder, assaulted their ears with a **RO——— AR!**

Raine squeezed Thaddeus' hand hard. "It's happening," she called out, determined to rid her thoughts of any and all fears. "It's happening as it should!"

Suddenly, the swirling atmosphere opened with a violent suction– making them feel as if they were being sucked down a giant drain! Rapidly then did the Tunnel wholly swallow Raine, Maggie, and Dr. Weatherby, as Aisling disappeared from their view in a brilliant burst of blue-white light, her voice rebounding after them, **"Bles–sed Beeeeeeeeeeeeeeeeeeeeeeeeeeeeeee!"**

Faster than any one of them could answer "Blessed be," the time-travelers were forcibly hauled deeper and deeper– into the long, black Tunnel of Time.

"Hold tight to one another!" Above the blustering din, Maggie's voice echoed through the Tunnel, **"We can't chance being separated!"**

"Whenever and wherever we go," Raine's words rumbled down the Passageway of Time, **"we go together!!"**

With a squeal, Raine landed on her firm, little *derrière*, the landing, on the forest floor, cushioned by a soft pile of leaves banked against a towering oak. The impact created, in woodland celebration of Goddess-bestowed blessings, a blazon of orange, gold, russet, and green leafy-confetti.

She glanced quickly around to see Maggie and Thaddeus slouched forward, their backs against a neighboring tree, on the leaf-covered damp earth next to her. Her heart swelled with gratitude and relief. "Thank you, God-Goddess," she whispered. She breathed in the crisp, cool air, fragrant with the woodsy autumn aroma of decaying leaves, her emerald gaze sweeping her surroundings. "It's definitely October," she announced needlessly. "And it seems to be about the right time of day that we programmed to land."

After giving her head a shake to still her surroundings, Maggie glanced curiously around to see where capricious Time had deposited them. "If all went as planned, we should be in Haleigh's Wood near the railroad tracks and the river. At least that's *where* we programmed to land."

Maggie's eyes shifted to the foliage, vivid even in the fading, late-afternoon light. "Oooh yes, it's definitely October. Let's just hope it's 11 October 1932." She started to say something else, when she stopped. "Great Goddess! I just realized– this landing was easier than our earlier passages! I was so hoping it would be this trip!" Her hands came up to lightly massage her temples, after which she turned toward Thaddeus. "Darlin', you really are a genius!"

"It *was* easier!" Raine exclaimed. *Yes, Virginia, there is a Santa Claus! Clap hands; I believe in faeries! And in Eva's Time-Will-Tell Tea!* she rejoiced inwardly, a satisfied smile curving the corners of her little-cat mouth, as she leaned back against the tall oak. An idea was coming to her. *If we add just one drop of Granny's flying potion– Yes, I think that would make it purrrrr-fect!*

"That will do the trick!" Maggie effervesced, beaming at Raine. "Doesn't need much. As you suggest, only a wee drop of Granny's flying potion. I'm not experiencing that horrid nausea and disorientation as I did with previous landings! And if I'm dizzy at all, it's with delight!" Maggie leaned over to kiss Thaddeus on the lips. "Thank you!"

"Don't thank me, though you're welcome to kiss me anytime," Dr. Weatherby grinned. "We must all thank Eva for her truly enchanting tea when we return to our own era. Thank her, that is, without telling her precisely why. And let's keep our voices down, no telling who is lurking about in these woods, who might hear us and zero in. I don't want to alarm you, ladies, but the Depression era, as well you know, was rife with crime."

His bright blue eyes probed deeply into the shadowy foliage and thick underbrush, searching as absorbedly as his ears were listening. A crow cawed raucously from the uppermost branches of a tall, dead tree that, groaning in the wind, gave forth a lonely, forlorn sound.

Maggie slipped a hand under the bodice of trench coat and dress and over the two talismans she was wearing– for reassurance. "Good," she breathed, running her fingers over the treasured amulets, while she let out a long breath. "Thank the God-Goddess!" She removed the scarf from over her head and hat then, her fingers making certain that Granny's brooch was still securely fastened to the green cloche. It was, and again she let out a held-in breath with a whispered prayer of thanks.

After making certain of her own talisman, along with her beret and brooch, Raine, too, breathed a faint sigh of relief. She drew from her purse her compact, and checking her appearance, adjusted her beret. Ever the most adventurous, she was the first to stand.

"Breathe!" she encouraged with gusto. "Deep, *deep* breaths. Ah! Trekking back in time does provide such nice, fresh, clean air!"

Thaddeus and Maggie stood and, following Raine's lead, breathed deeply of the cool, crisp 1932 autumn air.

"Delicious!" Maggie concurred.

"Now that we're acclimated to our surroundings, let's get moving," Thaddeus pushed. "I'll feel better when we're out of these darkening woods."

"Hold it right there!" a deep, gruff voice behind them growled. "I got a convincer pointed right at you. Don't turn around. Drop your wallet, mister, and those purses you ladies got. Drop 'em nice 'n easy to the ground."

The time-travelers had frozen in their tracks at their accoster's first words.

"Do it!" the mugger roared with impatience.

Close to Thaddeus, Maggie was able to whisper into his ear, "It's not a gun; it's a knife."

"Whadya whisperin' about?! Knock it off! Now drop your money 'n any jewelry you're wearin' or, I swear, I'll plug ya full-a lead, all three of ya!"

"I don't think you really want to know if I am a good witch or a bad witch!" ~ Dr. Raine McDonough, PhD

Chapter Seventeen

Before the Sisters could say "Wiz-zard!" Dr. Weatherby whipped round with a knock-for-six karate kick that flung the assailant's knife high into the air. The stunned man seemed to freeze, recovering to attempt a lunge toward Thaddeus, fists poised for battle. But before he could make contact, the professor had spun round a second time, landing a powerhouse kick that hurled the mugger furiously backward.

Whilst the man was still on the ground, Thaddeus yanked his wallet from his suit-trousers' pocket, the action causing Maggie to whisper, "What're you doing?!"

Dr. Weatherby flashed his opened wallet before the woozy man's face. "Take a look, buster! We're federal agents on assignment, and we haven't time for the likes of you. Make tracks outta here fast, or I'm liable to change my mind and run ya in!" Thaddeus looked keenly at their accoster, adding, "So you know. An attack on a federal agent is a *federal* offense. Anymore trouble from you, and you're goin' 'inside for all day'! Clear?!"

Good thing we prepared ourselves for this trip with a good dose of Eva's tea, or we wouldn't have been fit to handle this, Raine told herself, fixing the would-be thief with her witchy stare.

With a groan, the beefy man gingerly sat up, shaking his head to clear it.

Thaddeus dipped into his pocket for a couple of the coins Hugh had given them, and reaching out to grasp the man's hand, he slapped them onto the open palm. "If you're hungry, this'll help. **Now go on! Get th' hell outta here!!**" he shouted, waving a deprecating hand at their staggered foe.

Eyeing the professor in a curious, cursory way, the man's gaze dropped to the palm where Thaddeus had deposited the coins. With a quick, sudden movement, he snapped his hand shut over the change, before he got warily to his feet.

Backing up slowly, the brute reeled and stumbled, his feet scrambling for traction on the damp leaves before he took off running, nearly falling face forward when his foot caught on an exposed tree root. His spouted oath reached the time-trekkers as he vanished from sight.

After she was sure the thug had fled, Maggie asked, "Darlin' what did you show him?"

The professor grinned, and his noble face lit up with the spirit of pure mischief. "My discount card for the Piggly-Wiggly Barbecue Pit."

The time-travelers reached Nellie Triggs' bungalow on Murphy Road just in time to see a tall, dark man banging a fist on her door. They pretended to ignore him, crossing the street, where they feigned interest in a vivid row of colorful fall mums lining a walkway.

"Nellie's sick in bed with the grippe," the gaunt, grey-haired woman, whom the time-travelers took to be Nellie's mother, answered at the door.

"I won't stay long," the ruggedly handsome man pleaded, "I just want to talk to her for a few minutes. Just give me five minutes with her; that's all I'm asking!"

"Why?! So's you can slap her around again?!" Nellie's mother's voice was suddenly louder and charged with exasperation. "I won't give ya five seconds with her! Biff, Nellie tole me t' tell you if ya came callin' that she never wants to see you again. Not after what you done to humiliate her in public. You're a damn nuisance; that's what you are! Now go away, and don't ever come back here again! If you do, we'll sic the coppers on ya! **Now get!**"

From their position across the street, the time-travelers heard the door slam shut. Out of their peripheral vision, they could see that the man started to knock again; but changing his mind, he started away, muttering under his breath.

When the Sisters and Thaddeus turned, they noted the look of anger stamped darkly on his features. They noticed, too, that his hands were balled into hard, tight fists.

"How are we going to keep an eye on Nellie's house without being seen?" Maggie whispered, her emerald gaze following Biff Valentine as he walked briskly away, muttering to himself. Her eyes swept the area for a good hiding place. "Later, we can cache ourselves between those hydrangea bushes and the house," she indicated with a jerk of her head, "but it's not quite dark enough to do that now. There's no place we can use as a lookout point right now, and we'll attract too much attention just standing here on this street."

"Y-yeah," Raine mused, "we'll have to follow Nellie when she exits the house to go to—"

Dr. Weatherby cut her short. "I've got an idea. Forgive me, Raine, but with a little luck this plan ought to fall into place."

They started walking slowly down the street.

"I propose," Dr. Weatherby began, "that we knock on Nellie's door, pretending to be from out-of-town and lost. We ask directions to an address very close to the house we think will turn out to be the ritual-murder house. We know she's going to be on her way there in a few, and she knows that her ex-boyfriend, Biff Valentine, wants to talk to her. She doesn't want to talk to him, and she fears he may be lurking about in the shadows, so when we ask directions to a place near her destination, I'm betting she'll say something like, 'I'm going that way myself. I'll be happy to walk with you to show you where it is you need to go.'" His blue eyes twinkled. "This way, since it's not completely dark yet, we won't have to worry that she'll think we're tailing her." He glanced about. "*Almost* dark though; so if she doesn't take the bait, we've lost nothing."

"Brilliant, darlin'!" Maggie remarked, patting the professor's shoulder. Leaning close, she whispered, "You know, you really do look like a handsome G-man in that trench coat and fedora." She shot him a wink. "Handsome and– *sexy*."

With a playful roll of her eyes, Raine checked the vintage wristwatch she remembered to wear. "It's only about a quarter till five. I'm thinking we have about fifteen minutes to kill before she's ready to set off on her walk to the target house."

"Let's amble up this street, keeping *her* house in sight. If she comes out, we'll simply ask for the directions without having to knock on her door," Dr. Weatherby stated. "That would be better anyway." He rubbed his hands together. "Being in motion, rather than standing still, will keep us warm."

As they walked, Maggie asked, "What address will we pretend to seek from Nellie?"

Raine and Thaddeus pondered for a reflective moment, with Raine answering, "Why not ask directions to the old– well, not so old in the era we're visiting– *Means* place? We know it was here then, and it isn't too far from where we think Nellie will be headed."

"Good choice!" Maggie concurred, silently forgiving Raine for the eye-roll. "And that would be a place that everyone back then– I mean *now*– would've been familiar with. Great Goddess, it's hard to keep one's tenses straight when time-traveling!"

"Head's up," Thaddeus cautioned under his breath. "It looks like Nellie's about to leave the house."

Since the trekkers had only gone about half a block, they hadn't far to go. Turning round, they started back down the street again, in the direction of Nellie's place. As they approached, she was bidding goodbye to her mother at the front door. Within a few seconds, they were following their subject, who set out at a brisk clip.

When they'd nearly caught up with her, Raine gave a **"Yoo-hoo! Excuse me!"**

Hailed by the unfamiliar voice, Nellie stopped and swung round, allowing the time-travelers to come up to her on the sidewalk. "Were you speaking to me, Miss?" The voice was soft and as pleasant as the face, the large, dark eyes soulful. Like Raine, she wore a black beret, with the collar of her trench coat turned up; but Nellie's belted coat was tan.

"Yes," Raine answered kindly, "I was. We were wondering if you'd be able to give us directions to the Means estate. We're from out-of-town, you see, and simply put, we're lost."

Nellie snorted, "You certainly are. This is the wrong side of the tracks for the Hamlet's mansions! I take it you came in on the train?"

"We did," Dr. Weatherby replied. "We were given instructions, but when we left the station, we must've made a wrong turn."

"I'll just bet you're from Pittsburgh," Nellie said mildly, tilting her head to study the three people before her in the dim light. "Our Hamlet gets a good many Pittsburgh folk here on business."

"That's a bet you'd win," Raine joked. "Do you know the Means place?"

"Who doesn't?" Nellie quipped. "Look, I'm headed that way myself; and truth be told, I'd welcome the company if you'd care to walk with me."

The time-trekkers traded glances. "Thank you!" they resounded, falling into step with the woman they knew would be dead, viciously murdered, around midnight. They couldn't help but feel sorry for her, so pretty, so young, and so sad-eyed.

Like most Old Souls, the Sleuth Sisters were empaths and, just as they could pick up the residue of energies left behind at historic sites, battlefields, old houses, and in vintage clothing and antiques, they could pick up the emotions of others. As they made their way down the street, they could sense that Nellie was troubled, for a whole circuitous route of emotions were swirling inside her, emotions the Sisters seized and pondered. That, coupled with the thought of Nellie's impending demise, made conversation difficult.

Once informal introductions had been made, the weighty silence prevailed for half a block. The Sisters purposely slowed their pace, with Nellie matching their steps. At the corner, they crossed a side street together, matching stride for stride, and it was Nellie who cracked the silence first with a sidelong look and the words:

"I've been down with the grippe all week. Still don't feel up to snuff, but I had to drag myself out of bed to run a couple errands that need tendin' to." She glanced nervously around, then looked at her walking companions with mixed feelings. "I'm awful glad for the company. I don't like walking in the dark. Not anymore. I used to enjoy the peacefulness of a moonlight walk, alone with my thoughts."

"The moon is a good friend for the lonely to talk to," Maggie said softly.

Nellie gave a half-nod, as a melancholy smile curved her lips. "Sometimes I'd walk fast to outdistance my thoughts, but most times, I'd use those moonlit walks to work through problems. I tidied up a lot of hitches that way. And I'd always end by tellin' myself that everything in my life right now is only temporary. That things will be better someday. One day, I'll *make* it better. I'm still young enough to do that, and this blasted Depression can't last forever, now can it?" She lowered her eyes. "Well, I'm glad you came along when you did."

The thought struck the Sisters and Thaddeus that the star-crossed woman was hungry for someone to confide in, someone who she sensed wouldn't repeat what she was saying. The fact that they were strangers, made it easier, in a way, for her to talk to them.

"Has something happened to change your mind?" Raine queried. "About walking alone in the dark, I mean?"

Nellie chewed her lower lip. "I–I have an ex-boyfriend I'd rather not run into."

"Then *I'm* glad, too, that we happened along when we did," Thaddeus put in, endeavoring to vanquish fear from the young woman's heart.

Nellie looked at the Sisters for a long moment before saying, "I don't know why I'm telling *you* this, but it's good to have *someone* to tell. It kind of lifts it off the heart, you know?"

"It does, yes," the Sisters replied, hoping the woman *would* unburden herself to them.

"My husband and I never got to have much of a marriage. Soon as we said 'I do,' he was sent off to war. When he came back, he wasn't the same. His last years were spent in the veterans' hospital in Pittsburgh. I want to remarry one day, but," she demurred, "I'm afraid."

"Of what exactly?" Raine asked.

Nellie took a deep breath, exhaling slowly. "Of making a mistake, of choosing the wrong fella." She lowered her eyes. "Folks talk if a woman has more than one beau. Before ya know it, word's out she's a real bearcat. I don't want people to gossip about me; but I have to, to use a popular expression, *play the field.* I *have* to be sure. I can't afford to make a mistake, because I won't be the only one to pay the price. My children and my mother would suffer too."

"I shouldn't worry about what others think," Maggie said, reaching out to touch Nellie's arm. "The best advice we could give you, or anyone, is to follow your heart."

"And we sense you have a good heart," Raine concluded truthfully. To Maggie, she sent the message, *Boyfriends or no, she's a **lonely** woman.*

"I never told anyone this before," Nellie stated quietly, "and, like I said, I don't know why I'm telling *you* these things; but I wonder if you would think me wicked if I tell you that every once in a while, when I'm feelin' especially blue, I wanna jump on a bus and escape, even if just for a day." In a split second, she added, "I never would, of course, but sometimes I can't help it. Sometimes I just feel so—" she hesitated, "*burdened.* I feel so guilty using that word, but that's what it feels like sometimes.

"Most times, it takes every cent I can scrape together just to make ends meet– and then something else happens. One of the kids gets sick, or my mother needs something, or something needs repaired or replaced in the house. Forgive me, but that's when I want to escape." For a second time, the woman quickly amended, "But I never would."

"We don't think you're wicked at all," Raine and Maggie answered nearly as one.

"It's normal to feel as you do sometimes, with all the responsibilities you have, not to mention that it's not the best of times." Maggie reached out, again, to pat the woman's arm.

Nellie smiled sadly. "Life can get heavy. Are you friends of Mrs. Means?" she asked unexpectedly. "Poor thing. I heard she's poor as a church mouse now. She'll have to give up her lovely home. I read in the paper that there's to be a grand auction up at her place. Everything will have to be sold, you know, to pay her husband's creditors and investors. When all's said and done, she'll have lost everything, including her husband." She lowered her voice, glancing quickly round again. "They say he jumped overboard from the ship he was traveling on last week." A sudden realization came over her. "Oh, but you know that, if you're going to the Means place. I hope you're here to help Mrs. Means. I really like her. She was a regular customer at the shop I manage. When she'd come in to browse or buy, she was never snooty like a lot of the highfalutin women in her class." Nellie's sad eyes held the Sisters, "Mrs. Means is a nice woman, a real lady, kind and considerate."

"Do *you* think J.D. committed suicide?" Maggie asked, rather abruptly for that particular Sister.

Nellie regarded Maggie sharply, hesitating with her response. It appeared to the Sisters that the ill-fated woman wanted to answer other than how she did. "I don't know," she mumbled, dropping her gaze. "All I know is that these are hard times, *hard times* for most." Nellie looked up to find anew the Sisters' steady regard. "I'm lucky to have the job I have."

"What did you say your line of work is?" Maggie asked, feigning ignorance.

"I manage an antique and curiosity shop here in the Hamlet," Nellie responded after a brief pause.

There was no doubt about it. The woman had avoided the Sisters' eyes again.

"One of several errands I need to do today is to pick up my pay for the week. And I've got to get some food in the house for my kids and my elderly mother. Bein' down sick really set me back." Nellie shot the Sisters the quickest of looks, an unreadable one. "My mom's a big help to me. She watches the kids when they're home from school, and she does the cooking and the light housekeeping."

"Antiques and curiosities. That sounds interesting," Raine remarked. "Do you enjoy your work?"

Nellie made a slight chortle. It was a short laugh completely devoid of humor. "Like I said, I'm lucky to have the job."

"I don't mean to sound nosy, but you sound as if you really don't like your job," Raine countered. "Don't worry. As we said, we're from a long way off, so your words are safe with us."

Nellie shrugged, her soft gaze dropping to the sidewalk. "I'm the breadwinner for my family, ma'am, so it's that job or the bread line." She glanced to her right, saying, "This is my turn-off. Just keep on this street another couple-a blocks, and you'll see, on the right, the wide, black wrought-iron gate at the entrance to the Means mansion. You'll see a large J on one gate, and a large D on the other, with a capital M in the center, where the gates meet. J.D.'s estate is called 'Oakmont.' You won't be able to miss it. The gates'll be closed, just press the buzzer, and either the butler or the housekeeper will answer. They're a husband and wife, and though Missus had to let all the servants go, those two stayed, out of loyalty to her."

Now that the time had come to say 'Goodbye,' the Sisters found it an even more difficult moment than they had anticipated.

"Thank you for the directions," Dr. Weatherby said.

"Yes, thank you!" the Sisters echoed hurriedly.

"You're very welcome," Nellie answered with her beautiful smile. "Thank you for the company and conversation. It did me good. I hope you can help Mrs. Means." Nellie lingered a moment, as if she wanted to say more, but all she voiced was, "*Goodbye.*"

As she started up the lane to her destination, she paused on the path to wave.

"Goodbye, Nellie," the time-trekkers replied, their voices muted with gloom. They watched sadly as the young woman walked away, thinking, as they did, that she had only a few more hours to live.

Raine, Maggie, and Thaddeus hadn't taken three steps, when Nellie wheeled round, and hurrying back to them, she whispered, "No, J.D. did not commit suicide."

Maggie reached out and, grasping both Nellie's hands, asked softly, "Please, tell us how you know this. It will aid us in clearing his name, and it will help his wife."

Terror leaped into Nellie's eyes. "I *don't* know it for certain." She shook her head. "I can't say anymore. Please don't press me."

With that, she turned and walked away; and this time, she did not look back.

When Nellie was out of earshot, Raine said to her companions, "What's our next step?"

"First of all," Thaddeus replied, "let's pretend we're going to Oakmont, in the event she looks over her shoulder and sees us still standing here." He grasped both Sisters by an arm, and they walked on, in the direction Nellie had indicated to them.

"We really *ought* to stop at Oakmont and speak with J.D.'s widow," Raine suggested.

"I think that's an excellent idea," Maggie agreed. "We hadn't planned on it, but it's always good to gather as much information as we can when connecting the dots in any puzzle. And this mystery is a *puzzle!*"

"More like a tangled web of evil," Raine mumbled.

"We don't have time now to speak with Mrs. Means," Thaddeus reminded them. "We've got to circle around and creep up on what we're almost certain now is the ritual-murder house."

Raine checked her watch. "I didn't mean speak with her *at this very moment*, Thad; but you're right, we'd better hurry. It's after five."

Within a few minutes, the time-travelers were picking their way along the shadows of the thick woods that bordered the house where Nellie had gone. Though it was now nearly completely dark, they did not walk up the driveway that led to the house. The moon on this night of 11 October 1932 was a waxing gibbous moon, ninety-two percent full, that, like the full moon they left behind in their own era, slid capriciously in and out of cloud cover.

From the tree line, revealed by the sudden reappearance of the moon, the time-travelers could see one side and the rear of the mansion. They immediately noted the period automobiles crowding the large, circular driveway, just as the crystal ball Athena had shown the Sisters.

"C'mon," Raine urged, "there's no time to lose. We've got to make a dash for those rhododendron bushes, so we can conceal ourselves sufficiently to peer through the ground-floor windows in the rear and, or the sides of the house."

"Let's wait *just* a bit," Dr. Weatherby replied, grasping Raine's arm. He was looking up at the moon. "Moon'll be gliding behind that huge cloud formation in a second."

Raine gave a silent nod, in the next moment, whispering, "C'mon! It's now or never!"

Keeping as low as they could and still moving fast, the threesome tore across the open yard to the bushes that hugged the house. There, they dodged behind the shrubbery to take up positions flush with the first-floor windows.

The Goth gal was just about to speak, when they heard the distinct sound of loud retching coming from somewhere behind them, in the trees not too distant from where they had been hiding. The sound was soon followed with a long groan. "My witchy intuition is telling me that is the robed figure who left the panel in the bookcase open when he hurriedly left the ritual, the same robed-and-hooded figure our crystal ball showed us surprising Nellie in the kitchen," she whispered to Maggie.

The redheaded Sister nodded, "Stands to reason."

Thaddeus, meanwhile, was cautiously peering, just above the sash, into a window. In a flash, he ducked down, resting his back against the brick wall of the house. "I saw Nellie. She's in the kitchen, alone. We need to keep still and quiet, crouched down behind these shrubs. We can't chance being discovered."

"Maggie or I will have to peek inside that window to be sure it's the same room Athena's magick movie showed us," Raine whispered. "It might as well be me. I'm lighter and more agile. Give me a hand, Thad."

"OK, but just a peek, and keep as low as you can," the professor answered. "Unless she moved, she won't see you." With his hands, he made a makeshift step. "See her?" he breathed.

"Put me down," Raine rasped. "Yep, saw her. It's the kitchen scene from Athena's crystal cave, all right."

Again the sickening sounds of retching pierced the hushed, dark night.

"Sounds like that one has no stomach for ritual-murder," Maggie stated. "We've got to find a window now that looks into the library."

"Stay low and quiet, and let's creep around the side of the house. Follow me," Dr. Weatherby whispered.

Crouched low and veiled by the thick shrubbery, the time-travelers skulked along, single file, until they came to a tall window on the side of the mansion. From the nearby woods, a fox barked, followed by a squeal; then all was again silent. Thaddeus raised himself eye level to the window sill, glanced furtively about, then peeked inside. "Damn," he whispered, ducking back down with his companions.

"What is it?" the Sisters asked in union, holding their voices to whispers.

"Those heavy drapes make it difficult to see, but there's a narrow chink you'll be able to peek through. Raine," he said, "you'd better try and see into that room. It looks to be the library."

Raine rose and, since the bushes were taller on this side of the manse, and the ground higher, she could stand and peek into the window without fear of discovery. No sooner did she begin peering through the slim separation in the draperies, than she spied Nellie inching gingerly into the room.

The raven-haired Sister waited, watched, and listened intently.

She could hear the faint sound of chanting through the window's single-pane of glass, and she could see that the room she was viewing now was the same one she and her fellow sisters of the moon had seen in their crystal ball. *There be dragons among us,* she told herself.

Meanwhile, Maggie and Thaddeus waited in vigilant silence, every once in a while turning to look over their shoulders for any sign of the lone robed figure, who was, as far as they knew, yet lingering somewhere in the flanking woods.

The moon rose higher, and, from time to time, the professor looked skyward. Maggie correctly surmised that he was using the moonrise as a clock.

In the shimmering moonlight, the thick grass of the clearing was a silvery-olive hue. More silvery was a white birch tree, surrounded by a ring of boulders, in the center of the lawn. Beyond that, the trees were dark, receding to black corridors in the seemingly endless forest.

From inside the house, behind the library's secret panel, the ritual chanting grew louder.

Raine would have liked to raise herself up a bit higher to see better, but the fear of discovery prevented her from doing that. Such as it was, she could see, but her view was limited. It would have to do.

Nellie was standing, luckily for Raine, at an angle, before a wall of shelved books with its partly open sliding panel, and the Sister perceived that Nellie appeared *spellbound* by what she was witnessing.

Both Nellie and Raine were seeing a ring of chanting, black-robed figures, hoods covering bowed heads, amid dozens of lit candles. The sinister dark forms encircled a naked man who was strapped to a large center table, the perimeters of which were covered with strange arcane symbols.

Nearly gasping in dismay and seemingly riveted to the spot where she stood, Nellie gaped, as the coven's leader stepped forth to speak into the ear of the bound man. Whilst another figure raised the naked man's head, a chalice-like cup was given into the hands of the leader, who held it to the lips of the victim.

Again the strange chanting rose in crescendo, as the man drank long and deep.

Unmoving, Nellie continued to stare at the bizarre scene, as Raine, joined now by Maggie, watched through the chink in the drapes.

Then, everything seemed to happen at once and in quick proximity. The transfixed Nellie looked as though she were holding her breath, as the coven leader raised the large ritual knife, holding it with both hands. At the moment when the chanting reached its climax, the leader plunged the wicked knife into the victim's heart, the bound man's glazed eyes staring unblinking at his killers.

It was an ugly death.

As Athena had shown the Sisters in the crystal ball's magickal movie, Raine and Maggie were witness again to Nellie's hand flying to her lips to stifle a scream. The staggered woman's mouth was stretched in a mute shriek, her eyes wide with shock and terror.

On the far side of the house's shrubbery, a twig snapped, then another. Someone, someone large, was coming through the nearby trees to the clearing of lawn with slow, measured, and almost furtive steps– creeping closer and closer, behind the Sisters and Thaddeus!

"Quick, get down!" Dr. Weatherby cautioned in a harsh whisper, a hand on each Sister's back, pressing each lower. In the moon's glow, the Sisters saw Thaddeus hold a warning finger to his lips. In a flash, they dropped even lower, hardly daring to breathe, as the robed figure passed precariously close to their hiding place.

Though it felt like an eternity, it was, in fact, but a few seconds before Thaddeus and the Sisters heard the manse's backdoor open and close.

Then, only moments beyond, the time-travelers watched as Nellie– with shock yet visible in the stunned, piteous eyes– sprang from the rear of the house and ran– ran for all she was worth, down the lane, to disappear into the night.

"Let's get out of here," Dr. Weatherby whispered.

Raine and Maggie breathed sighs of relief, while–

The wind blew damp and chill, but that was not the sole reason Maggie breathed out a shuddering sigh. "Horrid!" she muttered. "Dreadfully horrid!"

As soon as a hurrying cloud hid the moon, the time-trekkers dashed across the lawn and into the relative safety of the woods, where they kept going until they stumbled onto a path that led to a street. Exiting the thick trees at a residential block of stately homes, they collapsed on a stone wall to catch their breaths and get their bearings.

"I'm glad that's over! God-Goddess, protect us!" Checking her wristwatch, Raine suggested, "Let's go downtown to a café. We can get warm and grab something to eat, whilst we form our plan for tonight." She shivered, as the frosty air whipped her face. "And I think we could all use a nice hot cup of tea or coffee."

"What a ghastly torment! How can you think of food right now?" Maggie retorted.

"Actually, Raine's plan is a good one," Thaddeus said. "It's not as if we didn't know what we'd be witnessing, ghastly though it was. We're garnering what we've come for. The break will do us good. We need to refresh in order to face what remains to be seen. And, I don't know about you, but I'm curious as to what our Hamlet looked like in 1932. Though it's dark now, there are streetlamps, and who knows what gossip and info we'll pick up in a café?"

"You're right, of course," Maggie relented. "We have to form a plan for tonight, and the ax murders won't unfold till about midnight." She raised her coat collar. "Great Goddess, this is one *cold* October. We really *are* experiencing global warming. In our own era, I mean."

"*Midnight*. That gives us about six hours to kill," Raine reminded her companions. She rose and looked up, then down, the street they were on. "I know where we are. This is Wills Road. C'mon, we're not far from Tara. Let's walk by it, and– maybe we could stop and visit with Granny!" the raven-haired Sister exclaimed, her face flushing with excitement.

They set off down the charming, tree-lined street in the direction of Tara, their footfalls echoing loudly on the sidewalk.

"In our excitement to connect the dots and untangle this web of mysteries, I never thought of visiting Tara and Granny!" Raine rattled. "I can't believe that I didn't think of it till now, but I didn't! Let's see, how old would Granny have been in 1932?"

Maggie screwed up her mouth, thinking aloud, "She was born in 1913, so–"

"Eighteen or nineteen, depending on her birthday," Dr. Weatherby quickly answered. "Your granny would be younger than you."

"Oooh, I don't know if this is such a good idea. I mean what will we say to her?" Maggie looked to her two companions, her gorgeous face mirroring concern.

"I didn't say it was a good idea, I said maybe we should do it. But not this second. We need a plan for that too. C'mon, I really am hungry," Raine stated more ardently this time. "Let's walk into town and get a bite to eat, and we can craft all our plans. That way, we'll be using each moment of our time-travel to the best possible advantage. And let's walk briskly; it's getting colder." She thrust her hands into the deep pockets of her coat.

"Raine's right," Thaddeus put in. "I could do with a sandwich myself."

Nearly twenty minutes later, the adventurers were seated in a booth at Herr's Drugstore, where they were studying the menu.

"I heard a man outside say that you can get a decent sandwich and cup of coffee here," Raine mentioned as she looked over the bill of fare.

"Would you look at these prices?" Maggie whispered. "A Swiss cheese sandwich with lettuce and tomato is all of a quarter. Toasted ham and cheese sandwich, thirty-five cents. Special fish sandwich, thirty cents. Bacon, lettuce and tomato sandwich, thirty cents. Hamburger, thirty cents; hotdog, twenty. Coffee, tea, or milk, one thin dime." She smiled. "It's not that this comes as a surprise, but nonetheless, I can't get over it."

"What are you going to order, Mags?" Raine asked. "I'm going to have a toasted ham and cheese with a cup of coffee."

When the waitress took their order, they made that three of the same.

As they sat eating and talking, their evening plans began to take shape.

"OK, here's what we're going to do," Raine said, reviewing what they had decided. "We walk from here to–"

Her words were cut short when the owner began a heated dialogue with his wife. "I am not going to put up with that boy much longer, Mabel! He should've been back here an hour ago. If he's been drinking again, that's *it* for him, cousin or no cousin!"

"Herbert, don't make any rash decisions. I'm sure Rodney's got a good excuse for what's keeping him," the matronly woman, whom the Sisters and Thaddeus recognized from the portrait on the wall as the owner's wife, answered in a pleading tone, with countenance to match.

"I'm sick to death of his excuses. He'd better have a reasonable explanation this time! Who's going to deliver this seltzer water to Mrs. McDonough? You?! That was her on the horn. Her husband's stomach is acting up again, and she wanted this seltzer delivered right away."

"Mr. Herr!" Raine called out impulsively.

The drugstore owner turned his head. "Yes?"

"I didn't mean to eavesdrop, but I couldn't help overhearing. As soon as we finish eating, we're going that way. We could deliver the seltzer for you. Do you mean Mrs. McDonough of Tara?"

Mr. Herr walked across the room from behind the cash register to the time-travelers' booth. Eyeing Maggie (who looked remarkably like her young granny), he asked, "Are you relatives? You look like you might be."

"Yes," the Sisters chorused.

Mr. Herr shrugged. "I don't see a problem with it. It's not prescription." He shrugged again, "Sure, why not? I'd be grateful." I'll get the seltzer water. Mabel baked pumpkin pies this morning. If you'd care for a slice each, it's on the house."

"That would be very nice," the Sisters answered.

"Ok, now here's our plan for the night," Raine leaned toward her companions to speak in whispers. "We go from here to Tara–"

"Walking through town so we can soak up the 1932 Hamlet," Thaddeus interposed.

"Settled," the Sisters rejoined.

"On pretext of delivering this seltzer, we visit for a bit with Granny, then head over to Oakmont, the Means estate, to speak with J.D.'s widow." Raine sipped her coffee. "This is the best coffee I think I've ever tasted. *Smoo–ooth*."

"It *is* good," Dr. Weatherby agreed.

"From Oakmont, we'll complete our sight-seeing tramp about the Hamlet, then we'll split up," Raine went on, "with Thaddeus taking up his watch at the house we know for sure now is the ritual-murder house, and Mags and I taking up our post at Nellie's bungalow."

"Right, that way we'll be certain to harvest all the data we can," Thaddeus asserted. "We can compare notes, so to speak, upon our return home. I'll follow the killer from the ritual-murder house to Nellie's and join you both there. Cache yourselves carefully between the hydrangea bushes and her bungalow. I'll find you. Whatever you do, don't make any noise, stay still and quiet and out-of-sight."

"I hope we can trust you, darlin', not to get into any mischief," Maggie reminded him gently.

"I gave you my word, and I'll keep it," the professor promised, tweaking her chin. "Let's finish up and get going."

"We still haven't decided what we'll say to our young granny," Raine said, swiping her mouth with the paper napkin before setting it on the table.

"I don't think we can plan that out," Maggie answered.

"You'll just have to play that one by ear," Thaddeus concluded, scooping up their check.

The time-travelers thoroughly enjoyed walking through 1932 Haleigh's Hamlet. It was as though they'd been plunged into a fabulous dream!

The wind had died a bit, and the food and hot coffee warmed them. Though their hometown was recognizable, significant changes occurred over the years. They passed businesses they'd only heard of or read about that no longer existed in their time. It was dark, but not late, only about six-forty-five, and the Victorian streetlamps lighted their way. The time-travelers reveled in the 1920s and early 1930s automobiles, as well as the period attire of the people they passed on the Hamlet's main street, Crawford Avenue.

"Look!" Raine pointed to a gas station across the way. "Gas was ten cents a gallon!"

As they passed the black Western Union sign with its bright yellow lettering, Maggie said, "I remember Granny mentioning that place."

"I wish we could take our time and *really* look round," Raine mused aloud, "but we'd better get this seltzer water up to Tara. I don't want Granny ringing up Herr's to ask what happened to her order, and I'm looking forward to meeting our grandpa."

"He died before you were born?" Thaddeus questioned, taking Maggie's hand as they walked along.

"Yes," said the Sisters in sync.

"A classic workaholic," Maggie put in.

"Look!" Raine aimed a finger at the building directly across the street from them. "There's the old Bell Telephone office. I recall Granny mentioning that too. One of her good friends worked there."

"Yes, I remember. Her name was Colleen. She came from the same county in Ireland as Granny," Maggie added. "Oh, there's the Crawford Tearoom! Granny used to say what fine dinners they served. Hamlet folks especially liked to frequent the Tearoom Sundays, after church. Best roast beef, pot roast, and–" she interrupted herself. "Look, Raine, the tablecloths are immaculate snowy-white, just as Granny described. "The Crawford Tearoom was Duncan Hines Certified," she stated proudly.

"What does, *did*, that mean exactly?" Dr. Weatherby questioned. He raised Maggie's hand to his lips to kiss it. It was something he did, unexpectedly, from time to time, and it never failed to please the redheaded Sister.

"Duncan Hines and his wife compiled a list of restaurants they visited and rated all across the country. Especially for the benefit of travelers, you see," Maggie explained. "Those restaurants that were Duncan Hines Certified meant travelers could eat there with confidence, knowing the establishment carried the highest rating."

Raine remained where she had paused, at the eatery's large glass window. "I don't see the endorsement on the window or door, so the

Duncan Hines certification must have occurred *after* 1932," she reasoned.

"Oh, I believe it did," Maggie replied. "Yes, it was the mid or late thirties when the Crawford Tearoom became certified. Hamlet old timers remember it. You know, just the other day, Eva told me her mother always said Duncan Hines mentioned in his book that the Crawford Tearoom, of Haleigh's Hamlet, Pennsylvania, was one of the best places to eat in the entire USA." She bent forward to peer inside, where diners were enjoying one of the legendary meals. "Just look at the gorgeous tin ceiling!"

"Ceiling's still there," Raine remarked, "and still just as nice. The Crawford Tearoom is Nancy Morris' Beauty Shop today. Er, you know what I'm saying– it's a beauty shop in our era."

"Oh, Raine, look! There's the big clock outside of Murtz Jewelry Store! Granny used to say how Hamlet folks would avail themselves of that clock for rendezvous. 'Meet me under the clock!' That was a popular Hamlet saying for decades. Many a romantic rendezvous started ... and ended there," she added wistfully.

They walked on.

"Ooooh, so *that's* where the Chinese laundry used to be," Raine murmured, "on Brimstone Corner. Lee Lee's Chinese Laundry was where Granny sent Grandpa's shirts. Lee Lee, she said, always managed to get the ink out of Grandpa's breast pocket."

"I always got a kick out of why that corner was christened 'Brimstone,'" Dr. Weatherby stated with a chortle. "There," he indicated with a wave of his hand, "in the mid-1800s, stood an imposing brick house with a general store on the first floor. A man named Thomas Ewing owned the building and the store. Ewing and his entire clan were such staunch Democrats, the political discussions that unfolded there– especially in the cold season, around the general store's pot-bellied stove– grew so hot with hellfire and brimstone– and I'm talking shades of Henry Ward Beecher– people began calling it 'Brimstone Corner.' Bear in mind that brimstone is another name for sulfur, and sulfur burns *very* hot."

Maggie laughed delightedly. "The descendants of those fellas have pretty much the same discussions, only, in our time, they sit round the stove at Sal-San-Tries."

"We'd better pick up our pace, or Granny's likely to ring Mr. Herr and ask where that seltzer water is!" Raine reminded. "We can continue the walking tour of our Hamlet after visiting with Granny and after interviewing the widow Means."

Some minutes later, they arrived at Tara.

"I didn't know the front porch used to be wooden," Maggie said almost to herself.

"That and the shrubbery, which isn't all that different, in the front anyway, are really the only major changes. The canvas awnings are even dark green as we have on Tara today. I mean on the future Tara— oh, you know what I mean," Raine babbled.

The Sisters exchanged excited looks with the traded thought, *Let's do this!*

After they rang the doorbell, Maggie shook her red head, commenting, "Same bell! Loud and annoying and reminiscent of the change-of-class bell at Haleigh College."

"Shhh," Dr. Weatherby shushed. "Someone's coming."

In a twinkling, the front door opened to reveal a gorgeous young woman with dark red hair piled on her head in a loose Edwardian coiffure, with several loose tendrils softening the look and framing her perfect, oval face. She wore a well-cut, soft grey afternoon dress with embroidered bodice and sleeves that puffed but ended fitting close to the arms just above the elbow. The dress' skirt skimmed her hips and flowed to her shins, flaring out a bit at the hem. Her two-toned, grey and black shoes very much resembled the thick-heeled oxfords worn by the Sisters at the moment. A large, oval, shell-pink cameo brooch was fastened at her neck, and small, gold wedding-band hoops graced her ears.

Maggie, especially, was struck by the woman's appearance. *It's like looking in a mirror!* she mused.

"May I help you?" the mistress of the mansion asked in a musical Irish brogue.

For once, Raine's steady and ready tongue failed her; thus, it was Maggie who answered.

"We've brought your seltzer water from Herr's Drug Store," the red-haired Sister said, though she, too, was mesmerized. She tried to continue but found she could not, as her emerald eyes misted over. For Maggie *and* the redheaded woman before her, it was like gazing into an enchanted looking-glass.

The young Granny eyed the red-haired Sister sharply.

Clearing her throat, Raine hurriedly picked up the story. "You see, Herr's regular delivery boy was indisposed, and since we were coming this way, we volunteered to carry it to you."

The stunning young woman wiped her hands on the towel she held. *"Is it you?"* she asked in her low, lilting voice, the query completely astounding her future granddaughters, as well as the *au fait* Dr. Weatherby.

For a weighty, protracted moment the Sisters did not, *could not*, respond; then, after trading quick looks, they pealed in a burst of enthusiasm, **"Yes!"**

"How could you know, Granny?" Raine blurted. "Levitation! It feels strange to address you with 'Granny'!"

The woman smiled. "I've known f'r some time now, an' last night, I dreamed of you."

The Sisters could not help noting that the young Granny's brogue was heavier and more pronounced than when they came of age in the same house with her.

"Why didn't you ever tell us about this?" Maggie questioned. Her expression exhibited a wee bit of hurt that the woman before her could not help but pick up.

The young Granny smiled the enigmatic smile that was hers and Maggie's alone. "If ye think on it, you'll find that I did. That is– I will. Oh!" she caught her breath with a slight gasp accompanied by a wave of an elegant hand, "'tis confusin'. No wonder *ye're* confused. Anyroad, if ya think, you'll recall that I did tell you 'bout this. Mayhap it sounded cryptic whin spoken at you; but think, whin you've a breather in time, an' you'll remember. And if ye're here, then you've *larned*– An' sure 'n aren't we f'river larnin'?– that you must always wur-rk things out f'r yerself. 'Tis the witch way, me darlin's." She peered behind her visitors, looking for her namesake. "Aisling?"

"No, Granny, she isn't with us," Maggie stated, her astonishment rekindled. "She has a little girl, Merry Fay, and so she refrains from time-travel."

"Aye," the woman nodded her fiery-red head. "'Tis risky business, that."

"In Aisling's stead, we've come to travel with this dear man." Maggie turned toward her beloved who was standing beside her, still holding her hand. "May I present Dr. Thaddeus Weatherby, the love of my life. Thaddeus, this is our granny, Mrs. Aisling McDonough."

Promptly stepping forward, Thaddeus picked up the hand of the pretty, young woman before him, brushing it with a kiss. "Charmed, dear lady. Utterly charmed."

"Granny, aren't you going to invite us in?!" the impetuous Raine let slip.

For a puzzling moment, Aisling, senior, said nothing. Then she staggered the three people on her porch yet again. "'Tis too dangerous. Wait here, till I get me wrap." The door was pushed partially closed, while their granny disappeared into the dimly lit foyer. Shortly, however, she reappeared enveloped in a long, fringed, emerald-green shawl.

"I figure ye're here on a mission, an' 'twudn't surprise me t' larn that the mission is connected to the shipboard disappearance of Jim Dandy Means."

The Sisters exchanged expressive looks.

"Sooo, I'm right, am I?" Granny shot a quick look inside to the dark foyer; then, leaning forward in a confidential manner, she said in a near-whisper, "'Tis dangerous f'r you to be here, at Tara, f'r I don't know what 'twill do to yer powers. Saints alive! You aren't even born yet, me darlin's! As ye stand afore me, you don't even have yer *real* powers yet; an' 'tisn't wise to do annythin' that could lessen th' powers ya do have, powers ye've wur-rked so hard t' earn. I mean *what's happenin' right here an' now* is, f'r all of us– an *unknown*."

"Granny," Raine intervened, "we've traveled further back in time than 1932, and–"

"But ye've a *strong* connection to Tara and to me, and I jus' don't know what 'twill do. Think, me darlin's, whin ye're lookin' at me, ye're lookin' into the past; and whin I'm lookin' at you, I'm lookin' inta th' future! I kin feel those energies," she clapped her little white hands together, "*clashin'*. And as I said, I don't know, at this point in me life, what 'twill do to yer powers."

Noting the disappointment on her granddaughters' faces, she tried to explain further, "Oooh, darlin's, I wish you could stay, an' we could clak on an' on over a nice cuppa tea; but, ya see, I'd find out things from you, and ye'd find out things from me, and that, in a way, wud be like alterin' history, especially considerin' how accomplished ye aire! You must be. *Ye're here!*"

Still noting their faces, the younger woman pushed on, "Don't ye see, lassies? Don't ye see?! We can't risk revealin' particulars to one another, not in light of yer talents and accomplishments. 'Twud be *tamperin'* with history, I tell ya, and *that* cud *well* put yer powers at risk!"

"Oh, but Granny," Raine cut in with a pleading tone, "Maggie and I *so* wanted to meet our grandfather!"

"Faith an' begorrah, child!" Granny exclaimed. "Time-travel's risky enough as 'tis. No sense verily temptin' the hand iv Fate. I don't want t' take th' chance on spoilin' yer powers an' all th' good wur-rks you'll be doin'! Time-travel's precarious enough!" she thought best to repeat.

Not to be put off, Raine pressed, "Granny, anything done in the name of Love is the right thing to do. YOU taught us that ... or you will!"

"Love is like a strong Circle of Protection," Maggie concurred. "Like a Sacred Circle, Love is eternal and infinite." She picked up her future granny's soft hand, touching her wide, gold wedding band. "Love, like a Circle, is forever."

"And when a person is chock-full of Love, unconditional Love, nothing can harm that person," Raine ended in near desperation.

The young Granny smiled then, considering. "Aye, a Sacred Circle has no beginnin' and no end. It is where many worlds exist at the same time; as the past, present and the future are all *lightnin'* swift. 'Tis part of the Magick 'n Mystery of why you are *here*, and it's all a facet of Love."

"Love is like faerie dust, Granny. It creates *magick* whenever you give it away," Raine grinned impishly, keenly sensing victory.

"F'r **sar**-tain," the young woman paused, studying her future granddaughters with intensely felt pride, "ye've larned well, so mayhap, 'twill be all right." She reached inside to pull the front door softly closed. "Come round back wi't me, an' we'll go inta th' kitchen. I think I know wha' might wur-rk! You too, Thaddeus! I'll fix ya a nice hot toddy t' warm yer inners, whilst the gurls and I sort this out."

Once in the warm, pleasant kitchen, the time-travelers glanced round to see that it looked almost identical to Raine and Maggie's Tara-kitchen.

"Sit, me darlin's, and keep yer voices down. Mr. McDonough," she uttered, using the formal appellation for her husband, as was the custom in that more formal era, "is sleepin' on the couch in the parlor, and I don't want to wake him. Not yet anyroad."

Without further ado, Aisling, senior, set about making Thaddeus his hot toddy. The Sisters could tell that it was a task she had performed many times in the past. "This good Irish whiskey– wha' we Irish call *uisce beatha*, 'water of life'– will warm ya, boost yer spirits, and kill whativer might be ailin' ya!" She handed what she called a "beaker" of the hot drink to Dr. Weatherby, who accepted the mug with gratitude, immediately taking a long draft.

"Now, here's th' plan," she smiled at the Sisters, who were sitting at Tara's round, oak, claw-footed table, chins-in-hands, studying their young granny's every movement, hanging on her every word. Granny poured a large glass of the seltzer water. "You gurls will take this inta the parlor to yer grandfither, tellin' him that ye wur-rk part-time f'r Mr. Herr at th' drug store. I want you t' do me and yer grandfither a whackin' good boon by tellin' him that he needs to stop wur-rkin' so long an' so hard. 'Tisn't healthy! 'Tis why he suffers stomach ailment. God n' Goddess only know wha' the wur-rk is doin' to th' good man's heart."

"That's a wizard idea!" Raine replied. "Visiting nurses … **all right!**"

"Don't hang about, though. As I said, no sense in temptin' Fate's unsteady hand."

Maggie carried the tray with the glass of seltzer water, as the Sisters followed young Granny into Tara's dimly lit parlor. Stretched out on the long, leather sofa, was their tall, muscular grandfather, James McDonough. His suit jacket was hooked over the back of a chair, and his suspenders hung down from the waist of his pants.

"Darlin'," young Granny whispered, kissing her husband's cheek and switching on a lamp. "These young ladies have been so kind as t' deliver yer seltzer water from Herr's. They wur-rk for Mr. Herr part-time, and they asked to have a wor-rd with ya, regardin' yer stomach ailment."

James opened his eyes, one at a time, when his wife gently laid a hand on his shoulder.

Looking at him closely, Raine and Maggie were instantly struck by how handsome he was with his wavy, ebony hair; his thick, cavalry mustache; and his piercing eyes, the deep, rich blue of the Lakes of Killarney.

Standing, James fixed his keen gaze on the Sisters. "What foine young ladies to show such kindness to a stranger!"

"Thank you," the Sisters echoed.

"Do sit down," Maggie beckoned, indicating the sofa with her hand. "You need to rest."

"We want to tell you," Raine began, "that medical research has shown that one must learn to balance work with rest, sir. If you can learn to do that, you will see a significant improvement in your health."

"My health is foine, lassies! There'll be plenty o' time t' rest whin I'm old an' feeble. For now, I will continue to make my way here in America." He leaned confidentially forward to whisper in a jesting, jolly way, "'Tis my destiny, you see."

Raine's gaze swept the elegant parlor. "You seem to be doing quite well, sir, and–"

"*Aye*, and I want to continue to do that," he smiled, deepening the elongated dimple in his left cheek. "These are tryin' times, lass, an' *no* time t' be a slacker. No time f'r slackers at all, at all!"

"*Séamus*," young Granny began, using her petname for her husband, the Irish for *James* that she pronounced 'Shamus,' "these gurls are quite knowledgeable in what they are about, so 'tis somethin' t'give serious thought to." Putting her arm around the Sisters, then, she led them back into the kitchen.

There, Thaddeus had just polished off his hot toddy, setting the beaker down on the table with a contented grin. "That hit the spot!" he declared to Granny.

"I am pleased that you enjoyed it," she responded. Then, turning to the Sisters, she ventured again, "I don't want to par-rt, but we must. You know that, darlin's."

"We do," the Sisters replied in unison and with sadness carried on their voices.

At the backdoor, they thanked their granny, and when she hugged them, it was difficult to break away.

"Godspeed 'n Goddess bless," Aisling, senior, whispered, a hand on each Sister's wet cheek.

"We love you so much, Granny," the Sisters breathed, kissing the young woman and hugging her again.

"Don't you fret about our powers," Maggie leaned forward to whisper. "If anything, this visit has energized us. There's no greater power than Love."

"Always remember that," their granny urged. "When you walk in Love and Light, nothin' kin harm you. Love *is* th' greatest power on earth, and 'tis the *only* thing we take with us whin we leave this earth."

Maggie answered softly, "I don't think we ever looked at it that way. That old saying, 'You can't take it with you,' isn't quite true, is it?"

Granny responded with a warm smile. "You take Love with you, for, like Spirit, it is indestructible and eternal."

"*That* we know, Granny. It's one of many things we learned, will learn, from you," the Sisters chimed.

Aisling, senior, studied her granddaughters for a magickal musing moment. "Remember, too– the Truth always matters, in any era. 'Tis the standard of the Spiritual Realm. And Truth is Freedom."

The Sisters bobbed their heads, unable to speak for the emotions swelling within each Celtic breast.

Ancient Wisdom from the Ancient Ancestors, they thought in union. *Passed down in magickal families from one generation to the next– **Empowerment**.*

"Be true to yerselves and laugh a lot– 'tis good f'r ya!" young Granny brightened. "Above all– *be happy*. Whin ye're happy, ye draw only good and an abundance of good. What we are, we draw.

"Happiness, ya know, kin be an *existence*, an' not just a mood. I've always likened it to simply pivotin'," she laughed, spinning suddenly and merrily around. "If somethin' 'r someone makes me feel bad, I pivot to somethin' that makes me smile an' feel good. Most people don't know how to live that way." She giggled. "But 'tis easy; 'tis fun– an' *'tis smart!*

"The Craft is a gift, a gift from me to you, but, first and foremost, from the God-Goddess. Live yer lives in happiness 'n harmony, for that is wha' the Craft is all about. That is what it will do for you. It will reveal Truths. It will set you Free, and it will let you live in Peace, Love, Happiness and Harmony. An' always remember that magick is not somethin' ya do," she patted each granddaughter on a cheek, breathing, "magick is somethin' you *are*."

"Thank you, Granny!" the Sisters chorused. "We'll remember."

"Witches' promise," Raine thought to add.

Young Granny hugged them warmly. It was difficult to say goodbye.

"Thank you, Mrs. McDonough, for the good Irish whiskey," Thaddeus stated.

"Take good care of me gurls!" she said passionately. "They have a foine Destiny to fulfill!"

The time-travelers walked out the door to the leaf-strewn cobblestone walk, when the young woman in the doorway came rushing out after them. Laying a hand on each Sister's shoulder, she turned them to face her. Then taking a hand of each of her future granddaughters between her own, she whispered with ardency as two tears rolled slowly down her cheeks, "Go where there is no path, me darlin's, and *blaze* one of yer own."

As the threesome walked in the direction of Oakmont, the Means estate, the Sisters were silent. It was like losing Granny all over again.

Thaddeus respected that Raine and Maggie wanted to be alone with their thoughts, but now he pronounced in his strong voice, "Your Granny is never far away. She's *always* with you. In fact, I daresay more and more is she with you."

"You're right," they replied, their spirits lifting.

"Let's get our minds right for this interview," Raine suggested with renewed energy. "I'm hoping we'll be able to harvest a couple more of the missing dots to solve our puzzle."

The time-trekkers arrived at Oakmont's tall, black wrought-iron gates to find them closed, the two gates bearing the huge initials "J" "D," the even larger "M" in the center where they locked.

"It's as though the legend himself were asking Haleigh's Hamlet and Braddock County at large not to forget him," Raine, the consummate storyteller, uttered.

For several moments, the would-be callers stood staring at the heavy gates, before Thaddeus stepped forward to pick up the intercom to the house. Speaking clearly and with confidence, he proclaimed, "We've come to speak with Mrs. Means."

"Is she expecting you?" the disembodied male voice asked in an efficient tone.

"No, but it will behoove her to speak with us," Dr. Weatherby replied.

There was a brief silence before the voice answered, "Come ahead. I'll open the gates."

Within a few moments, the visitors were walking up the leaf-littered path toward the majestic mansion, behind which the beautiful, intricate gardens extended for some acres.

Built over rich seams of coal on a lush, rolling landscape, the palatial palace was designed by Daniel P. Burnham of Chicago, one of America's leading architects of the twentieth century. Behind a low stone wall, this Hamlet jewel crowned a rise of extensive lawns sprinkled abundantly with magnificent trees imported from various countries around the world that the Means couple had visited.

"This house was built to last," Dr. Weatherby reminded the Sisters. "J.D. had an inordinate fear that fire might destroy Oakmont. Thus, he had his home constructed with a strong steel skeleton and as much steel, iron, concrete, stone and brick as possible to prevent ruin by flames. The place is a virtual fortress."

Maggie made a sound of agreement. "Means laid out a literal fortune to construct and furnish his forty-two room home with unique treasures from all over Europe, Asia, and Africa."

"Must've been the butler, Mr. Brazini, who answered," Raine said. "Nellie told us Mrs. Means had to let all the servants go when J.D.'s bank failed, but the Brazinis, husband and wife, stayed on, out of loyalty, as butler and housekeeper."

Maggie recalled a fragment from one of her lesson plans. "Oakmont, a cross between a museum and a country club, was said to be, in its heyday, one of the richest homes in America." She reached out a hand to ring the doorbell, the sound akin to Tara's antique bell. A black wreath, symbolic of death, hung on one side of the huge, ornate double doors.

Forthwith, one of the doors opened to reveal a dignified man, with salt-and-pepper hair, wearing a dark grey suit and tie. His upper left arm bore a black mourning band, and his eyes expertly scanned the callers. The satisfied expression that settled on his dignified face told them he recognized respectability when he saw it.

"I'm Pascal Brazini, the butler. This way, please. Mrs. Means is in the parlor. Who shall I announce is calling?" the pleasant man queried.

"Friends," Dr. Weatherby replied flatly. "We'll explain ourselves to your mistress straightaway."

"Very good, sir." Brazini led the way through the vast entrance hall.

The time-trekkers could not help but be impressed with the sumptuous manse. Silk and precious tapestries covered the walls, whilst ultra-expensive carpets checkered the gleaming expanse of parquet floors. Imported marble fireplaces with elaborate mantels added to the splendor and warmth of the great house.

The Sisters exchanged the thought, *Everything will soon be sold at auction to pay back investors.*

Embossed leather portières accented the intricately leaded windows and doorways. Between a pair of tall standing, pre-Tiffany stained-glass lamps from Germany, positioned opposite the richly carved oak staircase in the foyer, stood an *immense* marble fireplace, large enough to walk into.

"What an extraordinary fireplace!" Raine exclaimed to no one in particular.

"On chilly days, Miss," Brazini offered, "it was filled with logs up to six feet in length." The butler's voice was rife with memories when he added, "The lighting of the Yule log, a Means family tradition, was always a festive occasion here at Oakmont." At the entrance to the parlor, he drew himself to attention, announcing in a cultured voice, "Friends have come to pay their respects, madam."

Mary Means, dressed from head to toe in black, nodded her head, saying, "Please come in and make yourselves comfortable." She set the book she had been reading aside, along with her spectacles. "Shall I ask Pasqual to bring refreshments?"

"No thank you," the Sisters echoed, fully aware that money was more than tight. Raine and Maggie sat, side by side, on the couch, and Thaddeus took a seat in a wingback chair in front of the lit fireplace that was dwarfed in comparison to the one in the reception area. Despite the fire, the room was damp and chilly.

"Were you friends of my husband?" the widow asked. Her voice was low and devoid of emotion, the voice of a woman determined at all costs to display self-control.

In that moment, the Sisters looked at Mrs. Means and instantly liked her. She was very much the *grande dame*. They liked her dignity and her simplicity. She had a noble, chiseled face with a patrician nose and chin. Understandably, she looked as though she had been crying. It was evident that the strain of her husband's strange death was telling on her. Her large eyes, exceedingly dark against the pallor of her face, were ringed with shadows. The widow Means wore her black hair, frosted lightly with grey, in a low, neat bun at the back of her neck. Appropriate for a lady in her former social position, the black dress she wore appeared to be of excellent cut and quality. Other than a pair of jet earrings, her only other adornment was her wide, gold wedding band.

Exchanging looks, the Sisters answered the woman's query. "We knew *of* your husband, but we did not know him personally."

"I don't understand why you've come to see me then," Mary said, not unkindly.

"Please," Dr. Weatherby said, coming to the rescue. "Tell no one of this visit. We cannot divulge our names or much else about why we are here, but suffice it to say that we are undercover agents on a mission."

"A mission?" Mary asked, raising one arched brow.

"Among other things, to clear your husband's name," Raine picked up the invisible magick wand, the one she wielded when she weaved the stories for which she was famous.

J.D.'s widow seemed to come to life. "Then you don't believe my husband committed suicide either," she stated, hoping it was true.

"We do not," Maggie replied.

"And please trust that, with the passage of time, we *will* clear your husband's good name," Raine concluded.

"I don't fully understand," the older woman replied. "I just know that this is uncommonly good of you to come here."

"Would you be willing to share with us anything you know, anything you can that might help us in this investigation?" Dr. Weatherby delivered his petition in a gentle manner.

The widow leaned her greying head a little to one side, as though in thought, then she asked a question of her own. "Do you have time for the whole story?" She sat up and squared her thin shoulders, as if shucking off fear.

Raine checked her watch. It was only a bit after seven in the evening. "We do."

The widow gave a quick nod, picking up a small bell to ring it. In a moment, the butler appeared in the doorway. "Pascal, please put another couple logs on the fire, and please ask Rosetta to prepare us tea."

With a slight bow, Brazini answered, "Very good, madam." The loyal servant tended the fire before he withdrew, on silent feet, from the room, at which time Mary embarked on her riveting tale, her words, at first anyway, rushing from her.

Now and again, one or other of the time-travelers interposed to ask a question, which Mary did her best to answer, sometimes clenching and unclenching a white handkerchief, edged in black that she had pulled from the pocket of her frock.

At one point, the butler, apologizing for the interruption, entered briefly to place a black, wool shawl over the woman's thin shoulders.

Toward the end of her account, the widow's voice, in response to one of the Sisters' queries, faltered and she lost her reserve, beginning to weep. No one moved as she went on crying, softly, her face in her handkerchief. Then– it seemed eternity– she began to regain control of herself. Little by little, the sobbing ceased.

Pulling the thick, black shawl tighter about her, Mary sat quite still, tightening her jaw. For several moments, her hands clutched and unclutched the black stuff of her dress. At last she was able to resume her story.

With bated breath and in sympathy, Mary's visitors sat quietly waiting, biding their time. However, even before the loyal butler, with a discreet cough, re-appeared at the door to collect the tea things, the widow delivered to their ears what the time-trekkers were waiting to hear.

It was nearly ten when Raine, Maggie and Thaddeus bid Mary Means good-night, assuring her that no one would ever know that she had spoken with them, and promising again that, with the passage of time, they would clear her husband's good name.

"What a lovely woman!" Maggie breathed as they headed for the town square.

"Yes, she was," Raine replied. "A real lady. I think once we make certain of the ax murders, we can return home. Everything is falling nicely into place."

"I dread witnessing those murders!" Maggie sighed. "Absolutely dread it."

"I know you do, Mags, and so do I, but we've no choice. We have to know with absolute certainty who perpetrated that vicious attack. It's the only way to know for sure." Raine glanced at her watch. "I hope something is still open where we can sit for an hour or so before we move to our final destination here tonight."

"Let's walk round the square and surely there'll be a diner or café open. It's not, after all, the wee hours." Dr. Weatherby picked up Maggie's hand to loop through his arm, patting it.

They walked on, in silence for several moments, until they came again to the town square. Almost immediately, they spotted a little café with lights on inside, and on the door hung the Open sign.

"Here we go. The Colonel's Café," Thaddeus read from the name printed on the front window with its faded image of Colonel Crawford. "Named," the history professor mentioned, though unnecessarily, "after the Hamlet's famous hero of the Colonial period. A good choice, wouldn't you say, ladies?"

"I hope," Maggie rejoined, raising her eyes to the Divine, "it's a good omen."

"Let's sit in the back," Raine suggested, as the bell on the door sounded their entrance. "We need to put our heads together, compare thoughts, and finalize our plans for tonight."

"Right," Maggie replied, with Thaddeus joining in.

"Sit anywhere," the proprietor, a thin man wearing a white, bib apron, called to them as they passed in front of the register. "Not busy tonight. Not busy any night anymore," he added under his breath. "Can I bring you coffee?"

"Yes," the threesome replied, glancing round.

There was only one table occupied, in the center of the small establishment, by two men drinking coffee from thick white mugs. As the time-travelers strode to a table in the back, they overheard the men talking, the conversation capturing their attention.

"Paper says the auction up at Oakmont will start this weekend. 'Everything Must Go' the headline read." The first man, dressed in dungarees topped with a flannel shirt picked up his mug to sip his coffee. "I don't know about you, but I never begrudged ole J.D. his fortune. He worked hard for his money, just like his pa done. Nothin' was ever handed to 'im. Damn shame about his bank goin' under." The man took another sip of coffee, shaking his grey head. "That hurt just about everybody around here, includin' me, but I'd-a never wished on him how things ended up."

The second man, dressed comparably in bibbed overalls and plaid flannel shirt, gave a grave nod, as he sipped his coffee. "Hurt us bad; that's for sure. J.D. guided a lot of us on how to invest our money during the boom. Made a lot of folks round here rich; but when his bank went, he took us all down with him. Never meant to;

but, even so, that's what he done. Guess he just couldn't handle it all. God rest him." He set his mug down with the finality of his next words, "I don't think the county will ever recover. Country either, for that matter." He stroked his cheek thoughtfully, adding, "But then again, time heals all, or so they say."

"Some folks are sayin' they don't believe ole J.D. jumped off that ship. Aw, I suspect folks are sayin' a lot of things," the first man chortled, "includin' who's behind J.D.'s *bank* takin' that deadly dive."

"Oh," the second man replied, glancing furtively around, "I don't think none of us have-ta think too long or too hard about who was behind that. And speakin' of deadly dives ..." He leaned forward, putting his head close to his companion's and finishing in low tones that the time-trekkers could not hear.

The proprietor brought the coffee, setting the thick, white mugs down in front of Raine, Maggie, and Thaddeus, respectively. "Cream?" he asked, and the look in his eyes told them that he was hoping for negative replies, which is what he got.

"Sugar's on the table," he stated before walking back to his station at the register, where he picked up the evening paper, slipping on his spectacles.

"You mean *you* think that–" Now it was the first man's turn to bend to his companion and converse in undertones, the rest of his sentence lost to the time-travelers, who, from that point on, only captured fragments of the other table's conversation.

"You won't believe who I caught sight of last night," the second man said once his coffee mate had finished spilling his gossip. He took a drink from his mug, his expression one of expectation.

"Who?" came the awaited reply.

"The Miller twins, that's who. Saw 'em right on the edge of town, and headed this way, the pair of 'em."

Halfway through a gulp of coffee, the first man choked. "N-n-n-aw! Couldn't-na been." He waved off his confidant's words with a gnarled hand. "You must-a been mistaken."

"I know those two when I see 'em; I'll tell ya that, and I know what I saw. By the looks on their faces, I suspected they was ..." the rest of the sentence was lost to the Sisters and Thaddeus. "When J.D.'s bank went under," the second man muttered, keeping his voice down so that the trekkers only caught fragments of dialogue, " ... Millers vowed and declared ... the last thing they'd do–" The second man abruptly lowered his voice again, as the time-travelers strained to catch as much as they could of the men's staccato conversation.

"Do you suppose they're the ones who–" And as the first man leaned in closer to his companion, the rest again faded to murmurs, after which the two men stood to leave the café, ambling over to the register, the final fragment of their gossip drifting back to the time-trekkers. "But why would they come back here? What ... or *who* would pull those two thugs back here?"

After the two men departed the coffee shop, Raine whispered, "Sounded like dialogue we've tossed back and forth among ourselves, huh?" She looked at her watch. "We should be leaving for our posts in five."

"Right," Maggie agreed.

"Are you sure you ladies will be all right by yourselves?" Dr. Weatherby asked, after draining his coffee mug.

"We'll be fine," the Sisters assured him.

Thaddeus spoke softly to the women, "I'll make certain to glean as much as I can up at the ritual-murder house before joining you at Nellie's bungalow."

"Please don't take any chances," Maggie breathed, reaching across the table to grasp her lover's hand.

The professor gave a brisk nod. "I'll say the same to you. *Both* of you."

"Thad, stay out of trouble," Raine delivered with her gamin grin.

Little did the Sisters know that *trouble* was precisely what was in store for them.

"The darkest nights produce the brightest stars."
~ Ceane O'Hanlon-Lincoln

Chapter Eighteen

It was about eleven-thirty when Dr. Weatherby's patient vigilance at the ritual-murder house was rewarded.

"About time," he grumbled to himself, as he scooched further down behind the bushes to the rear of the brick manse. *I'm getting stiff crouched down like this in the chill of this damp, cold night.*

A figure wearing a man's long, dark overcoat slipped through the backdoor and sped across the moonlit backyard to a small brick edifice that harmonized with the brick of the main house.

"Bingo," Thaddeus muttered, as he gaped through the foliage to what he was sure was the gardener's shed. *I'll wait till the murderer gets inside*, he told himself.

As soon as he noted that the figure had ducked inside the small building, he dashed across the moonlit lawn to the side of the shed, staying low and peering into the sole window.

Inside, the dark figure was shucking off the coat. Through the window, Thaddeus saw that it was a woman with wavy, medium-length, platinum hair, a slender woman wearing white satin pajamas and bedroom slippers. Laying the overcoat on the work table, the silvery blonde proceeded to the near wall, where, from a hook, she lifted off what looked to be the gardener's work clothes– dark corduroy trousers, a plaid flannel shirt, a scruffy, brown jacket, and a battered, brown fedora.

The professor continued to watch as the woman swiftly pulled the gardener's clothing over her satin pajamas. Lowering herself to the seat of what looked to be a discarded kitchen chair in a corner, she pulled off her slippers to yank on a pair of work boots positioned next to the chair. After hastily lacing them up, she returned to the worktable for the overcoat.

In the moonlight streaming through the window, Thaddeus saw her draw, from one of the coat's pockets, a small revolver and a pair of leather gloves, which she pulled on, working the fingers for a snug fit. Expertly, she checked the chamber before slipping the gun into the pocket of her donned jacket. After thoroughly tucking her hair up under the fedora, she pulled the hat down over her forehead and hurried out of the shed, closing the door and vanishing into the night.

Approximately fifteen minutes earlier, Raine and Maggie, cached between the hydrangea bushes and the alley-side of Nellie Triggs' bungalow, were experiencing the start of a string of troubles that would plague them for the next couple of days.

A large, fearsome dog, that spotted them whilst chasing a neighbor's cat, had crouched down and began making its cantankerous way to the secreted Sisters, with ears laid back and formidable teeth showing. Growling low in its throat, the Rottweiler inched toward them, rousing Maggie to poke Raine painfully in the ribs, "Do your thing! Do your thing! He's going to tear us to shreds!"

Unruffled, Raine patted her cousin and sister of the moon on the shoulder, saying, in a soothing tone, "I won't let him harm you, Mags. Just keep quiet. Don't move a muscle and don't look at him, not in the eyes anyway. I'm waiting till he gets a bit closer."

Maggie groaned. *Just what we need!*

It's nothing I can't handle, Mags. Raine didn't have long to wait. Straightaway, the growling dog was within inches of them, when the Goth gal zapped him a strong message: *Stop that! You behave yourself, mister! This is not your yard, and you have no business coming here and threatening us. We mean you no harm.*

The menacing dog stopped creeping toward them, tilting his dark head one way, then the other.

Noticing the collar, the Sister added, *Now you get home, and don't come back here ever!*

The animal had ceased growling, but he didn't move, which caused Maggie to zoom a telepathic message of her own– to Raine. *Why isn't he leaving? Make him leave!*

Relax. He's just curious. Raine reached out a tentative hand, palm down, to the dog's mouth. Whilst he sniffed her, the Sister told him, *I think you're a really good dog, but the family you guard doesn't give you nearly the attention you crave, isn't that right?*

In answer, the dog barked.

I thought that was it. If you'd stop being so cantankerous, you would get more affection. And another thing– you stop chasing and treeing the neighborhood cats, and I mean it! Or I'll come back and turn you into a toad! Now get on home! We have work to do, and I need you to leave us alone. The raven-haired Sister reached out and petted the dog then, scratching its ears.

With a delighted squeal, the huge animal sprang forward to lick Raine's face before turning and, freeing itself from the restraining bushes, loped off.

"Whew!" Maggie breathed. "That was close. I'm sure glad you took care of him. The murderer ought to be showing up any second now."

Raine opened her mouth to respond when a strong hand clamped forcefully over her mouth. Her eyes widened to see that Maggie, too, had a hand clamped over her mouth. Whoever their stealthy assailant was, he was right behind them.

The Sisters waited, their hearts beating rapidly, for the first words.

"Don't move; don't make a sound. Understand?" a raspy male voice whispered.

Raine and Maggie bobbed their heads in sync.

"It's me, Thaddeus. I couldn't risk startling you." He removed his hands from their mouths. "Heads up, ladies," he continued in low tones. "The killer will be at Nellie's door momentarily. I jogged most of the way, to beat her down here."

"Gallopin' gargoyles! You gave us a start!" Raine hissed. "Any surprises?" she questioned, after getting hold of herself. "I mean from what we told you we saw in our crystal ball?"

"None. The scene unfolded precisely as you and Maggie described it." Thaddeus turned his head sharply.

A rapping sound at the front of the bungalow alerted the time-travelers that the killer had reached Nellie's shack.

Motioning to the Sisters, Dr. Weatherby signaled for quiet, as they waited with pounding hearts and bated breath.

The rapping continued for several seconds before the trekkers heard the killer call out, "Nellie! Open the door! Nellie, open up!"

In the next few moments, they heard Nellie's voice, "Who is it? It's late. My mother and my kids are asleep."

"Elsa. I have your pay." The words were delivered so softly that the astute professors could not help thinking it was to prevent the neighbors from hearing the spoken name rather than the waking of those inside Nellie's house.

The front door opened, after which Raine, Maggie and Thaddeus heard the killer's dialogue to Nellie Triggs, before the door was pulled shut.

"I'm sorry to drop by so late, but our fancy dress ball only started winding down a few minutes ago." Elsa laughed then. "It was an all-day affair, and like children, we played a lot of silly games. As you can see, I'm still wearing my costume," she laughed again. "It's so cold tonight, colder than it usually is this time of year. Let me in to warm myself by your stove before I start out again. With all the cars in our driveway, I couldn't get either of our vehicles out of the garage to drive down here. Had to hoof it."

There was a pause, as if Nellie were digesting what the soon-to-be killer was feeding her. Then, the time-travelers heard the blonde woman speak softly again.

"Earlier this evening, one of our masqueraders told me you had stopped by. I figured you need your pay to shop for food." She shivered and hugged her body. "I took a short-cut through the woods, but I'm freezing!"

Those in the bushes did not hear Nellie's reply, if, in fact, she made a reply. They did, however, hear the sound of the door creak further open, and then clack shut.

"We have to peer into the kitchen window," Raine whispered. "And there's no time to lose."

Since they'd had time to scout round the exterior of the house before Thaddeus' arrival, the Sisters knew which window was the kitchen window. It was the one that looked out onto the back alley, and it was the one, now, into which Raine dared to peer. What she saw, though she and Maggie had pieced the scenario together pretty well, nonetheless, horrified her.

Inside the humble kitchen, Nellie, in a long, white nightgown, was backing up, step by step, toward the corner and the wood-burning stove, with Elsa coming toward her, inch by inch. Raine could see the killer's right hand dip into the man's jacket she was wearing.

"Thought you could snare *my* husband, did you?" Elsa Fane hissed through clenched teeth. "Thought you'd landed yourself a real sugar-daddy, huh? Is that what you thought?!"

"Noo," Nellie stammered. "No! That's never how it was. I never meant ... I told Adrian I couldn't see him anymore, I–"

"*Adrian*?! Is that what you called him, not 'Mr. Fane,' as you always did in *my* presence?" Elsa rejoined acidly. "What a two-faced little liar you are!"

Nellie's soulful eyes were pleading as fear flooded her. "I never planned any of it; it just happened. I never felt right about it. I–I knew I had to break it off, and I did. I **ended** it! I never meant to hurt you. I never meant for any of it to happen. Truly, I didn't. Please believe me!"

Nellie was nearly to the stove now, and it looked to Raine as though she were reaching, feeling, for something behind her.

"But it *did* happen, you little bitch! And stop lying to me! We women may fool men, but we never fool one another, do we?" she sneered. "Everything comes at a price, *Nellie*," Elsa's face darkened, as she pronounced the name with hatred. "And there's a really *high* price tag on what you did with my husband! I hope it was worth it to you." Elsa's words, carried on a hissing, malicious voice, matched the frightful expression on her sharp features as she loomed over her victim– a victim who seemed to sense that she was doomed. "Huh, was it worth your life?"

Nellie stopped, her back to the stove and the corner. "Please go. Please leave me alone! I broke it off; it's over! Please, I have children and an elderly mother who need me. *Please!*"

Elsa howled with laughter, and this time, it was a laugh steeped in evil. "*Plea-ssssss-e*," she mimicked with an ugly grimace. She was directly in front of Nellie now, inches from the frightened face, and still laughing.

It was then Raine saw what Nellie had been reaching for, feeling for with nervous, shaking fingers– the family ax. In an instant, the young woman brought it out in front of her, to ward off what she expected might be a blow from her attacker.

Like lightning, a snarling Elsa dropped the revolver and, with the fury of a demon, leaped forward to wrest the ax from her stunned, terrified prey. With super-human force, the crazed woman swung the weapon, with both hands, downward. The ferocious whack hit a dodging Nellie's shoulder, whilst her first shriek blended perfectly with the long, screaming whistle of the incoming freight train passing through on the nearby tracks.

As the evil woman's adrenaline kicked in, her revenge and hatred rendered her a *powerhouse*. Over and yet again, she wielded the ax, bringing it down with the strength of a giant, raining most of the blows about Nellie's face and head.

The profusely bleeding woman screamed several times; but, though the Sisters and Thaddeus were just below the kitchen window, the screams were stifled by the noisy clacking of the long freight train that passed through the area at midnight. And, as the *Hamlet Herald* had always reported, the train noise, from the onset, was accompanied by the loud barking of the neighborhood dogs.

This was the clue that convinced the watching Raine that Elsa had visited Nellie's shack on previous occasions. *That* was what the killer had been waiting for, toying as she'd done with her victim until– the loud cacophony of freight train and barking dogs began.

It was obvious to the watching Raine that the murderer had originally planned to *shoot* Nellie and her family as the train passed through; but when Nellie produced the ax, *that* became the vengeful, ruthless woman's weapon of choice.

In the glow from the kitchen's dim night-light, Raine could see that blood spattered the killer, as well as the kitchen walls, floor, appliances and furniture. Horrorstruck, she swallowed the bile that had risen in her throat. *No wonder the police thought the ax murders had been committed by a large man!*

A little girl in a pink flannel nightgown, eyes wide in fear and shock, appeared for an instant in the kitchen doorway. Coming upon the grisly scene, the child opened her mouth and screamed in terror, her small hands splayed in shock, before fleeing into the dark recesses of the house. Having caught sight of the preteen, the killer paused in her bloody work, giving the mangled, bleeding Nellie a chance for escape through the kitchen window.

But Elsa Fane was too quick, and making a furious grab for Nellie, before she could run for help, she brought the ax down in a vicious attempt to behead her victim. When Nellie sidestepped, the blow nearly severed her collar bone.

When the raven-haired Sister saw the bloody woman heading for the window, and as the killer's eyes were riveted on the child, she ducked down and, pulling her two companions with her, dashed farther under cover in the thick bushes.

If Nellie spied Raine in the window, she took that to the grave with her.

Making themselves as small and as invisible as possible, the sudden sound of broken glass caused the time-travelers to freeze, when Nellie came flying through the kitchen window to land only inches from where they were hiding.

Incredibly, the mutilated woman, her face unrecognizable, her broken arm dangling, struggled to her feet. Unable to see for the blood in her eyes and stumbling for several steps, the dying woman just managed to gasp out *"Murder!"* before collapsing in a grotesque, gory heap into the alley.

There Nellie Triggs would remain till her lifeless body was discovered the next morning by the neighbor boy.

Not wanting Raine to witness any more of the horror, Dr. Weatherby crept along the back of the house to peer into one of the two windows there.

When he rejoined the Sisters, several minutes later, he said nearly inaudibly, "She axed them all." It was all he could manage to relate at the time.

The final cars of the long freight train clacked and rattled past, though the neighborhood dogs were still loudly barking their midnight chorus.

Thaddeus motioned to the Sisters for quiet, a cautioning finger to his lips. While they listened, they heard the sound of Nellie's front door open and close. Creeping along the side of the house, undercover of the shrubbery, Thaddeus watched as the killer tucked the unfired revolver back into her jacket pocket. After glancing warily about, she hurried off, carrying something wrapped in a bloody bedsheet.

Joined now by Maggie and Raine, Dr. Weatherby breathed out a huge sigh. "By the size and shape of what she was carrying, I'd wager it was the murder weapon."

Maggie, who was visibly shaken, gave a somber nod.

Raine rumbled, "I never thought I'd be the first one to say this, on one of our time-treks, but I'm *more* than ready to go home!"

"Blessed be!" Maggie replied, as they eased out of the bushes and started for the woods.

Shortly, and none too soon for the three of them, they came to the tree line of Haleigh's Wood, and as they entered the darker, black void of forest, each Sister looped arms with Dr. Weatherby, who added, in reference to the murder weapon. "Since we know the Triggs family ax was never found, and since their bungalow was so close to the Yough, and we *saw* Elsa headed in that direction, I'm *convinced* she hurled the murder weapon into the river en route back to Fane Manor. River's high, so anything tossed in there now would be damned-near impossible to find."

"Our Youghiogheny has secreted more than one mystery in our county's layered history," Maggie concurred.

"Right, and I'd lay a wager that the killer burns those gardener's clothes upon her return to the Manor tonight," Raine ventured. "I noted a burning pit out back, behind the gardener's shed. Doubtless, she'll burn the bloody sheet she wrapped round the ax too."

"A woman scorned," Maggie drawled, "makes a formidable enemy."

"I'll remember that," Thaddeus stated, sending his beloved a loaded look.

When they'd gone deep enough into the woods, they paused. Maggie drew their small, travel *Book of Shadows* from her purse. Opening the grimoire to the ribboned final pages, the three time-travelers clasped hands tightly to begin the ancient Gaelic invocation– *the magickal Key that would unlock the door of Time–* and take them home.

When they landed in their own Haleigh's Wood, they found Aisling sitting on a log, a half-fallen tree that made a fine seat, and the lighted lantern still hanging from the limb where they left it when they embarked on their 1932 quest.

"So tell me," Aisling said, getting to her feet, "how did it go this trip? Did you ferret out everything we need to crack this messy mystery?" She checked her watch, and as before with their time-treks, not a minute had passed since their departure. It was only a few seconds after midnight, the precise time the threesome had departed for 1932 Haleigh's Wood.

This phenomenon never failed to inspire them. What a genius, a true genius, Albert Einstein was when he taught that the past, present, and the future all unfolded simultaneously!

"Oooooh, wait till you hear what all we ascertained!" Raine replied to Aisling's query, after picking herself up from the damp forest floor and brushing herself off. "We've so much to tell you!"

Dr. Weatherby, meanwhile, was helping Maggie to her feet.

The time-travelers never had much discomfort returning *from* their time-treks, since when they returned, it was always to their own era.

"Any trouble this trip?" Aisling questioned, eyeing the voyagers with her seasoned detective's discernment.

Raine chortled. "Nothing we couldn't handle."

Maggie lifted Aisling's talisman off to return it. "Thank you, darlin'," she whispered, handing the amulet over and giving her cousin and fellow sister of the moon a warm hug.

"More than welcome," the blonde with the wand replied, slipping the sacred necklace over her silvery head.

"Merry meet, pilgrims," Cara called from Aisling's bag of magickal tools.

Raine was just about to retort, since she and the poppet always enjoyed their verbal jousts, when a loud explosion interrupted her thought. "God's nightgown! What was that?!" she shouted with eyes wide as the proverbial saucers.

The Sisters and Thaddeus looked up, in the direction of the explosion to see a fiery drama. Above them, through the tangle of trees, the moon had slid behind some clouds, rendering the sky inky black. But the horizon was not at all dark. Rather, it was shot with crimson, like an ugly splash of fresh blood. The wind was right, and the smoke blew toward them.

"That's coming from Fane Manor!" Dr. Weatherby yelled. "Has to be. It tops the highest hill around here, and it's the right direction."

As the Sisters' minds ran riot, Aisling, with long legs already stretched in a sprint, yelled, "C'mon, let's drive up there and see what's going on!"

In Aisling's SUV, the Sisters and Thaddeus headed for the Fane estate. They only drove a quarter mile when they realized that Dr. Weatherby was right– the manor house was on fire.

"Something caused the place to explode first," Aisling stated, behind the wheel.

"And something's caused a really *hot* fire," Raine added, leaning forward with her elbows on the front seat's backrest.

"Gas, I suppose. I'll try and get as close as I can," Aisling answered. "Looks like the fire department and the police are already here."

"Oh, hell, there's a crowd of the ghoulishly curious already gathering too!" Maggie put in, gazing out the large vehicle's side window.

"Looks like everyone's headed the same place. No sense being stuck on this lane. Let's get out and walk up. I'll pull off and leave the car here." Aisling put the vehicle in park and unbuckled her seat belt.

Everyone piled out, and the group started walking up Manor Hill toward the hellishly burning mansion. As they got in close, they waved and called out to Chief Fitzpatrick, whose voice boomed above the clamor. Spying the Sisters, he started toward them, parting the crowd as Moses parted the Red Sea. "Let them through! Let them through! Go on now; go home! There's nothing more to see!"

Grumbling at being dismissed, the crowd began to dissipate, allowing the Sisters and Thaddeus to join the chief, who, roused from his bed, had hastily yanked on his uniform.

"Pretty hot fire, Chief," Raine said *sotto voce*. "What do you make of it?"

At that, Kevin Hurley, the chief of the Hamlet fire department, who walked over to confer with the chief of the Hamlet PD, pronounced, recognizing the Sleuth Sisters, "*Arson.* No doubt whatsoever. We found the evidence."

"And?" Fitzpatrick asked. His long years in law enforcement told him there was more.

"My men brought out a body, Fitz. It's a woman, but she's too charred for identification," the fire chief answered in somber tones, after glancing about to make sure they were still alone. "No one else in the house. No pets."

"Looks like someone went to a lot of trouble to see Mada Fane dead," Fitzpatrick mused, looking at the Sisters.

Raine pursed her mouth. "Yyy-eah, looks that way, Chief."

"Didn't you say she seemed frightened when you talked with her about the ax murders?" Fitzpatrick questioned, keeping his gaze on the three women sleuths he had come to trust.

"Yes, we most certainly did," Maggie replied. "And her body language gave us to believe she was holding back information. At least that was the impression we got."

"Well, like I said, someone's gone to a lot of trouble to make sure she didn't share that info," the police chief declared. "And I know you're gonna tell me that *this*," he threw an arm out in the direction of the burning mansion, "ties in with the Hamlet's unsolved ax murders, as well as the skeletons you discovered in Haleigh's Wood, right?"

"Right," the Sisters stated earnestly.

Raine turned her head to spot old Mr. Steward, Mada Fane's caretaker, who resided in the still-standing, though somewhat damaged, carriage house, staring at the burning manse. His lips, in the glow from moon and fire, appeared to be moving in a silent, private petition.

"I assume, Chief, that you've already questioned the estate caretaker." Raine cocked her head in the direction of Steward, who stood staring at the blazing fire. "Did he see or hear anything?"

Fitzpatrick scrunched his mouth into a grimace, shaking his head. "Nothing." It looked as though the chief were about to add something when a familiar voice called out to them.

Catching sight of the Braddock County Coroner, Dr. Benjamin Wight, Raine decided to wait before uttering the thought that was pressing on her mind.

After having parked his vehicle near to where the Sisters, Thaddeus and the fire and police chiefs were gathered, Dr. Wight walked briskly toward them. "Got your call, Chief," he nodded to Fitzpatrick. "What do you have for me?"

"One charred body we think is female. In all probability the owner of this house, who resided here sporadically. Dr. Mada Fane," Fitzpatrick replied.

While they continued talking, Mada's caretaker was joined by what appeared to be a younger man, who, noting the savvy sleuths at the scene, seemed more than anxious to lead Mr. Steward quickly away.

"Who's that with the caretaker?" Raine put sharply to Maggie and Aisling.

"Can't tell from here," Maggie answered, with Aisling responding in a similar way.

"Both men turned and looked at us before they hurried off to the younger fella's car," Raine said, her thoughts leaping to a different angle of the mystery.

"Wind's kickin' up. That ain't good," Fitzpatrick remarked.

"Arson," Aisling was muttering to herself, as she ruminated over the current situation.

"What'dja say?!" the police chief nearly shouted.

A sudden gust of wind hurled his shout back into his teeth.

"Arson!" Aisling repeated with vigor.

"A *definite* arson," the fire chief echoed, quickly placing his white helmet back on his head.

"Arson and *murder*," Fitzpatrick mused aloud. His face was grim, and his jaw was firmly set. "Gonna be a lot to sort through here, what with the evidence Kevin found," he glanced in the direction of the fire chief, who had rejoined his men; "the body; whatever the forensic team uncovers; and then what *you*," he looked to the coroner, "conclude."

Raine waited till they finished speaking before she turned to Dr. Wight, who, even past midnight, called out to a suspect explosion and fire, looked as though he had just stepped from the pages of *GQ*. "Ben," she began, "I," she shot a glance at her cousins and fellow sisters of the moon as she spoke, "*we*," she amended, "feel pretty sure that when you begin your forensic investigation ..."

Chapter Nineteen

At their breakfast table the following morning, Raine and Maggie were enjoying their second cup of coffee.

Gazing out the window, Maggie thought: *It's one of those days a happy person records for mental posterity. Pennsylvania summer's end. A dreamy landscape, faultless sky, bursting sunlight, birds singing, and that magickal play of light and shadow among the trees. All the ingredients for a perfect day. Then why do I feel as though something wicked this way comes?* She shook off the thought quickly before Raine could pick it up.

Preoccupied, Raine's emerald gaze was traveling round Tara's cozy kitchen. "Every time I come in here from now on, I shall think of Granny," she declared, brushing toast crumbs from her green, gauzy summer dress. "Not that I never did before, of course, but you know what I mean."

"I do," Maggie replied, setting the morning paper aside with its pictures of the flame-engulfed Fane Manor. "Once we tie up the last few strings of this muddle of connected mysteries, let's conjure Granny. I have a few questions I want to put to her." She fastened a missed button on the coral blouse she was wearing. With its matching skirt, the outfit was cool and becoming to the red-haired Sister.

"You bet!" Raine exclaimed. "I have a couple questions of my own for Granny. What were you thinking about a moment ago? I was too fixed on my own thoughts to read you."

Maggie shrugged. "I was looking out the window at the woods and thinking that autumn is starting to show itself. Not outright. But secretly. I notice it early in the mornings and late in the evenings, don't you?" She prattled on, not waiting for an answer and not really wanting one.

"Did I hear you rattling round the house in the wee hours this morning, or have we another spirit in this house besides Granny?" Maggie took a sip of the coffee and sat back in her chair to listen to what a hunch told her Raine was about to say. The sun, streaming through a stained-glass window, caught her dark-red hair, surrounding her head with a glowing aureole.

Raine smiled. "You look like one of those holy images on a church window. But in answer to your query, I couldn't sleep, so I got up and started researching something I happened to remember in the middle of the night. Or maybe it was a dream. I don't know, but my research got me what I was looking for. A very *interesting* read, as it turned out."

"Do tell." Maggie put her cup down on the table and freshened her coffee from the pot.

When we were interviewing Mada Fane in the Manor's library, I happened to glance up at the ceiling." The Goth gal jerked her head. "Remember the ornate ceiling medallion that encircled the chandelier there?"

Maggie considered. "I think so." She sat back in her chair with the fresh cup of coffee.

"Well, get this. Some five hundred years ago, give or take a week or so," Raine quipped, "a very covert society was formed in Europe called the 'Four Ps,' which is said to have been created for gaining Perception, Prosperity, Prestige, and Power. Membership is for life, and a blood oath is taken for secrecy. The coven– yes, they call themselves a coven, though, God and Goddess know that their magick involves only the very blackest kind ... ."

Raine paused, absent in thought, as a chilling image flashed across her mind's eye. "Oooh, I lost my train of discussion!" She reflected for a bit, shaking off the disturbing vision. "At any rate, the coven members– twelve plus a leader– are said to include some of the most powerful people in the world. Participants pass the membership down in families, and those families are among the most wealthy, influential, and powerful dynasties across the globe. I'm talking finance, politics and government, research and science, *et cetera*."

Maggie raised a perfectly arched brow. "What has this to do with–"

"The ceiling medallion in Fane Manor's library bore four Ps," Raine cut in, anticipating Maggie's question.

"Age-old ritual killings for gain, for the four Ps! It makes perfect sense. Go on," the redheaded Sister prompted. "I'm all ears."

"Gives a whole new meaning to the phrase, 'No pain, no gain,' huh?"

When Maggie grimaced, Raine lifted her shoulders, flinging out her hands, palms up. "That's it for now. On that subject anyway. But I've a feeling we're going to learn a lot more about that bizarre circle within the next day or so." Raine picked up the pot to refresh the coffee in her cup.

"Who were you talking to on the phone this morning?" Maggie asked, taking the last bite of her toast.

"Train Nellie and Ben." Raine swallowed some coffee before continuing. "Nellie left a message to call her back, so I did. She wanted to know if we'd made any progress at all on her great-aunt's murder. I told her we'd telephone her to set up a meeting in a couple days, that we were very close to wrapping the cold case. Of course, I didn't divulge how or *any* details really, just that we were close. When we do talk with train Nellie, we can always say we can't reveal our sources for some of the particulars."

Raine pursed her pouting mouth. "You know, Mags, if we hadn't returned home from our time-travel to encounter the arson-murder at Fane Manor, and I hadn't developed a sudden case of insomnia last night, consequently thinking of the Four Ps, I might have set up that meeting with train Nellie today, but there's more to all this. *There's more*, Mags."

Maggie nodded, pensive, as she sipped her coffee. "Did you say that Ben was the second person with whom you spoke on the phone this morning? I was catching up on my sleep, so I was just getting up, around nine-thirty it must've been, when I heard you talking."

"Ben, yes," Raine replied. "I rang him for news, left a message, and he rang me back. He has nothing new to report on the skeletons, but that's no surprise, is it? I mean he's such a thorough coroner, what else would there be to report from his initial forensic investigation? I didn't share anything with him yet from *our* findings. That can wait till we unravel the last bit of this tangled mess; and like I said, my witch's intuition is telling me that very soon now, it *will* all be untangled.

"Once we solve the arson-murder at Fane Manor, our remaining questions should be answered. Even though," Raine sighed, "my research this morning pointed out there was never any proof *whatsoever* that the Four Ps really existed, I'm *convinced* it did and *does* exist, and that certain members of the Fane family have been, for centuries, a significant part of it, **and**–"

"Uh, huh," Maggie murmured to herself complacently, as a new thought entered her head. "Not all *our* relatives are practitioners of the Craft. Needless to say, I'm *not* likening the Craft to the Four Ps, but there would very likely be members of those powerful Four-P families who never belonged to that evil circle. Mada wasn't the only descendant of Adrian and Elsa Fane, was she?"

"No, she was *not* the only descendant of Adrian and Elsa. I uncovered in my research this morning that there are Fanes, from her line, scattered all over the world," Raine disclosed.

"I remember that Mada looked frightened when we brought up the ax murders and the unearthed skeletons," Maggie recalled. "Yyyy-es," she mused, her voice momentarily trailing off. "I remember her eyes when she asked if we thought the ax murders and the skeletons were connected. And there was that flicker of fear again when we asked her about her family. That is certainly something to consider in this arson-murder. Some relative or other could have killed Mada to keep her quiet. Perhaps said relative discovered that she'd talked with us. We are, after all, pretty well-known."

Maggie sucked in her full lower lip. "You said that you were returning a call that train Nellie made to us, but she didn't ring this morning, right?"

"She rang yesterday."

"But," Maggie wrinkled her brow, "I heard the phone ring twice."

"Oh, the other call must've been a wrong number. When I answered, no one replied. They just hung up. Though," Raine amended, tilting her head, "afterward, I couldn't shirk the lurking feeling that whoever it was wanted to–"

"Good-morning, chickadees!" Hannah sang on the outside of the screen at the backdoor.

"C'mon in!" the Sisters replied.

"Have a cup of coffee before you start the cleaning!" Maggie suggested. "It's fresh."

The housekeeper was wearing a particularly garish Hawaiian muumuu this morning and, with it, her signature purple sneakers. "Noticed this envelop sticking in the door out front when I drove up," she announced, handing the missive to Maggie. No name on it." She poured herself a cup of ambition from the coffee pot and plopped down in a kitchen chair.

Glancing over at the *Hamlet Herald* on the table before her, with its front-page photo of Fane Manor engulfed in flames and its blazing headline: "Historic Hamlet Mansion Destroyed by Fire! Suspected Arson-Murder!" Hannah shook her head. "What a great loss to our Hamlet! Poor Mada Fane, burned up like that!" She picked up the paper, read a bit, then went on, "My cousin who's a firefighter said she looked like a chunk-a charcoal! Poor woman! I didn't know her personally, of course, but I have a niece who's on the hospital auxiliary in town here, and she mentioned, more than once, how the hospital board could always count on Dr. Fane for whatever Haleigh Hospital needed. Remember when the hospital got the new wing? Well, Dr. Fane was the one who paid for the whole thing. Gave generously to this town, she did."

"Yes," the Sisters said, exchanging glances. "She contributed to the college too."

Hannah took a long drink of her coffee before adding, "She always greeted Hamlet people with a warm smile and a kind word, even though she hardly spent much time here. Traveled constantly, yet she never deserted the Hamlet when we needed something.

"She must have loved her hometown very much," Hannah remarked, removing her spectacles and wiping an eye. "Always held on to the Manor. Oh, it was too big a place for one person, her being a spinster and all; but seemed like she could never part with it, didn't it? I heard talk that she'd planned to leave the Manor to the town, or the college, or maybe even the hospital. Who knows?"

Hannah's eyes swept the front page of the paper again. "Oh, and I ran into Mada Fane's caretaker, old Mr. Steward, early this morning at the Quick-Stop, where I always play my daily number. He was with his son and daughter-in-law. They told me they got him to finally agree to move in with them. The windas are all blown out in the carriage house. Wind blew embers that caused roof damage too. Old man Steward said the police questioned him at the scene of the fire, you know, as to whether he had seen or heard anything unusual before the explosion, but he wasn't home when the firebug was sneakin' around the place. His daughter-in-law told me he was over visiting them, *but* he was on his way home when he heard the explosion and saw the flames shoot into the sky."

Again, the kindly housekeeper shook her grey head, sounding out a trilogy of *tsks* that was her habit. "Life is short, and death is sure, but somebody wanted to make *really* sure that poor woman was dead– *good and dead.* I can't imagine what the reason was," she looked up at Raine and Maggie, "but I'm certain you girls will find out! And, if I know you, you're probably already on the case."

Passing a look between them, the Sisters answered, "Oh, we're on it!"

Hannah shuddered as she drained her coffee cup. "Looked like a chunk-a charcoal my cousin said." Standing, she posed the rhetorical question, as she carried the cups to the sink for washing. "How could something this evil happen here, in our Hamlet?!"

Maggie frowned. "Bad things happen everywhere, darlin'." The redheaded Sister tore open the envelope, the housekeeper had pulled from the front door, to read the single-sheet, pencil-scribbled note inside: *Meet me at the ruins of Fane Manor at eleven-thirty this morning. Don't be late. I can't keep this information to myself any longer. I will reveal all. Come alone.*

Maggie's eyes grew large, as she sprang out of her chair, handing the note to a startled Raine, who also leaped to her feet with one of her favorite expressions, "Levitation!"

"What's wrong?!" Hannah nearly shouted.

"Have to meet someone up at the Fane property in fifteen minutes," Raine responded. "Lock up when you leave. I don't know how long we'll be."

The Sisters grabbed their purses, which were hanging from hooks near the backdoor.

Watching them scurry, the housekeeper tilted her grey head. "I'll be in and out. I wanna finish the outside of the windas on the main floor today. Shouldn't take me long, then I'll lock up for ya. I'll leave a tea tray on the counter. And whatever you're up to– **you be careful!"**

"Always!" Raine tossed over her shoulder as she and Maggie dashed out the backdoor to the driveway and the redheaded Sister's Land Rover.

***

After the explosion and fire, Fane Manor was in total ruin. A single chimney stood like a lone sentry over the heaps of rubble. Yellow police tape surrounded the remnants of what had once been the Hamlet's greatest house, identifying it as a crime scene. Several yards distant, the carriage house stood looking forlorn minus its windows and with its blackened roof. A ghostly curtain fluttered from one of the blown-out windows.

Raine and Maggie stepped from the dark green Land Rover to gaze upon the desolate tableau. No other vehicle did they see, and no one was about. Though it was late summer, a chill slithered along Raine's spine, as though a cold wintery wind had blown at her back. *Brrr!* she shivered. *Someone's walking over my grave.* She cocked her head, pressing her bejeweled hands together to listen to the breeze in the encompassing woods.

Nothing. Not even the wind had a message for the Sisters.

"No sign of anyone," Raine remarked, glancing around anew.

Checking her watch, Maggie said, "We made it up here on time. Let's just wait."

The Sisters walked around the outside perimeter of the police tape in musing silence, every once in a while, glancing back at the long drive, flanked by tall trees, that led to what *was* the grand house.

"I'm starting to think someone has chosen to play a bad joke on us, Mags," Raine stated. "But why?"

"Out of sheer meanness, I suppose, and I'm anything but amused." Maggie gave a little shrug. "Let's wait another ten minutes, just to make sure no one's going to show up."

"Fine by me," Raine answered. "C'mon let's walk around up here to see if we can find any clues."

Something startled a group of crows in a nearby tree, sending them cawing loudly into the air with sudden fright. Little did the pair realize that, at that very moment, a pair of narrowed eyes glared at them from the trees.

Eyes that belonged to a murderer.

After scanning the grounds for nearly fifteen minutes, the Sisters started walking back to Maggie's Land Rover, having come across nary a clue, and convinced that someone, for whatever reason, had played a shameless practical joke on them.

In the surrounding trees, the birds were hushed now. It seemed too quiet.

When they came to the parked vehicle, Raine, whose sense of smell was very sharp, sniffed the air. Following the odor she detected, she took several steps, glancing down to find a smoldering cigarette on the gravel. Stooping down, she studied it carefully. A witchy flash told her it had been dropped in haste.

Plunging a hand into her purse, she extracted a tissue and a small tin of mints. Flinging out the remaining pastilles, she reached with the tissue and carefully picked up and snuffed out the smoldering cigarette, depositing it into the empty tin, then dropping the tin into her bag.

Maggie, meanwhile, was gazing at the mansion ruins, trying to imagine who would have played this joke on them, if, indeed, it was a joke.

Again, from the nearby trees, the crows grew raucous. "I used to wonder why a flock of crows was called a 'murder of crows,'" Raine mused aloud. "It's because when they're startled, they sound as if they're screaming 'Bloody murder!'" *I think this is a message, an omen,* she told herself, and her face looked anxious.

"Mags," Raine called from the exterior passenger side of the Land Rover, "we've got to make one important stop before heading home."

The red-haired Sister was just about to ask Raine *where*, when, up the long, steep lane that led to the Fane Manor ruins, came a Hamlet police car, hell-bent-for-leather. Behind the wheel was Chief Fitzpatrick with one of his juniors beside him in the passenger seat. The Sisters paused, standing on opposite sides of the Land Rover, each with a hand on a door handle.

"Wonder what's up?" Raine asked.

"Whatever it is, it must be major!" Maggie exclaimed.

Pulling up alongside Maggie's vehicle, the chief lowered his window to call out, "Your housekeeper told me you'd be up here. You were right. Ben just phoned me. Wait till you hear what he found! Get in, both of you. My junior can drive your car. We're going to the coroner's now; he's expecting us."

Maggie and Raine slid into the police vehicle next to the chief, whilst the junior officer jumped into the Land Rover. The way the cars were positioned, it was easier for the junior to start down the lane first, with the chief and the Sisters following in the black-and-white. No sooner had the cars started down the long, winding, steep lane, when the Rover's left front tire shimmied violently before flying off, causing the vehicle to careen wildly out of control! Sparks shot off the road as the front of the vintage car struck and scraped the gravel!

"Great Goddess," Maggie screamed, "help Officer Keogh!!"

Raine reached over and grasped her cousin and sister of the moon's hand, squeezing it hard. "It'll be OK. Stay calm!"

Instantly, the chief slowed, pumping the brakes. "We're lucky that's my best emergency driver," he said. "He'll get it under control." His voice and his words, however, masked his true feelings, as the Land Rover headed perilously for the trees.

In the next moment, and by the Divine grace of the great Goddess, the officer somehow managed to get the Rover stationary, though the car did graze a stately oak in the process.

Once Fitzpatrick stopped the black-and-white, the Sisters scrambled out. "Are you all right?!" they called, running toward Maggie's vehicle.

The junior looked a bit shaken, but other than that, he seemed uninjured. "Lug nuts must have been loose ... or loosened," he managed to state.

"I'm relieved that you're OK. *Are* you OK?" Maggie asked with anxious voice and expression.

"I'm fine," he said, making eye contact with the chief, who was standing next to the Sisters.

"Good work, Jerry! You handled the situation like a real pro!" Fitzpatrick declared with gusto, thumping the young officer on the back.

"Oh, but look at my baby," Maggie moaned. "I just had her to the Auto Doctor's, and now she will be right back in there." She looked to Raine, "Great Hecate's nightie! You don't suppose they neglected to tighten all the lugs when they rotated the tires, do you?"

Before Raine could answer, the chief, who was down on one knee examining the front of the Land Rover, said, "Looks like your baby won't be going right back to the Auto Doctor's, Miss Maggie. She's evidence now. Someone may have tampered with this wheel. Not to worry, we'll send her over to the Auto Doctor's when we're through with 'er."

"You mean to say that someone lured Raine and me up here with the intention of *killing* us?" Maggie looked keenly at Fitzpatrick before turning her emerald regard on her sister of the moon.

"That's *exactly* what I'm saying," the chief replied point-blank. "I've been in law enforcement a long time, and my gut is telling me that someone loosened the lug nuts on that wheel."

"And I believe I know who that someone was," Raine answered. "I've some real evidence to turn over to our clued-in coroner. Did you say we're going now to meet with Dr. Wight, Chief?"

"Roger that." Fitzpatrick pulled his cell phone out of his shirt pocket and began punching in a call. "Just as soon as I call for a tow for your Rover."

Meanwhile, Raine was speed-dialing Aisling.

***

When all *three* of the Sleuth Sisters entered Tara's kitchen door some time later, they were still talking about what they had discussed with Chief Fitzpatrick and Coroner Dr. Wight.

"Kudos to you, Raine," Aisling said, patting her cousin and fellow Sister on the shoulder. "We'll soon have everything we need to connect and wrap these entangled mysteries."

"Oh look," Maggie exclaimed with delight, "our dear Hannah remembered to ready a tea tray for us. Bless her!"

"I'm dying for a good cup of our tea!" Raine stepped up to the counter, where she washed her hands in the farm sink. However, before she had a chance to begin brewing their tea, she glanced round, wondering where Tara's three Merlin cats were. It was always their habit to greet the Sisters at the door. *I hope they're not shut in my closet! They have a habit of darting in there as soon as my back is turned.* "I've got to dash upstairs for a second," she said aloud. "Be right back. Then I'll brew our tea."

Raine raced upstairs, whilst Maggie and Aisling began washing their hands.

Within a few moments, the raven-haired Sister reentered the kitchen, a tad breathless. "I thought I'd accidentally locked the cats in my closet before we left the house earlier, but no problem. They're napping in a sunny window. Before I forget, Aisling, I want to give you that contact info you asked me for," Raine said, her vivid green eyes locking with the senior Sister's own McDonough gaze. "The contact info for the seamstress Maggie and I use." Seeing the puzzled look on Aisling's face, Raine quickly added with a slight movement of her head, "I'll write her name and phone number down for you."

By this point, the blonde with the wand, her mouth open in halted speech, refrained from voicing the question on the tip of her tongue, allowing Raine time to play out whatever it was she was plotting.

The Goth gal hurriedly sniffed the opened package of tea on the tray that Hannah had set out for them. Then she grabbed a pad and pen from the kitchen drawer where she stood to dash off the message: *Someone's in the house. After drinking tea, act as if poisoned 'n paralyzed. Follow my lead.*

She purposefully did not telecommunicate a message to Maggie. Rather, she scribbled the following postscript to her, showing the

- 330 -

note to *both* Sisters: *Do NOT send me any mind-messages. Person in house might read them.* ***Veil our thoughts now!***

The raven-haired Sister kept talking as much as she could all the while, "Yes, we love Mitzy. She's a great seamstress and a lovely person as well." Raine chose that name, for as far as she knew, not one of the three of them knew anyone by that name. The ruse was working as a warning to her Sisters. She could sense that all three of them were veiling their thoughts.

Veiling thoughts was similar to a shimmer of glamor with which a sister of the Craft could envelop herself, so that anyone gazing upon her would see her as gorgeous no matter what she looked like on a particular day. All three Sisters had learned, from Granny McDonough, when they were each quite young, to veil their thoughts when they felt treachery of any kind from another of the Craft whose intent was rooted in the Dark Arts. When the Sisters were wee girls, Granny invented a game they would play to test their ability to do this, for it was a difficult spell to master, requiring years of practice.

The spell veiled their true thoughts with brainwaves of mundane notions sent out to mislead mind-reading practitioners who meant them harm. It was one of the spells with which Granny had drilled them– and she had taught them well.

All the while now, Raine was pretending to prepare their tea with the opened package on the tray, when, in essence, she had slyly substituted it for another tea. Washing out the tea pot and cups with boiling-hot water, she said, "Every time I do this, I am reminded of **Granny**. How she taught us to make proper tea, and how she enjoyed the ritual of teatime."

Using their powerful thought-veiling spell, the three Sisters silently and secretly called upon Granny for help and protection.

Again, Raine quickly and quietly jotted a note: *Follow my lead– after tea, act paralyzed & don't move a muscle!*

Not wanting the murderer, who was somewhere in the house, to find the notes, after showing that last one to Maggie and Aisling, seated now at table, she quickly stuffed the small slips from the kitchen notepad into the latter's purse, saying aloud, "I'll put Mitzy's contact info in your bag, Aisling, so you don't forget it."

Busying herself with the tea things, Raine paused to reach into her own purse, which she had set on the kitchen counter. Extracting her smart phone, she switched on the recorder, letting the cell rest on the counter.

"Tea's ready!" she exclaimed, setting the tray on the table and taking a seat there with her Sisters.

It was then that Maggie's cell sounded with the rapid trilogy of musical notes that told her she had a text message. She pulled the phone from her bag, and read the brief but commanding missive from Eva Novak: **YOU ARE IN DANGER! SOMEONE IS IN YOUR HOUSE!**

The redheaded Sister flashed the text to her Sisters at table. No one spoke, as they drank the tea Raine had just prepared.

After a few moments, Raine said in a weak and shaky voice, "I feel strange," she slumped in her chair, "like I've been drugged. I can't move my arms and legs!"

And their invisible intruder was pleased to hear the note of panic in the Sister's voice.

Maggie and Aisling, too, were quickly taking on the appearance of having been drugged.

Unable to speak, Maggie croaked out something that sounded like a cross between a groan of pain and a cry for help.

It was at that deadly moment when their unseen, uninvited guest made her appearance from behind the open cellar door.

"Soooo, you were going to reveal the long-kept Fane secret, were you?" Mada asked in a dry voice, her face, so different from the Sisters' first encounter with her, now a reflection of evil, as she towered over them– savage and triumphant. "My family made use of worthless vagrants for their ritual killings, blood offerings that brought them, via an eclectic *mélange* of ancient secrets– Perception, Prosperity, Prestige, and Power."

She ran a hand through her short, wavy, honey-blonde hair, sending her victims a derisive look, her tone jeering, "The celebrated Sleuth Sisters everyone makes such a fuss about!" Mada clucked a mocking, disapproving sound. "I'm disappointed– in a way I am– that you're not as bright as everybody always said you were. I like a challenge, you see."

She tilted her head, studying the magickal threesome, who could only stare back at her, unmoving. "Well now, you're wondering what I put in the tea, aren't you? I was worried that you might sniff out the poison and do a switcharoo, so I tainted every bit of tea I could find and not just the pack on the tray, including your chai tea that masks the poison's faint odor. Ah," the wicked woman heaved a sigh, tilting her head and sending the Sisters a cunning sidelong look. "Curare is such an extraordinary poison. It's my personal favorite. I told you I learned many useful things living among the Jivaro headhunters of the Amazon; and," she leaned toward them, "to you I admit, I am a *malicious* creature, and I *revel* in it."

In a manner as if conducting one of her archeology lectures, Mada proceeded to explain to her victims what the powerful poison had done to them, paralyzing them and rendering them unable to move a muscle, "… though," she reminded them, "the horror of curare is that you will see, hear, and *feel* all that is done to you. But you won't be able to move!" She laughed chillingly.

"For this very special job, I had to take on a partner, whom you will meet," she gave a short scornful snort, "in a manner of speaking, in a few minutes. He's a local undertaker, though *scoundrel* is a better choice of word; and like all his sort, his work comes dear. It's costing me a cool million for each of you." Mada leaned forward, putting her face near the Sisters, to add in a raspy whisper, "Or so he thinks. What the stupid sod doesn't realize is that he's a dead man. I won't chance blackmail later.

"For now, however, I need the big lug to help me get rid of you three pests. I've fretted about you for a couple years now, *but no more!* From here, you'll be carted off by my ill-advised accomplice, when he gets here, to the crematory. I sent him a message a few moments ago from your cellar."

With a hideous expression contorting her features, Mada talked on, her voice, contrary to her face and plan, as sweet and soft as it had been the first time the Sisters had met with her. "Allow me to describe the cremation process to you, my pretties. Basically, cremation of a human body is carried out at a temperature ranging from 1400 to 1800 degrees Fahrenheit. The intense heat helps reduce the body to its basic elements and dried bone fragments. Bone is so difficult to burn."

Mada sighed with pleasure, her expression sly. "*Habeas Corpus.* Very basically– 'No bodies, no crimes.' And to cut a long story short, no one can charge me with your deaths. *I'm dead and gone– it's perfect!* By the way, I used the same M.O. as my family always used. Ritual murder of a homeless vagrant. No one reports them missing to the authorities, and their deaths are a boon to society. You see, it's a win-win situation," she finished triumphantly.

Mada fidgeted for a second or so with the collar of the tan safari dress she was wearing, as if debating whether or not to divulge to the Sisters what she had done. When ego won out, she couldn't help but brag. "After I filled Fane Manor with gas from the fireplaces in the library and the twin parlors, I left the house, wearing a disguise. Inside was the dead body of the homeless woman– my height, weight, and age– I had lured into my web, along with one of my cell phones and the ignition device I'd created. All I had to do was get a safe enough distance away, then call that cell phone with a burner phone, which, of course, I've since disposed of. The call ignited the spark," her face darkened, her eyes again sly, the lips curving into a chilling smile, "and," she lifted her hands, flinging them out in opposite directions, "**boom!!**

"There you have it! As the papers stated, 'The acclaimed Mada Fane victim of an arson-murder, her body burned beyond recognition.' The stupid Hamlet police will file it as another unsolved case, just as they did the 1932 triple ax murders."

The monstrous woman actually pinched off a piece of teacake from the tray and started munching, her hip slung casually against the kitchen counter, as she continued her disgusting discourse. "Little Nellie Triggs got an eye-full, so she had to be killed. My great-grandmother Elsa had no choice, in addition to the fact that she had every *right* to ax her after the stupid bitch's affair with my great-grandfather!"

Mada picked off another bit of teacake. "Your housekeeper whips up a great teacake. When I saw her from the woods, washing the windows, I had no trouble getting in here. I darted inside when she was busy on the opposite end of the house." She swallowed. "Too bad there's no good tea left to wash this down," she grunted.

"But getting back to what I was saying: Nellie left my great-grandmother Elsa no choice. She had to kill her. Just as Josie Means left me no choice." Mada's lips curled in a wicked grin. "We all weave and spin, each of us, our own fate; wouldn't you agree?" She regarded the Sisters cunningly. "And I'm certain you'd accede that my staging of Josie Means' death was genius? I was thrilled that the foolish woman– she was an odd sort, don't you think? Anyway, it was a stroke of luck for me that the dotty old puss had those two horrid cats. The fact that she did, inspired my clever plan to do away with her.

"There was really nothing else I could do!" she screeched of a sudden, the necessity to talk growing upon her. "It was simply a matter of time before author Josie Means – and she was such a *prolific* writer– only a matter of time before she wrote a book about her grandfather J.D. You understand, I'm certain, that I simply couldn't let her do that. She was bent on clearing his name, very sure he had not committed suicide by jumping from that ship.

"Using a fake passport and wearing a disguise, Adrian Fane was on that ship with J.D. Means, bound for England. Money can buy just about anything; so a fake passport was," she plucked another pinch of teacake from the tray, popping the morsel into her mouth, "*a piece of cake.*

"I couldn't let Josie spill into *your* ears what she'd been collecting on the whole affair for so many years. Josie never had any *concrete* proof that my great-grandfather Adrian pushed J.D. Means off that ship, but I knew that if she showed *you* all the information she'd laid hands on over the years, you'd find the proof somehow. So I killed her, staging that vase-lamp accident scene in her house, and I lifted the file on J.D. and my great-grandparents that she had very conveniently left lying on a table in her parlor. The file revealed to me that Josie knew, or had guessed, far too much.

"My great-grandfather Adrian very much wanted J.D.'s coal lands, but the stubborn man wouldn't sell them to him. You see, Adrian and Elsa were world travelers, and they knew the winds of another global war were already howling in Europe. Adrian was a good business man, *the best*, thus he wanted those coal lands, knowing what he did about Germany and their secret preparation for World War II. Coal would be in great demand for making steel– steel for armaments. As history professors, you *clearly* see what I mean.

"The only way to get those coal lands from a man as stubborn as J.D. Means was to *ruin* him, *bring him to his knees*! So my great-grandfather put out the rumor that J.D.'s bank was in trouble. A rumor like that at the height of the Great Depression worked like a charm. In a few days, Goody-Goody Jim Dandy's bank experienced a wild run, and it failed. Long story short– Great-Grandfather Adrian got what he wanted, the rich coal lands that, during the upcoming war, added significantly to his coffers." Mada passed her tongue over her dry lips. "As I said, he was a *shrewd* business man.

"And *you?*" she spat the word viciously, pointing a finger in a gesture of irritation. "What will happen to you three super-snoops?" Mada's voice took on a supercilious tone. "You'll simply disappear. How fitting that you'll vanish into a Black Hole of History! Think about that? Isn't it all pure genius?!"

The sorceress laughed darkly, a peal of laughter that sounded very much like an evil witch's cackling. "Your close friend, that nerdie professor, will think you time-traveled and just couldn't make it back without his assistance."

Unable to speak, the Sisters' eyes echoed shock. Mada Fane's words hit them like a punch to the gut, the jolt turning quickly to outrage. *But all they could do was gawk.*

Raine, however, launched Maggie a telepathic message, neglecting, in her state, to veil the thought: *She knows about our time-travel! How?!*

"Yes, I know all about your time-travel, your– and I must add *brilliant*– Time-Key." From her brown leather shoulder bag, the wicked woman whipped out the Sisters' portable *Book of Shadows* that contained the ancient, arcane chant that was their Time-Key!

Though the Sisters did not move, again three pairs of McDonough eyes mirrored shock and, rare to their essences, *fear,* as a thousand questions rebounded in their heads.

Pleased, Mada smiled her chilling smile, a false, unnatural thing. She was like a dark shadow standing there, appraising the Sisters, as she was, with her hollow eyes, eyes behind which there appeared to be no soul. Or one so black it seemed there was none.

"I know a lot of things, including what I've ascertained about you," Mada was saying in a condescending voice. "You thought you were in sole possession of so much knowledge, so many secrets! Had the world by the tail you thought, didn't you? *News flash*– the world doesn't revolve, as you thought it did, around the three of you! I know about your poppet too," she pronounced with relish. "My family has collected curiosities and artifacts for centuries, including *haunted* items, such as dolls; but I am smart enough to know– the spirit in *that* poppet," she flung a pointing finger toward Cara, who was sitting quietly on the kitchen counter, "will serve only you. She'd be more trouble to me than she's worth!"

Mada's hands met in a gesture of delight, and her nasty smile widened. "I intend to make use of your precious Time-Key to uncover untold ancient treasures, ancient secrets, and all sorts of unknown, undiscovered arcane, esoteric knowledge!" The woman's face went utterly Satanic, the expression ugly and calculating with something of triumph too. "I'll soon be the most powerful person in the world, the most powerful individual the world has ever known! I daresay this whole mess has produced its rewards!"

The malevolent creature inclined her honey-blonde head, as she pulled a gold cigarette case and matching lighter from her shoulder bag, lighting up and inhaling deeply. "Awww, feeling sad and rather stupid, aren't you?" Her manner was fawning and utterly repulsive. "You tried to protect the Key from falling into the wrong hands, I know; and, I must admit, you did a pretty good job of that, but not quite good enough!" Full of importance, she laughed longer this time.

"And now the Key has fallen into *my* hands, and your worst nightmare has come to pass! My fake passport is already in the works, and I'll have a whole new identity. They say that money can't buy everything. **Not true!** What it can't *actually* buy, it can procure some pretty good substitutions." She spewed her wicked laugh. "My whole life has been an exhilarating series of adventures, and I am so looking forward to this next one– with my newly acquired Time-Key! And my ticket to, who knows– *immortality!"*

Feeling deadly sick, the Sisters saw that the unusual ring she was wearing sparked and flashed in the light from the sun that was streaming into the kitchen through the stained-glass window.

The sound of a vehicle pulling into the driveway sent the mad woman flying to that window, where, peering through a panel of clear glass, she gave a theatrical sigh, "Ah, here's my oversized flunkie now. I'm certain you three will have a really hot time of it when he carries you away with him!" She took a last drag of her cigarette, before flicking it to the floor, where she snuffed it out with the toe of her shoe. Picking it up, she wrapped it in a napkin, depositing it into the pocket of her safari dress.

Mada was muttering something to herself when a gigantic, scowling man opened the backdoor and stepped into the kitchen, filling the doorway with his bulk. For several moments he remained motionless, curiously staring at the three Sisters who looked frozen in time.

"What the hell took you so long?!" Not waiting for an answer, she rushed on, "I thought you'd never get here! Carry the bitches out to your vehicle, and don't dawdle!" the Fane woman ordered, flinging a pointing finger toward the door. She jerked her head in the direction of the driveway, where he had parked a panel truck, to say, "I'm glad to see you were smart enough to take my advice and use an *unmarked* vehicle."

When the hulk– hitherto staring at the Sisters– didn't move, she roared, **"Don't stand there like a tree full of owls! Get them out to the truck!! I want them incinerated without delay!"**

It was at this juncture that everything started happening fast, furiously, and nearly simultaneously.

At the express moment when the undertaker started forward, reaching huge paws for Raine, the front door burst open through which stormed Beau, Ian and Thaddeus. When the hulk reeled to look in the direction of the charging men, the Sisters, whose hearts were hammering in their chests, shot out of their chairs.

Ian and Thaddeus sprang forward to subdue the giant, whilst Beau, most familiar with Tara, hastened to the back porch for a length of rope.

"What the–?!" To the evil enchantress' utter dismay–

Raine quipped, "Shall we say the drama is over?!" as she snatched the portable *Book of Shadows* from Mada's hand, tossing it to Maggie, who ran with it from the room.

Not ready to give up the valuable Time-Key so easily, Mada– having taken a step after Maggie– and Raine grappled for several moments, when, unbeknownst to the Sister or the Fane woman, the protective, black magick ring the latter was wearing fell soundlessly to the braided rug, bouncing under the kitchen table.

Straightaway, Aisling spied it, and scrambling for it on all fours, she scooped it into a plastic zip-lock bag she'd seized from a drawer, thinking, as she did, that the ring must possess a cauldron of hidden powers. The wise Sister would be certain to take the foul thing out of the bag and bury it deep, at the earliest possible moment. As soon as her fingers had made contact with the ring, she gasped as an image flashed across her mind. Dozens of lit candles. A circle of dark figures in hooded black robes. Voices chanting. And eyes. A pair of yellow eyes with vertical black pupils glaring at her through the flames.

Concurrently, Raine was doing fierce battle with Mada Fane. Despite the fact that the Goth gal was years younger, she had her work cut out for her and could not believe the strength the older woman exhibited, though that was somewhat diminished with the loss of her empowering ring. Raine, however, was wearing the protective aquamarine ring gifted to her at *Beltane* by High Priestess Robin, and she could feel its energy shooting through her body.

When Mada lunged, arms extended, to claw at Raine's eyes, the Sister deftly dodged the blow, as her left fist faked her adversary out to land a power-house right that firmly caught the jaw, sharply turning Mada's head.

With a warrior cry, Raine leaped to make a wild grab for the tall can of wasp spray that Cara– spouting, "More trouble than I'm worth, eh?! More trouble than she knows!!"– kicked off the counter, shooting the substance into the Fane woman's angry face. The vile sorceress screamed, her hands flying to her burning eyes. For the first time, a spasm of fear flitted across her expression, but her investment in evil goaded her on!

Masterfully thrashing the colossal undertaker with his ace karate, Thaddeus walloped him to the kitchen floor, after which Ian and Beau fell upon him and began tying him up with the strong rope Beau had snatched from the back porch. In tandem, Aisling and Maggie (who was just re-entering the kitchen) scrambled for their cells to ring the police chief.

With super-human strength, Mada tore away from Raine (who had dived for her), slamming the Sister backward– **Wham**!– against the counter, as she darted for the kitchen door.

"Don't let her get away!" Maggie and Aisling shouted.

"Boost my besom!" Raine snapped in exasperation, pulling herself upright and massaging the small of her back, "She has the strength of ten demons!"

Having bolted free of the house, the now-desperate woman sprang into the undertaker's panel truck, the keys in it, to roar down Tara's drive– Witch-Way– like the proverbial bat out of Hell.

At the door, a determined Raine, afire with anger and suspense, was nearly shaking with frustration. "Goddess, don't let her get away!" She rubbed the magickal aquamarine ring on her hand before flinging a pointing finger, like a powerful wand, in Mada's direction. **"STOP HER!!"**

At that precise point in the happenings, the chief, in his police car and speeding off the main road with siren blasting, wheeled into Tara's lane, nearly crashing head-on with the three vehicles left there by Ian, Beau and Thaddeus to block the entrance. Fitzpatrick slammed on the brakes, careening to a screeching stop, before jumping out of the black-and-white with his junior.

Watching at the house from the driveway, the Sisters were relieved. "It's the chief!" they chorused. Putting two fingers to her mouth, Raine gave a loud whistle, blowing a signal that she and Fitzpatrick used on occasion.

The four cars blocking her exit at the end of the lane, spurred Mada, speeding down from the house, to veer, sharply turning the top-heavy vehicle to avoid a head-on. Instantly, the panel truck rolled over, flinging the evil woman– who was not wearing a seat belt, and whose burning eyes were watering so badly she could not see where she was going– out of the vehicle, crushing her beneath.

"Great balls of fire!" Raine yelled. "She's flipped over!"

At the same moment, Aisling exclaimed, a hand to her breast, "The chief'll collar her!"

The undertaker's truck lay on its side, tires spinning– ironically, directly under the Witch-Way sign posted to the huge, ancient oak tree at the entrance of the lane to Tara.

Back at the house, Maggie and Aisling turned to Raine. "Mada told us," Aisling probed, "that she tainted *all* the tea she could lay hands on here in the kitchen. I was expecting any moment to be paralyzed! What tea did you use?"

"Huh! It occurred to me she might've done that. A very shrewd mind had been at work here I reasoned. I didn't want to take any chances," the raven-haired Sister replied. "Mada, as you recall from her books, was a very *thorough* woman with a methodical, analytical mind. My back was to you, so neither you nor Mada, hiding behind the cellar door, could tell what I was doing. I happened to have some of Eva's tea in my purse, so that's what I brewed. I always have a few packets of tea in my bag, in case we stop to eat somewhere that doesn't have tea I fancy."

"Damn good detective work!" Ian acclaimed, the praise prompting a snappy salute from Raine in response.

"And how did you three big, strong men know to come to our rescue?" Maggie directed her words and gaze to Ian, Beau and Thaddeus, who were standing in the kitchen over the trussed, dazed undertaker. "I'll just bet Thaddeus got a feeling we needed help and telephoned you," the gorgeous redhead remarked to Beau and Ian.

Dr. Weatherby shook his head. "I can't take credit for that, my Maggie. Actually Beau is the one who got a feeling you were in need of assistance and telephoned Ian and me to meet him here on the double."

"Right after Thaddeus called me, I telephoned the chief and asked him to get here as quickly as he could," Ian related.

"We didn't hear a car pull into the drive before you burst in," Raine and Maggie said at once.

"We left our cars down at the entrance to the lane to block it, and we snuck up the drive to surprise the owner of that strange truck we sighted next to the house," Ian answered.

When Raine pressed Beau on how he knew to come to their rescue, he ducked his head briefly and faltered in his story, finally declaring, "Let's just leave it at what Thad told you. I had an uneasy feeling you were in need of some help."

"Wiz-zard!" Raine uttered under her breath. Fixing Beau with her witchy stare, she curled her index finger toward herself in a come-hither gesture that matched her expression. When he stepped to her side, she flung her arms around him. *I like to think we have no secrets from one another, but I wonder if he could be the—* Her thought was interrupted when—

Hastening his robust physique through Tara's kitchen door, the chief bellowed, "I left Officer Keogh in charge down there. Wanted to come up here to see what the situation is at the house. Is everyone OK?" He stopped, out of breath.

"Everyone's fine, Chief!" Maggie and Aisling reacted.

Raine snapped off another quick salute then turned back into the kitchen from whence she regarded Beau with a sidelong glance. *Or maybe he figures if he can't stop me from sleuthing, he might as well join me. He's different of late, and he's up to something ...*

"We got Mada Fane's accomplice trussed up like a Thanksgiving turkey," Ian chuckled, unceremoniously yanking the hulk to his feet before pushing the undertaker forward toward Fitzpatrick.

"Good work, fellas! How about taking him down to my junior."

"Wi-th pleasure!" Ian replied, taking hold of the mammoth mortician, who, regaining his equanimity, puffed out his massive chest and began an on-the-spot explanation that Ian quickly nipped in the bud. "Tell your story walkin'!"

"Y-you've got this all wrong! I-I g-got a call t-to pick up a body, and that's why I was here when you burst in. I had *no* idea what was going down here!" the hulk spluttered, struggling to ingratiate himself with those in the room. "You gotta believe me! All I knew is that I was to pick up–"

"Yeah," Ian grunted, cutting him off and giving the man a shove.

"You've got this all wrong; I tell you! **I'm innocent!**" the undertaker barked.

"I wish I had a buck for every time I've heard that," Ian muttered, giving his prisoner another push to keep him moving. "I could retire in style!" Then with a boot to the protesting man's ample posterior, he marshaled him off down the lane.

"Chief," an excited Raine half-shouted, holding up her smart phone and rushing out the kitchen door to the driveway, where everyone had congregated, "We took an awful chance not leaping out of our chairs to overwhelm Mada Fane before her accomplice got here, but we had to get it all recorded!" Her magnificent eyes flashed green fire.

"Not to mention that we wanted to find out who the accomplice was. We didn't want to hazard scaring him off," Maggie added.

Raine raised the cell phone she held. "I got it all right here, Chief. The devil couldn't help but brag about her dirty deeds, and I recorded them all! Now we've got all the missing dots we needed to link this Pandora's box of murder and mayhem, the old mysteries to the current ones. We got her, Chief. We got her dead to rights!"

"Dead *is* right," Fitzpatrick answered. He cocked his head with its shock of white hair, grinning at the Sleuth Sisters, who never ceased to amaze him. "Soooo, Mada Fane spilled her guts, did she?" He gave a short laugh. "They say the dead tell no tales, but I'm happy to discover that isn't always the case."

Chapter Twenty

[Three days hence …]

The Gypsy Tearoom's banquet hall, on the former armory's ground floor, rang with merriment, as the Sisters and their sleuthing set celebrated another of the magickal trio's successes. Gathered for the festivities with the Sisters were Ian, Beau and Thaddeus, Hugh and Betty, in addition to the Tearoom proprietress Eva Novak, who was hosting the party. Yet to arrive were Chief Fitzpatrick, Coroner Dr. Wight, and train Nellie Triggs.

Dressed in their choice black evening dresses and looking like the most bewitching witchy-women who ever waved a wand to weave a spell, the Sisters were sorting out the cobwebs of this particularly mystifying case.

Eva had delightfully decorated the banquet room table with a gorgeous crystal-ball centerpiece. And to the Sisters' delight, an enchanting shadow-light cast images of crystal balls, magnifying glasses, and silhouettes of trench-coated Nancy Drew type figures on the walls in the Victorian room that was romantically lit with flickering wall sconces. The dear, sweet woman had even gone so far as to ask the Sisters about their favorite music. Softly playing was Rowena of the Glen's *Book of Shadows* album. It was all so purrrr-fect!

A long tray of delectable hors d'oeuvres occupied a buffet table on one side of the room. The Sisters' 'other halves' thoughtfully provided champagne; and now, Ian popped the corks from a couple of bottles to begin filling the glasses, as Beau and Thaddeus passed them round.

"As Auntie Merry said last spring in Salem, "We all have our little secrets," Raine commented, as she accepted a glass with a kiss from her Beau, his sapphire eyes dancing with humor at her remark. *Now– **there!** What's he inwardly laughing about?!* she asked herself. *I've noticed that he doesn't take nearly as many fits as he used to over the dangers of my time-travel and 'cross-the-board sleuthing. In fact, he seems to have resigned himself to it all. It's as if he's decided to accept it and pitch in–*

"Unbelievable!" Taking a short break from the food preparation to join the sleuthing set for a glass of the bubbly, Eva gave a long sigh, "I'm shocked, shocked to the core, over Mada Fane and rather vexed at myself. All these years, I thought she had high principles. I would never have dreamed–" She stopped, looking a tad discomfited. "An educated, respected woman like that– the picture of respectability! Never a breath of suspicion ..." she shook her head with the realization.

"When we interviewed her, Mada Fane was most amiable toward us," Maggie supplied, glancing in the direction of Raine and Aisling. "The woman was *extraordinarily* skilled at cloaking her real thoughts and feelings."

"Highly gifted, super intelligent, and barking mad," Raine muttered.

"The whole thing is incredible! I just can't get over the fact that she was a murderess," Eva said with sudden force. "And one of such *heartlessness* and ... *magnitude!* She was always so *nice* to me, to everyone. *Really* she was!"

"Some murderers are methodically 'nice,'" Ian cut in, gesturing invisible quote marks. "I have been a detective for many years now, first on the Pittsburgh police force and, in the past several years, as co-owner," he turned to Aisling, "of our Black Cat Detective Agency. Anyway, it's always been my personal opinion that murderers are set apart from the rest of us. Each of us has a conscience, an inner voice that tells us that murder is morally wrong, but that's not the case with murderers."

"They're wired differently," Aisling interjected. "I never cease to be appalled at the workings of the mind of a murderer. They want something badly, and they *kill* to get it. The brake that operates within the rest of us– you know, that stops us when something is wrong– doesn't function with them. I've always wondered if, perhaps, murderers are morally undeveloped. What I mean is this: a child does something wrong, is punished, and learns right from wrong. A murderer, some anyway, do not feel that what they are doing is evil. And the ones who do realize that it's wrong, do not *feel* it. They have no remorse."

"For them, it, *murder,* is 'necessary' and the 'only way.' You don't know," Ian let drop, "how many times a murderer has told me, 'I had no choice.' And I'm not talkin' self-defense here. No," the seasoned detective shook his head, "I've never met a murderer yet who really felt remorse."

"The mark of Cain," Betty, who had been listening with gravity, put in. The thought struck her that she had uttered that same phrase this past spring, in Salem, where the Sisters had solved another puzzling mystery.

"I'll second that," train Nellie stated with ardor. "When murder touches your family, you never again look at it from the outside. You don't go on thinking that it can never come close to you." As the great-niece of axed Nellie Triggs walked into the banquet room, the Sisters could not get over how much she looked like the ill-fated woman. Even her style of dress and her mannerisms matched her great-aunt's.

Raine sent Maggie the thought, *She truly has her ancestor's soulful eyes.*

"We're so glad you could come to this little gathering we put together," the Sisters said, rushing forward to greet Nellie, who instantly initiated a group hug.

"I wouldn't have missed this for the world! I'm so grateful to you for giving our family closure after all these long years of not knowing who killed my aunt and why she and her household were butchered."

Beau handed Nellie a glass of champagne, which, tearing up as she was, she accepted with a warm smile, taking a sip. "It's all over now," he said softly.

"We've more to tell you than what we said over the phone, of course," Maggie said. The red-haired Sister sent Raine an encouraging look.

Once the raven-haired raconteur finished filling Nellie in on all that had transpired, leaving out only their crystal-ball gazing and time-travel, the grateful woman was silent, as she processed all that was conveyed.

Maggie shot Raine the thought: *Thank the great Goddess that Mada Fane chose to reveal to us, not only her own dirty secrets, but her family's too. Hence no one outside our sleuthing set has questioned how we came about certain details of this intertwined intrigue.*

Indeed, we must continue to protect the Time-Key, Raine fired back.

Maggie fixed her McDonough gaze on Eva, who was picking up a tray of hors d'oeuvres to pass among her guests. "Don't beat yourself up over Mada. I daresay retribution, or what," her glance took in her fellow sisters of the moon, "we like to call 'Karma,' finally caught up with her as she raced down our Witch-Way Lane. She had a powerful way of veiling her evil, and she had *a lot* of people fooled, including us for a while, not to mention our wise old housekeeper Hannah Gilbert, who can usually spot a fake in a New-York minute."

Aisling quickly jumped in. "Hannah's worked for our family a *long* time, and we've come to recognize what a good judge of character she is. Like you, she's got good common sense, that, by the way, Ian and I have discovered isn't such a common thing at all. Besides serving as Raine and Maggie's housekeeper, Hannah's our little girl's nanny, which is why she isn't here with us tonight; and trust me, she is *wizard* at figuring out every one of our Merry Fay's clever little schemes. You were right on target, though, when you texted us that someone was in the house, and that we were in danger."

"A bit late though, wasn't I?" Eva laughed. The Tearoom owner was looking quite youthful this evening in her Gypsy, off-the-shoulder, crimson blouse and long red-and-black skirt.

"Not really," Maggie replied to the query.

"It reached us about the same time Granny and our Merlin cats told me that someone was in the house," Raine said. "When our familiars weren't at the door to greet us, I felt instantly that something was wrong, so I rushed upstairs to see, firstly, if I had closed them, by mistake, in my closet. Not finding them there, I dashed up to the attic; and lo and behold, there they were, napping in their favorite bed under a watchful Granny standing sentinel in the attic mirror. She had called our Merlin cats up to the attic, to keep them safe from Mada, and closed the attic door after them. Out of sight, out of mind– Mada's mind, who was too busy tainting all our tea to think about the cats." She bit into a crab-stuffed mushroom, exclaiming, "Mmm, Eva, you've outdone yourself this time! These are excellent!"

The proprietress smiled, "Glad you like them." After a moment, a thought crossed her mind, and she, too, exclaimed, though not over a savory, "And our Hamlet undertaker Jason Holt!" Eva gasped. "I saw him as a big, friendly old boy! To think that he–" She gave a little shudder, concluding, "I suppose he's mighty sorry now that he got mixed up with the likes of Mada Fane!"

"Horsefeathers!" Chief Fitzpatrick bellowed, entering the hall from the coatroom entrance, "I don't believe, in my experience of criminals, that any murderer has ever truly felt regret for what he or she did." He shook his head with its thick white hair. "No, my friends, a murderer is never really sorry. Oh, they're always *mighty* sorry they're going to prison, but there's no genuine, heart-felt remorse." He accepted a glass of champagne with a nod of thanks to Ian. "I tell you that just like some folks are born without an organ, an arm or a leg, some are born without a conscience. And when you look into a murderer's eyes, there's nothing behind those eyes. *Nothing!* No conscience, soul, or whatever you choose to call it. Mada Fane was a monster."

"My stars, murder is such a vile business!" Betty tsked, shaking herself free of the images the Sisters had conjured earlier whilst revealing the details of their newly solved case. "And to think that no one until *you*," she regarded the Sisters, "could ever uncover a single clue in regard to our Hamlet's triple ax murders, the connected ritual murders, which no one knew *anything* about, and our historic figure J.D. Means' suspicious suicide. Not to mention Josie Mean's murder. You figured it all out, tying it all together! Such clever girls! Our Hamlet owes you so much!" She handed Hugh a stuffed mushroom from the little plate she held.

The Sisters looked pleased, though a bit embarrassed by Betty's praise. "Thank you, Betty," they replied nearly simultaneously.

"Where there's a witch," Raine cast a look to her cousins and fellow sisters of the moon, "or *three*, there's a way, you see. Witch-way!" she quipped with a giggle.

"It was an interesting case," Hugh responded. "Chock-full of twists and turns– and surprises. An interesting case," he repeated, patting Betty's hand.

"Ah hemm!" Cara cleared her throat as loudly as she could, the cough coming off as Maggie's. The Sisters' crafty little poppet was sticking halfway out of the side pocket of Maggie's large designer purse. It was the doll's preferred mode of transportation, for she rarely missed seeing or hearing anything.

"As always, we had help from family and friends," Raine, via Cara's prompt, rejoined to Betty's praise, with Maggie and Aisling heartily agreeing.

"An especial Thank-You to Ian, Beau, and Thaddeus!" the Sisters chorused loudly.

Maggie patted the ragdoll's faded yarn-covered head, as Raine sent the poppet a psychic message: *Thank you, sweetie, for kicking me that can of wasp spray! I wouldn't have thought to spray it in Mada Fane's eyes! Good work!*

Th' Divil you say! Cara shot back telepathically. *She knew 'bout the Time-Key! We had t' stop 'er!*

"There was so much to untangle in this unlocked Pandora's box, as you called it," Betty reiterated.

"Especially since people as shrewd as Adrian, Elsa, and Mada Fane had everything so meticulously plotted out," Hugh put in, huffing into his cavalry mustache. *"Diabolical."*

"True, **but**," Maggie voiced, "in *our* experience," Raine jumped in to complete the sentence, "a murderer makes at least one mistake."

Ian and Aisling were gently bobbing their heads. As detectives, they had seen and heard it all when it came to murder and just about every other crime the Sisters could shake their wands at.

"Like a lot of murderers, Mada Fane, it seemed, had an overblown ego," Hugh mused.

"Arrogance!" Aisling blurted. "Ian and I never met a murderer yet who wasn't arrogant."

"That's it!" Ian replied, "Like I told you when you solved that case last spring, it's his or her own cockiness, nine times out of ten, that leads to a murderer's downfall."

The chief chortled, "Right you are! They always think they're too bloody clever to be caught. Yet so many of them are chompin' at the bit to tell someone what they did, to *crow* about their crime." He advanced to the buffet table where he fixed a small plate of hors d'oeuvres for himself.

"Our cousin Sean, a brilliant philosopher, offered the explanation at Salem when we were gathered there for Great-Aunt Merry's hundredth birthday bash, "that having committed a murder puts a killer in a position of great loneliness and separation," Raine recounted. "But you're spot-on, Chief! Mada could not resist bragging about all her family's murders, including her own. Little did she realize that I was recording every word on my phone!"

"Arrogance," Fitzpatrick repeated. "The murderer's nemesis."

"My, my," Betty mused aloud, heaving a sigh of reminiscence. "Last year, when Hugh and I were away for an amusing mystery weekend in New England, someone asked me if Haleigh's Hamlet was a nice village. I remember answering, 'It's quite a *pretty* village. There are some nice people living in it, and some extremely unpleasant ones as well. Little did we know then, did we, Hugh?"

"Ah, I find I am just in time for the *dénouement*," the Coroner Dr. Wight pronounced in the proper French manner as he strolled smartly into the banquet room, "to yet another Sleuth Sisters success. From the fragment I caught thus far, I am in total agreement that one cannot simply dismiss the criminal with a doctrine of original sin, or the deliberate disregard of the laws of the land."

Looking as elegant as always, Wight declared in his resonant voice, directing his intense grey-eyed gaze at the Sisters, "I must say, I am always impressed by the sleuthing skills of these ladies, but never so much as I was on this case." He lifted a glass of champagne from the tray in Beau's hands. "Thank you, kind sir."

The Sisters went rather pink as they verbalized their thanks.

"As educators, we've," Raine gestured toward Maggie and Thaddeus, "had to acquire a good working knowledge of psychology. Aisling and Ian, too, given their background."

"Decidedly." Wight sipped the effervescent wine, then redirected his focus on Raine, Maggie and Aisling who were standing together with their significant others. "However, noting the shade of lipstick on that smoldering cigarette you found at the Fane Manor ruins was quick-witted sleuthing."

"Oh, Ben, that wasn't anything really," Raine countered. "Mada just happened to wear a unique shade of lipstick, a sort of pinkish-beige." She took of sip of her wine. "Though she didn't smoke in the house that day we interviewed her, I noted fine lines above her mouth, the lines smokers get from puckering their lips. Other than that, her complexion was perfect."

"Your suggestion about the teeth was," to use one of your own expressions, 'bang on,'" the coroner continued. "The teeth in that charred body could not have belonged to someone with as much affluence as Mada Fane, and the saliva on that cigarette proved helpful in my DNA collection for this case."

"It dawned on us," Maggie put in, "that night, as we stood and watched the Manor reduced to ashes, that she just might've staged her own death, using the Fane's M.O. of sacrificing a vagrant, though in her case, she was hoping to pass the homeless person off as herself. She bragged about that to us in our kitchen when she thought we were drugged with curare."

"Nasty business." Ian took a swallow of champagne.

"Mada staged the arson-murder to destroy any evidence of the ritual-murder room," Aisling disclosed. "She never intended to donate that mansion to the college, as she told us when we interviewed her!"

"Not bloody likely!" Raine interjected.

"Right," Aisling pressed on. "No way could she do that. She knew that at some point, toward the end of her life, she would have to destroy Fane Manor for the secrets it held hidden away in that ritual-murder room, and–"

"So she could be free to murder the three of us," Raine, Maggie and Aisling stated in sync.

"Oh my dears," Eva uttered softly, a hand to her ample breast. "Mada was like the evil witch in a Grimm's faerie tale."

"Faerie tales are more than true," Aisling nodded, "not just because the evil people really exist, but because they can never win."

"Mada Fane *was* an evil witch," Ian remarked.

"That *witch* does not kill us, can only make us stronger!" the magickal threesome quoted with a touch of merriment.

"She was convinced it would be the perfect crime." Aisling spoke the words with derision on her voice.

The chief caught at the phrase. "No such thing as the perfect crime!" he bellowed. "I'm happy to report that when we confiscated Mada Fane's phone, it led us to the off-the-beaten-path Starlight Motel where she'd been hiding out; and that's where we nabbed her laptop. There's enough information on phone and computer to round up her gang, the Four-P *circle*, as our Sleuth Sisters called it.

"Inasmuch as the others in Fane's ring are spread out, across the globe, we turned everything over to the FBI, who, in turn, contacted Interpol. Thank God," Fitzpatrick's gaze leaped to the ceiling, "Mada Fane was the only member of that bizarre bunch around here."

A great sigh went up from the gathering as the chief lowered his gaze to the plate he held in his hand. The smile remained on his broad face as he chose his next hors d'oeuvre with overt bliss.

"About five hundred years ago," Maggie stated, "there was a very covert society formed in Europe called the 'Four Ps,' said to have been created for gaining Perception, Prosperity, Prestige, and Power. More evil, ethereal, and elusive than any cabal of conspirators that ever was. No one could ever prove its existence, less known who its members might be. Membership was nattered to be for life, handed down for generations in the same families, with blood oaths taken for secrecy. Their magick was rumored to involve the very blackest kind."

The redheaded Sister glanced over at Raine, who seemed to be studying her ebony fingernails. "Raine uncovered the unconfirmed information about the evil circle through research, after spying the four intertwined capital P's on the ceiling medallion in Fane Manor's library. It put us on the right track."

"Their days of crime and vice are numbered," the chief interposed. "I wouldn't be at all surprised to learn they've all been rounded up already."

"When we interviewed Mada in the library at the Manor," Raine remembered, "we noted that she had quite a few curiosities, antiques and artifacts on display in that room. Mayan, Aztec, Egyptian, Celtic, and Native American cultures, particularly the Pawnee, were all represented. As professors of history and archeology, we knew those cultures, at some period in their histories, made use of human sacrifice."

"The artifacts all looked to be genuine," Maggie asserted, having made that call upon sight with an unerring eye.

"And lo and behold, among the lot was a large, wicked looking, obsidian ritual knife– for human sacrifice. Aztec," Raine revealed. "Centuries old– the real McCoy.

"The day of our interview with her, Mada rattled on and on about the Jivaro headhunters of the Amazon, and how they used curare on their poison darts to paralyze their victims in order to decapitate them and shrink their heads down to the size of an orange."

"She mentioned that she'd learned several things from the Jivaro, living among them, as she did, for field study," Maggie reflected. "And truth be known, we were impressed with the range and completeness of her knowledge, as well as the dramatic way in which she presented it."

Raine's kitten face took on a look of scorn. "Oooh, that noodle of hers was crammed to overflowing with information all right, and she clearly enjoyed exhibiting what she believed was her superior knowledge. Got to be a tad tiresome," she muttered. "You know what I'm saying. Very superior and civilized," the Goth gal rotated her shoulders in a "la-dee-da" imitation of Mada Fane, "with belief in that 'Ole Black Magick' very close to the surface."

"There is no good or bad magick, only good and bad people," Aisling let drop. "By the way, the crime lab report indicated that she'd tainted all the tea on your kitchen shelf with curare," Aisling divulged, her eyes on Raine and Maggie. "Thank the Goddess that *you*," she pushed a playful finger into Raine's belly, "had the gut-feeling you did about the tea."

"It was all a matter of connecting the dots, as we say," Raine remarked with a dimpled grin. "I knew from my research that curare gives off a slightly tar-ry odor. I have an especially good sniffer." She reached over and plucked a smoked salmon canapé from Beau's plate to slip into her mouth. As she chewed, an old Irish proverb Granny had taught came to her: *Be humble, for you are made of earth. Be noble, for you are made of stars.*

"I don't know how you did it with so many dots to connect, but again, let me tell you how grateful I am," Nellie said kindly. "The ax murders rendered our family less than devoted. I can't help thinking that poor Billy always blamed his uncle Clyde for the ax murders. He went to his grave, hating him. Sad, isn't it?"

"Quite," Raine began, clucking her tongue sympathetically. "We noted from old photographs of Clyde, Beatrice Hart showed us, that he habitually wore a fedora. Mada mentioned that her great-grandmother Elsa disguised herself in men's clothing, complete with a fedora that she'd pulled down over her forehead the night she axed her victims."

The smug Mada Fane hadn't mentioned that during her harangue of bragging in Tara's kitchen, but Raine could hardly disclose how they *really* found out about this. It was a white lie that harmed no one and protected their Time-Key.

"Henry Moretti told us that he and his brothers caught sight of a prowler at Nellie's boarded-up bungalow, the house they called the 'murder house,' a couple of weeks after the killings, at Hallowe'en. The intruder wore a fedora, pulled low over the face. Whether it was Nellie's brother Clyde, looking for clues the police might have missed, or Elsa returned to the scene of the crime, or someone else entirely, someone out, perhaps, on a Hallowe'en dare or ghost hunt, we'll never know," Maggie concluded.

"Anyway," Nellie went on to reveal her earlier thought, "the Billy-Clyde conflict caused a rift in our family that, passed down, still exists to this day."

"We noted that too, when we interviewed Clyde's direct descendant Dale Hardiman," Raine let drop.

"Hah!" Nellie guffawed. "And a more disagreeable fellow, I'd wager, you'd be hard-pressed to find anywhere."

"I'm sorry to say you're right about that," answered Aisling.

"Sticky sort," Maggie muttered to herself, rolling her eyes.

"What Nellie's brother Clyde likely meant when he told police that she 'was straying onto a dark path,' was that she had taken a married lover. He'd probably heard the gossip about his sister, and he came up here to try and talk some sense into her," Raine reasoned. "Maggie and I thought, at first, that she had fallen into the dark side of the Occult, but that was not the case; though she did depend, more and more, on readings from Eva's great-granny Anna. Not to say there was anything *whatsoever* sinister about Anna; but, as Eva told us, Nellie was using the readings increasingly like a crutch."

"Revenge, then, was part of Elsa's motive for axing Nellie," the chief pondered aloud, fitting together various scraps of the entwined murders in his mind. "Her husband, Adrian Fane, was Nellie's elusive 'secret lover' mentioned in the police records."

"Right," Raine and Maggie agreed in unison. "That and the fact that Nellie had witnessed a ritual murder at Fane Manor."

Nellie frowned. "I must confess I always suspected Aunt Nellie did have a secret lover." She dipped her head for a second, raising her eyes to the Sisters and adding, "I never told you that. And though, I'm grateful to have closure, it's disturbing, really *disturbing*, to think my aunt fell for someone like Adrian Fane. How? How could she have fallen for *him*?!"

"Bad luck that. We don't believe she planned to fall for him, though our keen intuitions are telling us *he* fell for her, and that's probably how the affair started," Maggie said. "Our granny always told us to be bold in what we stand for and careful, *very* careful, what we fall for. She often said, 'We are the choices we make. Our choices show us who we really are.' My sixth sense is also telling me that Nellie realized what Adrian was pretty quick and broke off their *liaison*."

"To his chagrin," Raine added. She tilted her dark head in thought. "Inside all of us is a wild thing. Granny also said that while forbidden fruit can taste the sweetest," she raised a brow, "it spoils the fastest."

- 353 -

"Nellie was a lonely woman who had the misfortune of succumbing to the wrong guy," Maggie said. "Loneliness and boredom, and the desire to escape her mundane, burdened existence led her into Fane's snare. Nellie desperately needed to keep her job with the Fanes, so she continued working for them. She worked more with the wife, Elsa, than she did with Adrian Fane, who probably only dropped into the shop on occasion. But then Nellie had the second misfortune of accidently witnessing a ritual killing; and, as they say, the rest is history."

"There were so many wretched things about this whole twisted mystery," declared the deep-feeling Maggie. "It assumed gigantic proportions. The evil things the Fanes did hurt and destroyed countless people world-wide. We'll never know how many people they and their circle murdered in their ritual killings, and we'll never know how many people they hurt in their unscrupulous, ruthless business dealings."

She thought for a protracted moment, adding, "A black thread of tragedy and terror that they wove around countless innocents. Those skeletons we discovered in Haleigh's Wood, for instance. How very sad. Those were homeless people of the cruel Depression, who had lost everything, likely even hope, and who then fell victim to an even crueler pillager. After which they were chucked, like refuse, into a hole and forgotten. No words said over them, nothing. No one even knows their names."

"I doubt any locals will recognize the forensic artist's facial reconstructions," Thaddeus remarked, "that the *Herald* published. In all probability those men weren't from around here, but Depression-era transients who rode in on a freight train, looking for work only to meet with disaster here in the Hamlet."

"When I went downtown yesterday," Raine began, "our Hamlet bench-sitters asked me if," she glanced over at her fellow Sisters, "we knew what happened to Old Milly. They hadn't seen hide nor hair of her for several days, and it wasn't like our colorful bag lady not to join the guys for their lively political discussions, especially now when there's so much in the news, this being an election year and–"

Aisling cleared her throat, a signal for Raine to cut to the chase, which she did.

"We happened to think," Raine went on, her voice breaking a bit, "that Milly was about the same size and age as Mada Fane. Milly

Murray was not your *usual* bag lady. Some folks might not remember, but she was a school teacher for many years. Taught political science at the high school. The poor woman lost all her savings and her home due to her husband's medical bills and her n'er-do-well son's shenanigans. I figured there would be dental records for Milly, and thus I immediately telephoned Ben."

"Your hunch was right," the coroner replied. "I regret to report that the charred body from Fane Manor proved to be Milly Murray."

"God rest her," Fitzpatrick droned, with the others joining in. "We all looked out for Milly," he let his voice trail off, shaking his head sadly.

"We tried to help her several times," Maggie said, brushing away a tear, "and we did, to a certain extent, but Milly was determined to keep her bag-lady status."

"Maggie's right," Aisling agreed. "She didn't want to have to worry about losing anything anymore."

"Well," the chief resolved, "to quote an old saying, 'When ya ain't got nothin', you ain't got nothin' to lose,' though ..." again, he let his words fade away.

"While pretending to be such noble philanthropists, the Fanes were a *cruel* lot. What Mada did to Milly and Josie ... what Elsa did to Nellie and her family, and what Adrian did to J.D.," Raine's eyes narrowed, "incredibly cruel and heartless. As for the Fanes concealing their evil with the benevolent mask of philanthropy, **huh!**" she scoffed. "None of them ever came close to our Hamlet's Addison McKenzie, the leader in funding our library, our theatre, and our college. He left behind generous trusts, as well as a myriad of good works."

Maggie and Thaddeus murmured their agreement, with Raine continuing, "For those of you who may not know this, Addison always told people he did not want the town named for him, that he was the man he was because of the good woman he had at his side, inspiring him to achieve. Thus," she said with a flourish of hand, "*Haleigh's Hamlet*. Now *there* was a philanthropist!

"But getting back on track," Raine blurted, "as history professors, Maggie and I knew a good bit about J.D. Means. He was *not* the type to commit suicide; and," the image of his sobbing widow flashed upon the movie screen of her mind, "we promised," she darted a wink to Maggie, "ourselves that with the passage of time, one day we would clear his name. J.D. was another of our early industrialists who really *did* help a lot of people."

"Indeed, this mystery had many layers," Thaddeus stated, popping a cheese canapé into his mouth.

"Hmm, along with a few bolts from the blue. You know," Maggie mused, "we were surprised to learn from Mada's bragging," she glanced toward Raine and Aisling, tossing them a half-nod, as if making a silent agreement with her sisters of the moon, before turning again toward Nellie, "that Mada's great-grandmother Elsa went to your great-aunt's bungalow with the intention of *shooting* her. When Nellie reached for the ax, the die was cast. Seemingly, Elsa could move as quickly as a panther, and her adrenaline rush rendered her as powerful when she wielded that ax! We," Maggie's magnificent green eyes swept over Raine and Aisling, "feel strongly that the evil entity that threatened us the night we did the séance was Elsa."

Nellie stood wordlessly still, adrift in reverie over all that was being discussed. She was seized with a sudden desire to cry, to laugh, to express both, until finally, she said, "Elsa Fane was a shadow that darkened the lives of a great many people. I am so sorry that I inadvertently opened a door with that Ouija board and let her in. I never meant to."

"Of course you didn't, dear, but it all worked out the way it was supposed to." Maggie reached out to take Nellie's hand. A change had visibly taken place within the woman, and the Sister looked at her with new eyes. "It takes courage to get through life, no matter the era."

"It does," Nellie whispered, her dark eyes shimmering with unshed tears. "I always believed that, despite her naiveté, my great-aunt was a courageous individual."

"She was," Maggie replied. The redheaded Sister would always be haunted by the image of the woman, bloody and hacked, as, refusing to die, she tried in vain to seek help to save her children and her mother.

Nellie gave a slight nod, her soulful eyes brightening with gratitude. "Life has knocked me down a few times. I've seen and experienced things I never want to again, but I've never stayed down."

The Sisters quickly exchanged looks to send Nellie a blessing. "May the positive energy of the Universe surround you, flow through you, and bring peace to your mind and love to your heart."

"Thank you," Nellie mouthed in a quiet tone, squeezing Maggie's hand. "It's never too late, in fiction or in life, to revise," the editor determined more to herself than to the Sister.

Man problems have troubled her with a rueful disquiet, Maggie thought.

Yes, but me thinks she means it when she said she intends to do a revision, Raine answered telepathically. "By the bye," she interjected aloud, snapping her fingers, "I just received the information I requested about the Fanes this morning. The family took the *Fane* surname– which, apropos, means 'Temple'– after they were forced, in the mid-eighteenth century, to leave their native Germany, due to corrupt deeds. The first of them to step foot on American soil– the 'master' he called himself– was Gerhard Meier, who changed his name to Adrian Fane. Adrian, I discovered in my research, translates 'Dark One.' It's a recurrent name in their family."

"What's in a name, huh? I must excuse myself to see about your dinner," Eva said of a sudden. "Arugula salad to start, eggplant pizza with fresh pesto and pine nuts, and chocolate-zucchini cupcakes for dessert– I call it an end-o'-summer harvest supper."

"Oh, don't remind us!" Raine moaned. "Before we know it, we'll be back in our classrooms for a new year at the college. I don't know where the summer went!"

"Hmm," Eva answered in agreement though somewhat absently, "there was a hint of autumn in the air this morning."

"The dinner sounds delicious," Maggie directed to Eva.

"It will be; I promise you. My eggplant and pesto pizza is not your ordinary, everyday pizza. It's in a class all by itself!" Eva started for the kitchen, then paused. "By the way," she asked, turning to face the group, "what's going to happen to those cats you were talking about when you first came in tonight, Josie Means' cats?"

"Her lawyer contacted me," the chief volunteered, swallowing a mouthful of shrimp appetizer. "You know how lawyers are. Can't get a straight answer out of any of 'em. Anyhow, he was asking about Miss Means' cats. Seems Josie left her house to a cousin who is allergic to cats. The attorney told me to tell whoever took them in to keep them if they wish. Just so they go to a good home. That's what Josie's cousin communicated to the lawyer." He took a drink of his champagne. "The attorney will forward the cats' papers to the new owner."

Raine and Maggie traded looks with a poignant thought.

"Eva," Raine began, "would we be right in saying you'd very much like to have Josie's cats? You're familiar with Abyssinians?" Not waiting for a response, she rushed on, "They are a feisty breed, but I assure you these particular Abbys are well trained now, and they are absolutely gorgeous. Affectionate and intelligent too. All we ask is that you give them a good home and keep them together. They really love one another."

Eva's comely face lit up like a *Samhain* bonfire, and her voice choked. "Oh, do you mean it?! I would *love* to have them! Thank you!! And not to worry, they'll have a great home with me, and I won't ever separate them."

Raine thought for a moment. "Please don't have them declawed."

"I won't!" Eva answered quickly. "I know how to safely trim a cat's claws, not to worry. I've had several cats in my day."

Raine smiled. "Maggie and I will deliver them to you tomorrow, along with their kitty things that go with them, as a token of an especial kindness you did for us."

"And what was that?" the Tearoom lady asked, a bit puzzled.

"Introducing us to your Time-Will-Tell Tea!" Raine and Maggie echoed with passion.

"Heavens, that was nothing!" Eva declared with a wave of hand.

"Ooooooh, it is *something*– something very special to us," the Sisters all replied in unison, "and we're deeply grateful."

"I'll second that," Thaddeus affirmed enthusiastically.

The smile sparkled yet in Raine's eyes. "Good thing, Eva, I had some of your tea in my purse, to substitute for the tea the *Fane* tainted in our kitchen."

"Your tea has served us well– in more ways than one," Maggie assured. "I hope it'll always be a part of your delightful offerings here at the Tearoom."

"Not to worry," Eva smiled.

"Mention of those cats reminds me," Dr. Wight interposed. "I confess that I was skeptical about your ability, Dr. McDonough," he aimed his keen grey gaze at the Goth gal, "to communicate with animals. However," his mouth curved in his rarely seen smile, "I must amend my earlier judgment due to what you ascertained after your warning message from that flock of crows at Fane Manor ruins, and after you had spoken, earlier on, with Author Means' felines."

Raine dimpled. "Hmmm, a flock of crows, also known as a 'murder of crows.' Thank you, Ben. Coming from you, that means a lot. The 'large book' that Josie's cats told me the murderer lifted from a table in her parlor was, as Maggie, Aisling and I thought, a *file*. A file that contained information on, not only her grandfather J.D. Means, but the Fanes as well. She had intended to use the material in a book to clear her grandfather's name and expose the Fanes for who they really were. Mada Fane destroyed the file, but no matter, as it turned out.

"I believe," Raine recounted, "when we interviewed Josie, a couple days before she was killed, she harbored fear that we would endanger her life with our findings. We don't think she'd planned on publishing her book on her grandfather and the Fanes till she knew it was her time to pass over, or she may have even thought about having the book published posthumously. Josie wasn't such a fool as to tangle with Mada."

The tall, elegant coroner nodded his understanding. "The question begging in my mind at this point is when and how you first realized that you could communicate with animals?"

"You've gone and done it now, Dr. Wight," Aisling laughed. "That is her favorite family story, and our Raine loves nothing better than to recount it whenever she can. We've all heard it so many times; we could recite it by heart."

"I've never heard it; and, I can't believe I'm saying this, but I'd very much like to," the coroner stated with his usual dignity.

"I'd like to hear it too," Nellie ventured softly.

"So would I," Eva called from the doorway that led into the kitchen.

Needing no real encouragement, Raine told it now again, running all the images through her mind, remembering everything, forgetting nothing.

"As you might know, Maggie and I enjoyed a *magickal* childhood with lots of perks, including travel." She cast a warm smile toward her red-haired cousin and fellow Sister. "Our parents are archaeologists, and we accompanied them on several digs, across the globe.

"I shall always remember one excursion especially. It was in Nepal the summer Maggie and I were nine. We were riding atop an elephant with our fathers when the beast sensed danger. A large tiger was in the area. Now, mind, tigers don't attack elephants ... *usually*. But *this* elephant didn't know that, and she started backing up– right into a tree. The jolt unseated Maggie and me, and we tumbled to the ground where we heard the tiger growl.

"He was close. *Mighty close.* He had recently marked a tree, and we could smell him."

The love of storytelling always seemed to fill Raine with boundless energy. "Did you know," she grinned, her dimple dancing in her cheek, "that tiger pee smells like buttered popcorn?" She pressed her pouty, crimson lips together with a solemn nod. "Ooh, *I'm no-joke serious.* So if you're ever strolling through the jungle, and you suddenly get the sense you're in the lobby of a movie theatre, *beware*," she wagged a warning finger at her listeners.

"As I was saying," Raine swept on, telling the story as though it had happened that day, "the tiger was close, but we didn't know just *where* he was until suddenly we spied him. I think Maggie and I both spotted him simultaneously as we locked eyes with him in the tall, gently swaying grass. And oh, those great golden eyes!

"In the interim, our fathers had bounded off the agitated elephant, and with their guns at the ready, they both took careful aim, all the while shouting at the poor tiger, as was our guide, who had begun banging loudly on a drum.

"Mind, this was all happening as fast as a jackrabbit before a prairie fire. With all the force we could muster, Maggie and I yelled at the top of our lungs, **'Don't shoot!'** To the tiger, I whispered, 'Go on now; **scat!**' Needless to say, that's exactly what he did, as we watched his tail quickly disappear in the high grass."

Raine thought for a moment, adding, "The Nepal incident made me realize that I could transfer thoughts to an animal, but I'd already begun to pick up mental images from animals." She tilted her head. "I can recall the very first time it happened. I had just turned five. It was a chilly, stormy April day when I caught the distinct sound of mewing on our back porch. I ran outside, and there, shivering and wet, was a tiny, brown tabby kitten, looking frightened and cold and hungry. When I reached down to pick him up, a terrible image flashed across the movie screen of my mind of a mean-faced man hurling the poor little creature out into the storm." Raine shook her dark head. "Needless to say, Granny let Maggie and me adopt the kitten." She smiled. "Tigger lived with us for many happy years, and I always said, ever after, that the best gifts are the gifts of April."

"Tell me," the coroner bade, his grey eyes penetrating, "though I think I can guess the answer, did the Nepal incident frighten you at all?"

Raine shook her head. "It might be difficult for some to believe, but no, Maggie and I weren't rattled by it– except when we tumbled from the elephant, that is."

Wide-eyed with admiration, Nellie exclaimed, "I know I would've been literally shaking in my shoes!"

"So would I!" Eva swooned.

A deep, rich chuckle rumbled in Raine's throat. "As a very wise and much-loved Lakota shaman once told us– and that's a whole other story cherished from a whole other dig– 'Everything has a voice and wants to communicate.'

"I like to say, if it has a beating heart, it has a soul. *Spirit.* You see, animals are teachers and messengers– and that tiger, *as Tigger,* delivered a significant message to me," she turned toward the red-haired Sister, "and to Maggie. In that suspended moment in time, gazing into the tiger's mesmerizing eyes, I felt my spirit merge with his." Raine closed her eyes, envisioning the eyes of the tiger, the eyes she would always see– each and every time she connected with an animal. *Inside each of us is a wild, untamed thing,*" she thought for the second time that evening.

"Maggie and I will never forget that summer in Nepal. It was *surreal,* like nothing before or since– *an epiphany.* Though I'd already received a few mental pictures from animals in my childhood, I needed that illuminating discovery in Nepal for the *full* realization of my gift. And that's how I recognized beyond a doubt that I could actually communicate with animals," the raven-haired Sister finished with a lightheartedness in her voice and a renewed sparkle in her own feline eyes.

Maggie and Aisling nodded in a way that bespoke harmony, raising their glasses slightly to acknowledge the truth of Raine's words. "Hear, hear, Sister!"

This inspired Nellie to lift her own glass of champagne. "To the Sleuth Sisters and their spectrum of … *extraordinary* talents!"

"Thank you for helping me to solve this complex case, cold and current!" Chief Fitzpatrick toasted, holding up his glass. He gave an avuncular beam. "I'm glad I learned over the years to trust your instincts."

Raine felt herself go red, before the next toast almost sent her reeling, a startled look flashing in her eyes.

Hoisting his drink a bit higher, Dr. Wight added with a warmth on his voice that both surprised and pleased the Sisters, "In addition to yet another *victoire célèbre*, ladies, thank you for always coming to the aid of those in need, no matter what the occasion."

My cup runneth over, Raine thought, lowering her gaze, her words catching in her throat.

"Every good and valuable thing done in life makes the world a better place to be," Aisling smiled.

"We were only doing what comes naturally to us," Maggie laughed her crystal laugh, the sound reminiscent of wind chimes on a caressing breeze. "In many ways, it's our life's work to connect the dots."

"Maggie and I do it all the time as professors of history and archeology," Raine declared. "Aisling too, as a former police detective and present-day private eye."

Maggie gave an approving nod. "Yes," she quickly agreed. "Historians and archeologists are, in essence, detectives. When we were working toward our doctorates, so many times did Raine and I slip into sleuthing mode to solve a few of history's diverse mysteries." She grinned like a contented cat with a nice bowl of cream. Now it was her turn to send Raine a wink, which seemed to say, *Well, well, haven't we come through this all quite nicely?*

So happy were they to be with kith and kin and to have untangled yet another mystery, all three Sisters virtually glowed. "*Slàinte!*" they toasted the gathering with the Irish for "Great Health and Life."

Eva had ducked out to tend to customers in the Tearoom's public area. "Only two customers out there this near to closing time. Two friends of yours," she announced, re-entering the banquet room. "Kathy Wise and Dr. Yore. They didn't come in together, and they're sitting at separate tables."

The Sisters exchanged looks. "Invite them to join us!" they rallied.

"I knew you'd say that," Eva pronounced, looking pleased, "so I asked them to bring their plates in here."

"They each played a part in solving this mystery!" Raine called out. To Maggie she fired off the thought, *Dr. Yore gave us one of our earliest heads-up about the Fane, remember? I nabbed her thought right after she mentioned that Mada's work was phenomenal.* Yore's thought was: *Fane is a phenomenon all right, but phenomena can be realized by those who seek.*

Maggie shot back, *I knew Liz didn't like Mada Fane– she distrusted her instinctively– but she was too much of a professional to say so. Or did she know that we would pick up her thought, and she wanted us to be wary of her? It's times like this that prompt me to wonder if our Dr. Yore could be the–*

"Wiz-zard!" Raine was saying aloud. "Yes, they're both very dear friends. With common denominators, I might add. Both believe in speaking their minds, bless them! Elizabeth Yore doesn't suffer fools gladly, and I doubt very much Savvy Kathy does. There's nothing of the humbug about either."

"None. It will do us a power of good to have them join us!" Maggie, who had an infallible accuracy for spotting both fools and fakes, laughed gaily.

At that moment, Savvy Kathy and the perspicacious Dr. Yore, never without one of her long capes or her staff, entered the banquet room, where they were greeted amiably by the Sisters and the group inside.

"We were just making a toast to the Sleuth Sisters for solving yet another mystery. In this case, a *tangle* of mysteries," Thaddeus prompted.

Having read some of the details in the *Hamlet Herald* the evening before, the new arrivals held up the champagne glasses Ian handed them.

"To the Sleuth Sisters!" chorused the voices of dearly beloved family and friends, as they smiled affectionately at the magickal trio.

With stars in their emerald eyes, at that moment not even the Universe could compete with the galaxies contained within the dynamic trilogy of those Sister souls!

"Hear! Hear!!" The response with its subsequent merry laughter seemed to waft and swirl, in an embracing manner, round the entire gathering.

Almost visible was the camaraderie in that banquet hall, diamond-like and glittering, as resonating warmly within the good and pure hearts of three very special Sisters of the Craft, the energies rose skyward, in gratitude– to the Goddess.

"Magick is essentially the higher understanding of Nature." ~ Anon

~ Epilogue ~

The first Saturday in October found Raine and Maggie happily engaged in decorating Tara for *Samhain*. It was their favorite time o' year, and the Sisters were really making use of their witchy talents to bedeck their home for the sabbat and the Celtic New Year.

Leaves were falling; the spicy, tart scent of apples hung on the crisp air; and mornings were delightfully frosty and brisk, when spider webs clung to Tara's hedges and ground cover. Afternoons, the sky above Haleigh's Hamlet was a cloudless, clear crystal blue. And when sunlight dwindled into twilight, and Raine and Maggie took their evening walks, after supper, the cozy smell of wood-burning fireplaces greeted them.

The Sisters could feel the approach of *Samhain* in the air, in which even the surrounding woods gave off a magickal scent. The spirit world drew closer and closer– the veil between the worlds grew ever thinner.

Samhain was a time for reflection. It was a time for ancestors. It was a time to celebrate the harvest and to thank for its bounty.

The front porch looked apropos for the season with three tall besoms– each one different and each special in its own way– resting against the wall, beneath which Raine set a black pair of witch shoes, adorned with silver buckles, the pointed toes turning up. The plaque she hung next to them read: *Witch Parking Only. All Others Will be Toad.* Next to the shoes, Maggie set a huge, orange pumpkin, and beside it, a ceramic toad.

Of course, the doormat announced – *The Witch Is In.* Tara's ornate, emerald-green front door looked especially charming surrounded by a string of faux autumn leaves that bore twinkling lights. A smaller besom, adorned with orange and black ribbons, the colors of *Samhain*, dangled from the front door, above which hung a primitive pentacle fashioned from grapevine. The Sisters, with Aisling for the Power of Three, cast everything with strong protection spells for Tara and all that the beloved home encompassed. The magickal threesome cast the same protective spells at Aisling's home in Haleigh's Wood.

"When witches go riding, and black cats are seen, the moon laughs and whispers, ''Tis near Hallowe'en!'" Maggie stood back to admire their work. Small ceramic jack o' lanterns rested on Tara's interior window sills, each housing a battery-operated flicking candle. Studying their handiwork for another few moments, she declared, "Everything looks purr-fectly enchanting."

Feeling the energies of *Samhain* all about her, the redheaded Sister whirled round to face the woods. Last evening, Beau and Thaddeus had come over to help Raine and Maggie fashion ghosts from wire and white gauze, which they hung from the surrounding trees. "The people we love become ghosts inside us, and in this way, they stay alive for *and* with us," she said, thinking of Granny.

"Blessed be!" Taking a needed break, Raine stretched, her arms reaching skyward. "Oh, Mags, smell the air! *October!* There's nothing like it! I am going to try and create this scent, which, of course, I shall call 'October,' with herbs and oils." She sniffed again, breathing in a great gulp of the tangy air. "Pumpkins, apples, and there's that indescribable perfume of leaves. I'm not talking about burning leaves, but the layered leaves carpeting the forest floor. It's a sort of nutty, woodsy smell that's bewitching and utterly and deliciously … *mysterious!*"

Maggie, too, paused to take in a draft of the fresh, crisp air. "Autumn is the hush before winter," she said quietly.

Her statement prompted Raine to lift her arms in a chant, "With night coming early, and dawn coming late, with ice on the walk and frost on the gate, our fires burn cozy and our kettles do sing, whilst Earth Mother lolls to rest till the spring!" She looked at the sky. "Gonna be a clear, starry night tonight."

"Is Beau coming over later?" Maggie asked, leaning against the porch wall.

"So far, that's the plan," Raine replied with her little cat smile. She purposefully scattered some colorful fallen leaves around the trio of tall besoms, witch shoes, pumpkin, and toad. "There, that's better. Earth Mother's own personal touch." She looked over at Maggie. "I just hope he doesn't get hauled out on a farm call. I have an emergency of my own that no one but Beau can dose," she expressed with a low sexy laugh.

"Well," Maggie answered, "you'll have Tara all to yourselves for the entire weekend. Thaddeus and I will be at his cabin in the woods."

"Who were you on the phone with a little while ago? I meant to ask you, then we got busy here, and I forgot." Maggie stared moodily at the autumn sky, and Raine picked up her thought. She was recollecting past *Samhains*, recreating an especially nice mélange of memories.

The raven-haired Sister tilted her head, quietly watching Maggie for a few moments before snapping her fingers with the thought that had entered her dark head. "High Priestess Robin. I don't know *how* I forgot to tell you. She called to invite us to the Keystone Coven's *Samhain* fest. This year, she will be hosting it at her home in Washingtonville." Raine's lips curved upward. "She said she hoped she could do as 'Crafty' a job as we did last year here at Tara."

"We did stage a wicked *Samhain* fest, didn't we? I daresay it was quite an excitement!" Maggie started packing away, in a box from the attic, the decorations they had not used. "I hope you told her the three of us would be honored and most happy to attend."

"I did, of course!" Raine exclaimed. "Though we aren't of the Coven, we do aid and support one another in just about everything. It's empowering to have sisters who have your back, huh Mags?"

"*Quite so.*"

"I called Aisling right after, and she said she'll drive." Raine bent to move the toad just an inch. "Washingtonville is such a pretty little hamlet, a yesteryear village, not unlike our own. Lots of rich history there too. That's the charm of our southwest corner of the commonwealth. We're unspoiled, and the reason is that the march of Time has passed us by," her pussycat face made a cute little moue, "though the Philadelphia side might be prone to say we're a lost cause," she giggled. The Goth gal slipped on her black leather jacket, over her black tee and jeans. "You know what my favorite Washingtonville bit of history is, Mags?"

"The Indian curse?!" the redheaded Sister supplied in a near shout.

"You got it in one! I love that story and the Hester Tree's, of course!" Raine slapped her palm to her forehead. "Levitation! I nearly forgot to tell you that High Priestess Robin not only rang to invite the three of us to the Coven's *Samhain* fest, but to ask for our assistance in saving the Witch Tree!"

"Is that dear old tree in jeopardy?!" Maggie asked, pausing in her cleanup around the porch.

"Seems that it is. I didn't get all the particulars, but Robin said there are some people, the worst sort of muggles apparently, who want to get hold of the land the Witch Tree is on to develop it for, I don't know which, commercial or industrial use; and if they *get* that land, they'll cut down the Witch Tree!"

Maggie's face went ghostly. "Cut down a healthy– magickal– 300-plus-year-old oak with a rich history?! It's sacrilegious! I get so sick and tired of people who think what *they* think is the only way *to* think!"

"Don't get your knickers in a twist, Mags. Together, we can stop these unenlightened twits," Raine pronounced. "C'mon, we're all done now. Grab that box. I'll get this other one, and let's break for a bracing cup of tea. I'm exhausted, and I want my tea," she said almost querulously. "We can rehash the Washingtonville tales, including the Witch Tree story. It's *the* time o' year for those ghostly tales. Then, we'll ring Robin and tell her she can count on our help in this matter. The Coven came to our rescue when we needed to rid our 'little theatre in the woods' of the *Macbeth* curse. And now, we need to let them know they can count on us to save the Witch Tree."

Once their tea was brewed, Raine and Maggie sat at their kitchen table in deep thought about nearby Washingtonville's famous Witch Tree, also known, far and wide, as the Hester Tree.

The whole of Braddock County, Pennsylvania, was a treasure chest of legend and lore, possessing a rich, *layered* history. The rustic glen abounded with chronicles of great men from the French and Indian and Revolutionary war eras. Raine and Maggie told their students that such tales thrive best in these sequestered, long-settled retreats.

After breathing its witching air, visitors, like the region's Celtic and German settlers, were captivated, for Washingtonville, as Haleigh's Hamlet, was an enchanting spot– a place to dream mysterious– cryptic– dreams, becoming all the more imaginative. That village, like the Sisters' own, attracted artsy people, as well as those interested in history– and, because of its legendary ghosts, the metaphysical.

Feeling refreshed after sipping her tea, Raine was saying, "I can't explain it, except to say that I love the *feel* of a place like our Hamlet and Washingtonville."

"Yes," Maggie agreed. "I thought that very same thing about our little corner of the commonwealth, when Thaddeus once took me for a sweeping, autumn helicopter ride. Over the years, this whole area has retained a sleepy, bucolic ambiance, a sense of peace that radiates from every doorway, from each well-tended yard or farm, from every blossoming garden."

"You're right," Raine put in. "I love the agelessness that both our Hamlet and Washingtonville possess." She took a long swallow of tea, reflecting, "There's a sense of reverence for that which has gone before, a determination to preserve things as they were, perhaps even an unwillingness to acknowledge things as they are, as they have become."

"I always enjoy the rustically beautiful drive from our Hamlet up to Washingtonville," Maggie stated. "Especially in the autumn, when the trees are sporting their fall colors of gold, orange, cordovan, red, and brown with just the right touches of green remaining; and the shedding leaves dash at our windshield like the great Goddess' confetti. Oh yes, there's nothing casual about the especial beauty of a Pennsylvania autumn. It's *visceral*, like the beauty of Ireland. Mystical. *Magickal*. Hmmm," she brought a hand to her chest, "with a thump to the heart."

Raine nodded. "And all along the route, from here to Washingtonville in the fall, pumpkins hauled in from the fields brighten roadside stands, together with rosy apples, jugs of apple cider, and jars of apple butter. I love seeing those neat little farms, as they begin preparing for another Pennsylvania winter, the smoky haze wafting over the cornfields, the captivating scarecrows standing watch, the cornstalks lying helter-skelter ..." her voice floated off with reminiscences – memories that dissolved into other memories– like so many autumn leaves that drift past Tara's stained-glass windows.

"I was just thinking how our little corner of Pennsylvania has more than its share of gripping stories. History is a collection of layered stories, *true* stories. I love Washingtonville's history as much as I do the Hamlet's," Raine rattled on. "Together, our little burgs have some *really* good ones." Her mind ran riot. "All the witching tales of their old houses and woodlands flood back to haunt me every time we take an autumn drive through the countryside: the legless figure in a long, black cloak, who searches the midnight roads for his lost love killed in the violence of a nor'easter over a century past; the White Lady of Haunted Rock, whose plaintive wails can be heard far and wide on the lonely, hollow wind; the reappearing faces in the mirrors at the manse of Fellowship Knoll; along with the misty, red-clad English soldiers, who cling to the old

Braddock Road, perchance chained to earth and nightly wanderings due to their ghastly fates when death wore feathers and garish paint on a long-ago day in 1755.

"The realms of heroes and villains from the past spring to life from fragments of history and myth– and from my own recited classroom tales of wonder," she dimpled. "In the eternal element of imagination, a symphony of phantom pioneers and dusky Native Americans– *all*– rise to spook me, and I love it! All along the route to Washingtonville, I can almost hear the bloodcurdling war cry of that old Seneca shaman shaking his gourd rattle at me and chanting into my ear his spun-out curse!"

"But, of course, the best tale of all is the one connected to the Witch Tree! Tell it again, Raine, I love to hear you tell it," Maggie coaxed.

Raine, however, never needed coaxing to spin a yarn. She was what the Irish call a *seanchaí*, a natural born storyteller, and so she readily wove the tale for her sister of the moon.

"Hester Duff was said to have been a beautiful woman. It was also said that she was a witch. According to legend, she had hair as black as midnight and eyes the deepest of blue, like a clear Scottish loch. Even her petname was mysterious, 'Dark Star,' given to her at birth by her Scottish parents, who came to this county with their remarkably pretty little girl sometime in the 1700s.

"The Duffs came to America's shores for the same reason so many left their homelands– to escape the old countries' class system. For freedom and what the newcomers called 'elbow room.' Here on the precarious Pennsylvania frontier, these pioneers, though they would've had to fight Indians, were equal to their neighbors and free of any government boot on their necks.

"It is thought that when Hester's parents were killed by Indians, she was taken in by another frontier family. Whether *they* passed away, were also killed by Indians, or she simply came of age and ventured out on her own, we don't know. All we know is that Hester lived alone in a simple log cabin deep in the woods here in Braddock County, in the vicinity of Washingtonville.

"There's no record as to what year Hester first showed up in the area. Like our Hamlet's mysterious hermit Rue Cameron, most of Hester's life was shrouded in mystery.

"Here is this beautiful young woman living in a crude hut hidden away in the dense forest with no one for company. She kept completely to herself. In such a remote and sequestered area of the frontier, folks became suspicious of Hester, as they were of all strangers, though they pretty much left her alone. That is, they did so in the beginning.

"Then, as fear will do, it fired their imaginations to run wild, and they began to 'notice' that every time Hester appeared at the blockhouse, a misfortune followed– a cow she touched went dry, a boy who taunted her suddenly took sick, a woman who gossiped about her behind a hand, tripped and broke a leg, a man who made a snide remark was found scalped in the forest, or some such occurrence."

"Same ole, same ole– misunderstanding and thus fear of witches." Maggie heaved a sigh. "It is what it is, Sister, what it always was."

Raine held up a bejeweled hand. "This new mystery is what it is but will become what *we* make it. Anyway, Hester's neighbors' imaginings– and their suspicions might've been quite unjustified– spread through the valley like wildfire, but no one ever lifted a hand against Hester Duff until one particular autumn.

"Thought to have been the autumn of 1787, the incident occurred after Hester joined the others, whose small farms were scattered round about, at the centrally located blockhouse, when a war party of painted Shawnee had been sighted by local rangers. The poor woman was met with derision and nearly drummed out of the protective walls of the log fortress. Though the gathered settlers grudgingly permitted her to stay, Hester was shunned and humiliated. Three days hence, a violent storm destroyed the frontier farmers' entire harvest.

"That October, close to *Samhain* it was, an angry mob rushed Hester's cabin and, taking her captive, tied her to an oak in the forest. Mind, there had never been any witch hunts or executions in Pennsylvania– nothing to speak of anyway– so what they intended to do to her is debatable; but they most certainly meant to frighten her enough to drive her out of the area.

"What I tend to think is that they were debating over what to do with her, shouting and arguing among themselves; when, in the time it would take to utter a curse, the sunny sky turned black as night, and thunder and lightning rumbled and crashed. Hester looked skyward, uttering her oath; and in a literal flash, a violent bolt of lightning crashed into the tree, covering it, Hester, and the onlookers in thick smoke.

"Now this is powerful sorcery that I'm talkin' about here. When the smoke cleared, the ropes that bound Hester to the tree were still there, but she was gone, never to be seen or heard from again. However, a sign that she existed remains to this day. By the power of the lightning bolt and that sister's strong magick, six letters were burned so deeply into the tree, they are *still* visible– H-E-S-T-E-R! Thus, the prevailing wind that blows through the village of Washingtonville is one of witchcraft and mystery.

"That tree is huge, a majestic oak, over three hundred years old," Raine concluded, picking up her teacup. "I just can't believe that some stupid muggle wants to cut it down!" Her face darkened from kitten to panther. "Not only would that be a damn shame and irreverent to Earth Mother, it would be downright *dangerous!*"

"You're right, of course. Some say Hester's *spirit* inhabits that tree! We'll do everything in our power to aid the Keystone Coven with this endeavor," Maggie vowed. "I sense there's more behind this new mystery that's fallen into our laps than meets the eye."

"Always is," Raine laughed shortly. "I didn't get all the particulars, but Robin said something about having gone to the man, who wants the land the tree is on, and entreating him to understand; but she said the coldness of his tone told her the 'frost is on the pumpkin.' Robin did mention that several strange events have occurred since this Witch Tree problem arose."

"You don't say!"

"Oh," Raine gave a brisk nod, "I *do* say."

"Well, we've sorted out long-buried secrets before, even those taken to the grave. It won't be our first time at the rodeo, or more apropos, our first trip back to Colonial times. We'll take this latest puzzle on, and *we'll solve it!*" Maggie stated with fire.

"You bet we will!" Raine laughed again, giving her sister of the moon an affable knock on the shoulder. "After all, folks don't call us the 'Sleuth Sisters' for nothing!"

As the Sisters stood and began washing up the tea things, they chanted softly, "Still around the corner a new road may wait. Just around the corner– ***another secret gate!***"

~About the Author~

Ceane O'Hanlon-Lincoln is a native of southwestern Pennsylvania, where she taught high school French until 1985. Already engaged in commercial writing, she immediately began pursuing a career writing both fiction and history.

In the tradition of a great Irish *seanchaí* (storyteller), O'Hanlon-Lincoln has been called by many a "state-of-the-heart" writer.

In 1987, at Robert Redford's Sundance Institute, two of her screenplays made the "top twenty-five," chosen from thousands of nationwide entries. In 1994, she optioned one of those scripts to Kevin Costner; the other screenplay she reworked and adapted, in 2014, to the first of her Sleuth Sisters Mysteries, ***The Witches' Time-Key,*** conceived years ago when Ceane first visited Ireland. As she stood on the sacred Hill of Tara, the wind whispered ancient voices– ancient secrets. *O'Hanlon-Lincoln never forgot that very mystical experience.*

Fire Burn and Cauldron Bubble is the second of the Sleuth Sisters Mysteries, ***The Witch's Silent Scream*** the third in the bewitching series. ***Which Witch is Which?*** is the fourth exciting Sleuth Sisters Mystery, and **Which-Way** the fifth adventure in the series.

Watch for ***The Witch Tree***, the sixth Sleuth Sisters Mystery– coming soon.

Ceane has also had a poem published in *Great Poems of Our Time*. Winner of the Editor's Choice Award, "The Man Who Holds the Reins" appears in the fore of her magickal short-story collection *Autumn Song*– the ultimate witchy-woman read!

William Colvin, a retired Pennsylvania theatre and English teacher, said of her ***Autumn Song***: "The tales rank with those of Rod Serling and the great O. Henry. O'Hanlon-Lincoln is a *master* storyteller."

Robert Matzen, writer/producer of Paladin Films said of ***Autumn Song***: "I like the flow of the words, almost like song lyrics. *Very evocative*."

World-renowned singer/actress Shirley Jones has lauded Ceane with these words: "She is an old friend whose literary work has distinguished her greatly."

In February 2004, O'Hanlon-Lincoln won the prestigious Athena, an award presented to professional "women of spirit" on local, national and international levels. The marble, bronze and crystal Athena sculpture symbolizes "career excellence and the light that emanates from the recipient."

Soon after the debut of the premier volume of her Pennsylvania history series, the talented author won for her ***County Chronicles*** a Citation/Special Recognition Award from the Pennsylvania House of Representatives, followed by a Special Recognition Award from the Senate of Pennsylvania. She has since won *both* awards a *third* time for ***County Chronicles***– the series.

In 2014, Ceane O'Hanlon-Lincoln was ceremoniously inducted into her historic hometown of Connellsville, Pennsylvania's Hall of Fame.

Ceane shares Tara, her 1907 Victorian home, with her beloved husband Phillip and their champion Bombay cats, Black Jade and Black Jack O'Lantern.

In addition to creating her own line of jewelry, which she calls *Enchanted Elements*, her hobbies include travel, nature walks, theatre, film, antiques, and reading "… everything I can on Pennsylvania, American, and Celtic history, legend and lore."

~ A message to her readers from *Mistress of Mystery and Magick–* Ceane O'Hanlon-Lincoln ~

"There's a little witch in every woman."

"I write because writing is, to me, like the Craft itself, *empowering*. Writing, as the Craft, is *creation*. When I take up a pen or sit at my computer, I am a goddess, a deity wielding that pen like a faerie godmother waves a wand.

"Via will, clever word-choice and placement, I can arrange symbols and characters to invoke a whole circuitous route of emotions, images, ideas, arm-chair travel– and, yes indeed, even time-travel. A writer can create– *magick*.

"I am often asked where I get my inspiration. The answer is 'From everything and everyone around me.' I love to travel, discover new places, and meet new people. And I have never been shy about talking to people I don't know. I love to talk, so over the years, I've had to train myself to be a good listener. One cannot learn anything new, talking.

"People also ask me if there is any truth to my stories about the Sleuth Sisters. To me, they are very real, though each is my own creation, and since I have always drawn from life when I write, I would have to say that there is a measure of truth in each of their essences– and in each of their adventures."

How much, though, like the author herself– *shall remain a mystery.*

~ ~ ~

A Magick Wand Production

**"Thoughts are magick wands powerful enough
to make anything happen– anything we choose!"**

Thank you for reading Ceane O'Hanlon-Lincoln's
Sleuth Sisters Mysteries.
The author invites you to visit her on Facebook, on her personal
page and on her *Sleuth Sisters Mysteries* page.

"The most beautiful experience we can have is the mysterious.
It is the fundamental emotion that stands at the cradle of true art and
true science." ~ Albert Einstein

Believe!

16145455R00234

Printed in Great Britain
by Amazon